FULL THROTTLE

Dawn Hawkins

DEDICATION

This book is dedicated to my two beautiful daughters, Daytona and Elizabeth, who have reminded me daily to follow my dreams. I hope you always remember to follow your own dreams no matter where they may take you.

To my best friend, my boyfriend, my lover, and soul mate Chad, for believing in me that I could accomplish this and encouraging me to continue writing no matter how discouraged I became. For loving me, and supporting me, and helping me through the difficult times. You may never know just how much that truly meant to me to have your love and support when all I wanted to do was hide from the world.

And to the countless friends and family who have stood by me throughout this journey to completing and publishing this next novel.

This is a work of fiction. Names, characters, places and incidents are the product of the author's imagination or are used fictitiously, and any resemblance to actual persons, living or dead, business establishments, events or locales is entirely coincidental. (The only exception being the circumstances surrounding the deaths of NASCAR drivers Alan Kulwicki and Dale Earnhardt Sr.)

Cover design: Jessica Jagmin, Simply Windsor Media Inc, Windsor, ON
Author photo: Susan Lindsay Photography

CHAPTER ONE
Mooresville, NC – June 2015

The door slammed and I could hear my seventeen year old daughter, Jessika, cursing as she stormed through the house. I looked at the clock on my office wall and sighed quietly. She was home early from her date. I had a feeling this was not going to be a good night. When I heard her bedroom door slam, I stood and slowly walked upstairs. I knocked lightly on her door before I poked my head inside.

"Can I come in?" I asked.

She nodded and I walked across the room to sit down on her bed with her. She was sitting in the middle of it, clutching a pillow to her chest as tears streamed down her face.

"I hate him, Mama," she sobbed. "He's such a jerk!"

"What happened, Jess? Did you have an argument with Jonathon tonight?"

"If you want to call it that. He didn't put up much of a fight. Do you know what I found out tonight? I found out that dating me wasn't enough for him. And not only was he dating Mandy, he was sleeping with that slut too!"

"Are you serious? How did you find out? Did he tell you?" I was shocked to say the least. They had been dating for almost a year now and I had always liked Jonathon, from the first time Jessika had brought him home to meet me. And Jess and Mandy had been friends since we'd moved to Mooresville.

"After I confronted him with what I knew, he had no choice but to admit his guilt. I was in the bathroom and heard Mandy laughing about it with her other friends. How they thought it was so hilarious that he was sleeping with her behind my back and that I had no idea. I hid in the bathroom until they were gone. I thought he loved me and I thought Mandy was my friend!"

"What did you say to him?"

"Well, I walked out to the table and sat back down casually. When I asked him how his other girlfriend was, he acted like he didn't know what I was talking about. So I told him exactly what I'd heard in the bathroom. By the time I was finished, I knew it was true, just by the look on his face. Then I stood up, poured my drink over his head and told him Mandy could take his sorry ass home because I was through being played for a fool. He just sat there and watched me walk out. Mama, why are boys such jerks?"

"I wish I knew honey. I've been trying to figure that out since I was your age. What I do know is that your heart is probably breaking into a million pieces right now. And I know it's gonna take time, but your heart will heal and eventually you'll fall in love again."

"No way. I'm never gonna fall in love again. And no man is ever gonna hurt me like he did," she vowed.

"Trust me, Jess. You will fall in love again. Maybe a hundred times more before you find a guy who's not going to break your heart. I've been there, said the exact same things as you, vowed never to feel anything for another man again and to never fall in love again and your Grandmother told me the same thing."

"Come on, Ma. Nobody could've broken your heart. You're just saying that to make me feel better."

"No, somebody did break my heart. Once. It was a long time ago, before I met your Dad. Wait here. I'll be right back. I think it's time I showed you something." I walked back downstairs to my office and returned to Jessika's room with a box.

"I packed this box up when I was twenty-one. I knew someday I'd open it again when your heart was broken the first time and go through everything with you. In this box, is almost two years worth of memories."

As I opened the box, and began telling Jessika the story, the memories came rushing back, as if it had all happened just yesterday.

* * * * *

CHAPTER TWO

Windsor, ON – 1993

The high-energy dance music was near-deafening as I made my rounds from table to table, taking drink orders and serving all the beer, shots and mixed drinks my section of customers could handle. I stopped at a table with two of my heavier drinkers, Todd and Brad.

"Are you boys ready for another round?" I asked, setting my tray on their table. They'd been drinking double White Russians for most of the night until they began experimenting with other drinks. It was only their second night together in the bar. The first time they had come to the bar, together with Jerry, another friend, they had sat near the dance floor most of the night. Conveniently, that was my section that night as well. During the night, Todd had flirted shamelessly with me, although I only half-heartedly reciprocated, since I was involved with somebody at the time. Brad, the louder and more obnoxious of the two, had been to the bar a number of times before and had been dating one of my friends, Jenna. The relationship had ended, however, when Jenna discovered him kissing another girl on the dance floor.

"Do you have a quarter?" the quieter one, Todd, asked me. I looked into his deep brown eyes as he spoke, wondering why he'd be interested in me, but also skeptical that he was only looking for a quick fling. He had wavy brown, almost black hair hanging down to his shirt collar. When he stood, he was not much taller than my five-eleven, and I estimated he was about six-one. He appeared to be in good shape, and he had mentioned that he worked out regularly. He was definitely somebody I would notice walking down the street, or in the bar, if I hadn't been working.

"I sure do," I answered, digging through the change on my tray.

"Good, because my mother told me to call her the minute I fell in love."

"Sorry, Todd. I told you already. I have a boyfriend." I laughed as I dropped the quarter back onto my tray. I should have known it was just another line of his. I was beginning to think I'd heard them all; and working in the bar, I had heard more than enough to last me a lifetime. He had been hitting on me since the first time I'd waited on them.

When I had first told him I wouldn't go out with him because I had a boyfriend, Todd had asked what he did for a living. I had told Todd my boyfriend was a police officer.

He had replied by explaining to me that we was going to school to be a cop and was working as a private security guard. I wasn't impressed with what he planned on becoming.

"Why would I want a wannabe when I've already got the real thing?" I had countered.

"Now, what would you boys like me to bring you this time?" I asked, picking up my tray again.

"I want something sweet," Brad announced.

"Well, I don't come in a drink, but I'll bring you something just as good," I answered with a mischievous smile and headed to the bar. When I returned with their drinks, and set the glasses down in front of them, Brad eyed his apprehensively.

"Is it strong?" he demanded.

"Yes," I replied. "There are three different kinds of alcohol in it."

"What is it?" Todd asked.

"It's one of the best drinks you'll get here; but you won't find it at any other bar anywhere. Just try it," I coaxed. Finally, they lifted their glasses and tested the concoction.

"Hey, this is good! What is it? Are you sure it has alcohol in it?" Brad spoke up first.

"It's called a Leg Spreader," I replied with a laugh and turned to walk away.

"Does your boyfriend buy these for you?" Brad asked, attempting to keep me at the table.

"He doesn't have to," I shot back, still laughing.

"So, have you done him yet?" Brad persisted.

"Nightly," I answered, beginning to tire of his line of questioning. I walked away as Brad fired another in my direction. His inquisition continued for the remainder of the night and for a number of weeks afterward.

I had been casually involved with a local police officer. We were both working nights, so most of the time that we saw each other was at Daytona's Sports Bar where I worked and where we had met, or after his shift was over at three o'clock in the morning. We'd spend a couple hours together after his shift was done, before he'd head home.

Eventually, I decided that my relationship with Rob wasn't going to progress and there were rumors that he was married. I thought I'd take a chance on Todd, but was hesitant to get involved with him. Partly because he was American and I was Canadian and living in a border town, I was used to seeing cross-border romances; and I was afraid that under all that charm, he was going to eventually turn out to be just like Brad.

I finally exchanged phone numbers with Todd and he called me just two days later. We talked for about half an hour that night and then spent the next week getting to know each other a little better through our telephone conversations. I had begun working as the public relations representative for the local junior hockey club and convinced Todd to come to a game when he asked me out on a date again.

I gave him directions to the arena and told him what time the game was starting. He said he'd see me there and I hung up the phone looking forward to the game. By the time I arrived at the arena that Tuesday, I was nervous about seeing Todd. I stood by the main doors, watching for him to show up, until the opening face-off. At that time, Jenna, who also did work for the team, came by and told me she'd watch for him so I could go into the game. By the time the second period had ended, I was angry that Todd had not arrived. After the game, I called the various media organizations in the city to notify them of the scores before going home. The phone was ringing as I walked in the door. It was Todd.

"What happened?" I demanded.

"My car broke down," he apologized. "I was five minutes from the border and Brad had to come out to help me. By the time he got there, I knew it was probably too late for me to meet you for the game. I'd really like to make it up to you though. Can I take you out to dinner sometime?"

"I'll get back to you," I answered. We talked a while longer and I told him about the game before we said good night and hung up.

* * *

We continued talking regularly and a month later I had figured out how he could redeem himself for standing me up. A neighbor's band, Jester, was playing at one of the local nightclubs that spotlighted area bands, California's. I asked Todd to go with me and my best friend, Maya and he agreed. We made plans to meet at Daytona's and I called Maya to let her know that Todd and I would be going.

I was surprised; he actually showed up Saturday night. I introduced him to Maya and we headed over to California's. We made it there in time for the first set and found a table near the stage. I had never heard the band perform live before and I was impressed.

However, Maya and I determined after the first set that rock was not Todd's favorite kind of music. We finished our beer and I suggested going back to Daytona's. Todd was more than agreeable and we were soon on our way.

After last call at Daytona's, Todd asked us if we wanted to go for something to eat. Maya declined, but Todd easily talked her into it and we went to one of the few twenty-four hour diners in the city.

We joked and laughed over our food and Maya and I kept exchanging looks. Finally, Todd asked what was up. I had introduced Maya to him as my little sister, just as I had introduced her to everybody else at the bar, since she was only eighteen.

"Should we tell him?" I asked her.

"Might as well. He's gonna find out soon enough anyways," she replied.

"Okay. Go ahead," I crossed my arms on the edge of the table.

"We'll both tell him."

"Tell me what?" Todd asked, looking at us both.

"We're not -- " Maya began.

" -- really sisters," I finished. We took turns explaining why we told everybody we were sisters. Seeing as Maya was only eighteen and the legal drinking age in Canada was nineteen, we had to figure out a way to get her into the bar so we could party together. Since I worked there and knew all the door staff, I had taken her there one night and introduced her to everybody as my sister so they wouldn't ask her for identification.

Once we were done explaining, Todd took care of the bill and drove us home. Maya lived across the street from me and three houses down, so Todd dropped her off first and then threw his car in reverse and backed up the hundred yards or so to my house. As we sat telling each other what a good time we'd had, Todd turned to me.

"So, do I get a good night kiss?" he asked.

"Um, sure," I replied, pulling my hair back from my face. I normally wore it in a ponytail at work, but had left it loose for the evening. I leaned over to kiss him, a kiss which he prolonged, deeply probing my mouth with his tongue. When I pulled away, I laughed softly and put my hand out to open the door.

"Yes, I still have my tonsils," I said.

He laughed and promised to call me soon. I climbed out of his car and headed up to my front door. As I lay in bed later, trying to fall asleep, I thought about the evening, and I decided I was glad I'd given Todd a chance.

* * *

Over the next few weeks, Todd would come out on Tuesday nights for the hockey games, although he never usually arrived until halfway through the second period. We would go out Friday nights as well for dinner and a movie.

Thursdays and most Saturdays were road trips for the hockey team and I quit my job at Daytona's so I could travel with the team. On the Saturdays that I wasn't with the team, I spent at the bowling alley with my parents, but on a team of my own.

At the beginning of November, my parents asked me to join them at a bowling banquet for some of the top bowlers in the city. I agreed and asked Todd to go with me. He said he thought it would be interesting and was eager to go. He picked me up at Maya's where I had stayed the night before since her parents were out of town visiting her brother. Since Maya and her boyfriend were not going with us, we arranged to meet at Daytona's later that evening.

Throughout the banquet, I talked to my father while Todd chatted with my mother and her friends. Everybody seemed impressed by my date; he was so polite and attentive and they all thought he was funny. When we could finally make an exit, we quickly slipped out and headed to Daytona's to meet Maya.

"So, how was the bowling banquet?" she asked.

I faked a yawn and we both laughed. She wasn't really into bowling and I only used it as a night out to have fun and socialize, not compete like a lot of the others on the league or in attendance at the banquet. We found a table big enough to accommodate everybody who had arrived in our combined circles of friends and Todd and I sat down together, our heads close, talking.

"You know, Brianna," he began. "We've been seeing each other for a month now, and I really like being with you. Will you be my girlfriend?"

I didn't tell him that I thought I already was; I simply nodded yes and he leaned over to kiss me. At the end of the night, we all piled into Todd's car and went back to Maya's where we turned on the television and started flipping through the satellite channels. Todd and I curled up on one sofa, while Maya and her boyfriend Steve occupied the other and our friend Tina took a chair.

Tina soon headed up to Maya's room to sleep, leaving the four of us watching a lame horror movie. When a shower scene came on, Steve and I got into an animated discussion on whether the squeaking sounds were the girls soaping up their wet breasts, or the door handle turning.

Finally, we agreed to disagree and Steve and Maya headed downstairs to sleep in the spare bedroom while Todd and I made our way to Maya's parent's room. Unfortunately, I didn't get any sleep that night. Todd did though. In fact, he slept very soundly. Very loudly, too. His snoring kept me awake all night and I finally crept out of bed at sunrise.

Once I was dressed, I jogged across the street to my house. Todd and I were going to the Detroit Lions game with my parents and some of their friends, and I wanted to get the tickets from my mother. When I walked in the door and explained why I was there, my mother eyed me suspiciously.

"Don't get excited. Maya and I slept in her room and Steve and Todd slept in the spare bedroom in the basement," I lied, although it was half true. How would she know otherwise? Nobody else in the house was going to confess the real sleeping arrangements. And it wasn't like anything had happened.

I returned to Maya's with the tickets and found that everybody else was finally awake, and Todd and Steve were in the kitchen, busily making breakfast. Once they had eaten and Todd was ready to go, we headed to the Pontiac Silverdome. He took me through Southfield and the Bloomfield Hills area, pointing out various landmarks.

* * *

After the game, Todd drove me back to his house because he wanted to introduce me to his mother, Elaine. She wasn't home when we got there, so he gave me a tour of the house before we settled in front of the television in the family room. The house was two-story, and beautifully spacious. Most of the main floor was done in a calming off-white, with white couches in the formal living room, offset by a black baby grand piano in one corner, bordering the dining room, which also held a black dining set. The color scheme flowed into the airy kitchen, where numerous plants prospered on the expansive counter space. In the family room, we relaxed on one of three peach-colored sofas, facing the big screen television.

When his mother came home a couple hours later, Todd introduced us and she quickly retreated to her own room on the second floor, but not before asking if I would be spending the night. If I hadn't been sitting down, I think I would've fallen over from the shock. How often do you hear a question like that from a mother who has just met her son's girlfriend? I pulled myself together and said no, explaining that I had to be at school at nine the next morning.

* * *

Two weeks after the football game, Todd picked me up at school, and we drove to his sister Jo-Ann's house for Thanksgiving dinner. There I met his sister, and her husband Brad. Jo-Ann was pregnant with her first baby and due in February. Also there, was one of Todd's brothers, Glen and his wife, Melissa. They had a little boy named Gerry, named after his grandfather, Elaine's late husband.

Everybody made me feel welcome and I easily fell in love with Todd's family. Brad's mother and Elaine also joined us for dinner. I also learned that Todd had another brother named Scott, who was married to Wendy. They didn't join us, however, because there had been some sort of fight between Todd and Scott after Todd had wrecked Scott's car, the night that we had met.

Over dinner, I was seated between Todd and Glen. Todd was talking to everybody at the table and Glen turned his attention to me.

"So Todd tells me you're Canadian eh?" he asked, chuckling.

"Yes, but not all of us say 'eh', y'know," I replied.

"Well, do you know how many Canadians it takes to screw in a light bulb?" I had already heard the joke and knew the answer, but figured I'd let him have his laugh.

"No. How many?" I asked.

"One hundred. One to hold the bulb up to the socket and ninety-nine to drink until the country spins."

"Well, you know… that's all we do is drink. That's why we've got a bar on every corner. We're all born with booze in our veins instead of blood so we have to keep our supply up. And when we're not all liquored-up, we're out racing our sled dogs and wrestling with our penguins and polar bears," I shot back, laughing.

After dinner, we returned to the living room to watch the football game. Todd and I left about an hour after dinner and he drove me back home.

* * * * *

CHAPTER THREE

December 1993

One month later, on my twentieth birthday, Todd showed up on my doorstep with a teddy bear and a card.

"I had something else for you, but it's not ready yet," he apologized. I thanked him for the bear and put the card in my purse to read later. We were supposed to meet the rest of my journalism class at the Windsor Press Club for a year-end party. After Christmas, we would all be heading in different directions as we worked as interns to complete our final year.

Over the past five months, the nine of us that had remained in the program had become close, spending most of our time together in, as well as out of, school. When we arrived, I introduced Todd to my classmates since this was the first time they'd really met him. The party was a jumble of mixed emotions as we looked forward to beginning the final leg of our journey towards our diplomas, but sad at the same time that we wouldn't be able to stay together.

"Aren't you going to read your card?" Todd asked as I passed out the Christmas cards I'd brought. I'd almost forgotten about it. I pulled it out of my purse and took the card from the envelope. I chuckled as I read the front, *"It's your birthday! Now get out there and celebate!"* then laughed as I opened it and read the inside, *"Oops! I meant celebrate. Jeez, I hope you didn't think I was implying that your sex life is dead or anything . . . I mean, sex is a very personal thing and what you do (or don't do) in your spare time is up to you, and – Oh, just forget it. (Not that I'm saying you should forget about having sex on your birthday. . .)"*

I showed it to my friends to read before tucking it back into my purse. As the evening passed, and I joked and laughed with my friends, I noticed Todd sat silently, choosing not to join in the conversations going on around him. My friends and I all tried drawing him in, but he would simply answer the questions asked him and then fall silent again.

I could tell he didn't really want to be there, so I asked him if he'd rather go to Daytona's where I had arranged to meet Maya. He couldn't seem to get out of the building fast enough and I hastily said my good-byes. Being at Daytona's wasn't much better though and I ended up yelling at Maya because she thought I should get drunk on my birthday and I didn't want to. Finally, the night was over and I had Todd take me home.

One week later, he met me at the bowling alley on Saturday night and gave me my birthday present. As I opened the box, I was surprised to find a watch. It was one that I had been looking for the past six months. On the face of the watch was Mighty Mouse. During the course of our conversations, I had told him that I was looking for a Mighty Mouse watch. When he asked why, I explained that I had been a big fan of the 1992 NASCAR Winston Cup Champion, Alan Kulwicki. He had died in a plane crash in April on his way to Bristol for a race. He'd had Mighty Mouse embroidered on his driver's suit. I even told Todd that I planned on getting a tattoo of Mighty Mouse the following summer. Maya and I were going together to get them. She was planning on getting a dolphin diving into a sunset.

I took off my old watch and replaced it with my new one. I gave Todd a kiss to thank him and we continued on our date.

* * *

A couple days before Christmas, Maya brought over a large box to place under our tree. She told me it was from Todd, but wouldn't let me pick it up or touch it at all. The only clue anybody would give me was that my gift was green, yellow and white. And it seemed everybody knew what it was.

Finally, Christmas Day arrived and my grandparents came over, bringing my great-grandmother with them. Todd arrived soon after and we made the introductions before we all began opening our gifts. My parents, brother and I had all exchanged earlier, as well as me and Maya. Everybody whispered to each other as my mother brought me over the box from Todd and set it in my lap. I ripped off the paper to find a Labatt Ice beer case.

"You bought me a case of beer," I exclaimed sarcastically. "But I drink Canadian Ice. Maya's the one that drinks Labatt." I broke open the box, knowing by the weight that it wasn't beer.

Suddenly I was looking at a box of popcorn. I thought to myself *"Green, yellow and white? Well, unless some of this shit's gone moldy, there's gotta be something else in here."*

"Start digging," Todd said.

"How 'bout I just dump it on you?" I asked, as I stuck my hand into the kernels. It came in contact with something very hard and I felt around for the edges, finally coming out with a brick.

I recognized it from Maya's backyard sidewalk as we'd each tripped over it numerous times cutting through the backyard. First popcorn, now a brick. I was not so amused anymore. I knew Todd and Maya were both practical jokers, but this was just getting ridiculous.

"Keep digging," somebody said. I think it was my mother. Back into the popcorn I went, and this time was rewarded with a small, pink velvet box.

Opening the box, I gasped as I discovered an emerald nestled between two diamonds on a thin gold band. It was beautiful. I took it out of the box and slipped it on my finger.

"It's beautiful. Thank you, Todd." I had worn an imitation emerald, and during a conversation at the hockey arena, Todd had asked me what my favorite gemstone was. After we had finished opening our gifts, we all sat down to dinner. With my ninety-two year old great-grandmother sitting between me and my mother, I had Todd to my left, and we talked quietly as the conversations flowed around us.

The day after Christmas, Brad and Todd came over to go with Maya and me to a friend's bar. When we got there, I introduced everybody to Don, the disc jockey. He'd been the deejay at Daytona's when it had first opened, and I'd met him just before I'd started working there. We joined my brother, John and his girlfriend, Amanda, at a table big enough to hold all of us. My parents were also planning on joining us. Maya and I got down to drinking right away and Brad and Todd kept us going, buying us round after round. Soon enough, we were starting to feel a good buzz, and Maya and I started racing with each of our drinks to see who could finish first, a trick we'd picked up to get drunk faster.

Too soon, the night was over and Todd drove us back home. He pulled up in front of my house and Maya and Brad began walking towards her house as Todd walked me up to my door. Suddenly Brad started running up the street until he reached Maya's house, then turned and ran back to mine. He continued doing this until Maya had reached her front door. My sides hurt from laughing so hard at Brad, but I still managed to continue my conversation with Todd. Maya and Brad had been bugging us all night to go out with them on New Year's Eve, but I had convinced Todd that it should be just the two of us. He agreed and was trying to get information out of me about what I had in mind.

"Trust me," was all I said, before kissing him goodnight and unlocking my door.

* * *

When he picked me up on New Year's Eve, I carefully packed everything that would be needed into the back seat of his red LeBaron convertible. I had prepared a beef and potato casserole for dinner and it required only minimal work to be ready.

Arriving at his house, I quickly got to work re-heating the main dish, setting the table and preparing the appetizers, salad as well as vegetables served in a green bell pepper dish. As we sat down to eat, Todd complimented me on everything and I was very proud of myself.

After a Kahlua mousse dessert, we settled in the basement on the sofa in his room to watch movies before turning on the traditional Dick Clark Special from Times Square.

When midnight neared, we made our way back upstairs to the family room where Todd cracked open the bottle of wine his mom had bought for us, filling a glass for each of us. I noticed that his glass drained and refilled a number of times, but chose to remain silent about it. I had greatly reduced my alcohol consumption during the previous months, drinking excessively only occasionally, but did not force my choice to remain sober on my friends. After all, it was New Year's.

At midnight, we toasted the New Year and drank together, wishing each other a Happy New Year. Todd took my glass after a few minutes and placed it with his on the floor, before leaning over to kiss me. We ended up horizontal on the couch, and our temperatures quickly rose. He finally suggested going downstairs to his room and I eagerly agreed. I had been anticipating a romantic evening, ending with us making love for the first time. He took my hand and led me down to his bedroom, where our clothes quickly fell to the floor. I was unsure of what to do as his hands traveled my body. My lack of knowledge and experience became obvious soon enough.

"I could use some help you know," he said suddenly.

"With what?" I replied, having no idea to what he was referring.

"Stanley."

Stanley, I learned, was what he had named his penis. Stanley? Mr Happy, I had heard of. Mr Big, I had heard of many times. How many guys didn't name their penis Mr Big? But Stanley? Reminded me of power tools. Exactly the idea, Todd revealed. But, I thought aloud, aren't Stanley power tools guaranteed to always work? Not knowing how to help, I asked him what he expected me to do. After a quick explanation from Todd, I decided he could help himself. I had very little sexual experience and there was no way I was going to touch 'Stanley'. And I sure as hell wasn't going to put it in my mouth. 'How gross,' I thought.

Eventually, as the wine wore off, 'Stanley' came back to life. Todd grabbed a condom, declaring, "We're in business now!" as he tore open the package and pulled the condom on. As he entered me, I stifled a scream. I wasn't a virgin, but it certainly hurt like I was.

Afterward, the after-sex glow I'd expected wasn't there. Instead, I felt like I'd been run over by a truck. I was so sore and my whole body felt battered and bruised. It seemed like I'd just had sex with Dr Jekyll and Mr Hyde.

During the foreplay, he was sweet and gentle, but actually having sex, he became fierce, almost crazed. It was as if he forgot there was a living, breathing, feeling person under him.

And then, to top it off, he expected me to rate him, compared to my former lovers, and my orgasm, which I had not had. Not wanting to hurt his feelings, or bruise his ego, I declared him the best. Eventually, I thought, I'd let him know he was a little too rough. But not yet. The rest of the night, we talked about our childhoods and before we knew it the sun had come up. We got up and showered and dressed before heading back to Windsor.

I was expected to travel to St Mary's for the junior hockey game between the St Mary's team and the Windsor team. I was not looking forward to the game, since the last time we'd played against the Lincs on their ice, half our team had been ejected, with one of our best players receiving a game misconduct and a four game suspension for mouthing off to the linesman. The ride to St Mary's was torturous as pain shot through me with each bump on the road. After returning to Windsor following the game, Todd and I met Maya at Daytona's where I filled her in on my evening.

Exhausted by the end of the evening, I gladly fell into my own bed and fell into a dreamless sleep. The next morning, I would be beginning my internship and didn't want to fall asleep on the job.

* * *

Todd's birthday was three days after New Year's Day and I had bought him a gold bracelet, which had cost me close to three hundred dollars, but was not ready in time because I was having it engraved with his name. The bracelet was ready on the Friday after his birthday and I gave it to him when he arrived for our date. Unfortunately, I'd had the flu all week and was unable to go out anywhere.

During the next few months, we got into the routine of going out on Friday nights and ending up at his place, where we inevitably ended up having sex. I was grateful that he calmed down a bit in bed and I didn't leave feeling so sore. He always brought me home Saturday morning before he went to work. There was one Saturday morning, however, when I was tempted to call my parents to come pick me up. Todd decided to blackmail me into performing oral sex on him. Something he knew I didn't like to do.

"I'm not taking you home until you give me head," he announced.

"What?" I asked, unsure I had heard him correctly.

"You heard me. You're not going home until you go down on me," he repeated. After debating the subject with him, and hoping he'd change his mind if I didn't do it, I finally gave in. It seemed an eternity before he was finally satisfied with me doing as I was told, and drove me back home again.

* * *

February 1994

Just after Valentine's Day, we went to see Starmites, the high school play that Maya was stage-manager of. Driving home after the play, Todd and I somehow got on the subject of children, which turned into a full-blown argument.

I had a strong mothering instinct, and wanted to have children, although not right away. Trying to explain it to Todd, he assumed I wanted to start a family that minute.

"No, dammit. That's not what I'm trying to say. I do want children, yes. But I'm not saying I want them right this instant. I'm trying to tell you that I'm planning on having a career as a Winston Cup driver by the year two thousand. So I want to have at least one child before then, because I absolutely refuse to start racing and then have to take a year or two off because I've gotten pregnant, or I'm planning on getting pregnant. It's too easy to be forgotten when you take time off in the sport and it's too difficult to get back into it, after being off the track for that length of time."

"But you don't even have your driver's license yet. How are you going to drive a race car?"

"Did I say I was jumping into a stock car tomorrow? No. But I will be getting my license soon enough."

"Well, I think you're setting your goals too high. You can't just hop into a Winston Cup stock car."

"I know that for crying out fucking loud! Do you think I don't know that? I know I have to work my way up and I'm planning on doing that. But when people ask what I want to do, I tell them my eventual goal, not that I think I'm going to run at a short-track somewhere for a few years, then find a Grand National team to drive for and eventually hope to drive a Winston Cup car."

The argument continued on his not wanting children, until finally I told him I no longer wanted to discuss the subject.

* * * * *

CHAPTER FOUR
April 1994

Our sixth month anniversary fell on a Saturday, after the conclusion of the local hockey season and Todd met me at the bowling alley. I hadn't thought he'd remember it was our anniversary, so I hadn't bothered getting him a card. However, he did remember and after bowling we went to buy cards for each other. Back in the car, we exchanged cards.

Opening mine, the outside read, "*On Our Anniversary, I still remember how I felt the first time you touched me – In that single moment, I became yours forever.*" The poem continued inside: "*And though we can never recreate that exact moment in time, what we share now is even better . . . Because our love is deeper, stronger and more exciting than either of us could have ever dreamed in that single moment so long ago when we first touched.*"

We had agreed that 'our' song was Doug Stone's latest release 'I Never Knew Love (Til I Was Loved by You)' and we had each added that quote to our cards.

At the end of the month, when I completed my internship, Todd suggested I bring a couple days worth of clothes and stay with him for a while. Eventually, we were practically living together. While he worked during the week, I would stay home and take care of laundry and making dinner. He would pick me up Saturday when he got off work at the Watchband Outlet and I'd stay until Thursday morning.

Every Thursday, he would drive me home and then head back to Pontiac for work. I didn't have my driver's license yet, only my learner's permit, so it was up to Todd when I went home. He was still driving the convertible, but said he hated driving it on the freeways, so that was his reasoning for having me stay at the house.

That, and the fact that he wanted to be able to see more of me, and it would be easier if I was at the house, instead of him having to drive forty-five minutes each way in order for us to go out.

When the warm weather arrived, we added the lake to our daily routine. There weren't many days we didn't spend at the lake with Brad and the jet skis. They were both jet ski fanatics, having both bought one and every spare minute was spent either racing them at the lake, in the garage with the two of them working side by side on their toys, or reading the latest issues of Splash and Watercraft World, learning different methods of increasing their speeds.

Brad had moved into Todd's after getting into a fight with his father and leaving home. They both kept trying to convince me to learn how to ride and eventually, I gave in and allowed Todd to try to teach me.

It took forever and after him yelling at me and me bursting into tears, I somehow managed to pull myself up into a kneeling position on the ride tray. After a minute or two, I lost my balance and was tossed into the water. Retrieving the jet ski, I couldn't pull myself back up and headed into shore, telling Todd I'd had enough for one lesson.

With Brad living at the house, there was no escaping him and that ultimately resulted in numerous arguments between me and Todd. Todd had this awful habit of telling Brad what went on between us in the bedroom, and of course, Brad had all the tact of a bull and would bring up what he knew, usually over dinner. I would repeatedly tell Todd that what we did was none of Brad's business and how would he feel if I told Maya everything we did? He always said he didn't care if I told her what we did, but I felt that it was something between us, that our friends didn't need to know.

Todd knew I was constantly irritated by Brad and his behavior and when Todd bought a new car, a Ford Probe, he told me that Brad was against his choice. When Todd asked him why, Brad had revealed that when he was younger, his parents had had a vehicle the same color, a metallic silver-blue. The color reminded him of his parents fighting all the time. When Todd shared this information with me, I decided to have some fun with Brad, and began starting arguments with Todd in front of him, so he would think it was the result of the color of the car. Todd knew what I was doing and always played along, although more often than not, we ended up laughing instead of arguing, which was fine with me. However, I was more than relieved when Brad finally made peace with his father and moved back home.

* * *

July 1994

After the holiday weekend, Todd planned a trip to northern Michigan and Higgins Lake. According to Brad, who had been there before, it was the best place to jet ski. Todd agreed to take me along with him. But only if I promised to ride the Jet Ski. Blindly, I made the promise. How was I to know what I was setting myself up for?

As soon as we reached the lake that first day, I regretted making that promise. Higgins Lake was huge. And it was packed with swimmers, boaters and other jet skiers. There was no way as a beginner that I would be able to jet ski on this lake.

Todd quickly made friends with a couple of guys with jet skis and spent the next two days riding with them while I swam or worked on my tan. He asked me a few times if I wanted to take the jet ski out. I declined every time, explaining that as inexperienced as I was, I wasn't ready for such a large body of water.

His new friends had recommended the Tobacco River, which was a short detour along the way home. Todd decided we'd stop there during the trip home. This time, I had no choice but to ride. Todd declared that we were not going home until I'd taken the jet ski out. I tried every excuse I could think of to get out of it, but to no avail.

"You promised," he growled. "And so far, you've broken that promise. I could've left you at home."

At his request, or rather demand, I pulled on a life jacket and slowly waded into the water. Firing the engine, I pointed the jet ski away from the dock where Todd stood, his hands clenched into fists on his hips. A few hundred feet out, I tried pulling my knees up into the ride tray. Over and over again, I tried with no luck. I had very little upper body strength and my legs felt like dead weight in the water. I managed to pull myself up as far as my hips, but could get no further than that. I soon became frustrated that I couldn't get my hips past the end of the ride tray. After a few minutes of struggling to pull myself up, I could hear Todd yelling something from shore and turned to find him waving for me to head back. I steered the jet ski towards the dock and as I got closer, I could hear what he was yelling at me.

"What the hell were you doing out there? I brought you with me to jet ski. Not sit on the beach for two days, and then let the ski drag you around," he yelled.

"I tried pulling myself up!" I yelled back.

"No, you didn't! I stood here watching you!"

"I did try! Were you out there with me? No! You don't know how many times I tried pulling myself onto the ride tray. I couldn't get my hips past the end and onto the jet ski and my arms are not strong enough. Besides, this sunburn is killing me," I countered.

"Forget it. Let's just go home," Todd angrily pulled the jet ski out of the water as I changed into dry clothes. By the time we reached his house, we weren't even speaking to each other. As we pulled into the driveway, we saw his mother working in the garden and Todd finally spoke to me again.

"Don't say a word to her about us fighting."

When we got out of the car, I tried to mask my emotions behind a smile, but his mother could tell right away, asking if everything was alright. Todd engaged in small talk with her, assuring her that all was fine, that we were both just tired. I was right behind him, feigning a headache. I followed him to his room, where he stretched out on the bed. When I tried to talk to him, he said he was tired and wanted to sleep. I curled up on my side, my back to him, and silently cried until I was exhausted.

Later that evening, after a tense dinner, the subject came up again as I washed the dishes. Elaine had gone out with friends and we had the house to ourselves.

"Fine," I finally burst out, having taken about all I could from him about the topic. "I'm so fucking sorry if I ruined your vacation. I lied about wanting to jet ski because I wanted to be with you. Are you happy now? I'm so sorry if I ruined your trip!"

"Do you mean that?" he asked gently, walking over to stand next to me.

"Yes," I nodded as he put his arms around me. I didn't mean it; I had thought I would jet ski when we got there, but I didn't think it was fair of him to complain that I had ruined his vacation, since he had claimed to be having a good time while we were there. But, I knew it would shut him up to hear my apology, since he seemed to think everything was always my fault, or so he conveyed to me through our arguments, and his mannerisms. The subject was dropped shortly after but only temporarily.

Throughout July and August, we spent most of our time arguing about how much time he spent with the jet ski. I'd jokingly say that I felt like a jet ski widow, even though we were not married, considering the amount of time he spent with the machine, and invariably, he'd take offense and ask what my problem was. When I'd explain to him that it felt like I had to compete with a machine for his affections and attention, he'd counter that I didn't want to learn how to ride. Another hot topic between us was sex, and we constantly argued about that too. He complained that I was frigid and a prude, because I didn't want to be turned into a human pretzel. He loved to have sex everywhere and anywhere it suited him. I considered myself to be open-minded to any suggestions he might have about sex. However, I wasn't open to the idea of the neighbors watching us having sex in the living room in front of his mother's floor to ceiling windows, especially considering that most of them had young children.

There was one day when I actually thought he was going to resort to physical violence. I was sitting on the couch in his room, reading a magazine when he came down from his morning shower. I had already taken mine, finished dressing and applying my makeup, and was waiting for him so we could begin our day. He dropped his towel as he strode towards me.

"Hey baby. How about some head?" he asked.

"I'm not interested," I answered.

"Well, I am, so you are," he replied, reaching me and pinning me down with his hands.

"No. I'm not," I said emphatically. He responded by moving up and pinning me down with his legs, swinging his penis in my face.

"Come on. Don't be a prude."

"I'm not being a prude. I'm just not interested in blowing you. I swear, Todd. Stick it in my mouth and I'll bite it," I warned.

Unfortunately for him, he didn't believe me and forced himself into my mouth. As I started applying a gentle pressure to let him know I meant what I said, but not enough to cause any pain, he panicked and pulled back, hurting himself more than I would have hurt him.

"You bitch!" he screamed, jumping off me and running across the room and into his bedroom.

"Hey, I warned you. It's your own damn fault you didn't believe me," I responded, standing up and following him into his bedroom, half-heartedly trying to apologize. He wanted no part of my apology and continued to complain about it for the rest of the day.

After that, if we weren't arguing about sex or the jet ski, Todd complained that I wasn't as interested in getting my drivers license or working out as I should be. I finally let him try to teach me how to drive, but that turned out to be too stressful for both of us, and he suggested having his mother teach me when she had time, although he thought I should be more eager to learn to drive. When I began to get self-conscious about my body, the arguments escalated and finally I told him that it was because of him complaining that I didn't work out enough that I felt so self-conscious.

"Well," he'd say. "If you worked out more often, you wouldn't have a reason to feel self-conscious." By the end of the summer, there wasn't much we weren't fighting about and we had another major blow-out when Todd announced he was going to Kentucky with Brad for a few days to jet ski. When he dropped me off Tuesday morning, I reminded him to pack condoms, which started another argument between us.

"Why the hell would I pack condoms?" he asked, laughing, trying to make a joke of it.

"Hey, I don't want you bringing anything home to me," I answered. The resulting argument reduced me to tears.

"We're just going to jet ski, nothing else," he finally snapped at me, in an effort to end the fight.

"Fine," I replied, and the subject was dropped, although I wasn't too happy about him leaving. I didn't trust him going with Brad to not cheat on me. He decided to leave me his pager while he was gone, and said he'd leave messages for me. True to his word, Thursday night, his pager started going off repeatedly while I was at work at Daytona's. I checked the messages when I got home that night.

"Hey, Boo. I just called to say hi, and I miss you. Brad and I are having fun down here. We drove into the next county, 'cause this one's dry, so we could get some beer and we're just hanging out at the hotel here, having a few drinks." Five minutes later, he paged me again.

"Hey, Boo. How come you haven't left me a message? I miss you. I don't know where you are or who you're out with, but give me a call when you get a chance, okay?"

I wasn't impressed when I heard that one, especially considering the condescending tone he was using, but continued listening for the next one, which had come through about ten minutes later.

"Hey, babe. I'm sorry about that last message. I forgot it's Thursday and you're at work. Leave me a message later when you get home from work, okay. I love you." Still pissed off at his first two messages, I called to leave a scathing one for him, so he would know I was not impressed with his antics or his attitude.

"Hey, Todd. I'm glad you're having such a great time. But I thought this was supposed to be a jet ski vacation for you, not a get drunk at the hotel with Brad vacation. I guess you're having so much fun drinking and partying it up that you forgot it's Thursday, the one day a week I work. See you when you get home."

* * * * *

CHAPTER FIVE

September 1994

While Todd was away in Kentucky, I busied myself trying to find a full-time job. I had been asked to be the maid of honor for one of my long-time friends. And I knew there was no way I could afford the bridal shower she expected, working only one night a week at the bar. I was called for an interview at one of the desktop publishing/copy shops I'd applied to.

Two days later, I got a call back, offering me a job typesetting and doing graphic design, if I still wanted it. I accepted it, and gave up my job at Daytona's again. I also signed up for driver's education, and things got better between me and Todd. He was happy that I'd finally decided to make an effort to get my driver's license, although he didn't seem too happy that he wouldn't have me at the house every day.

The next few weeks were hectic. The other two people hired, according to my new bosses, had changed their minds about the positions they were offered and I was asked to work the front counter of the main store. I agreed, since they told me it was just going to be until they found somebody else, but that I was still going to be doing some design work. I was working full-time days and taking driving lessons at night. The day of my road test, I was extremely nervous and by the time we arrived back at the Ministry of Transportation office, I was positive I'd failed the test. To my delight and surprise however, I passed.

The week after my road test was our one-year anniversary and we celebrated at the Plaza Hotel in Detroit. Elaine was dating one of the hotel's owners, so she arranged for the room for us. I had bought Todd a Star Trek poster and a copy of 'The Nitpickers Guide to Star Trek: The Next Generation' which outlined each episode and listed any discrepancies in the plot or props.

He bought me another watch because he thought it was time I wore a more 'adult' watch than one with Mighty Mouse on the face. This new one was silver and gold with a black face. Although I loved the Mighty Mouse one, I had learned that Todd's opinions were his way of telling me what he thought I should do, and began wearing the new one all the time, putting the Mighty Mouse watch away in my jewelry box.

* * *

Halloween weekend, we had another blow-up that resulted in Todd giving me the silent treatment for two days. Thursday night we argued on the phone because I hadn't been to the gym all week to work out. Finally, I gave in and told him I'd go work out the next day after work and he could pick me up at the gym. We set a time and I thought the subject was dropped.

The next day, however, I was running late and called his pager to let him know to give me an extra hour. Apparently, he didn't receive the message and showed up at the originally decided time. He stormed into the all-women's facility and glared at me as I did leg lifts. I hurriedly dropped the weight I'd been using and smiled as I jogged over to him, kissing him quickly.

"Didn't you get my message? I needed an extra half-hour or so. I've been running behind all day," I explained.

"No. All I got was your code. I tried calling your house, but got no answer. Are you almost done?"

"Yeah. Give me twenty minutes and I'll meet you out front." He stormed out and I headed to the locker room to shower and change. Twenty minutes later I hopped into his car, only to be greeted with a stony silence.

"I just have to stop at home and grab my clothes and then I'll be ready to go," I said. He merely nodded and sped out of the parking lot. During the entire ride to his house, he answered my questions in monosyllables and said little else to me.

* * *

I spent Saturday alone, having no idea what had brought on this treatment, while Todd was at work and decided to have dinner ready and waiting for him when he got home. I timed it perfectly and he seemed surprised when he walked in the door.

We talked very little over dinner and as I was clearing the table, he suddenly asked if I wanted to go to one of the area haunted houses. I agreed and we were soon on our way. Upon arriving at the haunted house, we engaged in small talk while we waited in line. I felt as if it was our first date again with the awkwardness.

When it was our turn to go through, I took Todd's hand as he pushed me ahead of him. He pulled his hand away as we entered, only to grab it again as we were enveloped in darkness. Once we made it through the haunted house, we laughed together about how scary it hadn't been, and headed back home.

At home, I broached the subject of the attitude and the silent treatment I'd been receiving from him and finally got him to admit it was because of our argument Thursday night and my lack of interest in working out.

"The silent treatment was the first step. If that hadn't worked, I would've stopped coming to see you for a while, until you realized how important it is to me that you work out regularly," he explained.

We discussed the subject further, until I tired of his juvenile attitude towards me doing what he wanted, and turned the discussion into an argument. I refused to be blackmailed into working out.

* * *

By the time my twenty-first birthday came around, there wasn't much we didn't argue about again. On my birthday, we had an all-out war. It all started because I didn't really care where we went for dinner. I never really had a specific preference where we dined, knowing that no matter where we went, I'd be able to find something on the menu I liked.

Todd finally told me that if I didn't provide an answer within thirty seconds, he was leaving. I was speechless when he told me that. Getting no response from me, he stormed out. Shocked, I began to cry even harder than I had been.

When he came back into the house, he ignored me and sat watching television. I busied myself putting away the laundry I'd done that day and planned on packing my things and going home. I'd gotten my car on the road the weekend before and had driven out to Todd's by myself.

He finally confronted me as I was getting my things together and started complaining that I never talked to him anymore. He said he wanted to know my thoughts, feelings and opinions. As he stood at the bottom of the basement stairs, looking up at me sitting on the top step, both of us crying, he exploded.

"I'll give up love for happiness if I have to," he threatened. "I don't want to, but I need these things from you."

A part of me wanted to tell him to end it all right then and there and go find his happiness. But I foolishly thought if I changed I'd be the one to make him happy. I had always done what he asked, or rather told, me to do. I colored my hair the shade of blonde he wanted, styled it how he wanted, dressed how he thought I should dress. I'd joined the gym at his insistence and worked out as often as I could. I had even chosen not to get my tattoo with Maya because he had told me not to get one.

"I don't want my future wife to have a tattoo. So, you're not getting one," he had said when we had discussed it before Maya left for university. To end the argument on my birthday, I finally promised to provide him with what he said he needed and Todd seemed happy.

* * *

30

Just before Christmas, I suggested we go to Greenfield Village in Dearborn to check out the displays. The radio advertisements had portrayed demonstrations from various eras, and I thought I would be able to add to my photography portfolio. Unfortunately, there was not as much going on as I had expected and I didn't take one picture.

However, the time there provided yet another argument for me and Todd concerning children. Exasperated, I told him that if he was so against me having children, I would go to the doctor and have a hysterectomy, so he would not have to worry about me accidentally getting pregnant.

"Don't be stupid. It's easier for me to have a vasectomy, because I know I don't want kids. But what happens if we break up and you and whoever you eventually marry decide you both want children?" he countered.

"We'll adopt," I shot back. "You say that like you know we're gonna eventually break up. Is there something you want to tell me?"

"No, I'm just saying it's a possibility," he replied.

* * *

At Christmas, Todd bought another jet ski, initially for me and said he was going to rebuild the engine so it wouldn't be as fast as his, so I could learn how to ride, and we could ride together during the upcoming summer. We made plans to personalize it for me, and we began thinking of names for them both.

Between Christmas and New Year's, we made a stop to our favorite country music radio station, WYCD. I had won a trivia contest a week before and they were holding a prize package of a tee shirt and a gift certificate for an area restaurant for me. While we were at the station, my favorite deejay was on the air and Todd talked him into letting us sit in the booth for a few minutes. Once we got in there, Todd asked the deejay, Doctor Don, how he could win a prize. Don was well-known for having listeners do the strangest things on his show and one of those things happened to be what was known as a 'five minute ride.'

During those five minutes, a contestant, usually female, went on the area freeways with one of the guys from the station. Listeners would be informed as to the participant's location and the game would begin. Listeners were encouraged to honk their horns at the car holding the participant, and for each honk, one article of clothing had to be removed until the contestant was completely naked. Todd suggested we do a five minute ride, but I was not agreeable, telling him that if he wanted the prize package, he was making an ass of himself, not me.

We threw ideas back and forth for a while, until Don came up with one of his own. Taking me out in the hall, he asked me how many times Todd and I had had sex during the past year that we'd been together. Armed with my answer, we returned to the broadcast booth and he asked Todd, explaining that if our answers were identical, he would win. Our answers were off by about two hundred, so he lost.

Finally, Don claimed he had an idea and ran from the room, returning a short while later with a pair of pliers. Back on the air, he explained the rules of the game to us. I was required to grasp Todd's tongue between the pliers while he sang a song, on the air. Laughing, I eagerly took the pliers I was offered. As the traffic report began, Don indicated for us to begin and Todd stuck his tongue out for me to take.

"Now keep in mind, if you stop singing, or she lets go, you lose," Don stipulated as Todd began singing Friends in Low Places. The traffic took a relatively short time to report and Todd still continued to sing, since he couldn't stop until Don told him to. With Todd sounding like a complete idiot, I could not help but laugh. The longer he had to sing, the harder I laughed. As I laughed, the pliers began to slip and I finally had to rest my elbow on the desk to avoid letting go of his tongue. Finally able to stop singing, I let go of Todd's tongue. He was awarded his tee-shirt and we left a short while later to go home.

* * *

New Year's Eve, we took our celebration to the Plaza Hotel, borrowing Elaine's boyfriend's suite since they were in New York for the holiday. Our celebration was short-lived however, and the arguments began again early in January. If it wasn't my inability to communicate with Todd, it was my lack of interest in working out or jet skiing. Over and over again, the arguments were always the same.

"I want you to do these things for you," he'd say.

"But you make me feel like I have to do it for you, to make you happy. You get angry with me and give me the silent treatment if I don't do what you tell me to. I feel like nothing I ever do is good enough for you," I'd reply. "And you make me feel self-conscious when you complain about how I look."

"Well," he'd answer. "If you went to the gym more often, and worked out, you wouldn't feel self-conscious. Do you think I'd have you do something that would hurt you?"

And still, the battle continued.

* * * * *

CHAPTER SIX

February 1995

On Valentine's Day, we drove to a nearby drugstore to buy Valentine's cards for each other and back at home, we exchanged them. I had complained on my birthday and at Christmas that he had not bought me a card for either occasion and mentioned it again on his birthday in January, since I had gotten a card for him for both occasions.

The inside of the card to me read: *"Sweetheart, ever since the day we met, I've known you were the one for me. No one else has ever made me feel as alive, as special, or as happy as you do. Wherever I am, you're with me, if only in thought and heart. You're a wonderful part of my life, and I now that if we hadn't met, I'd still be looking for happiness! Happy Valentine's Day."*

Underneath his signature, he'd added a postscript: *"Happy birthday and Merry Christmas."*

Touched by the poem in the card, I kissed him and told him I felt the same way about him, and the fighting ended for a while.

As usual, the truce was brief and the arguments soon returned, although in a different direction for a change. Later in the month, as we laid in bed one night talking, Todd asked me something that I thought had come completely out of left field.

"What would you say if I told you I was engaged before?" he asked. I was slightly taken aback by his question and it took me a minute to respond.

"Well, I guess I'd want to know who you were engaged to, first of all," I answered slowly.

"It was this biker bitch I dated," he replied. "She was about three hundred and fifty pounds. She rode a Harley and was covered in tattoos."

I knew from previous conversations that he looked down upon that image. He hated tattoos and considered anybody who was overweight and didn't have a clean-cut appearance to be disreputable and beneath him socially. When he was done with his description, I laughed.

"Okay, now who were you really engaged to?" I turned serious.

"Brenda," he replied hesitantly.

I almost went through the roof. Brenda, I knew, was Todd's last girlfriend before me. She had also been the subject of many fights between us. She had moved to Dallas prior to my meeting Todd, but still continued to call his pager, usually in the middle of the night, leaving messages to say she still loved him, although she knew he was dating me, and had even made a few references to me, a couple times when she had paged him.

"Brenda?" I repeated. "You were engaged to Brenda, yet you've had nothing but negative things to say about marriage when we talk about it. Why are you willing to marry her and not me? Or is it because you were engaged to her that you don't want to marry me?"

"You've got to understand. When Brenda left for Dallas, I thought I'd never date again. So, before she moved away, I gave her my Social Security number and told her when she turned twenty-five to get in touch with me. Then, if we were both single and unhappy, we'd get married," he explained.

"When does she turn twenty-five?" I asked stiffly.

"September of the year two thousand," was his reply.

"So, you're telling me that in September of the year two thousand, Brenda's gonna come knocking on our door, and you're going to run off and leave me to marry her. Am I right?" I demanded.

"No. I told her that it was only if we were both single and unhappy. If I'm with somebody, unless I'm unhappy, I'm not gonna marry Brenda. Besides, you and I may not even be together then."

I refused to speak to him after that, knowing that as angry as I was, I'd end up saying something I was going to regret in the long run. During the next day, I spoke to him only when it was absolutely necessary. I figured if he could give me the silent treatment when he felt I hadn't worked out enough, then I could give him the silent treatment for this.

"Tell you what," he finally brought the subject up again on Sunday.

"What?" I snapped.

"I'll make you a deal. If we make it to our sixth anniversary of dating, we'll get engaged."

"What? You have got to be joking!" I exclaimed.

"Why?" he asked, looking confused.

"You've just applied for a job with the Michigan State Police and the Oakland County Sheriff's Department, and said if you get State, we'll get a house and move in together," I replied.

"Yeah, so?"

"So, when we reach our sixth anniversary, we will probably have been living together for close to four years. And you will have had all the conveniences of marriage without the paper or putting a ring on my finger. Why would you want to marry me then? Like the old saying goes, why buy the cow, when you've got the milk for free?" I exploded.

"Who said anything about marriage? I said we'd get engaged," he clarified.

"Even better. Put a ring on my finger to shut me up. Why even bother with that?"

"Eventually, we'll get married."

"Why?"

"To have kids, of course."

"Why? We've already discussed that issue to death. You said you don't want any. And by the time you change your mind, I'll be too old for making babies. And I've already told you, I'm not going to race for a year, and then have you decide you want kids and me have to take two years off to have a baby."

"You will not be too old. Lots of women are waiting until their forties and even fifties to have children."

"Let's just drop the subject. I'm tired of arguing about this," I answered.

* * * * *

CHAPTER SEVEN

A couple weeks after our argument about Todd's offer of marriage, I was sent to work at the copy center my bosses had opened on the campus of the university. One of the first days there, I met a first-year law student, Jeff, and we began talking. I was working on a report about crime scene investigations for Todd for school, just another example of how I would do anything to please him. He didn't like to read anything that wasn't jet ski-related, so he had asked me to do the report for him. Somehow, Jeff and I got to talking about the report and I passed it off as mine. He wished me luck on finishing it on time, since I only had a week to do it, and had just been given the books by Todd.

Over the next two weeks, Jeff became a regular, almost daily, visitor, either for copies of his notes, or just to say hi and chat for a few minutes. Usually, we talked about school, and since I knew what Todd was doing in class, I could talk about how classes were going and told Jeff that I got a ninety-eight on my paper. Although, in actuality, Todd had received that grade on my paper. One day, the conversation took a more personal route.

"So, are you married?" Jeff asked me.

"No," I answered honestly.

"Are you planning on getting married anytime soon?"

"No." By this time, I had resigned myself to the fact that Todd and I would not be getting married until he decided he wanted children, if we were ever married. Although I loved Todd dearly, working at the university provided a lot of temptation to cheat on him.

"Can I take you out to dinner sometime?" Jeff asked. I hesitated before answering.

"Um, how about we start with a phone number and get to know each other a little better first?"

He wrote his number, then waited patiently for me to write down mine. Impulsively, when I saw Todd that weekend, I told him about the exchange and he almost went through the roof.

"Why didn't you tell him you had a boyfriend?" he demanded.

"He didn't ask."

"So you couldn't volunteer the information?"

"Do you tell girls that flirt with you that you have a girlfriend? No. You tell them that your friend's mother bought you that cool Mickey Mouse shirt that all the girls love. When you flirt, I become just a friend, so why should I act any differently?" I exclaimed.

"But I don't give them my phone number," he yelled.

The argument continued and finally I admitted that I knew I was wrong, only to shut him up. I figured if he could relegate me to being just a friend when girls flirted with him, or being his 'associate' when he took me along on anything pertaining to his jet ski repair business, then what was the harm in me 'forgetting' I had a boyfriend once in a while? Besides, I rationalized to myself, it was only harmless flirtation. Or so I thought.

Shortly after that argument, I met Joe. He was about six five and built to perfection. He made my knees weak and my heart pound every time he talked to me. From the beginning, our conversations were purely sexual and I knew it was only a matter of time before I slept with him and ultimately cheated on Todd. One Thursday night, as I was leaving the university, I ran into Joe. He invited me over to his apartment and I eagerly accepted the invitation. Knowing why we were both there, he led me directly to his bedroom and began undressing me as he kissed me. He pushed my hands away as I began to remove his clothes and slowly lowered me to the bed. Quickly shedding his clothes, he joined me and our kisses continued. His caresses and kisses were tender and sweet as he teased me and increased my anticipation and arousal. When I thought I could stand it no more and was virtually begging him, he began to purposefully and expertly make love to me.

We spent hours alone in his apartment that night, and many nights following that one, and each encounter seemed to be better than the one before. I had never thought it possible, but Joe knew exactly what to do to my body. Indisputably, he was the best lover I'd ever had so far. He knew from the beginning about Todd, but he seemed to have no problems with the fact that I had a boyfriend. One night, early on in our affair, he told me it was more of a turn-on knowing that I was somebody else's girlfriend. And I had to admit, there was a certain thrill in knowing that Todd had no idea that I was going to another man for the satisfaction I wasn't able to get from him.

Somehow, Joe made me more aware of my body, accepting me as I was and I was less inhibited with him than I had ever been with Todd. Knowing the arrangement was only temporary, I still dreaded having to say good-bye to Joe when the time came.

* * *

My last day of work before the Easter weekend, Jeff showed up to give me a creme-filled chocolate egg and wished me a Happy Easter. Todd arrived shortly after to pick me up for the weekend. When he saw the egg, he demanded to know why I'd bought it, considering he'd just lectured me the weekend before about how much fat was in chocolate.

"Jeff gave it to me," was my reply and Todd exploded.

"Haven't you told him yet that you have a boyfriend?" he demanded.

"Today's the first day I've seen him since we exchanged numbers. And he only stayed long enough to drop off the egg because I was busy and he had a class. I haven't had a chance to tell him," I lied. In all honesty, I had seen him almost every day. I just didn't feel it necessary to tell Todd that fact.

"Well, since you won't be eating this, I'll just get rid of it for you," he replied, and promptly tossed it into the garbage can down the hall. It seemed we argued the entire weekend about it, and I couldn't wait to be back in Joe's arms.

Two weeks later, came the dreaded day when I had to say good-bye to Joe. The end of the semester was near and he would be returning home to Kingston and I would be transferred over to the main store for the summer months. We had our last night together on the last Thursday before exams and I told Todd on Friday that I would be returning to the main store on Monday. He seemed happy about the move and I knew it was because he knew I would not be seeing Jeff at work any more. However, I knew I was going to miss the other friends that I had made during the past few months and hoped that I would be moved back to that location when classes resumed in the fall. Most of all, I knew I'd miss Joe, but I'd always remember the time we'd had together and if I returned to the university in the fall, there was a possibility we could resume our affair.

Without Jeff around everyday, I figured things would get better between me and Todd and that the arguing would subside, if not cease.

* * *

Just after Easter, I chose to change my hair color. I had wanted to become a strawberry blonde for some time. But Todd had always disagreed. Finally, I talked his mother into trying it for me. If I didn't like it, I knew I could change it in a few weeks. One Saturday afternoon, while Todd was at work, we did it. Finishing up late in the afternoon, I was drying my hair as he came home. He stopped in his tracks when he saw me.

"What the fuck did you do?" he asked.

"I had your mother color my hair today."

"It's red."

"I know." It had come out a darker shade of red than I'd planned, but I knew in a few days it would begin to wash out and fade.

"Well, when you can do it again, my mother'll do it blonde for you again." I held my tongue. He didn't ask if I liked it; didn't even seem to care what my opinion was. He only seemed to care that he didn't like it. For the next week, until the color had begun to fade, he demanded I wear a baseball cap whenever he was around, claiming he hated it and didn't want to look at it. However, if I was wearing a blue shirt or sweater, he said the color of my hair looked better and I could pass on the cap. I happened to like it and decided I would continue to color it red, although I thought I might move to a lighter shade, so it would not be quite so shocking.

* * * * *

CHAPTER EIGHT

When Todd started a new job as a security officer at The Plaza, I was happy for him. It was a great opportunity for him. He was happier, and every night on the weekends while I was there, when he came home, he would tell me how his shift had gone. I was happy that is, until he came home one night in late-April and told me he'd made a new friend, Virginia.

Virginia, I learned, worked the front desk at the Plaza Hotel. Todd explained to me that they had met while he was covering the exit of the hotel's bar. It had been a fairly quiet night and he looked over to find Virginia smiling at him as she twirled a lock of her hair around her finger. He mimicked her and laughed. One of their co-workers called him over shortly after to talk.

"Would you strip for four thousand dollars?" the co-worker had asked.

"I'd strip for free if there was an audience," Todd laughed. He went on to explain to me that Virginia had looked at him and stated matter-of-factly: "I'll be your audience." I was not impressed and told Todd exactly what I thought.

"You were flirting with her," I said. "Does she know you have a girlfriend?"

"I was not flirting with her," he denied. "Of course she knows about you. She's seen you before when you've stopped by the hotel."

"So she just doesn't care," I said.

"Of course she cares. She's just a friend. Don't be stupid," Todd snapped.

I had even less reason to be impressed the next night when he came home from work and told me about his shift and having taken his lunch break with her. During the course of the conversation, Virginia declared that her goal was to prove to Todd that the city of Detroit was not as bad as its image portrayed.

Living in the suburbs most of his life, Todd believed the image that Detroit was a city overrun with guns and drug dealers on each corner. It apparently wasn't that bad, but according to Todd, Virginia owned a gun and had used it when a man had broken into her house, shooting him in the leg. Todd had then decided that his goal was to prove to her that not all guys are jerks.

"But Todd, how are you going to prove to her that not all guys are jerks?" I asked. "It's not like you can sweep her off her feet and be her knight in shining armor, riding off into the sunset, unless you're planning on leaving me for her."

"Of course I'm not going to leave you for her. She lives in one of the worst neighborhoods in Detroit. I'm not gonna put my life in danger just for a date. Don't be stupid. I'm going to prove it by being her friend," he explained to me. After that, I dropped the subject, although I still wasn't comfortable with the situation and did not trust her even one little bit.

* * *

The following weekend, Todd was late coming home from work. Not half an hour, or even one hour. But he was four hours late. My body had become accustomed to waking up at two-thirty every morning when I was at his house, when he was working nights, since that was the time he usually got home. On this night, it was no different for me. Once I was awake, I would drift off to sleep for a few minutes, but somehow, my body continued to wake me up repeatedly, knowing that he wasn't beside me. The hours seemed to drag endlessly, and as six thirty neared, I finally decided to get up to see if maybe he was upstairs in the family room watching television.

There was no sign of him anywhere in the house, and as a last resort, I checked the driveway, thinking that maybe his garage door opener was malfunctioning again. And since I had his front door key, he wouldn't have been able to come in that way. His car wasn't in the driveway, however, the newly fallen snow was still undisturbed, and I slowly made my way back downstairs to bed. As I pulled the covers back over me, I finally heard the garage door open. Minutes later, Todd was hanging up his suit in the closet before quietly crawling into bed beside me.

"Awfully late night, dear," I said, startling him. "Sorry, I've been awake since two thirty, waiting for you."

"One of the elevators got stuck between floors," he hurriedly explained. "I was the only one on duty at the time, so I had to wait for the repair man to get there." He went on to tell me that he'd had to work on keeping everybody calm who was in the elevator, and somebody had said there was a gun and they were going to start shooting if they didn't get out soon. Therefore, the police had to be called in. When the situation was finally resolved and everybody was safely out of the elevator, Todd was able to leave.

The entire weekend, he claimed to be exhausted and all he wanted to do was sleep. He had no interest in doing anything else. After repeatedly turning down my sexual advances, I was worried. He never turned down sex. And I had never known him to be too tired, as he was claiming to be.

I considered voicing my innermost thoughts about it and saying *'You know, if you keep turning me down, I'm gonna start wondering if you're sleeping with Virginia.'* But I chose to remain silent and hoped things would return to normal the next weekend.

* * *

Instead of things getting better, they got worse. On Friday when Todd picked me up, he told me that him and Virginia were going out for dinner the following Monday. Right away, warning bells started going off in my head and we began arguing about it. I said that in my opinion, it was a date, but he claimed it was just two friends going out for dinner.

Finally, after an hour of arguing heatedly about her intentions, Todd and I called a truce, agreeing to be supportive of each other's friendships. After all, Todd pointed out: I had male friends that I went out with occasionally. Although I countered that when I went out with my friends, it was a spur of the moment thing, not planned a week in advance, I agreed to be supportive of his friendship with her, as long as she didn't interfere with our time together and that he didn't stand me up to go out with her. He claimed I had nothing to worry about and I left the subject alone.

The next day, however, I could not help but comment. When he came home from work that afternoon, his pager began going off repeatedly with messages from her. I was not happy about that at all. He had promised me she wouldn't interfere with our time together. He also claimed that she didn't want to hurt him and that she knew if we broke up because of her, he'd be hurt. By the time he drove me home Sunday night, I was thoroughly pissed and my newly resurfaced intuition warned me to be wary of her intentions. Before he left my house, knowing he was going out with her the next night, I laid it all out for him in the plainest and simplest terms I could think of to let him know I was serious about not trusting her.

"I'll tell you right now," I said. "I don't feel even the slightest bit comfortable with this. My gut reaction is that Virginia is looking for more than just a friendship from you. So here are my ground rules. You go ahead and have your dinner date with her. But I'll tell you right now, if you fuck her, don't even bother coming back to me on Tuesday when we're supposed to go out. I love you, and I want to trust you, but I don't want her leftovers."

He seemed upset with my terms, mostly because I wasn't willing to share him with her, I assumed, but I didn't care. I had always told him that if he ever cheated on me, as long as he told me about it, and it only happened with one person, I would forgive him. I told him I'd forgive him, but I wouldn't forget. If it happened a second time, I told him, we were through.

I didn't want to appear hypocritical, but I had been discreet and made sure that my affair with Joe hadn't interfered with my relationship with Todd and I had never thrown it in Todd's face that there was somebody else in my life. Most importantly, I had never had any intention of breaking up with Todd for Joe.

However, all I'd heard about all weekend was Virginia. Todd couldn't seem to go one hour without making some mention of her. Although I had told him I'd forgive him the first time he cheated, I was not willing to be so open-minded about him being with Virginia. I felt threatened by her presence and was going to do anything I possibly could to keep him from leaving me for her, even if it meant threatening to leave him.

* * * * *

CHAPTER NINE

I kept myself busy Monday to keep my mind off the fact that my boyfriend was out with another woman. Monday night I went to nearby Lincoln Park with my father to go shopping for something for my mother for Mother's Day, since she was in Arizona for a bowling tournament. During the drive, I told him about Todd's plans to have dinner with Virginia that evening. Upset, I tearfully revealed my insecurities regarding the situation.

By Tuesday, I was so tense, I spent the entire day pacing at work, wondering if he would show up. At five o'clock when he walked through the door, I was so relieved, I almost fainted. I felt like I was walking on air as we walked out to his new truck. He'd been looking at it since he'd started his new job and had finally picked it up that day. I should have known my euphoria would be short-lived. We stopped at my house so I could change before we went to dinner. As we stood on my front porch with my father, talking about Todd's new truck, the conversation turned to dinner, when Todd asked me where I wanted to go. Before I knew it, I could hear myself asking about the night before.

"So, where did you go for dinner?" I asked as we got into the truck.

"Outback," Todd replied. Outback was one of my favorite restaurants near his house and we often ate there. However, there was also one closer to Virginia's house.

"The one down on Eureka? Wow, Dad and I were over that way looking for a shirt Mom wanted," I answered.

"No. We went to the one on Orchard Lake Road."

"Why would you go to one so far from her place?" I asked innocently, although I could hear the warning bells again, this time louder than the last.

"Virginia wanted to get out of her neighborhood," he explained as he drove.

"So why doesn't she just move out of it?" I snapped, wondering why it was up to Todd to get her out of her neighborhood. In the back of my mind, I could see her thinking that since Todd lived in West Bloomfield, if she dated him, she could quickly move up the social and economic ladder.

44

"It's not that simple. She can't just sell her house."

"Why not? I thought Detroit wasn't that bad a place to live. She should be able to sell her house fairly easily. So tell me how your evening was."

"Well, I went and picked her up. Right after we left her place, the Gang Squad flew by us Code Three, so she told me to follow them."

"Hold on. What's a Code Three?"

"Lights and siren."

"Did you follow them?" I asked, silently hoping his answer was no.

"Of course. As far as I could anyway. The last we saw of them, they were skidding around a corner. I lost them after that," he sounded disappointed.

"Great friends you pick," I replied sarcastically.

"What's that supposed to mean?" he demanded.

"Well, I don't know about you, but I try not to pick friends that are going to purposely put my life in danger," I began.

"What are you talking about?" he interrupted.

"My friends wouldn't ask me to pick them up in a bad neighborhood, first of all, where there are drugs and guns on every corner. And second, my friends wouldn't endanger my life by telling me to chase a Code Three Gang Squad, not knowing what's at the other end. Especially in Detroit, and even if they did, at least I'd be smart enough not to do it."

"What's the big deal?"

"What's the big deal?" I repeated, dumbfounded that he would ask such a question. "Think about it from my side for just a minute here. How do you think I would've felt if you had been able to keep up with the Gang Squad? Do you honestly think I would really enjoy getting a call from your mother saying you'd driven right into the middle of a gang fight and that you were laying in a hospital shot? Or that you'd been killed? Just because Virginia wanted you do to something so stupid as to chase the Gang Squad and you decide to be a fucking macho stud and did it. I don't give a shit about Virginia, but I happen to love you," I finished emphatically.

"But I'm fine. Nothing happened to me. Now lighten up, or I'm taking you home," he joked.

"Why don't you do that then? Go take Virginia out to dinner," I sneered as I began to cry. Todd stopped the truck as he pulled into the parking lot at the restaurant.

"Remember what I said before about living with the consequences of what you say? Hey what's with the tears?"

"Nothing." I angrily swiped at my tears, wishing I could easily stop them.

"What's your problem? I didn't get killed last night. I'm here. Why are you crying?" he demanded impatiently.

"I am just so goddamn sick and tired of hearing about her all the time okay. I'm tired of competing with her!" I exclaimed.

"Why would you be competing with her? She's just a friend."

"Because she's everything I'm not."

"Where the hell did you get that from?" he asked.

"You said it yourself. Remember when your mother and Ted broke up because he was screwing his ex wife? You told your mother that if a man can't find what he wants with one woman, he's going to look for it somewhere else."

"So what does that have to do with Virginia?"

"We've been arguing for months now that you don't think I'm athletic enough and that I never talk to you anymore or give you my opinions, right? Well, along comes Virginia, who's just full of opinions, who talks to you and works out every day. So what else am I supposed to think but that you're getting from her what you don't think I'm giving you? Of course I feel like I have to compete with her!"

"But you don't have to!" he burst out.

"But I feel like I do! All I've heard about for the passed month is Virginia. Every single time I talk to you, you mention her. I feel like she's your goddamn girlfriend and I'm just a friend you're spending time with," I yelled. An overweight woman got out of a car close by and Todd pointed her out.

"If Virginia looked like that, would you be threatened by her, or think you had to compete with her?" he asked.

"Of course not. Because I know you don't date girls who are overweight," I replied. "But Virginia doesn't look like her. That's the problem."

We sat in silence for a few minutes, both of us absorbed in our thoughts. I could've kicked myself for opening my mouth in the first place. If only I'd not said anything and just pretended it didn't bother me, I thought to myself.

"Look. Just forget I said anything. It's no big deal. Obviously you're going to have friends that are women; who talk; and work out. And I can't continue to feel jealous and threatened by your friendships," I tried some damage control.

"Well, I think if we are going to continue our relationship, there's going to be some changes," Todd began as he put the truck in gear and pulled out of the parking lot. "I don't feel like eating now. I've lost my appetite. So I think we should try talking." I started to tell him how my day had gone, before he cut me off.

"That's not what I meant. We have to deal with this problem first." When we pulled up in front of my house, the fireworks began again.

"Look; you know I need these things from you that we've been arguing about for the past year," Todd said.

"And I know I can give you what you need. I did before; I can do it again," I cried out.

"But how do I know you won't stop talking to me again? I think we've forgotten how to be friends."

"So what are we supposed to do?" I asked, petrified of what his response might be.

"Maybe we should put our relationship on hold until we can get the hang of being friends again. Instead of dating, we'll just be friends for a while," he suggested.

"So what are you saying? Do you want to break up?" I asked.

"I'm saying we stop sleeping together; no more weekends together until we can work through this. All we're going to do is spend time together as friends. And when we can handle that, we'll pick up the rest of our relationship again. It may take a week, a month or a year. But no matter how long it takes, this is something we have to do."

"But why can't we keep our weekends? At least it would give us time to talk. I'll even sleep in the spare bedroom," I asked.

"Don't you understand? Are you stupid? If we keep our weekends, there'll be no change in our relationship."

"So you're willing to just throw away the last two years?"

"No I'm not throwing away two years. We just need to work on our relationship, that's all. And even if this doesn't work, I won't regret any part of the past two years," he explained. I nodded silently as I pulled his house key off my key ring and handed it back to him.

"You don't have to give this back to me now," he said.

"I won't be needing it," I replied.

"I'll give yours back to you next time I see you. Now go in the house. I need some time to think. Give me a call when you're ready to try being friends."

As I leaned over to give him a hug, I noticed he was crying too. I slowly climbed from the truck and crossed the street. Walking in the house, I began sobbing uncontrollably and my father immediately pulled me into his arms to hold me as I cried. When my tears finally subsided, I managed to explain to him what had happened. We talked well into the night, and he gave me advice about what had happened. When I finally went to bed that night, I cried until I was exhausted, but still I could not sleep. I tossed and turned all night, finally turning my light back on and began to write a letter to Todd, until I had to begin getting ready for work. I planned to ask for a few days off and hoped we could resolve our differences during that time, and possibly go away for a few days. I also planned on looking for a new job, seeing as it was right around the same time I'd started working there that the arguments had begun.

I hadn't really been happy with my job, since I had been told I was being hired for typesetting and graphic design, but as yet, had done very little of it. Eight months after being hired, I was till making photocopies and working the front counter. Todd had repeatedly told me I should rectify the situation, but I had chosen to remain silent, not wanting to make waves. When the time came for me to get the raise my bosses had promised me, Todd had felt I should push them for it, saying that since they had promised it to me, I should be getting it when they claimed I would, instead of a month later when I finally did receive it.

* * * * *

CHAPTER TEN

My bosses were willing to give me some time off and I spent my days either calling Todd's pager to let him know I wanted to talk, or writing him letters pouring my heart out to him. Wednesday, my father drove me over to Todd's to drop off the first letter. He wasn't home when we got there, so I left it in the door.

Maya called me on Friday, when she got back to Windsor from London, where she'd been going to school. I told her everything that had happened, and she talked me into going out and managed to cheer me up a little, until Saturday.

That afternoon, I called Todd's house but got no answer. Finally, I decided to call him at work. Eventually, he had to talk to me. My heart was racing as I waited for the front desk to connect me with the Security Office. I was sure it had been Virginia that had answered the phone.

"Hi Todd. I'm sorry to call you at work," I began when he picked up the phone. "But I just wanted to make sure you got my letter on Wednesday."

"Yeah, I got it," he answered gruffly.

"So are you going to come over tomorrow?" I asked quietly.

"No. Tomorrow's not good."

"Why not? I want you to come over so we can talk about us."

"There isn't an us anymore."

"How can you say that?" I cried out.

"Because I've been doing a lot of thinking this week and I just don't think it's going to work."

"But I can be everything you need. I know I can! Didn't you read my letter?"

"I read it. But I don't want to have to work that hard on a relationship."

"You don't have to; I know what to do now. I just never realized how important it was to you," I persisted.

"But I don't want to have to worry about when you're gonna stop doing those things again."

"I won't stop now that I see how important it is to you."

"Yes, you will."

"No! Don't give up on us, Todd," I begged.

"It's too late. I just feel more comfortable being by myself and playing Nintendo than being with anybody right now."

"Well, I'm sorry if I was such a terrible girlfriend for you and just wasted two years of your life," I replied bitterly.

"Don't start."

"What?" I cried.

"You want me to dump on you and I'm not going to do it," he replied.

"No. I want you to level with me. I can't believe you're willing to just throw away the passed two years. Obviously, I don't mean shit to you. You know I was going through all the cards you gave me during our relationship and the two that mean the most to me were our six month anniversary and Valentine's Day this year. Can I read them to you?"

"No. It's too late for that."

"Then I guess they were really just empty words. And here I thought maybe you actually meant what was written in them. I guess our relationship was a lie right from the beginning. Do you even care that you're ripping my heart out and shredding it into a million pieces?"

"Look, you'll get over it. I think right now you need to get out and start dating other people," Todd said. Suddenly, the picture was becoming all too clear to me.

"That's what this is all about, isn't it?" I demanded angrily.

"What?"

"You want to date her, and fuck her, without having to feel guilty about cheating on me!" I accused.

"No! That's not it at all! I just need some time to myself right now. Give me some time to get over the bad parts of our relationship, and then maybe we can be friends again. Give me a call once in a while to say hi and if I'm ready to talk to you, I'll call you back."

"How much time do you want?" I asked.

"I don't know."

"Well, thank you very much for having the balls to break up with me in person."

"Hey, I'm sorry if I don't, but I think it's better this way."

"Why? So you don't have to see how you're ripping my heart out?"

"Because in person, I'll see you crying and then I'll end up doing something I'll regret."

"What? Like saying we'll give us another chance?"

"Yes."

"So why can't we?"

"Because it just won't work."

We argued a while longer as I tried to convince him that we could make it work. Finally, I gave up, exhausted with having to put up such a fight. I knew every relationship needed work to keep it going, but I wasn't going to kill myself trying to get him back. I resigned myself to the fact that there was no way I could change his mind. I felt like my heart was breaking into a million pieces as I hung up the phone. My intuition told me that he was breaking up with me to be with Virginia. He just seemed too defensive about her.

* * * * *

CHAPTER ELEVEN

Mooresville, NC – June 2015

By the time I had finished telling Jessika about my relationship with Todd, and our break up, it was well after midnight. Her tears had long since dried and she looked at me expectantly when I paused.

"He sounds like a no-good rotten creep. Why did you want to stay with him? I would've kicked his sorry ass to the curb," she offered.

"Because I was young and thought he really loved me. And I thought that I could change to be what he wanted," I explained.

"But he should've been able to accept you the way you were. That's what you've always told me. Don't change who you are for anybody."

"Unfortunately, Todd wasn't able to accept anybody unless they were exactly what he wanted them to be. Everybody had to be perfect by Todd's standards. And I was so blinded by my love for him that I couldn't see that there was a serious problem with how he treated me. I thought that if you really and truly loved someone, you'd change to be whatever they wanted, no matter what. I didn't realize until much later that his treatment of me bordered on psychological and emotional abuse. And my relationship with him is why I've always tell you to not change for anybody."

"So, how did you manage to get over him? Obviously you fell in love again. With Daddy. Otherwise I wouldn't be here."

"That, my dear, is something I will tell you about in the morning. Because right now, it's time for bed."

"But school's done," she protested.

"Hey, you might not have school tomorrow, but I have to go to work in the morning."

"You're the boss. Can't you take one day off?"

"Jess, you know we leave for Michigan the day after tomorrow. And you know the shop is always busy right before we leave," I paused. "Tell you what. Come to the shop with me in the morning and we'll take off for the afternoon and go shopping."

"Okay," she readily agreed. I closed up the box of mementos and headed for the door as she stood up to change.

"Good night, Jess."

"Night Mom."

I returned the box to the file drawer in my office where it had sat since we moved in, before I headed to bed. I laid awake for hours thinking about everything I had just told Jessika. I had thought about Todd over the years, but those thoughts had become less frequent, now coming only around the anniversary of our first date, and that of our break-up. I had kept in touch with his mother through the years, sending her photos of me and Jessika. She told me what was going on in Todd's life when I asked, but we didn't mention him often.

I had seen him a few times when I'd been to see Elaine, but for the most part, he would completely ignore my presence. I had worked through my anger and my feelings of betrayal and hurt and was willing to talk to him. Todd, however, was not so amicable, although I couldn't understand why he would act such a way towards me. After all, he had been the one who had so blatantly cheated on me and lied to me. I didn't think he had any reason whatsoever to have any ill feelings towards me.

* * *

The next morning, we were both exhausted from our late night, but Jessika already had coffee made and was ready to go by the time I showered and headed downstairs. During the drive to the shop, Jessika read parts of the paper to me, as had become our routine on the days she came with me. When we walked in the front door, I felt like I'd walked into a florist's shop. Every available space held a vase of flowers, or a plant of some sort. I looked at my receptionist, perplexed.

"Kara, when I left yesterday, this was still a Sprint Cup facility. When did I change careers and become a florist?" I asked, taking the mail she held out to me.

"This morning, Ms Lane. There were two delivery vans waiting in the lot when I came in. They just kept unloading them," she explained.

"Do any of them have cards?" I inquired.

"Yes ma'am. All addressed to Jessika," Kara answered, handing over a pile of cards. "It's not her birthday already, is it?"

"No," I turned to Jessika, handing her the cards. "Do you want to look at these?"

"Who are they all from?" she asked, tearing open the first envelope. I watched as the color drained from her face and she dropped the remainder of the cards to the floor.

"Guess we know who they're from," I said, surprised when I took the card from her and found I was wrong, although close in my guess. I pulled her into my arms as she began to cry again.

52

I walked her up to my office as my team began arriving for work. Most of the guys thought of Jess as a little sister and more than a few had already threatened her dates with bodily harm if she was ever hurt.

I convinced her to stay in my office for the morning, instead of accompanying me on my rounds of the shop, as she normally did when she was off school. My first task was to dispose of the jungle in my lobby. I instructed Kara to call the florist that had delivered them to pick them up again and take them to nearby retirement homes. That done, I checked on the rest of the shop, ensuring that everything was running smoothly and that the primary and back-up cars were ready for us to take to Michigan for the next race. My engine department had been working overtime trying to improve what we already had. Confident that all was fine, I returned to my office to find Jessika telling my crew chief, Kyle, about the events of the previous night.

"Trust me, Jess. Your mother knows what she's talking about," he was assuring her as I walked in, stopping in the doorway.

"I know. She told me all about that no-good creep, Todd, who broke her heart. But she still hasn't told me how she got even, or how she got over him." Kyle chuckled before responding.

"She's probably afraid you'll do the same thing."

"You know! I forgot you knew her back then! Please tell me," Jessika begged. Kyle saw me standing in the doorway then and shook his head.

"Sorry. That's your mother's story to tell. But I can guarantee you that it is a good story."

"Kyle, are you here to see me or to flirt with my daughter?" I asked as I crossed the room and sat behind my desk.

"Just here to flirt," he replied. "But you should know by now that it's with both of you."

"Well just remember, she's young enough to be your daughter too."

"Mom!" Jessika shrieked.

"Chill, Jess. Kyle knows I'm only joking around. Now, are you ready to go?"

"Yeah, I think so. But I don't want to have to look at those damn flowers again."

"No need to worry. As we speak, that jungle you received today is being delivered to a retirement home or two."

"I think you should've sent them over to Doug's shop. That way, he can see what his daughter is doing with that credit card he so freely gives her, and pays for," Kyle suggested.

"Oh, he'll be finding out anyways," I answered. "Doug and I are going to have a nice, long talk about his precious Mandy this weekend while we're in Michigan. Now, I don't know about you young lady, but I think it's time for us to hit the mall and I'll continue my story."

"Cool," Jessika jumped up and gave Kyle a hug before bouncing out of the office. I talked to Kyle for a few minutes, discussing which cars I wanted to take to Michigan before heading downstairs to go shopping with Jessika. I caught up with her in the lobby, as she joked with a couple of my mechanics. As we walked out to my truck, I continued my story.

* * * * *

CHAPTER TWELVE

Windsor, ON – May 1995

After I hung up the phone from talking to Todd, I called Maya in tears.

"It's over Maya. He just told me he'd rather be alone than with me," I sobbed.

"I'll be over as soon as I can get there and we'll go out," she assured me.

An hour later, she was outside. I ran out to the car and we drove off. She had our friend Justin with her and we were dropping him off before we went out. When we arrived at his house, Maya talked me into going inside for a few minutes to talk to his mother. Upon hearing my story, she offered her advice.

"You're young. Go out and have some fun. Start doing things for yourself. Travel. Do things you want to do," she advised. Back in the car, I told Maya everything Todd had said on the phone, and she asked if I wanted to spend the night at her place.

"No, I think I want to stay home tonight. I have to get used to being at home again on the weekends," I replied. "Fuck, I hate him so much right now. To think, I was going to give up my job and move in with him, and work at the hotel. He's such a bastard." By the time she dropped me off again, I was feeling a little better, and my father had gotten home from bowling. I had to go over the story again, after he asked where I went. He said he'd gotten worried when he got home and found I wasn't there, considering how upset I'd been when he left.

Sunday night, my mother arrived home from her bowling tournament in Arizona and I had to tell her everything that had happened during the week that she had been gone. By the time I was done, I was exhausted, physically as well as mentally, and she sent me up to bed to try to sleep, since I had to work in the morning.

Monday morning, I woke up feverish and sick, and asked my mother to call in to work for me to explain why I would not be in that day. Tuesday, I managed to go to work, although I was still not feeling well. By late afternoon, when I went home, I felt even worse and was suffering from severe stomach pains. Worried, my mother took me to the emergency room, where I was rushed in with a possible appendix rupture.

Upon examination, it was discovered that I was in actuality, two and a half months pregnant and in the midst of a miscarriage. I was immediately wheeled into an operating room, where the distressed fetus was removed. My parents came into my hospital room as soon as I was allowed visitors and sat by my bedside.

"Why didn't you tell us?" my mother asked, taking my hand.

"I didn't even know until they told me I was miscarrying," I replied quietly. "I had no idea. No signs. No morning sickness. Nothing."

I was kept for observation for the rest of the day, as well as the next, to make sure there were no complications and finally went home Wednesday night. I was back at work Thursday morning as if nothing had happened, although I was still an emotional wreck and still in pain.

To avoid having to talk about it, I saw as few people as possible and told only my closest friends about the miscarriage. I decided I would never tell Todd I had been pregnant, although I knew he probably wouldn't care if I did tell him, since he had not wanted children, recalling vividly an argument we'd had about me having an abortion if I ever got pregnant and we were not married. The biggest reason why I chose to keep the miscarriage a secret though, was because I had no idea if the baby had been Todd's or Joe's.

* * *

One day, shortly after Mother's Day, Todd's mother phoned me.

"Hello, Brianna. It's Elaine. How are you doing?" she asked. The concern was apparent in her voice.

"I'm surviving," I replied, struggling to hold back the tears. I was still suffering emotionally from the break up and miscarriage and found it quite difficult to control my emotions and my tears. I would find myself losing control and sobbing at the simplest of things.

"I had no idea. I just found out the other day. Did you expect this?"

"No. We'd been arguing. But I didn't think it was this bad," I revealed.

"Jo-Ann called me up at the golf course on Sunday to ask me where you were and who the girl was that Todd had taken over to the house. I told her I had no idea, but that I'd call you when I got home and find out what was going on. Can we get together sometime this week to have dinner and talk?"

"I'd really like that."

"Okay. I'll call you later in the week to arrange something. But I just wanted to call you and let you know that I'm thinking of you and I love you."

"I love you too," I replied, before hanging up, relieved that she wasn't angry with me, or blaming me for the breakup. We had become close during my relationship with Todd and I hoped her and I could continue our friendship, even though things had not worked out so well with Todd.

* * *

On Friday, Elaine picked me up and we went to The Plaza for dinner. Both Todd and Virginia would be off this day; Elaine had checked before deciding to go there. During the ride there, I filled her in on everything that had transpired. When I told her about their dinner on the Monday evening before we broke up, she offered her opinion.

"That was a date."

"I know that, and you know that, but he refuses to see it as that," I replied.

"So you want the truth?" she asked.

"Yes, I've wondered, and I have my opinion, but I need to hear it."

"They're dating," she stated bluntly.

"Oh God," I moaned. Somehow, I wanted to believe that it wasn't true; that it was all just a bad dream. But I knew it wasn't; it was reality.

"I'm so sorry Brianna. But I thought you had a right to know."

"It's okay. I'll survive." I pulled myself together as we got out of the car and walked into the hotel. Over dinner, Elaine described her initial meeting of Virginia.

"Wednesday morning, I'm sitting in my bedroom and this gal comes waltzing into my bedroom wearing nothing but a robe and says to me 'Hi. We haven't met, but I'm Virginia, Todd's girlfriend'."

"What robe was she wearing?" was my first question.

"Oh, it wasn't yours," Elaine quickly explained. "It was a little red one." The conversation turned to her opinion of Virginia before we returned to why Todd and I broke up.

"Why did he tell you he was breaking up with you?" she asked.

"Basically, it came down to the fact that I wasn't talkative, opinionated or athletic enough for him. He said originally, that we needed to learn how to be friends again before we could resume the rest of our relationship. And then, he told me he didn't want to have to work that hard on a relationship anymore," I explained.

"He told me it was because you weren't assertive enough," she revealed.

After dinner, we moved to the lounge for a drink. As we passed a table, Elaine paused to comment to the gentleman at the table how much he resembled Judge Ito who had recently become famous during the murder trial of OJ Simpson. When we sat down in the lounge, Elaine turned to me.

"Would you do something like that?" she asked me.

"What? Make a remark like that to somebody? Of course; if it were true," I answered emphatically.

"You know. Todd told me that he had to order dinner for you every time you two went out because you could never order for yourself."

"That bastard!" I burst out laughing. "He never had to order dinner for me. I always did it for myself."

The lounge piano player, Freddy, came over then and joined us for the evening. Before she left, Elaine asked him to drive me home, since I wanted to stay at the hotel longer than she did. I had originally planned to meet another one of my friends there after dinner with Elaine, but he never showed up. Freddy agreed and even said I could drive his car, a convertible Z-28 Camaro.

The drive home was exhilarating and a real confidence-booster for me. We had the top down, and it was a busy night at the border, since Detroit was hosting the annual country-music Downtown Hoe-down in Hart Plaza. I got many appreciative, second glances from guys in other cars and those walking down the street.

By the time we reached my house and I'd had time to think about everything that had happened, I was more than a little pissed off at Todd. After I had changed out of my dress and pumps, into my jeans I wandered through the house, collecting photos of Todd and the two of us together. Once I had them all gathered up, I began methodically shredding them, one by one, until my father came home from work, stopping me.

When he questioned my actions, I exploded in a fit of rage, describing what I'd learned from Elaine that evening. He managed to calm me down somewhat and soon after I went up to my room to think and try to sleep. I laid awake for quite a while, thinking about the events of the past two weeks and my anger grew. Reflecting on my relationship with Todd, I realized that I had blindly chosen to do everything he suggested I do, such as how I had colored and styled my hair, how I had dressed, and acted as well as working out, although I had never been athletically inclined.

Although he had complained that I rarely offered my opinions or feelings about things, I realized that I had chosen not to because when I did, he told me I was being stupid or irrational. So, I had stopped providing my thoughts and opinions because I didn't feel it was necessary, considering he repeatedly put me down for my thoughts.

The next morning, I went through my closet, finding all the shirts I had confiscated from him during our relationship. Elaine and I had made plans to get together on Monday, since it was Victoria Day in Canada and I had the day off work. I had decided I would return all of Todd's shirts then and move my things out of the house, although he had told me on the phone when we had broken up that I could keep whatever shirts of his I had. However, I wanted no reminders of him.

* * *

Monday morning, I piled everything into my parents' minivan and we headed over. When we got to the house, I started to take Todd's shirts downstairs to his bedroom, but Elaine stopped me, taking them out of my hands.

"I'll take these down later," she said.

"No. I'll do it. I have to get my things anyways," I protested.

"But Todd got your things together," she explained.

"He wouldn't have gotten everything. I know there are things he would've forgotten and I don't want that bitch touching anything of mine," I replied.

"I don't think it's a good idea. You can do it another time," Elaine argued.

"I have to do it now. Now is the best time for me to do it. I need to get it over with and not put it off any longer," I began to cry.

"I just don't want you to be hurt. And I know there are things down there that you're going to see that are going to hurt you," she paused then handed the shirts back to me. "Okay, if you feel that strongly about it, I'm not going to stop you."

"Thank you." I took the shirts and headed down the stairs. My step faltered briefly as I rounded the corner to find a pile of women's clothes on the floor. I continued on my way into the bedroom we had shared, thinking I'd found the worst of it. Unfortunately, I was in for a bigger shock when I walked into the bedroom and turned on the light. Strewn across the bed and floor were her clothes mixed with his. The entire room was in disarray. There were clothes all over the bed and floor, the bed sheets were all tangled and pulled halfway off the bed. I took a deep breath and walked into the closet to hang his shirts.

Walking out of the closet, I began collecting my things that Todd hadn't bothered to put with the rest. As I moved through the room and discovered more of Virginia's bras and panties, my anger quickly built. I decided I was not going to leave any reminders of me for him. I opened the drawer in his night table that held all the cards and letters I'd given him over the nineteen months we'd been together. I debated removing the cards and letters as I picked up my black leather change purse. It held his stash of condoms, and as I pulled them out to drop back into the drawer, a glint of metal caught my eye. It was a large safety pin.

Suddenly, an idea lit up in my head. As I reached for the pin, I noticed a vibrator further back in the drawer. I knew it hadn't been there the last time I was and it definitely did not belong to me. With a renewed determination, I picked up the pin and proceeded to puncture every one of the condoms the drawer held. As I dropped each one back into the drawer, I thought back to my conversation on Friday with Elaine and the fact that Todd had told her he didn't think I was assertive enough.

"Well Todd", I thought, *"assert this, you lying, cheating, deceitful bastard"*, dropping the last condom back into the drawer.

After nineteen months, I knew him well enough to know that he never bothered to inspect a condom before wearing it, so I was confident that he would not notice a pin hole. I closed the drawer, having completely forgotten about the cards in my anger.

I packed up the rest of my things from the basement and headed back upstairs, putting the condoms out of my mind. Reaching the main floor, I remembered my Hawaii beach towel and returned to the basement. I came up empty-handed in my search, having torn the floor apart, tossing their clothes haphazardly around the room, not that anybody would detect an alteration of the current mess.

I returned to my packing and decided to clear my things out of the bathroom before tackling the office we shared for our two businesses. As I opened the drawer I kept my razors in, I found an envelope addressed to Todd, resting on top of everything else.

Knowing the writing was not mine or even Brenda's, curiosity got the better of me, and I pulled the letter out, assuming it was only one or two days old. Checking the calendar, I discovered that it was written the day after we'd broken up.

5-7-95
Hi Honey,

It's 9:42 pm. I'm still in my office waiting for 11:00pm to roll around. I miss you. This is so new, so different. I have NEVER felt this way before, whenever I see you I get this warm fuzzy feeling inside of me. You make me so happy!

When I get home tonite I'm gonna finish the tape I'm making you. I really don't want to go to court in the morning, it all seems so pointless – a waste of **our** time. Hopefully, it will be all over with soon. Anyways! When are you gonna teach me how to ride the jet ski? I'm getting excited! I wanna go away soon – very soon! Just you and I alone for a couple days.

As you can see I'm using a different pen now. We just got slammed! About 60 people just checked in! It's now 10:42pm. I can't wait to get outta here! I can't wait to see you tomorrow. I miss you lots & lots! I see you tomorrow – I Love You!
Love,
Virginia

Furious, I headed back downstairs. I flew out the door, waving the letter at Elaine and my mother as they stood outside talking.

"I know this is none of my business," I interrupted. "But I found this letter in the bathroom, when I was clearing my things out of the drawer." I quickly re-capped for them what the letter had said.

"Put it back where you found it. And pretend you never saw it. Let's go shopping and get you smiling and laughing again," Elaine tried to calm me. I returned the letter to the drawer and put it out of my mind. We spent a fun day at a nearby outlet mall, laughing and joking and I never once thought about Todd.

* * *

When we returned to the house later in the day, I headed into the office to tackle the job of sorting our paperwork and removing everything connected to my public relations business. I found that most of the desk had already been organized, but mixed in with my paperwork, I found another letter to Todd. This one was dated the day we broke up, and she had even included the time: nine-twenty. Thinking back, I did a mental calculation; it was roughly two and a half hours after I had hung up the phone from talking to him.

5-6-95
Dear Todd;

Hi honey. It's about 9:20pm (you just poked your head in the door!) I want you to know that I'm not mad anymore. I was a little upset, but now I'm fine. You should be aware of one thing. I am VERY possessive! I don't think I should have to compete with anyone.
I know we are gonna be together for a very long time and I know we have a lot to learn about one another, it's gonna take time, every minute I'm with you my feelings grow stronger. It scares the hell out of me.
I'm sure as time goes on my fears will subside, but right now it all seems so new. I'm a rookie in this game. I just don't want to burst the bubble. I look forward to spending the rest of my life w/you.
I Love You,
Love,
Virginia

I handed the letter to Elaine to read after I was finished. As she read it, I finished packing up my paperwork.
"Now, if that doesn't prove that he was cheating on me and he left me for her, I don't know what does," I said.
As Elaine and my mother left the room to begin loading my things into the van, I slipped the letter into my pocket, and retrieved the second from the bathroom drawer.

Once the office was cleared of my things, I headed into the garage and emptied our photo album, removing every picture of me or us, except my college graduation picture. When my things were all safely stowed in the back of the van, I asked Elaine to get my spare house key from Todd, as well as to ask him about my beach towel.

We hugged, with promises to keep in touch. My mother and I were soon on our way to return to Canada. During the ride home, my mother turned to me.

"Elaine really thinks that Todd never meant to hurt you."

"That's bullshit. You and I both know it. If he never meant to hurt me, he wouldn't have cheated on me with that skank-whore. He wouldn't have lied about his relationship with her and he wouldn't have left me for her. And he would've had the balls to face me today. But where is he right now? Probably sticking it in her as we speak. But no, he didn't mean to hurt me. You can damn well bet the farm, he meant to hurt me. He knew exactly what he was doing the second he decided to get involved with her. And he knew I was gonna get hurt by his actions," I exploded. The rest of the trip home was spent in silence as we were both absorbed in our own thoughts.

* * * * *

CHAPTER THIRTEEN

The day after I moved my things out of Todd's, one of my best friends from college called me at work.

"Do you want to go for dinner after work today?" Paul asked.

"Sure. Can we go to the mall and we'll have dinner there?"

"Well, yeah. But why do you want to go to the mall?"

"Because I want to get my ears pierced again," I replied.

I explained that Todd had told me that he didn't want me to get my ears pierced a third time. So, like my tattoo, I hadn't done it, but now I figured there was nothing stopping me from doing any of the things he hadn't approved of.

At three-thirty that afternoon, Paul picked me up at work and by four, my ears were pierced again and we were on our way to West Bloomfield for dinner. During the drive to the mall, he had talked me into going to Outback. Since it was one of my favorite restaurants, it wasn't difficult to convince me.

Over dinner, I told him about moving my things out the day before. When I told him about the condoms, he almost choked.

"Brianna! What are you going to do if she gets pregnant?"

"It won't be my problem. I'll send a card and congratulate them," I paused. "But you know what would be better if she does get pregnant?"

"Uh-oh. What?"

"If I hadn't miscarried," I laughed. "I'd love to see the look on his face for both of us to be pregnant, although there's no guarantee that it was his baby. But I'd love to make him squirm."

Paul was one of the few people that I had revealed my fears to about who the father might have been, as well as the fact that I'd had the affair. Our discussion continued and soon turned to other things. When I got home that night, I called Maya.

"What are you doing the weekend after this one? It's the first weekend in June," I asked.

"Nothing. Why?"

"I'll put gas in your car, and we're going to London," I answered.

"What for?"

"Because I want to go to the Blue Dragon," I explained.

"Cool. I'll pick you up from work on the Friday and we'll leave from there. We'll make a whole weekend of it." We finalized the plans and I was impatient for the time to pass.

* * *

The next two weeks flew by and before I knew it, we were in her car on our way to London. When we got into the city, she gave me a tour of her apartment and introduced me to her roommate, Marilyn. It was still early, so we sat down to a couple games of euchre before heading to the bars. That night, we all got pretty drunk, but I was the worst of us. I got so drunk, I was sick. To make matters worse, I started feeling sorry for myself because Todd and I had broken up and Maya began polling guys that walked by, asking them if they thought I was attractive.

One in particular stopped to talk to us, and Maya began a conversation with him, finding out more about him, presumably for me. As soon as we got back to the apartment, I passed out until morning. I awoke the next morning to the sound of the buzzer going off for the door. I tuned it out as Maya answered it, and heard her tell Marilyn that her boyfriend, Martin, was on his way up.

I finally dragged my protesting body out of bed about half an hour later although it was only eight o'clock. I still felt sick and my head was pounding. I wasn't surprised. It was the first time I'd been really drunk in almost two years. I managed to stay up for almost half an hour, but decided I was too hung over and went back to Maya's room to sleep it off after swallowing two Tylenol. At eleven-thirty, I woke again, feeling better but still had a massive headache. I felt like I'd been run over by a truck.

After showering and dressing, I felt better and curled up in a corner of the couch to watch country videos. Lorrie Morgan's newest release, 'I Didn't Know my Own Strength' came on and Maya spoke.

"This is my song to you," she said.

"Why?" I had never heard the song before.

"Because it's so you. I mean, Todd broke your heart and you're getting through it. You're a lot stronger than you think you are," she explained. We fell silent again until it came time to go to the Blue Dragon. When we walked in the door, I was nervous. I told the man what I wanted and showed him the picture I'd brought. He handed me a release form to fill out and sign before anything could be done. After I paid my money, the stencil was applied to my left hip and I was instructed to lie down on the table. As he prepared to begin the outline, I nervously looked up at Maya.

"Just relax," she said. "Once he's done the outline, the whole area will be numb and you won't feel a thing. Here; hold my hand and just squeeze if it starts to hurt too much."

I took her hand and nodded that I was ready to begin. I jumped as the needle first pierced my flesh. He made quick work of the outline of the body, but paused before beginning to trace the face. As planned, I was getting Mighty Mouse. When he resumed his work, I almost screamed. The face was directly on my hip bone, and no part of it had gone numb yet.

"Holy shit this hurts, Maya!" I cried out, the tears beginning to form in the corners of my eyes.

"It shouldn't," she replied. "Hasn't it gone numb yet?"

"No dammit. I think I'd rather go through labor than have another one done," I said.

"You obviously don't have any children," the tattoo artist interrupted. "Watch your language, young lady."

"This is all just a dream, right?" I asked Maya as he began to work on filling in the color. "I'm gonna wake up and there's not gonna be a tattoo on my hip. I'm gonna wake up at Todd's and Virginia is not going to exist." Maya looked down at me, frowning.

"Does this feel like a dream?"

"Hell, no! My dreams never hurt quite so much," I replied with a laugh. The tattoo artist paused as my laughter caused my leg to move. By the time he finished filling in the color, I had muscle spasms in my leg from keeping it immobile and flexed for so long. He covered it with a bandage before giving me instructions on how to care for it until it healed.

After pulling my jogging pants back up, I emerged into the sunlight with Maya and carefully climbed back into her car. Returning to her apartment, I curled up in a corner of the couch again as we settled in front of the television to watch The Lion King.

By the time we drove back to Windsor that night, the pain in my hip had subsided to a dull ache. During the drive home, we relived the night before and Maya told me everything she had learned about the guy she had picked up for me, telling me I should've gotten into the conversation.

He had even bought a drink for me, although I had ended up giving it to Maya because I knew I wouldn't be able to stomach yet another bottle of beer. The last time I'd been even close to being drunk had been that day after Christmas when Todd and I had gone out with Brad and Maya.

I crawled into bed when I got home, careful not to lie on my left side or nudge the tender spot on my hip. It was difficult however, because I had forgotten when I instructed him as to where I wanted it, that I always slept on my left side.

The next two weeks were hellish as I tried not to hurt the area as it healed. But it seemed the harder I tried, the more I would hurt it. Between rolling over onto it in my sleep, to leaning on the counters at work, I was in almost constant pain. But once there was no longer the painful reminder of my decision, I would temporarily forget that Mighty Mouse clung to my hip.

I spent a few weeks after being momentarily surprised when I would see it in the shower or when I changed my clothes, but for the most part, it was the fact that I couldn't believe I'd actually gone through with it and gotten a tattoo.

However, I was proud of it and was more than willing to show it to anybody who wanted to see it. But I had to be careful to hide it from my parents, since they had told me they didn't want me to get one. My father had told me it was my decision whether or not I got it, but that he didn't like the idea of me having one, and my mother told me that I absolutely could not get a tattoo. She even went so far as to tell me that if I ever came home with a tattoo, I had better be moving out that day. However, she made that declaration after I'd already gone under the needle and I figured since it was on my hip, it wouldn't be too difficult to keep hidden. I had a few close calls when I thought my father saw it, but if he did, he never mentioned it.

* * * * *

CHAPTER FOURTEEN

North Carolina – June 2015

"Did you ever tell Gran about Mighty Mouse?"

"Eventually. But not until after I moved out and came here. Then it didn't matter if she knew. She wasn't happy about it, but there was nothing she could really do since I had already had it done. I explained to her that I'd carefully considered it before I went and got it and that I knew I wouldn't regret getting it in ten or even twenty years. And I was right. To this day, I still do not regret getting it or any of my other tattoos done."

I had also gotten a poppy done on my shoulder blade as well as a palm tree on my ankle and a hibiscus arm band.

"You really stuck a pin through his condoms to get even? That is so cool. I never woulda thought of doing that. But did you ever consider that he might change his mind about breaking up with you and want to work things out? Is that what Kyle meant when he said about you getting even with Todd?"

"By that time, I knew that no matter what Todd said or did, there was no way I'd reconcile with him. At the beginning, I told Maya that for me to even consider getting back together with him, he was going to be putting a ring on my finger, and setting a wedding date that was within a year. But by the time I knew he was dating Virginia, I decided that I didn't want him back. It took a while to realize that he was very controlling; everything had to be his way. I knew that no matter how much I loved him, I was better off without him," I explained as we pulled back into the driveway after our afternoon of shopping.

"Was it difficult to adjust to him not being around?" she asked.

"In the beginning it was extremely difficult. I had to get used to doing things because I wanted to, instead of the things he expected me to do. Getting the tattoo and my ears pierced again helped, along with other things."

"Like what?"

"Like continuing to color my hair red," I replied.

"He had hated it the last time I'd done it before we broke up and I didn't really want any reminders of my life with him. I basically started new after the break up. I changed everything about myself. My whole attitude changed too. It took quite a while before I was able to really feel comfortable with myself. I became extremely self-conscious about my body. I even went so far as to practically starve myself. I worked out every day to make sure I stayed in shape. You might say I was anorexic.

"Oh sure, the guys all noticed me. Quite a few asked me out, but I spent months telling myself that there must be something wrong with me and wouldn't let myself get close to any guys because I figured they'd just leave too. I completely buried my emotions until I met your Dad, because I knew that if I didn't feel anything towards the guys I was dating, it wouldn't hurt so much when they left. I became what we all called a player. I dated a number of guys, but left when things got too serious, or they expected a commitment, or if a guy came along that I thought was better than the one I was with.

"And even when I was dating somebody, half the time, I was dating somebody else at the same time, only none of them ever knew it. I even resumed my relationship with Joe, because I knew our entire relationship was just sex. There were no expectations aside from that. He knew I didn't want a serious relationship and we both knew that there were no strings attached to what we had going."

"Did you ever see Todd again after you moved your stuff out?"

"Once, not too long after. I went over to go shopping with Elaine, about five months after we'd broken up. And Elaine and I have kept in touch over the years. There have been a few times that I've been at her house and he's shown up."

"What happened? Was it awful seeing him again? Was he still with Virginia? Did he have her with him? Did you knock him or her out?" Jessika began firing the questions.

"Slow down honey. I can only answer one question at a time. And I was very civil to both of them. I was still hurting, but I wasn't about to let him know how much. I gotten good enough at hiding my true emotions that I knew seeing him wouldn't make a difference. Even though I had worked through my emotions regarding our break up, we had never really discussed it, and I had a lot of things I wanted to say to him. Unfortunately, he wouldn't face me alone and I wasn't going to force him to talk to me, even though I wanted an honest explanation from him about why he'd broken up with me. I knew it was for Virginia, but I wanted to hear him say it," I answered as we dropped our bags on my bed to sort through as we talked.

We sat down in the center of the bed with the bags surrounding us as I began to tell her about the first time I saw Todd again.

* * * * *

CHAPTER FIFTEEN

Pontiac, MI – October 1995

It was Thanksgiving in Canada, Columbus Day in the States. Since I had the day off work, I'd made plans to spend the day with Elaine. I had originally planned on going over for the primary reason of dissolving my business, Victory Lane Media Services, as it was in both my name and Todd's. I had sent him a letter stating my intentions and had gotten a call back from Elaine that it wasn't necessary, but that she'd still like to see me if I was going to be over. I wasn't surprised that he'd had her call. I'd had a feeling he wasn't going to ever call me.

How I knew this was because of the fact that I had called his pager at the end of July, when they'd had to put the dog to sleep. I had offered to talk to him, if he felt like talking and wanted to call me back. He had not called though, and Maya had gone up one side of me and down the other when I told her, saying that he didn't deserve for me to be nice to him, after the way he had treated me. Ironically, Thanksgiving in Canada fell on what would have been our second anniversary and I wondered if he would remember.

My parents dropped me off early in the afternoon and arranged to pick me up later that evening, to give me and Elaine almost the entire day together. Going into the house, Elaine gave me my mail that had accumulated since my last visit and I quickly flipped through it as she went upstairs to finish getting ready. The phone rang while she was upstairs and out of habit, I began walking towards it to answer it, but she got the extension in her room before coming back down.

Ten minutes later, as we backed out of the garage, I glanced over at the jet skis to see if he'd made any changes to mine. I was contemplating telling him that since he'd bought it for me, that I was taking it home with me. I had to take a second look as I realized my towel was draped across the hull of his.

"That's my beach towel!" I exclaimed, pointing at it. Elaine stopped the car.

"Do you want to get it now?"

"No. I'll grab it when we come back." As we pulled out of the driveway and headed down Birch Harbor, Elaine spoke again.

"You know, when I asked him about it, he said he didn't know what towel I was talking about."

"He knew; he just doesn't want to give it up. And I can't understand why. I mean, it's not like he's been to Hawaii. The towel was mine. I brought it over for when we went to the lake."

As we stopped at the sign at Pine Lake and Birch Harbor, Todd came speeding around the corner. I managed a quick glimpse at his face before he passed us. Elaine turned to look at me.

"Do we know that lunatic?" she asked.

"That was your son," I replied, with a laugh.

As we headed to a nearby mall, we caught up on what we'd each been doing. She was concerned that I wasn't happy, but I assured her that I was, and that although I wasn't dating anybody exclusively, I was dating and not sitting at home moping over Todd. I wasn't going to tell her that since we'd broken up, I hadn't trusted myself to make a commitment to anybody in particular.

Since I'd lost so much weight after the break up and my miscarriage in May, I decided to buy new jeans and found that I'd gone from a size ten to a seven. I changed into one of the new pairs and walked out of the store, my confidence boosted.

We headed to Hudson's to check out their sale and get a frozen yogurt. Elaine commented about my drastic weight loss and asked if I was alright, but I decided not to tell her the entire reason for it, and the miscarriage. Since I knew that I would probably never know if the baby was Joe's or Todd's, I figured it would be best if I didn't tell her.

Leaving Hudson's, we wandered aimlessly and halfway through the mall, I was surprised to see Todd walking towards us. I did a double take when I saw a blonde hanging on his arm. As they got closer, I looked Todd in the eye and smiled.

"Hi Todd!" I exclaimed cheerfully, hoping to let him know that I had gotten on with my life and to show I had no hard feelings towards him or Virginia. He refused to acknowledge me and would not even look at me once I said hi to him. Virginia spoke up right away, directing her comments at Elaine.

"I've gotta show you something."

"This really isn't a good time," Elaine replied.

"But I gotta show you something," Virginia repeated, as she pulled her aside. I could easily see the lights bouncing off the diamond-laden gold band on Virginia's left ring finger as she displayed it to Elaine. I looked up at Todd's face to see he still wouldn't meet my look. Disinterested, I turned and walked into the nearest shop to browse as I waited for Elaine. She joined me a few minutes later and began apologizing profusely.

"It's no big deal," I reassured her. "He's getting on with his life, and he's happy. I'm cool with that. I'm getting on with my life."

"But you're hurt. I can see it in your eyes."

"A little. But only because he was so set against marriage with me."

I went on to explain about our argument concerning his engagement to Brenda. She continued to apologize throughout the day about running into them at the mall. Each time she apologized, I would reassure her that I was okay with the engagement. I even asked her to let me know when they'd set a date and I would send a card. But Elaine advised me not to waste my time.

When we got back to the house at the end of our day together, both of their cars were parked in the driveway.

"Let's wait out here since your parents will be here soon. I don't want you to be uncomfortable by being in the house with them," Elaine explained as we drove up.

"I'll be okay," I replied, determined to be strong and not let it bother me, no matter what Todd did.

"No. No. We'll wait out here. I'll just go in and get your mail and we'll sit out here and chat until your parents get here." She jumped out of the car before I could protest and headed into the house through the garage. When she rejoined me a few minutes later, she handed me the bag with my mail in it and I asked her where my towel was.

"It's gone from the jet ski. I went into the family room and asked Todd where it was. He shrugged his shoulders. So I said to him, 'Todd, it was on the jet ski when we left. Where'd it go?' He still said he didn't know. I don't understand what he wants with a towel," she explained.

"He's just being childish. As long as he's got the towel, there's still some sort of connection between us. I really don't care about the towel. It's the principle of the matter. It's my towel and I don't want him to keep it as a reminder of me. Let him live with his damn memories," I replied. A little while later, I saw the basement light go on as we talked and mentioned to Elaine that they must have gone downstairs to bed.

"Well, let's go inside and we'll sit in my bedroom until your parents get here." She pulled the car into the garage and we walked around to the front of the house. Ten minutes later, my parents arrived and I bounced back down the stairs to greet them. I told them about Todd's engagement as Elaine joined us on the front porch. They looked surprised and Elaine began apologizing again. My mother and I both reassured her that I would be fine.

"She's grown a lot emotionally since May," my mother explained. She and I had talked extensively after the break up and she had provided some much-needed advice. After talking a while longer, and promising again to keep in touch, my parents and I climbed into the van and returned to Canada. During the ride home, I described my day with Elaine, running into Todd and Virginia and the incident with the towel.

Once I was done relating the story, my mother revealed that they too, had seen Todd. My father explained that as they pulled out of the driveway when they dropped me off, he had noticed a white Chevy pick up truck parked in the cul-de-sac which was almost directly across from the house. Even from a distance, both my parents recognized Todd.

"So apparently, he saw you both drop me off, but he called the house anyways and asked Elaine if I'd gotten there yet. Why would he do that, when he already knew I was there, since he saw you both drop me off?" I wondered. It also made me wonder if Elaine had told him where we would be going and he took it upon himself to make an appearance.

* * *

The next morning, I took my mail with me into work to sort through during the slow periods. I had been transferred back to the university and it was always slow from the time I opened at eight o'clock, until about ten every morning. Halfway through, two photos fell out from between two envelopes. Picking them up, I realized they were of Virginia, presumable before she colored her hair blonde. Turning them over, I read the back. One said "I've thought it over and yes, I will marry you, love, Virginia."

When I got home from work that evening, I was still puzzled as to why I had been given the photos and wondered just who had put them in with my mail. The mystery was solved when Elaine called. She instructed me to go ahead and send the engagement card I had mentioned, and told me about the pictures. Apparently, Todd had volunteered the information that he had slipped the photos into my mail, but didn't say why. I assumed it was because he hadn't gotten the reaction he had expected at the announcement of his engagement. Unfortunately for him, I wasn't going to make a big deal out of the photos either, so he had wasted his time in giving them to me.

* * * * *

CHAPTER SIXTEEN
Charlotte, NC – June 2015

After telling Jessika about running into Todd, we finished sorting through our bags and packed our things for the weekend in Michigan.

Wednesday afternoon, we headed to Michigan as planned. As we were checking into the hotel, I noticed Doug strolling through the lobby towards the door. I called his name and he slowly turned to me. I waved him over and he hesitated briefly before changing direction and walking towards us.

"Mom, don't do this here, please," Jessika pleaded, gripping my arm tightly.

"Don't worry dear. Just smile and say hello," I replied quietly. I smiled brightly as Doug reached us and cheerfully greeted him.

"Hello Brianna. Such a pleasant surprise running into you and your lovely daughter as well. You're certainly growing up fast Jessika. If I didn't know better, I'd swear you were Brianna's little sister," Doug responded. "You should come by the house sometime. I'm sure Mandy would love to see you. I remember. . . " He trailed off as Jessika walked away.

"Would you have time for us to get together to talk sometime this weekend Doug? It's rather important," I hastily spoke up.

"Is it about teaching that daughter of yours some manners? Because I will gladly do that. Really, Brianna. I thought you'd brought Jessika up better than that. Perhaps she needs a steady male influence around to keep her in line," Doug replied.

"Like your daughter maybe? Don't preach to me about Jessika until you've taken a long, hard look at your precious Mandy," I shot back angrily.

"My daughter is every bit a lady," he snarled.

"Maybe around you she is, but trust me; Jessika has more class in her little finger than Mandy has in her entire body."

"How dare you insult my daughter! This attack is totally unprovoked. You know, I can understand that you and I are in a battle for points, but it's not necessary to bring our children into this," Doug lectured.

"Our children are in their own battle Doug, and I really don't want to discuss it here in the lobby. Come up to my room. I'd like to show you something."

"I don't have time. I'm late for an appointment," Doug replied, before turning and walking away.

I sighed and picked up my bag, heading to the elevator. Walking into the room I was sharing with Jessika, I dropped my bag on the bed and apologized to her.

"I should've known he'd bring her up, since you two hung around together when we first moved to Mooresville."

"It's okay Mom. I guess I should apologize to Doug for walking away from him," she answered.

"You'll do no such thing, young lady," I reprimanded her gently. "He had the nerve to complain about your manners and practically called Mandy a saint. Tomorrow when we get to the track, I am going to show him exactly what she's been doing to you. Now, let's go see your grandparents. You know your grandmother complains that she never gets to see you."

Heading out to the parking lot, we ran into Kyle and Jessika invited him to come with us. Ever since I'd bought the team, and hired Kyle as my crew chief, she'd always found any excuse to have him around. Jessika's father had been killed shortly before I'd gotten the team together and I often wondered if she was looking to Kyle as a substitute father, or what her intentions were. He seemed hesitant to join us, but Jessika had a way of talking him into anything and we climbed into my rental car.

The two hour drive to the border passed quickly and we joked and laughed as Jessika sang along with the radio, changing the words to make Kyle and me laugh even more. When we got to the Canadian side of the border, I was surprised when the customs official recognized me. I was still getting used to being recognized whenever I was out anywhere.

"Can I have your autograph?" he asked, coming out of the booth to stand beside the car.

"Sure thing. Jess, hand me a postcard out of the box, would you please?" Jessika handed me one over the back of the seat as Kyle handed me a pen.

After I had signed the card, I gave it to Kyle and Jessika for them to both add their autographs as well. As I passed it out the window to the customs officer, he thanked me and wished me luck on the upcoming weekend's race before waving me through.

Reaching my parent's house, we found a number of family members and friends awaiting our arrival. Jessika was quickly out of the car and in her grandparents' arms as they rushed out to the car. They hadn't seen us since February and the season-opener Daytona 500. Kyle and I got out of the car and slowly walked up to the house where we were greeted with hugs from everyone.

My entire family adored Kyle and eagerly welcomed him whenever he joined us. We'd met when I was working at the university and he was taking classes. Our interests were similar and we'd quickly become friends.

When I'd been looking for a crew chief, I knew without a doubt, it was Kyle I wanted. Luckily, he'd accepted right away.

After spending a few hours with my family, we headed back to our hotel, promising I'd see my parents at the track on Sunday. I'd brought them team passes which would enable them to come into the garage prior to the race, although I knew they would choose to return to their seats in the grandstands for the race.

* * *

Thursday afternoon, I walked into Doug's trailer as he sat talking to his crew. He looked up as I walked in, then turned back to his crew and continued talking as if I wasn't even there. I leaned on the counter and let his rudeness pass for a few minutes. When he paused, I interrupted him.

"Doug. I want to talk to you. We need to discuss something."

"I'm busy, Brianna. I'm sure it can wait," he answered impatiently.

"No, it cannot wait. However, your tales of last night's escapades with your Michigan pit bunny can wait," I replied.

"If you're going to run my daughter's name into the mud some more, I'll warn you right now, I won't stand for it and I don't want to hear it."

"Well, guess what? You are going to hear it, whether you like it or not!" I slammed the side of my fist into the countertop, shocking the men into silence. His crew quickly vacated the hauler, leaving me and Doug alone.

"Now that I've got your undivided attention, let me enlighten you on your daughter's activities, Doug. And I can tell you that my facts can be verified by a number of people," I continued and proceeded to repeat Jessika's story. I paused before telling him about the flowers.

"Mandy would never do something like that. I'm sure Jessika simply misunderstood."

"Try again, Doug. Tuesday morning, I arrived at my shop to find a jungle in my reception area. All the cards were addressed to Jessika and signed from Mandy. And none of them can be misunderstood. Have a look and judge for yourself. I think they'll make for very interesting reading for you." I dropped the cards in his lap and walked out.

Jessika was waiting in my hauler and we left the track for a public appearance and autograph session at one of the area Ford dealerships. During the drive, I filled her in on my conversation with Doug and offered her some advice.

The day passed quickly and we soon headed back to the hotel for dinner with the team. After dinner, half the team converged on the games room while the other half headed to the gym or the pool. Jessika talked me into going with her to the games room where we were soon engaged in a competitive pool game, playing doubles against Kyle and one of my newest crew members, Mark.

After playing a number of games, Jessika and Mark wandered over to the air hockey game. Kyle and I sat down at a nearby table, watching them. I had bought a pool table as well as an air hockey game for our basement and Jessika and I had spent many rainy summer days playing against each other, when I didn't have to go to the shop, or after I had returned home for the day.

"She'll be okay, you know," Kyle broke into my thoughts. "She's strong. Like her mother."

"I know. She's too much like me, I think. And it worries me sometimes. I remember what I was like growing up. And what I was like after Todd and I broke up."

"She's a good kid. You don't have anything to worry about."

"Yeah, that's what my parents thought. And look at what a hell raiser I was," I laughed.

"But it was different when you were Jess' age. You and her act more like sisters than mother and daughter."

"Maybe so. But I can't help but worry. It's what mothers do. It's my job to worry about her, and wonder if I'm raising her okay. It's not easy being a single parent."

"Well, it's not like you had a choice. I mean, being divorced from Craig would've been one thing. But he was killed Brianna. It was part of the job. You knew it and so did he."

"And his death could've been prevented. That bullet Craig took was meant for me. If I had recognized that creep before we arranged the bust neither one of us would've taken a bullet. But I screwed up. I was the one who should've known who he was, and that he was a threat to us. After all, it was me and Craig that helped put him away. It's no surprise he wanted revenge."

"But it's a chance you took. You knew there was that risk when you chose to become a cop. Just like you know the risks every time you strap yourself into that race car. You can't blame yourself for Craig's death," Kyle reasoned.

"I know, and I don't now as much as I did before. But I was the one who was in charge of the bust and I should've known who was involved in that drug circle. The hard part is I know Jess misses him more than she lets on. I mean, I could accept his death a little easier because I knew the risks and I took them too. And I'm grateful for the time Craig and I did have together. But she's so young. She needs a father figure in her life.

"And I don't think she fully understands the risks we took as cops. After all, it looks so easy when you catch the bad guys and they get put away for life, but then there are the dirt bags that get away, or that have their lawyers get them off. Then they're back on the streets, selling drugs to kids, or killing again. And look at the image portrayed on the television. The profession gets glamorized everyday on these TV shows.

"But we agreed that we didn't want Jessika to see the harsh realities of our jobs until she was old enough to understand. And let's face it, how many twelve year olds are going to be able to relate to their parents being cops, let alone understand that Daddy's not coming home ever again? The hardest thing I've ever had to do was explain to her why Craig was killed."

"I know. But you're doing a great job of raising her." We were interrupted as Jessika and Mark joined us.

"Mark and I are gonna go swimming. Is that okay?" she asked.

"Of course. Just be careful," I cautioned.

"I know. Don't wait up," she called over her shoulder after giving me a quick kiss on the cheek.

"Just don't be out too late. Remember, we all have to be at the track early tomorrow!" I called after them. After she left, Kyle and I continued our conversation and he walked me up to my room. At the door, he gave me a hug and reassured me that Jessika would be fine. I unlocked my door as he walked down the hall to his room, thinking about the events of the day.

* * * * *

CHAPTER SEVENTEEN

Friday was a busy day, with qualifying and two public appearances scheduled for the day. I took my qualifying run early in the morning's session and did not do as well as I had hoped I would. Kyle walked with me from the garage to the motorhome after my qualifying lap.

"Do you want any changes made before practice?" he asked.

"See what you can do to it. I've got two appearances today. I doubt I'll be back to the track before practice tomorrow," I explained.

"Okay. We'll play around with it and see if we can get some more speed. Fine tune the engine a bit. I'll see ya back at the hotel tonight," Kyle replied before heading back to the garage.

After changing out of my driver's suit, Jessika and I drove to Dearborn and Ford Headquarters for my first public appearance. I was among five of the Ford drivers present with our show cars on display for an autograph session. By the time the last autograph had been signed and all the fans had left, the five of us had a friendly argument going about who was going to win that weekend. Many of the fans in attendance knew that I was from Windsor, which wasn't that far from Dearborn and everybody came to the conclusion that I was the odds-on favorite to win, although a number of the fans providing their opinion felt that other drivers were the favorite. After a brief luncheon put on for us by the company, a film crew was brought in to shoot a commercial with us on the dangers of drinking and driving.

Since I'd brought Jessika with me, the executives at Ford decided to shoot a second spot with just me and Jessika. It came out well and everybody was pleased with it. The production department promised to send us a copy before it was released to the television networks. Leaving Dearborn, Jessika and I drove to Southfield to one of the area country radio stations for an on-air interview. The afternoon passed quickly and all too soon it was time to head back to the hotel for dinner with the team.

Regretfully, we left the station after an afternoon of laughs and promising to stop by in August when we returned to the area.

Before getting on the freeway back to the hotel, I took Jessika for a drive through Pontiac and West Bloomfield, so she could see the area that I had described to her during my story about Todd.

I sat for a few minutes in front of Todd's old house, although I knew Elaine had moved out just over ten years earlier.

Putting the car in gear again, I drove away. I pointed out Orchard Lake as we drove by, explaining that was the lake where I had spent most of my summer with Todd. Waiting for the light to turn green at Orchard Lake and Pontiac Trail, Jessika tapped my arm and pointed across me to the next lane.

"Mom, do you know that man in the next car? He keeps staring and waving."

"What man, Jess?" I turned my head towards the other car she was referring to and got the shock of my life. It was Todd. I turned my attention back to the light just as it changed. Instead of driving right through though, I made a sharp right turn onto Pontiac Trail.

"Hang on honey. We're going to take the scenic route back to the hotel," I gunned the gas and quickly picked up speed. I had a feeling he would follow us and I wanted to get far enough ahead of him to hopefully outrun him.

"Cool. Who was that? Ohmigod! Was that . . .? It wasn't him, was it? It was! Holy shit! I don't believe it!"

"Yes, Jessika. It was him." I slowed down as the road curved and looked in my rearview mirror. "Shit! How did he catch up to us?" I muttered and sped up again. Reaching Haggerty Road, I had enough distance on him that when I ran the yellow light, he got stuck at the red. I laughed, knowing how frustrated he'd be. I kept my foot to the floor and made sure I was quite a distance from the light before I decided to pull into a parking lot and waited for him to pass.

He raced by a few minutes later, and I waited for traffic to clear before I pulled back out onto the road. There were about five cars between us, so I knew there was no chance he'd see me. Jessika had been with me before when I'd play what she called highway hide and seek with Kyle or one of the guys on the team, so she knew exactly what I was doing. As luck would have it, the road widened to two lanes in either direction and the cars between us all chose to take the right lane, while Todd took the left.

I pulled into the right lane behind everybody else. Minutes later, I found myself almost even with him and shifted to a higher gear to shoot by him, remembering that the freeway was close by. I ducked in and out of traffic, watching him mimic my every move. For a while, I stayed in the left lane, making sure there were no cars in the right lane next to me. At the last possible second, I abruptly changed lanes to get on the freeway. Jessika and I laughed as I merged with traffic, knowing he wouldn't be able to catch up to us now. We were still laughing about it when we joined the rest of the team and Jessika quickly filled them in. Kyle and I sat together and I noticed that although there was an empty seat next to us, Jessika chose to sit at another table next to Mark.

"So you outran him on his own turf, eh? That must've pissed him off," Kyle laughed.

"I hope so," I answered, pre-occupied with my thoughts as I watched Mark absorb everything Jessika said.

"Hello! Earth to Brianna. Anybody home?" Kyle said a few minutes later, breaking into my thoughts.

"I'm sorry. What did you say?" I asked, turning my attention back to him.

"I asked how everything went in Dearborn today and at the radio station. Would you relax? I already had a talk with the boy. He knows what happened Monday night with Jessika and he's not gonna push her into anything."

"I just don't want to see her rush into another relationship so soon. She's at a very vulnerable stage right now. And I know how easily she can be hurt."

"She's a big girl, Brianna. I think she knows what she's doing. And the guys are all looking out for her. Besides, I think Mark really likes her. Now, tell me how everything went today," Kyle changed the subject. I told him about my day and the second drunk driving spot as well as how popular Jessika had been at the radio station. We laughed again as I described seeing Todd at the traffic light.

"I couldn't believe it. Here, I'd just finished telling Jessika about my relationship with him. And I had just shown her the house. And there he was, sitting at the light. I was kinda surprised when Jess pointed him out. Especially considering the last time I saw him, he wouldn't even look at me."

"Maybe he regrets the decisions he made in the past," Kyle suggested.

"Of course he does. Think about it Kyle. Virginia divorced him and took him for everything he had. I've got a successful race team and had a great career as a cop. People recognize me everywhere I go because I'm in the top five in points, only the second woman to run full-time on the circuit and the first woman to be successful in the sport since Daytona Hudson. Why wouldn't he regret leaving me for her? If he'd stayed with me, he'd be living the good life now, savoring the fruits of my hard work, instead of still working the same dead-end security job he was in when we broke up," I explained.

"Hey, everybody makes mistakes," Kyle reasoned.

"Yeah. And mine was dating him," I laughed. The conversation turned to the day's qualifying as one of my mechanics interrupted us, and Kyle described the changes they'd made to the car.

After dinner, I changed and headed to the gym to work out. There, I was joined by Kyle and a number of the other crew members. We went to the pool afterward to relax, but ended up getting pulled into a competitive game of volleyball. When I finally fell into bed that night, I was exhausted.

* * * * *

CHAPTER EIGHTEEN

Saturday was hectic with more public appearances as well as two interviews with area television news stations. The second interview included Doug, since we were fighting for the top spot in the point's standings. He stopped me as I left the media building at the conclusion of the interview.

"Do you have a minute Brianna?" he asked. I stopped walking and turned to face him, crossing my arms over my chest. I was prepared to argue with him further about our daughters' feud. I was totally unprepared, however, for what he did say. "Look, Brianna, I want to apologize for what I said the other day. I called the florist and they confirmed the order. Mandy tried to deny it at first when I called to ask her about it. But when she knew I'd talked to you and read the cards, she admitted to sending the flowers. I'm sorry about the way she's treated Jess. And I'm going to make sure she apologizes when we get home."

"Thanks, Doug. I really appreciate you doing that. If you'd seen how upset Jessika was by it all," I trailed off, looking up at him.

"Well, I thought about how I would feel if it was the other way around. She looks like she's doing okay though," Doug answered.

"Yeah, well, she's strong. But she hides her emotions a lot. If she wasn't my daughter, I'd never know how much she's hurting by it all," I explained.

"I don't know about that Brianna. The past coupla times I've seen her, she's looked pretty happy hanging around with that new mechanic of yours. They're starting to look pretty cozy."

"Oh, don't start! If she wants to go out and have fun, I think it's great. I don't want her sitting around feeling sorry for herself. If she's spending time with other people, it means she's not thinking about everything that's happened. I'm happy she's getting out already, and personally, I like Mark; he's a nice boy and a good kid."

"Yeah, I guess," Doug relented.

"Besides," I continued, as we walked out into the sunshine. "It could be worse."

"How?" he asked, looking puzzled.

"She could've taken up with one of the guys on your team," I laughed.

"Oh, really? And what's wrong with the guys on my team?" Doug feigned a hurt look.

"Besides the fact that they work for you? On a Chevy team? Shall I continue?" I joked as we reached my hauler.

"I'd rather push a Chevy, than drive a Ford!" Dough shot back. "And at least my guys don't have to worry about getting fired just because I have PMS."

"That's because PMS is a requirement to work for you. Pretending to be macho studs is mandatory on their resumes!"

"Oh yeah? Well, at least my team can spell PMS."

I looked at him and could tell that he knew he was losing this one; he hated to give up arguments to me, even when it was obvious he was grasping at nothing to try to salvage it.

"Only on a good day," I answered. "And, that's only when you hold up cue cards with the letters on them. Even then, they'll stare at the cards for an hour like monkeys doing a math problem before they get it right." I waited for Doug's response. He stood there, just watching me, totally at a loss for words. I could almost see his thoughts forming and breaking apart as he struggled for a retort.

"I'll think of something," he finally spoke. "Just give me some time."

"Take all the time you need. I'm going to get some practice in before it gets too late," I said before walking into the back of the hauler to change. Doug met me out on the track a short time later and we drag raced down the straight-aways for a few laps before I pulled ahead and left him behind. When we pulled into the garage after the day's practice session was over, our crews surrounded our cars and began making adjustments for the next day's race. By the time I was changed back into my street clothes, the crew was done with the car and we arranged to meet later.

I left the team playing pool after dinner, and headed back to my room to sleep. I'd learned early that it was too difficult to keep focused on the race after staying out too late the night before.

* * * * *

CHAPTER NINETEEN

Race day, Doug sat with me during the drivers' meeting, and walked me to my car after driver introductions. He gave me a hug and wished me luck before jogging up to the second row and his car. I was starting twentieth. Kyle met me as I climbed into the car.

"What was that all about?" he asked.

"You know, I have no idea. I've been trying to figure it out myself. He's been overly attentive today for some reason. Oh well," I shrugged. "I'm not going to worry about it. I'm more concerned about finishing well today."

"Yeah. We need those points to take the lead from Doug," Kyle agreed, pausing. "Hey, maybe that's why he's being so attentive. So you'll back off on the chase."

"No. Doug knows better than to try to pull a stunt like that," I replied. Conversation was impossible as the grand marshal was introduced.

"Gentlemen," he paused. "Excuse me. Drivers . . . start . . . your . . . engines!" The field roared to life and Kyle and I chuckled at the blunder.

Although there had been one other woman, Daytona Hudson to run full-time on the circuit previously, whose team I had bought following her retirement, I was currently the only woman doing it. Being the only woman, I had grown accustomed to the mistake.

Kyle hooked up my lines and radio and I secured the safety harnesses and locked the steering wheel into place. He gave me the thumbs up before putting up the window net and locking it into place.

The field began rolling down pit road and I put my car in gear. I slowed down as I neared my parents' seats and waved. They had made a banner and put it up in the grandstands wishing me luck and the whole crowd waved when they saw my car. Luckily, I'd been able to get the pit stall right in front of their seats.

When the green flag flew, I accelerated with the rest of the field and quickly began fighting my way to the front. Somehow, Kyle and my guys had managed to play around with the set-up and my car was much faster than it had run earlier. Before I knew it, I was on Doug's rear bumper. We stayed running bumper-to-bumper and pitted together at the halfway point.

His pit was directly in front of mine, and our pit times were identical, putting him back out on the track right ahead of me again.

Rejoining the field and getting back up to race speed, I heard Jess' voice coming through the radio. She worked as my spotter at every race.

"Wreck in Two. Go high."

"Brianna, caution's out. There's a bad wreck in Turn Two. Take the high line," Kyle explained as I headed into Turn Four. Doug had gotten back up to speed faster than I had and was a short distance ahead of me.

"Ten-four." I held my breath as Doug's car fishtailed in Turn One, but he easily regained control as I released some of the pressure I had on the accelerator and down-shifted. I looked ahead of us as we approached the second turn and swore as I saw a car come back up the track, crossing our path.

"Shit! Move, move, move. Doug, take your foot out of it!" I yelled, although I knew he couldn't hear me. I hit the brakes to slow down, causing my car to fish-tail and spun into the outside wall. I couldn't do anything but watch as his car hit the other. I could hear myself scream as the back end of Doug's Chevy began to lift and suddenly, it was flying over the concrete retaining wall.

Luckily there were no seats in Turn Two or down the backstretch. My car slid along the wall and I began pulling off my helmet and safety belts before I had even come to a complete stop. Dropping the window net, I climbed out the window and crawled across the hood to scramble over the wall. I raced down the hill to Doug's car and squeezed in through the passenger side window.

His Chevy was mangled to the point that it was difficult even for me to climb into the car and at five feet nine inches tall, I was one of the smaller drivers on the circuit. There were only a couple that were shorter than I was, but most were at least six feet or taller. The roof had caved in so far that it was almost touching Doug's head. The windows had all either shattered or been blown out by the flip.

I could hear the sirens of the safety crew faintly as the sounds of the race died away. I leaned over and dropped Doug's window net and carefully lifted the visor on his helmet. The safety crew arrived then to assess the wreck to figure out the best way to get him out.

Luckily, the HANS device which had become mandatory after Dale Earnhardt's fatal crash in Daytona Beach in 2001 looked to have worked, but Doug had been knocked around enough in the car that he was unconscious.

Somebody began furiously cutting away the roof of Doug's car to make it easier to get him out. Once the roof was peeled back, we worked on getting him secured to a back board and only then did we slowly remove his helmet. When they had him loaded onto a stretcher, I picked up his helmet and followed them to the ambulance as a wrecker arrived to take his car back to the garage. Kyle and Ricky, Doug's crew chief, caught up to me in the infield care center as I spoke to one of the emergency workers and we inspected Doug's helmet.

Shortly after, they wheeled him out and explained that although he was now conscious, they were airlifting him to Foote Memorial in nearby Jackson for more tests.

I walked alongside the stretcher and Doug took my hand as we made our way to the helicopter.

"Brie. Call Mandy. I'm okay," Doug struggled with his words.

"Of course, Doug," I assured him, and then pulled the doctor aside. "He's not okay, is he?"

"We won't know until we get him to the hospital and they run more tests. He's in pretty rough shape though." Kyle and Ricky looked at me expectantly when the doctor headed back inside to call the hospital and notify the emergency room that Doug was on his way. I shrugged my shoulders and walked over to them.

"They don't know shit around here. I'm going to the hospital. I'll call Mandy on the way. Should I have her fly up?" I looked to Ricky, but it was Kyle who spoke.

"What about the race?" he asked.

"Mine's over. I'm pretty sure I wadded up the back end good when I hit the brakes to avoid the original wreck and smacked the wall. I'm too many laps down by now to salvage today's run. I wouldn't be able to concentrate on the race now anyways, not after seeing that wreck. Pack up and relax. Ricky?"

"Yeah. I know what you're thinking. I agree. It might be a good idea to have her come up. I'll call and have the other plane ready. And one of the guys can pick her up at the airport in Jackson," Ricky answered. We each headed in different directions then to accomplish our various tasks. I ran to the hauler and grabbed my keys, wallet and cell phone.

Leaving the track, a state trooper directing traffic stopped me and jogged over to my car, explaining that he'd heard about the wreck, and asked if I was going to the hospital. I nodded.

"Want an escort so you can legally speed?"

"I'd love one," I answered with a smile. He immediately jumped in his car and we were off. He turned on his lights and siren and I could see him talking on the radio as I picked up my cell phone and dialed Doug's home number. Somebody picked up on the second ring and I could hear Mandy crying and screaming in the background.

I knew she always watched the races at home when she didn't travel with Doug's team and was all at once grateful that Jessika was my spotter, so she was always at the track with me.

"Mandy, calm down already. I'm sure your Dad's okay. Hello?" a male voice answered.

"Obviously, Mandy's in no shape to come to the phone. This is Brianna Lane. Is this Jonathon?"

"Y-yes, ma'am. It is," he replied hesitantly. "Do you want to talk to Mandy?"

"No. I'd rather talk to you. I want you to get Mandy on her father's plane. It's going to be ready to bring you both up here. There'll be a crew member from either my team or Doug's waiting to bring you to the hospital," I explained.

"Is he. . . ?"

"No, Jonathon. He's not dead. But he is in pretty bad shape. I'm on my way to the hospital right now and I'll see the two of you in about two hours. Now, get a move on and get your asses on that plane."

I hung up, hoping he'd be able to get Mandy on the plane without too many problems.

Arriving at the hospital, I waved to the state trooper to thank him as I ran into Emergency. I explained to the nurse at the desk why I was there and she eyed me suspiciously before picking up the phone and calling a doctor. She spoke to him briefly before turning back to me.

"Ma'am, your husband is being prepped for surgery. If you'd like to fill out these forms and sign them."

She held out a clipboard. I took it from her and began filling in the forms she'd indicated, not bothering to correct her on my relationship with Doug. When I reached questions I couldn't answer, I called Ricky on his cell phone.

I hurriedly explained what was going on and got the information I needed. Thanking him, I signed the release form and hung up as I returned the clipboard to the nurse.

"You do not know your husband's medical information?" she asked haughtily, looking pointedly at my phone.

"No. Because he's not my husband," I held up my hand as she began to protest. "Relax. I'll take responsibility because I'm the only one here. His crew chief has given me authorization to do so. I was right behind him when he crashed and I got to his car before the safety crew. Take a chill pill a'ight? Now, if you'll do me the favor of directing me to where the operating room is."

I headed down the hall in the direction she sent me and found a seating area outside the operating room she'd told me he was in. Shortly after, I was joined by Ricky and half of Doug's crew. My crew began arriving and Jessika walked in with Kyle. The mood was somber since we had no idea what condition Doug was in, and eventually other drivers and their crews began wandering in for news on Doug's condition.

Soon the entire hall around the operating room was full of various uniforms. Most of the teams still wore some sort of indication as to what team they were a part of. Traffic through the corridor that was not related to the racing community looked at me oddly and I finally realized the reason why.

I hadn't bothered to take the time to change out of my uniform into my street clothes, since I'd left so quickly to head to the hospital. I chuckled softly and Kyle looked at me.

"What's so funny?" he asked.

"Look at me. I was in such a hurry to get here, I didn't bother to change into my street clothes. No wonder everybody is looking at me so strangely. I was starting to wonder if I was still wearing my helmet or something."

"I guess it's a good thing Jess thought to get your stuff out of the motorhome then. I was just gonna leave your bag there, thinking you had already changed. Your bag's out in the car. I'll get it for you so you can change." Kyle shook his head as he chuckled, heading out to the car for my clothes.

*****

CHAPTER TWENTY

When Mandy arrived, Doug was still on the operating table. She was sobbing hysterically and I assumed she hadn't stopped since she saw the crash. Despite the events of the past week, Jessika hesitantly stood when I did and walked with me to where Mandy had stopped. I put my arms around her to try to calm her down a little, knowing Doug wouldn't want her to fall apart. Her mother had walked out on Doug when Mandy was only a baby, so I knew she'd need a comforting shoulder to lean on the next little while.

"I can't believe he's dead," she sobbed. "Last time we talked, we got into a huge fight and I told him I hated him. I didn't mean it though. Honest, Brianna. I really loved my dad." She looked up at me and I took her tear-stained face in my hands and smiled.

"Mandy, your Dad's not dead. He's very much alive. He's just in surgery right now. He's gonna be okay. Trust me," I explained quietly.

"He's really okay?" she asked, her tears subsiding slightly.

"He had a real bad wreck, and I'm not gonna lie to you. We don't know how serious his condition is; but there's an excellent team of doctors and nurses in there with him. Your dad's very strong too, and he's got a lot of people out here who love him and are praying for him. Come over here and have a seat," I led her over to where I'd been sitting and sat her down. Jessika sat on the floor in front of us and I could see Kyle out of the corner of my eye as he signaled the rest of the crews to follow him down the hall to another waiting room. I also noticed he took Jonathon with him, so the only ones left in the room were me, Jessika and Mandy.

"D-don't you hate me?" she hiccupped between sobs.

"No, honey. We don't hate you. I'm a little disappointed and I know Jessika is hurt by what you did, but we certainly don't hate you," I exclaimed.

"I'm sorry Jessika. I know I was wrong. I was jealous of what you and Jonathon had. And I wouldn't blame you if you never forgive me. If I were you, I wouldn't forgive me," she apologized.

"Well, it's gonna take a while for me to forgive you. The only reason I'm still here is because I know how I'd be upset if it was my mother in that operating room and I'm not a vindictive person. I'm not gonna be a bitch to you now when your Dad's the one in there," Jessika replied quietly, taking her hand.

Mandy smiled weakly as I covered both their hands with mine. A short time later, the operating room door opened and the surgeon emerged, removing his mask. The three of us stood as one and he slowly walked over to us. He shook my hand as he introduced himself.

"You must be Brianna Lane. Dr Matthews. Pleased to meet you. And thank you. Your input about the scratches on the helmet were a lot of help to us in determining what injuries we should be looking for."

"How's my Dad?" Mandy interrupted.

"He's going to be fine. In another few minutes, we'll be moving him to a recovery room and tonight he'll be in a private room," he replied.

"How badly was he hurt?" I inquired.

"Well, he could be worse, considering the occupation and the severity of the wreck. But I'm not going to lecture you on career choices. He has a concussion and minor bruising of his brain. That should subside in a couple days. His major injury is a broken femur; that's the bone in his thigh. But we did the usual plates and rods to repair it, and he'll have to go through therapy after it heals. And he'll have to wear a brace on it for about six weeks, much like Darrell Waltrip did back in ninety-two and one of my former patients, Daytona Hudson, did back in ninety-eight," he explained.

"Is there going to be any long term damage?" I questioned.

"Obviously, he's going to walk with a limp because of the broken bone. As for the concussion, we'll be monitoring him while he's here. There's a possibility of brain damage and diplopia, which is more commonly known as double vision. He's also going to have quite a headache and might be confused or disoriented for a while from the trauma of the accident as well as the morphine we've given him for the pain. But we'll be able to take care of all that here."

"When can I see him?" Mandy demanded.

"Just as soon as we move him into a recovery room and he wakes up. It's probably going to be another hour or so before he wakes up. I'd suggest going for a walk or something. Don't wait around here. Y'all have been here too long," Dr Matthews replied.

"Come on girls. Let's follow the doctor's orders. I'll have Kyle call us when Doug wakes up."

I led them down the hall and quietly informed Kyle that we were going for dinner, leaving instructions with him not to call unless it was an emergency. I also told him to send our crews home since Doug was out of the operating room. I joined Jessika and Mandy out at the car, where they were whispering and giggling to each other. As I pulled out of the parking lot, I turned to Jessika, surprised at her change of attitude about Mandy. But I realized that she probably understood that Mandy needed to be cheered up at the moment.

"What's with the giggles?" I asked.

"Nothing, Brianna," Mandy spoke up from the back seat. "Jess and I were just talking."

"I see you've forgotten what it's like to spend time with us. 'Fess up, Jess. What's the deal?"

"Mandy was just commenting on how hot Kyle is. So I explained to her that he's your man if you two ever get your shit together. And that I didn't think you'd take too kindly to her trying to do to you what she did to me."

"Jessika!" I admonished her, not for her cursing, but rather for her bluntness about me and Kyle.

"Well, it's true. It's obvious he likes you, and I know you're crazy about him."

"Yeah, well -- "

"Well, nothing', Ma. I swear, ever since Daddy died, you've practically become a nun. It'd be real nice to have a man in the house again, beside the guys on the team, that is. And Kyle's cool," Jessika explained.

"Hey, I'd do him if he'd give me the time of day," Mandy piped up from the backseat.

"Mandy, you'd do anything with a penis and a pulse if they gave you the time of day," Jessika said sarcastically as Mandy pouted.

"That's not true, Jessika. I turned down the O'Connor boy and I haven't slept with every guy I've dated. And I stayed a virgin longer than you did," Mandy shot back.

"You turned down the O'Connor boy because of the rumor that he's got shit Medicare don't cover!" Jessika retorted as we got out of the car at the restaurant.

"I wouldn't have done him anyway. He wanted me to be part of a threesome with some other chick he picked up. I don't do that shit. One at a time and men only please and thank you," Mandy explained as the waitress seated us. We quieted down briefly as we looked over the menu. After the waitress took our order and brought our drinks, I overheard two guys at a nearby table arguing.

"It's her, I tell ya," the one said.

"How could it be? What would she be doing here?" the second one asked.

"I'll betcha. Go ask 'er."

"You go ask. I'm not gonna look like an ass."

"Fine," the first one replied, standing up. "I will go ask and you'll see I'm right." He walked over to our booth and stood looking down at me nervously. I looked up at him and smiled. "Excuse me. My buddy and I over there were just having a debate about you. I was just wondering if you'd clear something up for us?" he asked me.

"Sure thing. What's the debate about?" I asked, assuming it was about whether or not I was a race car driver.

"Were you Playmate of the Year back around ninety-eight or ninety-nine?" he asked hesitantly, surprising me. I didn't think anybody would recognize me from those pictures all those years ago.

"That's a long time ago. Do you really think it's possible to recognize a person from a photo taken, what, sixteen, seventeen years ago?" I asked.

"It was a face I'd never forget, not in a million years. She had the most amazing blue eyes; I fell in love with her. She was all I dreamt about. I woulda given anything to meet her," he replied, looking dejected.

"Well, you don't have to give anything, 'cause it's free to meet me. Although I am surprised that you remembered me after all these years," I answered. He smiled as he realized what I'd said, then leaned down and looked into my eyes, frowning.

"Nah, it's not you. Yer eyes are a different blue," he accused.

"They were colored contacts," I explained gently.

"Prove to me you're really her," he demanded. I looked at Jessika, wondering how I could prove it. She knew about the layout, but I could tell from the shocked look on Mandy's face that Jessika hadn't told her.

"Hey, Mom. I'm mighty proud of you, if you know what I mean," Jessika said, referring to my tattoo. I stood up and winked at her.

"Thanks, dear." While he stared at me, looking confused, I unzipped my denim shorts and pulled down one side, exposing my Mighty Mouse tattoo. I'd gone back once to have the color retouched and it still looked fairly new. His jaw dropped when he saw the tattoo and he grinned at his friend as he was proved right about who I was.

"I have a copy of the issue in my car. Would you autograph it for me?" he inquired as I returned to my seat.

"I'd be more than happy to sign it for you, as long as you're discreet in bringing it in. There's children here that I don't think need an early education in female anatomy," I agreed. He quickly rushed out and returned a few minutes later with the magazine tucked into his jacket pocket. He quietly set it down on the table and I opened it to the centerfold. As I began to sign it, I heard a voice complaining to the waitress and turned around to face the speaker, seated in the booth behind me.

"I can't believe such smut is permitted in this establishment. I demand to be moved to another table and I want to talk to the manager."

The woman looked to be about sixty-five and well past her prime. I looked at her companion, who I assumed was her husband. He was wearing a grin from ear to ear and I winked at him and laughed quietly as I held up the centerfold for him to see. I dropped the magazine back down on the table and turned back to Jessika and Mandy as the woman turned to confront me.

"That's utterly disgusting. For a woman to display herself like that. It's immoral and degrading. And to be proud of being so loose. I'm glad I'm not your mother."

I slowly slid out of the booth and stood up, turning to the woman. I leaned over, with one hand on the table, and the other on the back of the bench seat we shared.

"Let me tell you something ma'am," I began. "Being proud and unashamed of your body is not disgusting, immoral or degrading. The layout was actually done quite tastefully. And the centerfold was not a nude shot. In fact, I'm sure your husband here probably had the issue. Just because I posed for Playboy does not mean I'm loose or easy. But I am proud of my sexuality and sensuality. It's how I was raised and it's how I'm raising my daughter. And by the way, my mother happens to be quite proud of me, as is my entire family, thank you very much. You see, not only did I pose for Playboy, but right now, I happen to be in the top five in the Sprint Cup point standings, only the second woman to accomplish that feat."

"Why, I never!" the woman exclaimed.

"Maybe you should sometime," I shot back. "You might enjoy it."

"Waitress? I demand to be moved to another table, preferably as far away from this one as possible. And I want to speak to the manager immediately," she demanded again.

"Ma'am? I think she understood you the first time. But I'm terribly sorry if near nakedness offends you," I spoke up, and then turned to her husband. "And I'm sorry for you that your wife is offended by the most natural thing in the world, sex and flesh. I commend you for accepting it. You're a wonderful man."

I rejoined my table and finished signing the magazine as the waitress led the couple away to another table. Jessika and Mandy howled with laughter as I handed the autographed magazine back to the man. He thanked me and happily returned to his own table. A short time later, the waitress returned with our dinner order and I noticed she was trying to fight her laughter.

"Go ahead and let it out," I laughed, as she smiled and began laughing with us.

"I can't believe the way you told off old Mrs Jenkins. You really gave her what-for. That was so cool. I could never do that. Enjoy your dinner, Ms Lane," she bounced away with a smile and I returned my attention back to Jessika and Mandy. I explained everything to Mandy as we ate dinner and answered all her questions, of which she had many. After we finished eating, the restaurant manager came over to apologize for the uproar, obviously worried the incident would affect me returning in the future.

"She was no bother. I'm sorry if I offended her, but I understand that not everybody has the same opinion of magazines such as Playboy. She had every right to voice her thoughts on it," I explained. "And I assure you that I will bring my team here in August when we come back."

"I don't know what you said to Mr Jenkins, but the entire time I was at the table, he had a grin on his face from one ear to the other. I think you really made his day."

"Well, I have a feeling he enjoyed the Playmate of the Year issue as that other gentleman did. If you had seen the way his face lit up when I flashed him the centerfold, I think you'd understand," I explained.

"I think every man who has every seen it, enjoyed it immensely. And often. To be perfectly honest, I personally cherished my issue. I subscribed for ten years, hoping to see you in it again. And when I heard you were going to be driving a stock car, I was ecstatic, knowing you'd be on my television every Sunday. I'm curious. Will you ever do another layout?"

I hesitated briefly, contemplating his question, before responding. I had never really considered the possibility of doing a second issue.

"If Playboy asks me, I will consider it. But I can't guarantee that I would do it again. After all, I don't know how NASCAR would feel about me posing again and I have a very impressionable teenage daughter. I'd have to consider how it would affect her to have her mother posing nude in a magazine at her age. And Playboy hasn't asked me yet, which I guess is the most important thing."

"Well, it was a pleasure talking to you and I look forward to your return in August." He nodded and walked away. I paid the bill, leaving a generous tip and my autograph for the waitress before taking Jessika and Mandy back to the hospital.

* * * * *

CHAPTER TWENTY-ONE

When we got back to the hospital, Kyle was in Doug's room and they were discussing the race and Doug's crash. Mandy looked at Kyle accusingly.

"Why didn't you call to tell us my Dad was awake?" she demanded.

"Calm down, kitten. I just woke up a short time ago and Kyle figured y'all would've been on your way back from dinner already. Did you have a good time with Jessika and Brianna?" Doug answered.

"Yes, Daddy. And I apologized already. I had the best time. Did you know Brianna was a Playboy Playmate? Oops, was it okay that I said something, Brianna?" she blushed. I opened my mouth to speak, but Doug cut me off before I could get a word out.

"Whoa. Hold the phone Mandy. What did you do that you had to apologize for?" he demanded.

"Daddy! How could you forget? You and I had that huge fight about it the other day when you called me. Is this your way of punishing me? By making me go over it again and again?" Mandy pouted.

"Mandy, your Dad has temporary amnesia. He doesn't remember anything about this past week," Kyle explained.

"Guess you shoulda kept your mouth shut Mandy," Jessika spoke up.

"I'm sorry Daddy," Mandy turned back to Doug. I could see she was on the verge of tears again and I put my arm around her.

"I think we've all had a pretty rough day, so I'm going to take the girls home. That way we can all get some rest," I told Doug.

"Are we going home or to a hotel?" Jessika asked. I looked to Doug and Kyle for their input. It was Doug who decided where we would go.

"I'm only going to be here for a day or two and then they're gonna send me home. Take them home. I'll be fine here by myself. Ricky's staying here anyway. Y'all go home and I'll see you in a couple days."

"Are you sure?" I asked, skeptical that maybe we should stay with him.

"Positive," Doug replied. "Would you mind keeping Mandy at your place until I get home?"

"Sure. She can stay as long as she wants, as long as her and Jess don't try to kill each other," I answered. "Don't worry about anything except getting out of here and coming home. I'll take good care of your daughter."

I leaned over and kissed him lightly on the cheek as Jessika and Mandy stood staring open-mouthed at me, their expressions identical. Out in the hall, Jessika confronted me.

"Are you out of your mind, Ma? Did you forget what we talked about? What were you doing back there?" she practically shrieked.

"Jessika, lower your voice please. Remember where you are. We'll discuss it later," I answered.

* * *

After returning the rental car, we met Kyle and Jonathon at the airport and boarded the team plane to fly back to North Carolina. The rest of the team had flown back with Doug's on his primary team plane after they'd gotten the news that he was awake and alert and had requested they head home.

Jessika and Mandy immediately headed to one side of the plane, whispering and giggling to each other. Kyle and I sat on the opposite side of the plane and Jonathon seemed unsure of what to do. Kyle called him over to sit with us. He hesitated briefly before coming to join us. As he fastened his seat belt, I leaned over and lightly touched his arm.

"It's okay Jonathon. I've decided I'm going to let you live. You hurt my daughter deeply. And I don't like that. But I don't fight Jessika's battles for her. I will warn you however, she is very strong-willed and inventive. If I were you, I'd expect just about anything from her," I explained sweetly.

"That's what I'm worried about. Especially seeing as her and Mandy are talking again," Jonathon groaned.

"Buddy, I can almost guarantee you that between the two of them, your life is going to be a living hell," Kyle laughed as the plane taxied down the runway and took off. Once we were in the air and had reached cruising altitude, Jessika called me over to join her and Mandy. I unfastened my seat belt and walked over, taking a seat facing them.

"What's up girls?" I asked.

"I was just telling Mandy about Todd and we want to hear more," Jessika explained. "What happened when you moved to North Carolina? I mean, I know you met Dad, but I'm sure there's more to the story then you've told me over the years."

"Why did you move down here"? Mandy inquired. "After all, we all know it wasn't just to drive a race car, 'cause you haven't been doing it that long."

"Actually, that was my ultimate intention. But the main reason why I moved here when I did was to go the University of North Carolina in Greensboro," I explained.

"Why?" Mandy questioned.

"To take Criminal Justice and become a cop, which I did. That's the career I retired from to drive a race car," I answered and began to tell them about my move.

* * * * *

CHAPTER TWENTY-TWO

Greensboro, NC – 1996

Shortly after Todd and I broke up, I'd decided it was time for a career change, and set my mind on becoming a police officer. I applied to the universities in North Carolina and was accepted to the Greensboro campus, moving down at the beginning of August. I found an affordable apartment close to campus and quickly became settled. I missed everybody back home, but my neighbors were friendly and I easily made friends. By the time the semester started, I had found a part-time job as a bartender. It was in a strip club, but the tips were great and I knew it would pay the bills.

When the semester began, I eagerly jumped into my studies and found that I had indeed chosen the right course. It was near the end of my second month in the program that I met Craig. A number of law enforcement officials had been invited to one of the classes to discuss the field and let us know what was to come if we continued to pursue the career choice. My attention was riveted to Craig the minute he began to speak. At six five, he was easily the tallest in the group addressing us. His ash blond hair and ice blue eyes topped off a beautifully muscled, well-taken-care of body. After the day's class, a group of us went to the university-run bar for a drink and to discuss what we'd learned. I got into a friendly game of air hockey with Peter, one of my classmates.

I was leading and needing only one goal to win, when somebody put their money down on the table for the next game. I paused briefly to see who it was, my gaze traveling slowly up the well-muscled arm, to the broad shoulders and finally to the face. He smiled as my eyes met his and I blushed, realizing he's witnessed my visual tour of his upper body.

"Do I get to play the winner?" he asked, still smiling at me.

"Sure," I replied slowly, and returned to the game, easily scoring the last point. He exchanged places with Peter and the game began. I was a little nervous playing against him and lost my paddle as I took a shot. He caught it and held it.

"Can I have my paddle back please?" I asked.

"Come and get it," he replied with a grin. I slowly walked over to his side of the table and stopped beside him, holding out my hand. Instead of returning my paddle, he took my hand and introduced himself.

"You're one of the new Crim students, aren't you?" he asked.

"Guilty," I smiled.

"Do you have a name?"

"Brianna."

"Well, Brianna, it's very nice to meet you. Would you care to make a friendly wager on this game?" he smiled mischievously.

"That depends," I answered. "What's the wager?"

"How's dinner sound?" I contemplated the bet and decided there were worse fates than dinner with a hot man.

"You're on. But you should know that I happen to be a pretty damn good air hockey player," I warned.

"Well, then. Show me what you've got," he grinned, handing my paddle back to me. I returned to my side of the table and the game resumed. It was a close game and we took turns swapping the lead. We were tied when I finally scored the last goal to win. Craig walked over to my end of the table and shook my hand.

"Congratulations, Brianna. Looks like I owe you dinner," he smiled shyly.

"Really, you don't have to," I replied.

"Oh, but I want to," he answered eagerly. "Are you free tonight?"

"No, I have to work," I looked at my watch. "Shit! I'm gonna be late if I don't get moving." I picked up my books and jacket.

"Do you need a lift?" he asked, walking with me out the door.

"No, I only live a couple blocks away, and my truck is parked at my apartment," I explained.

"Well, at least allow me to walk you home. It's gonna be dark soon and the streets aren't safe. But then, I don't need to tell you that, do I?"

I agreed and we headed in the direction of my apartment.

"So, where do you work?" Craig asked.

"Déjà vu," I replied nonchalantly. "Have you ever been there?"

"Once or twice. For bachelor parties, usually. But I don't make it a regular hangout. Why would you want to work there?"

"Because they were hiring. I had the experience from back home and it pays the bills," I explained, knowing right away that he was assuming I was a dancer.

"Would you mind if I came to see you at work sometime?" he asked hesitantly.

"Not at all. I only work Monday to Thursday usually," I answered as we reached my building. "Do you want to come up? It'll only take me a minute to drop off my books and I can drop you back at your car."

"Um, sure."

I unlocked the front door and we headed up in the elevator after I emptied my mailbox. In my apartment, I left him in the living room as I walked into my bedroom to get my bag.

I usually wore tight fitting tee shirts and shorts with running shoes to work in, but always changed into whatever I was going to wear once I got to work.

When I walked back into the living room, Craig was looking at my computer. I always left it on, usually hooked up to the internet to receive messages.

"You have messages."

My friends back home were constantly sending me messages on the internet, since it was faster than sending letters in the mail and easier than calling back and forth playing telephone tag. I sat down in front of the monitor and accessed my mailbox, quickly retrieving and scanning my messages. I sent back a few responses, saying I had to work but that I would be back home and on the internet after three o'clock. That done, I stood up and picked up my bag, heading for the door.

"I probably shouldn't have taken the time to do that, but I haven't talked to some of those people in a couple days. And my friends back home tend to worry if they don't hear from me on a regular basis," I explained as I locked my door and we headed to the parking garage.

"Where's home?" Craig asked.

"Canada."

"Gee, could you be a little more vague? Canada's a big country."

"Sorry. I'm from Windsor. It's right across the border from Detroit."

"I know where Windsor is. Nice truck." I had bought myself a year-old Ford Explorer when I had moved, trading in my beat up old Grand Marquis. The truck was red, my favorite color, and I'd needed no convincing from the salesman that this was the truck I wanted.

"Thanks. Now, where will I find your car?" I asked as I pulled out of the parking garage and headed back to the campus. Following his directions, I stopped beside a shiny new black Mustang. He got out and walked around to my side of the truck as I rolled the window down.

"Well, Brianna. Thanks for the lift. It was very nice meeting you and I will get in touch with you for that dinner."

"I'm looking forward to it," I answered and put the truck back in gear. I waved as I pulled away and headed to the bar, thinking I would probably never hear from him again.

I was pleasantly surprised to find I was wrong. He showed up with a few friends that very night. He seemed surprised to find me with my clothes on and took a seat at the bar. As I served their drinks, he introduced me to his friends.

"Why didn't you tell me you were only a bartender?" he asked after draining half his beer.

"Because you didn't ask. Is it my fault you assumed I was a stripper just because I work here?"

"No. I'm sorry. I just figured with your body. . . " he apologized, blushing.

"It's okay. They've been trying to talk me into dancing since I started working here," I revealed.

"So why don't you do it?" one of his friends asked. I looked at Craig questioningly.

"Go for it," was all he would say. Just then, the bar manager came over to me.

"Hey, Brianna. Jayde just called in. Her old man beat the crap out of her again and she's not gonna be able to come in for a while, at least a week. I guess he really messed her up good this time. Can I talk you into filling in for her?" he asked. Jayde was one of the most popular girls he had, and I knew it would be difficult to replace her on such short notice.

"I don't know, Jack."

"Please Brianna. I'm begging. I'm two girls short tonight to begin with, before Jayde calling in. I know you can handle it, 'cause I've seen Jayde and Sapphire giving you pointers and teaching you their stuff after hours. I trust you to be able to go up there. I wouldn't ask you if I didn't." I could tell he was desperate and hesitated briefly before walking by him and heading to the dressing room to borrow an outfit from Jayde's back up stash that she always left at the bar. We were close in size and she had offered to let me use her stuff anytime I needed to. The outfits she kept at the bar she never used anyway. When I emerged a few minutes later, I slowly walked up onto the stage.

"Gentlemen, please welcome our newest dancer, Karma, to the stage." I heard the deejay introduce me as another song began. The girls had come up with a stage name for me, hoping I would decide to use it soon. In fact, they had gone so far as to stop calling me by my given name and would even introduce me to their boyfriends as Karma. Sapphire came over to join me and I began to slowly relax as I tuned in to the music. Most of the time when I was at work, I didn't really pay any attention to what songs the girls chose to dance to.

Out of the corner of my eye, I could see Craig watching me intently, but I would not look directly at him. By the time my turn on stage was done, I felt more comfortable about being up there, and Sapphire had been replaced by Shanda. After the last of the three songs ended, I headed off stage and re-dressed in my shorts and tee shirt, pocketing the money I had made. I nervously walked over to Jack, who was still standing with Craig.

"You did good kid. Like a real pro. Don't forget you're up there once more tonight," Jack praised me before walking away. I turned to head back behind the bar when Craig put his hand on my arm to stop me. I hesitantly looked into his eyes as he spoke.

"He's right. You were great up there."

"Thanks."

I went back to work and took my last turn on the stage later in the night. By the end of the night, I had made over five hundred dollars from dancing, and another one-fifty from bartending. Not bad, I thought, for only six hours work. I told Jack before I left that I would continue to bartend as well, so he wouldn't have to try to find another bartender on such short notice.

Since I wasn't on stage that long during each set, and Jayde would be back in another week or so, I agreed I'd fill in for her and whenever he was in a real bind for another dancer. When I walked out to my truck, Craig was leaning on the fender.

"I thought you would've been gone a long time ago," I said, unlocking the driver's door and climbing in. He blocked the way of me closing the door and leaned on the frame.

"I wanted to talk to you again before you went home. I was just wondering if tomorrow was okay for dinner?" he asked.

"You still want to do it?" I was surprised. "Even though I'm a stripper, even part-time?"

"I don't care what you do for a living. I'd really like to get to know you better," Craig replied.

"Yeah, sure. Tomorrow is fine, I guess. What time are you thinking?"

"I'll pick you up at seven."

"How should I dress?"

"Just casual."

"Okay then. I guess I'll see you at seven tomorrow," I started my truck while he moved out of the way and closed the door. I waved as I drove off and headed home, still surprised that he was interested in getting to know me, even though I took my clothes off for a living, even if it was only part time. It wasn't one of the most respectable professions I could've gotten into. And I didn't know many law enforcement officers who dated strippers.

* * * * *

CHAPTER TWENTY-THREE

I had spent most of the night on the internet, talking to my friends back home and did not wake up until almost two Friday afternoon. I had no Friday classes, and usually spent the day doing homework or cleaning the apartment. On this day, I chose to clean so the place would look a little better when Craig arrived.

Although the apartment wasn't a mess, there were books and a couple newspapers lying around and I hadn't dusted or vacuumed in about three weeks. Once my apartment was in order, I decided flowers would brighten the place up and headed out to a nearby florist.

I carefully chose a number of attractive arrangements and gently placed them in my truck and drove home. It took two trips in the elevator to get them all into my apartment and I easily placed them in various rooms. They were all bright and colorful, each making the rooms more attractive.

By the time I was satisfied with how the apartment looked, it was almost six o'clock and I decided to start getting ready. After my shower, I wrapped myself in a towel and opened my closet, trying to figure out what to wear.

"Dress casual," I said out loud. "Sure, but how casual? Or should I go with a skirt? What do you think Smoke?" I looked over at my cat. He was busily washing his paws, and paused to look at me, meowing his displeasure at me interrupting his bath. I pulled a pair of jeans out and he gave himself an all-over shake. I took that to mean no and replaced the jeans with my favorite skirt. I tossed in on my bed, and followed it with a shirt to match.

Heading back into the bathroom to apply my make-up, Smoke jumped off the chair he'd been perched on to sit on the bathroom counter to watch me. My make-up done, I began to tackle drying and styling my hair. I had continued to color it a lighter shade of red, almost a strawberry-blonde and kept it fairly long. Leaving it straight, it fell to halfway down my back.

Satisfied with my hair and make-up, I turned to walk back into my bedroom to dress. Just then, there was a knock on my door. I looked that the clock on the wall and saw that it was just past six-thirty. I didn't think it would be Craig already, but was surprised to find him standing in the hall when I opened the door.

"Hi. You're early," I said.

"Sorry. I'm a little over-eager, I guess," he paused, his gaze wandering down my body. "You know, when I said casual, I didn't think you'd take me quite so seriously." I looked down and realized I was still wearing just a towel. Horrified, I self-consciously tried pulling it tighter around me, but knew that would only make matters worse. Blushing, I turned and practically ran to my bedroom.

"Come in and make yourself comfortable. I'll just be a minute," I called over my shoulder.

I heard the door click softly shut and Craig chuckle as I frantically pulled on my clothes. As I slipped my bra straps onto my shoulders, I laughed quietly to myself, realizing how silly it was of me to be embarrassed about answering a door in a towel. After all, Craig had seen me almost completely naked the night before. Once I was dressed, I calmly walked back out to the living room. I found Craig standing outside on my balcony and quietly stepped out to join him. My apartment was on the twentieth floor and the view was fantastic. The sun was beginning to set as we looked out over the city.

"You've got a great view here," Craig spoke, breaking the silence.

"Yeah, it was one of the selling points for me. Besides being close to campus and affordable. I love to sit out here after a busy day and just watch the sun set," I revealed. "Sometimes, I come out here after I get home from work and just look up at the stars. It's great for relaxing."

"I can imagine. Are you ready to go?"

"Yep. I just have to grab my keys and a jacket," I replied, turning to walk back inside. Craig followed me, locking the balcony door behind us.

"Where are we going anyway?" I asked, grabbing my jacket out of the hall closet.

"How's my place sound?" he answered. I paused, my jacket half on. He laughed at my expression; I guess I looked shocked.

"I thought I'd make you dinner," he explained. "I'm a terrific cook."

"Um. Sure." I finished pulling on my jacket and smiled up at him. As we waited for the elevator, I nervously rattled my keys. It was a bad habit I'd picked up during recent months.

"Do you want to follow me in your truck?" he asked suddenly.

"What?" I hadn't really heard what he said, and he laughed, seeing how nervous I was.

"Do you want to follow me in your truck?" he asked again. "Then you can leave anytime you want, if you decide to."

"Why would I want to do that?" I asked as the elevator doors opened and I pushed the button for the lobby. "I trust you're not going to bore me to tears."

When we reached his car, Craig opened the door for me. During the drive to his apartment, I asked him why he chose law enforcement. He was silent for a minute before answering.

"I think for the same reason everybody else chooses it. To help make the streets a little safer. You know, make the world a safer place to live and raise our kids in," he explained.

"Do you have any children?" I wondered aloud.

"Me? No. The women I've dated either didn't want to marry a cop because of the danger I face everyday and didn't want to have to worry about if I was coming home every time I walked out the door to go to work. Or they were cops and were more interested in climbing the department ladder than having a baby." He turned to me. "What about you? Why do you want to be a cop?"

"To get rid of the drug pushers, the rapists, the murderers, the wife beaters. You know, make the streets safe again. It makes me crazy every time Jayde calls in and tells us her drugged-out boyfriend beat her up again. She refuses to press charges against the bastard because she says he doesn't really mean to hurt her; that he doesn't know what he's doing when he's high. One day, he's going to kill her. I just know it."

"I know it's rough to see it happen. But there are a lot of women out there like Jayde. But hey, that's why we're cops. Or rather, why I'm a cop and you're going to be one. To help, right? Maybe you will be able to convince Jayde to leave someday before it's too late. Now, come on in. Make yourself comfortable." I slipped my jacket off and he hung it up as I set my keys on the hall table. He directed me to the living room as he ducked into the kitchen. I stepped out onto his balcony. Looking out across the city, I realized I could see my apartment building.

"Wine?" I jumped as Craig spoke a short time later. I turned to see him holding a glass out to me. He laughed at my reaction and I took the glass.

"Do you always sneak up on people like that?" I demanded, trying, and failing, to sound annoyed.

"I'm sorry. I didn't mean to startle you. Do you want to listen to some music while I finish making dinner?"

"Yeah, sure." We both walked back inside and he headed into the kitchen as I checked out his cd collection. After making a selection, I took my wine glass and joined him in the kitchen as the apartment was filled with the beginning of Tim McGraw's 'I Like It, I Love It.' I sat down on a stool and watched as Craig cut tomatoes for salad.

"You like Tim?" he asked, not turning around.

"Yeah. I've got all his cd's at home," I replied, watching his movements. "Do you need help with anything?"

"Nah, I've got everything taken care of. I've got chicken and potatoes in the oven. They'll probably take another fifteen minutes or so. And the salad's almost ready. Would you like more wine?" He pulled the bottle from the fridge and re-filled my glass, not waiting for an answer.

"Trying to get me drunk?" I asked, laughing.

"I'm sorry. Would you like something else instead? Pop? Coffee?" He pulled open the fridge again.

"The wine is fine, Craig. I was only joking Relax," I assured him.

"Sorry. I guess I'm just a little nervous about this."

"First date in a while?" I asked gently.

"How'd you guess?" he looked at me, surprised. I smiled shyly as I answered.

"Because you're trying too hard to impress me. And you don't have to." The conversation turned to my classes as we returned to the balcony to wait for the rest of dinner to be ready. When the timer beeped, and Craig had checked that everything was ready, he lit the candles on his dining room table and dimmed the lights.

As we sat down, I commented on the romantic atmosphere. In the candlelight, I could see Craig's cheeks color. He recovered quickly however, and began telling me stories about arrests he'd made. Clearing the table after dinner, I paused as I set down our plates in the kitchen sink.

"Do you believe in love at first sight?" Craig had asked me as we walked into the kitchen. He stood next to me as he waited for my response.

"I think there's a possibility for it to happen. But I think it's more lust and physical attraction than love. You can't really love someone who you don't know. At least I can't," I looked up at him, wondering why he had asked. As I looked into his eyes, I completely lost myself and was mesmerized. He slowly leaned down to kiss me and I put my hands on his chest as I returned the kiss.

Eventually, he broke the kiss and began dropping feather-light kisses along my jaw line to my ear. When he reached the sensitive area of my neck right below my ear, he chuckled as I moaned softly. He paused to whisper in my ear.

"I want to make love to you until I die."

Without another word, he picked me up and carried me into his bedroom, setting me down on his bed. As we continued to kiss, he began to undress me, until I was down to just my bra and matching thong. When I reached up to unbutton his shirt, he gently pushed my hand away to do it himself.

We began kissing again and he made quick work of discarding the rest of my clothing. As his hands expertly traveled my body, I ran mine down his back, feeling the muscles perfectly formed. He began trailing kisses across my chest, taking one nipple at a time in his mouth. He continued down my stomach and gently eased my legs apart. As I felt his warm breath on me, I shivered, anticipating what he was about to do.

When he was lying next to me again, I began kissing his chest, working my way down along his stomach, when he took my arm and gently pulled me back up, rolling me over and pinning me underneath him. As he began kissing me again, and making love to me, I thought it was almost as if we'd been made for each other. As he held me in his arms afterwards, I wondered if I'd been too hasty in my response to him asking about love at first sight.

"What are you thinking about?" he asked, lightly tracing my jaw line with his fingertip.

"Just wondering if I can change my answer from earlier," I replied, rolling onto my side and propping myself up on one elbow to look at him.

"And what answer is that?"

"Whether or not I believe in love at first sight."

"Are you becoming a believer?" Craig questioned.

"I think so. Or at least I'm not so skeptical that it's not possible."

"Is there a specific reason why you didn't want to believe in it before?" I nodded silently, biting my lip. Laying back down with his arms around me, I began to tell him about my relationship with Todd. After I was finished, Craig kissed me tenderly and looked into my eyes.

"I can promise you I will never hurt you intentionally. And I will never do to you what he did. I can't believe anybody would be so stupid as to give you up. I don't know if I should say this or not; I don't want to scare you off. But I know I love you. And someday, I'm going to make you my wife," he promised.

"I think I love you too," I whispered. I rested my head on his shoulder and closed my eyes, smiling. Before I knew it, I was asleep.

* * * * *

CHAPTER TWENTY-FOUR

Over the next month and a half, Craig and I spent as much time together as our schedules would permit. I continued dancing a couple nights a week and averaged between five and six hundred dollars in tips. I had three papers due before exams, so I was spending a lot of time doing research or studying for my exams when I wasn't at work. Craig helped me out with whatever he could and finally the semester was over. Relaxing at his place after my last exam, our conversation turned to Christmas.

"Are you going to decorate your apartment?" Craig asked. I shook my head.

"I don't think so. I'm flying home to spend Christmas with my folks. I'd like to, since it's my first Christmas in my apartment, but there really isn't a point," I explained.

"When do you leave?"

"I think I'm going to wait until the twenty-third and then I'll be back on the twenty-sixth. That doesn't give me a lot of time to spend with my family, but I want to be back here for New Years."

We spent the rest of the day touring the malls, doing our Christmas shopping and finding decorations for Craig's apartment, since his parents would be visiting him during the holiday. Although they also lived in Greensboro, Craig didn't see much of them because of his schedule, but he had been hoping I could meet them at Christmas. Returning to his place, we decorated the entire apartment before falling into bed.

He drove me to the airport the day I was flying home, after promising to feed Smoke while I was gone. Although I was looking forward to seeing my family and friends again, I wanted to stay and spend the time with Craig. But I knew it would only be a couple days until I was back and he would be picking me up at the airport.

The flight home was uneventful and I practically flew into my parents' arms as they stood waiting at the gate for me. I had been talking to them once a week during the semester, and updated them on what had been going on during the previous week. I had taken pictures of my apartment, the campus and the area, and pulled them out to show to my parents when we got to the house.

"Who's taking care of Smoke while you're home?" my mother asked.

"Craig, of course," I answered, realizing too late that I hadn't told them about Craig.

"Craig? Who's Craig?"

"The guy I've been dating," I explained.

"Is it serious?"

"I think so. I mean, we have a lot in common and we have fun together. He treats me real well."

"How old is he? What does he do? Is he a student? What does he look like?" my mother began firing the questions at me. I flipped through the pictures before answering, knowing I had a couple of the two of us. I handed them to her.

"He's twenty-nine. He's not a student, but we did meet at the university. He's an undercover cop in Greensboro."

"A cop, Brianna? You're not really dating a cop are you? Do you realize how dangerous that is? If you ever get married to him, you're gonna wonder every time he walks out the door to go to work, if he's coming home at the end of the day," my mother lectured. I think sometimes she forgot what I was taking in school; either that or she was hoping I would not pursue the career once I graduated.

"Mom, I'm going to school to become a cop, remember. I know what the dangers are. And I'm gonna be taking the same risks he is. I'm happy being with Craig. Can't you be happy for me?"

"I'm sorry. I just don't want to see you get hurt again. I remember all too well the last time still."

"Trust me. Craig's not going to hurt me. I can feel it. I think it's the real thing this time. Craig is nothing like Todd. They couldn't be more different," I changed the subject then, asking about different happenings around the city. I called Craig later to let him know I'd gotten there in one piece and promised to call again on Christmas Day.

* * *

The days passed quickly and I was soon back in Craig's arms in Greensboro. We chose to go to my apartment when my plane landed, since I'd been neglecting Smoke. I was pre-occupied with my thoughts and Craig had to keep repeating himself as my mind wandered. I was worried that I might be pregnant and wondered how to approach the subject with Craig.

Finally, after dinner, we exchanged our gifts. As I opened mine, I gasped. Inside the tiny box was a beautiful diamond ring. When he got down on one knee, I knew what was coming and I held my breath.

"Brianna, will you marry me?" he asked quietly. I burst into tears and he pulled me into his arms. "What's wrong Brie? I thought you'd be happy, but those don't look like joyful tears."

"I think I'm pregnant," I blurted out suddenly. Craig pulled back and looked into my eyes.

"Are you serious?" he whispered. I nodded silently, sniffling and trying not to cry. I was petrified of what his reaction would be to my news.

"Have you been to a doctor yet? Are you positive?" he asked, sounding worried. I shook my head.

"I was gonna go tomorrow. I've got a few of the obvious signs. I've missed my period twice now, but thought it was just stress from my schoolwork. But I've been feeling kinda sick every morning for the past week," I explained.

"Wow. This is so cool. A baby. Now, just put that ring on your finger and tell me you'll marry me. You've just given me the best Christmas present ever." I stood up and walked across the room to stand at the balcony door, my back to Craig. He came to stand behind me, his hands resting lightly on my shoulders.

"What's wrong, Brie?" he asked quietly. I turned to face him.

"What's wrong? What's right? I don't want to sound selfish, but how can I have a baby? I still have two and a half years of university to finish. Plus the Academy," I demanded.

"We'll work something out. I promise. You'll still be able to finish school. And go to the Academy. I can take time off. And I'm sure my parents will help out with babysitting. Don't you worry about a thing, except taking care of you and our baby." He put his arms around me to hold me. I started to feel better, but I was still scared. Silently, I took the ring out of the box and slipped it on my finger. Craig looked down as I put my hand on his chest. Seeing the ring, he picked me up and spun me around. Setting me down, he kissed me deeply before carrying me into the bedroom.

A few hours later, we were woken up by a knock on the door. I looked at the clock and saw that it was two-thirty in the morning. The knocking became more insistent as I climbed out of bed and pulled on my robe. Craig was close behind me as I opened the door. Jayde almost collapsed when she saw me; luckily, Craig caught her before she fell, leading her into the apartment. Taking one look at her bleeding and bruised face, I knew what had happened.

"Jayde, you gotta press charges this time. You can't keep letting him get away with this. Next time, he might kill you," I pleaded, knowing that if she'd left him and come to me, she was finally willing to go to the police. She nodded silently and Craig moved to call one of his friends in the domestic violence unit.

By the time they arrived, I had made coffee and gotten the story from Jayde about what had happened. Craig let them in and quietly briefed them before introducing us. They quickly went to work to get a statement from Jayde. When they were done, she was exhausted and I led her to my bedroom as Craig filled two more coffee mugs.

Joining them back in the living room, Craig put his arm around me, handing me a glass of milk. I looked at him questioningly.

"Sorry, babe. No more caffeine for you. I'm putting you on a healthy diet from now until the baby comes," he apologized.

His two friends looked at us, both amused and confused, until he held out my hand for them to see the engagement ring.

"Congratulations, folks. When's the big day?" the older one, Jeff, asked.

"We don't know yet," Craig shrugged his shoulders. "We'll find out tomorrow."

"Well, we better go find this loser and get him into lock-up before he figures out where she is." Craig showed them out, as I put the coffee mugs in the sink.

He left his gun with me, with instructions to use it if I needed to, and headed back to his apartment, promising to return that afternoon. I crawled into bed beside Jayde, putting my arms around her to comfort her, and dreamt of her boyfriend showing up.

When Craig returned, I packed up a few things and told Jayde she could stay as long as she needed to. I left her the number for Craig's place and my cell number and made her promise to call if she needed anything. Craig made her promise not to let her boyfriend in if he showed up and to keep the door locked.

We left, and Craig followed me to the doctor's office where we were told I was definitely pregnant and the doctor estimated I was due the beginning of August. I scheduled an appointment for late-January for a check-up and we went back to Craig's apartment.

The next couple of days were spent trying to figure out what I was going to do about school. I knew I'd be able to finish the next semester without a problem, since I wasn't due until August. But I knew that my final two years might be difficult to complete.

"Look, Brianna. I can take time off work to take care of the baby while you finish school. Or I'll work part time. I think before we worry about that, we'd better figure out where we're going to put the baby. I mean, let's face it. We both have one bedroom apartments. Why don't we look for a house?"

And so began the search for a house. We decided to look for something small since it would be our first and there would only be three of us.

* * *

We had decided that I would continue to dance until I started to show and I was scheduled to work for Jayde the night before New Year's Eve. As I walked in the door of Craig's apartment after work, the phone was ringing. He was at work, so I knew it wouldn't be him, but I had a bad feeling it was Jayde.

"Hello?"

"Brianna? He found out I'm here. He called and said he's coming over to finish what he started. Oh God, Brie. I'm so scared," she sobbed.

"Okay, Jayde. Call the police. I'll be right there. Don't let anybody in except the police. Do you understand?"

"Y-yes. Hurry, please." I hung up and grabbed my cell phone, dialing Craig's as I looked for his off-duty revolver. He had already taught me how to use it and I knew I wouldn't hesitate to use it on Jayde's boyfriend. I left him a message about what was happening and ran out the door to my truck. I managed to beat the police there and stopped in my tracks as the elevator door opened on my floor. My apartment door had been kicked in. I clicked the safety off of Craig's gun and cautiously entered the apartment. The living room was in shambles, with the coffee table tipped over and my lamps smashed on the floor. I listened for any movement inside and jumped at Smoke rubbed against my ankles.

"Jayde? Are you here?" As I rounded the corner to my living room and looked down the hall to my bedroom, I could see Jayde's arm on the floor, coming out of the bathroom. I rushed in and fell to my knees beside her, cradling her head in my lap. She was covered in blood and I couldn't find a pulse. I bent my head and silently began to cry.

That was how Craig and the two uniformed officers found me a few minutes later. Craig helped me to my feet and led me out of the bathroom as one of the uniforms called for the medical examiner and forensics. Before I knew it, my apartment was crawling with the forensics unit, the medical examiner, a photographer and a dozen more uniforms. One of the uniforms began harassing me for a statement, until Craig blew up.

"You'll get a goddamn statement from her tomorrow, okay."

"But --"

"No buts about it. That happens to be my fiancée there, and she's pregnant. She's suffered enough trauma tonight, finding her friend murdered. I don't want her to be under any more stress. Do you understand what I'm saying?" Craig exploded.

"Yes, sir. I'm sorry." The officer quickly backed out of the room and Craig returned to my side. He held me in his arms until the apartment was almost empty again. Gathering up the few necessities for Smoke and tucking him into his carrier, Craig closed up the apartment and led me downstairs to his car. The drive to his place was spent in silence. As we walked into the apartment and I freed Smoke, I suddenly burst into tears, sobbing uncontrollably. Craig picked me up and carried me into the bedroom, holding me as I cried until I fell asleep.

* * *

The day after New Year's, Jayde was buried following a simple service. The dancers and everybody else who had worked with Jayde attended. There were also a number of police officers in case Jayde's boyfriend showed up. After he had killed Jayde, he had disappeared and none of his friends were helpful in finding him.

It took almost a month to find him, but he was finally arrested and charged. The trial took less than a week and he was found guilty and sentenced to life in prison. Unfortunately, he was eligible for parole in ten years, if he agreed to go through a substance abuse program.

I moved out of my apartment, putting my furniture into storage and Smoke and I took up residence in Craig's apartment until we could find a house. Calling my mother to let her know, I simply told her that I'd moved into Craig's place, rather than explaining to her that there had been a murder in my apartment. I knew she'd worry too much and ask me to move back home if she found that out.

* * * * *

CHAPTER TWENTY-FIVE

The week after Jayde's funeral, I began my second semester and it quickly flew by. Craig and I found a house and moved in the day after my last exam. Once we were settled, I called to tell my parents. Up until that point, I had kept my pregnancy a secret, not wanting to upset them. I was nervous about telling them, but Craig squeezed my hand to reassure me as I talked to my mother.

"So, how are classes going dear?" my mother asked after the usual discussion about the weather and how work was going. They knew I was bartending, but not that it was in a strip club, and definitely not that I had been dancing as well.

"They're done, Mom. I just wrote my last exam a couple days ago and I think I did really well."

"Well, that's good. I guess you'll be coming home soon for the summer break?"

"Actually, that's why I called. Craig and I would like you and Dad to come down here and stay with us for a week or so. We found this perfect little house and I'd love for you to see it and meet Craig. And we have great news for you. Craig and I are getting married."

"Married? My baby's getting married! Did you set a date yet?"

"Not yet, Mom. But I think we're going to wait until after I graduate. I'm in no hurry. And I don't think Craig is either. He understands how important my career is to me. I can't wait for you to meet him."

"Well, then. I guess we should come down then. I'll call you back in a couple days to let you know when we'll be there. Talk to you soon."

Less than a week later, I was nervously pacing in the living room, hoping everything was in place, and wondering how my parents would react to the news of my pregnancy. Craig stepped in front of me, putting his hands on my shoulders and looking into my eyes.

"Relax, Brianna. Everything's going to be fine. Trust me."

"Yeah. Easy for you to say. Your parents fell in love with me on the spot and asked when I was going to marry you and give them grandchildren. I don't know about you, but I've never heard 'nice to meet you' phrased quite that way."

Just then, the doorbell rang. I slowly walked to the door, with Craig close behind. I smiled as I opened the door, and welcomed my parents into the house. I gave them each a hug and introduced them to Craig.

"Would you like a quick tour of the house, or would you rather relax and have a cold drink first?" I asked.

"I'd love a cold drink," my mother answered.

"Craig, would you take my parents into the den and I'll be right in with some iced tea?"

I headed back into the kitchen as Craig led them down the hall. As I walked into the den with our drinks, Smoke marched into the room and jumped onto the back of the sofa. He waited until I sat down, then settled himself on my lap, purring softly.

"You're got to get him to stop doing that, Brianna," Craig spoke up as I stroked Smoke's back.

"I know and I will," I paused as I noticed my mother looking at me intently.

"Brianna, have you gotten bigger since you were home at Christmas? You know you really should cut down on your weight lifting. I realize you need to be strong to be a police officer. But don't you think you're overdoing it a little?" she asked.

"Actually, Mom, I've cut back on the weight lifting for now. It's been about a month now since I cut back. Doctors' orders," I replied.

"Why? You didn't hurt yourself, did you?" she asked, sounding concerned.

"No. I didn't hurt myself. And I cut back so that I wouldn't hurt myself. Or your grandchild. Mom, Dad, I'm pregnant."

"You're what?" they both asked at once.

"Pregnant. You know, having a baby."

"Oh my. How? I mean, when did this happen? I think we all know how it happened," my mother stammered.

"The doctor figures right around the beginning of November. I'm due the first week of August," I answered.

"November? Why didn't you tell us when you were home at Christmas?"

"Because I didn't know until after I got back here. And after I found out, all hell broke loose. One of my friends was killed by her boyfriend, so the police were looking for him. My boss asked me to take over her shifts at work until he could replace her. I had schoolwork to take care of. Craig and I were trying to find a house. There was the trial. Just everything happened all at once."

The conversation turned to what I was going to do about school and Craig took over. He explained that I would still be going full-time and that he would be staying home to take care of the baby until he or she was old enough that we could find a sitter. Afterwards, we gave my parents a tour of the house before taking them out for a tour of the city and dinner.

They stayed for a week and I showed them more of the city, taking them to the campus and showed them around the entire area. When they left, I promised to keep them updated on my pregnancy and call them as soon as the baby was born.

* * * * *

CHAPTER TWENTY-SIX
August 1997

In the early morning hours of August first, I woke up with an unbearable back ache. I quietly slipped out of bed, trying not to wake Craig. I tried to walk some of the pain off, since I didn't want to take any painkillers, but the pain only intensified. Going back to the bedroom, I gently shook Craig's shoulder.

"Craig? I think it's time to go."

"What honey? Where do you want to go? Can't it wait until morning?" He'd only been asleep a couple hours after working late.

"No, Craig. It can't wait. It's time to go to the hospital. I'm in labor." Suddenly, he was wide awake and getting dressed. As I changed into a pair of jogging shorts and a tee-shirt, he tore through the house, trying to find his car keys. Once he found them, he helped me out to the car and rushed me to the hospital. By the time we got there, the pain was worse and the nurses wheeled me directly into a delivery room.

The doctor arrived a short time later and the first light of dawn shone on our newborn baby. Exhausted from pushing, I cried as I heard her wail after taking her first breaths. Craig kissed my forehead, smiling at me.

"Congratulations," the doctor said, handing the baby to me. "It's a girl."

As I held her, she quieted and looked up at me sleepily, almost as if she knew I was her mother. I turned to Craig and returned his smile, before handing the baby to him. He nervously held her and the doctor chuckled.

"Don't worry, Dad. You won't break her," the doctor joked.

"But she's so tiny," Craig protested. The nurse took her back a few minutes later, to weigh and measure her.

"Have you thought of a name for her yet?" the doctor asked. I looked at Craig. One thing we hadn't discussed was a name.

"How's Victoria sound?" Craig asked me.

"Victoria Lane? Do you realize how much teasing she'll go through growing up? How about Jessika?"

"Let's compromise. We'll go with both."

"Fine," I turned back to the doctor. "We're going to name her Jessika Victoria."

Later, after I had slept, Craig and I walked with his parents down to the nursery to see Jessika. He had called both our families while I slept, to share the news. His parents had arrived with flowers right before I woke up. Craig put his arms around me as we stood at the nursery window, watching our daughter sleep. They would be bringing her down to my room to be with me after letting me rest.

"Can you believe it? I made that," he boasted.

"We made that," I corrected him. "You contributed, but don't forget, I'm the one who carried that little person around with me everywhere I went for nine months. And went through the pain of labor and delivery. So don't even think about taking all the credit for our daughter's birth."

"Okay, okay. I helped make her," he acknowledged meekly as his parents laughed.

Late the next afternoon, I was able to go home and Craig carefully helped us into the car when we left the hospital. Walking into the house, Craig made me close my eyes and carefully led me upstairs and down the hall. Opening my eyes, I gasped. Overnight, he had managed to put the entire nursery together. He carefully hugged me as I held Jessika before we put her down in her new crib to sleep.

* * * * *

CHAPTER TWENTY-SEVEN

Just after school resumed and I began my second year, I took Jessika with me to show her off to my friends and professors. They all fell in love with her and my professors congratulated me on continuing my studies. Leaving the campus, I decided to stop by Déjà vu, to thank the girls for the flowers they'd sent and to let them see the baby. I knew the next shift would be starting when I got there, and it wouldn't be too busy in the bar.

Carrying Jessika inside in her car seat, I got a few strange looks from customers who didn't know me, but a few of the regulars recognized me and came over to see the baby. The girls that weren't on stage surrounded me and all oohed and aahed over Jessika. Jack walked over after a while and sent the girls back to their customers.

"So this is the little bundle that took away one of my best dancers?" he asked, stroking her cheek with one finger. I knew he had a soft spot for kids, although he didn't have any of his own.

"I'm afraid so, Jack. But I'm only as good as my teachers were," I replied. Sapphire had chosen to retire shortly after Jayde's funeral.

"Think you'll ever come back?"

"Probably not. Between school and taking care of Jessika, I have almost no time to myself."

"Oh! I almost forgot! Just after you left, some photographer guy came in looking for you. He said he'd seen you dance a couple of times and thought you might like to pose for him. He left his card in case you came back and he's called a couple times since. Hang on a sec. I'll get it from the office." Jack rushed off and returned a few minutes later, handing me a card.

"Jack, this is Playboy. Holy shit! Playboy wants me? This is so cool. I have to tell Craig. Thanks Jack. I'll be in touch."

I bundled Jessika back into the truck and headed back home. When I burst into the house, Craig was sitting in the den with a couple friends from work. I put Jessika down for a nap before joining them.

I had lost most of the weight I'd gained during my pregnancy and was just waiting for the okay from my doctor to start working out again.

When we were finally alone, I told Craig about my visit to the bar and my conversation with Jack. He urged me to go ahead and pose; practically dialing the phone.

When I got the photographer on the phone, I explained who I was and why I was calling.

"Of course, Karma. I remember you. I was very impressed with your stage routine. I think you'd look great in front of the camera. First of all, I guess I should ask if you would be willing to pose for me. And second, when do you think you'd be ready for a camera session?"

"Well, I'm in school until mid-April. Would the beginning of May be okay?" I asked.

"Sure. I'll be in touch with you to make the arrangements."

We kept in touch over the next couple months, finalizing the details and before I knew it, the day of the photo session arrived. I'd finally been able to start working out again, and it didn't take me long to get back into shape. We used a number of different locations and it took two days to get all the photos he wanted. A couple of weeks after the photographs were taken, he called me again.

"The photos turned out fantastic! And you'll never guess what. When I showed them to my boss, he loves them. So much that he wants you to be our Playmate of the Year. Isn't that wonderful?" he exclaimed.

The issue came out right before school resumed for my senior year and a number of the guys on campus recognized me and asked me to sign their copy. I was worried that there would be problems with me being on campus so soon after the issue came out, but nobody seemed to have any negative comments about it; if they did, they kept them to themselves. I broke the news to my parents in my weekly phone call to them and although they weren't happy with it, they told me that it was my choice.

My final year passed quickly and Craig and I were married the second weekend in May. My family and friends flew down, with Maya standing up as my maid of honor, and Craig's best friend, James, was his best man. I had even sent an invitation to Elaine and she came with congratulations from Jo-Ann and Brad, but no comment from Todd. The day after we returned from our honeymoon, I received my acceptance from the Police Academy in Raleigh. I had already been accepted to the Greensboro undercover unit and needed only to graduate from the Academy to be sworn in as an officer.

Reluctantly, I packed up and headed to the Academy on September first, leaving Craig and Jessika in Greensboro. Fortunately, I would be able to go home most weekends to see them. The eighteen weeks passed quickly and both my family and Craig's drove in for the ceremony.

* * * * *

CHAPTER TWENTY-EIGHT

Mooresville, NC – June 2015

As the plane touched down in Mooresville, I finished telling Jessika and Mandy about meeting Jessika's father. Jonathon's car was at the airport, along with my truck and Kyle's car. Jonathon offered to drive the girls home, but they declined, opting to come home with me. Kyle left shortly after Jonathon, saying he'd see me at the shop in the morning. The girls and I piled into my truck and headed back to the house. They immediately went up to Jessika's room as I walked into my office to check my mail and messages. That done, I climbed the stairs to my bedroom and fell asleep exhausted.

The next morning, Jessika and Mandy rushed into the kitchen as I made breakfast. They were bubbling with their plans for the day and were eager to get going, protesting as I made them sit down to eat. Once I was satisfied, they talked me into dropping them off at Mandy's on my way to the shop. When I got there, Kyle followed me into my office.

"So, how was your night with the girls?" he asked, sitting down.

"Surprisingly it was quiet. They stayed in Jess' room, and I didn't hear anything from them until they got up this morning."

"You mean they didn't try to kill each other? I'm shocked. I mean, after Jess finding out only a week ago that Mandy had stolen her boyfriend."

"Yeah, I know. I was surprised too. But I think they talked most of the night about what happened between the two of them and Jessika's beginning to forgive Mandy. I'm glad though. I know Jess loves hanging around here and being with me, but I know she doesn't always want to be with me. She wants to be with kids her own age."

We were interrupted a few minutes later by a knock on my office door. Kara walked in with a vase of flowers.

"Somebody sent you roses, Ms Lane," she said, setting them down on my desk. I opened the card she handed me and read the note. It said simply, 'Thinking of you.'

"Any idea where they came from?" I asked Kara. "The card's not signed."

"No. But I can call the florist and find out for you," she answered, heading back out of the office.

She called me a few minutes later and explained that it was a cash transaction, so nobody took the person's name and the receipt had no salesperson's initials.

"Guess you have a secret admirer," Kyle said as I picked up the card again.

"Well, I don't have time right now to wonder who it is. I'm sure I'll find out sooner or later. Right now, I have a team to run." I stood up and began my rounds of the shop, with Kyle at my side.

That night, when I got home, I found that Jessika and Mandy had made dinner. They ushered me into the dining room, revealing an elaborate table setting. As I sat down, they began bringing dishes in from the kitchen. As they took their places across the table from me, I looked at the two of them, my eyebrows and curiosity, raised.

"What are the two of you up to?" I asked suspiciously, wondering what kind of trouble they'd gotten into.

"Nothing," Jessika answered. "We just wanted to do something nice for you, that's all."

"Okay, what do you want to do?"

"Nothing," Mandy spoke this time. "Since you agreed to take me into your home until my dad gets back, I wanted to do something nice for you and Jess suggested dinner."

"So, how was your day, Mom?" Jessika asked as we began to eat. I told them about receiving the flowers and the unsigned card.

"Cool. A secret admirer. Maybe it's Kyle," Mandy squealed.

"I don't think so. He was there when they were delivered and he seemed as surprised as I was," I answered.

"What about Todd? After all, he did chase us for miles trying to talk to you," Jessika suggested.

"What? You never told me that!" Mandy burst out, turning to Jessika. Jessika then relayed the story of our game of hide and seek with Todd. By the time she was done, we had finished our dinner and cleared the table. We moved into the family room and Mandy turned back to me.

"Will you tell me about your decision to quit being a cop and become a race car driver? If it's not too painful for you, that is. I mean, I know about you buying the team from Matthew after Daytona was shot, but I never heard the story leading up to you buying the team."

I looked at Jessika before responding. I hadn't really told her the whole story surrounding her father's death, but I figured she was old enough now to hear the details. She nodded and I began my story.

* * * * *

CHAPTER TWENTY-NINE

Greensboro, NC – September 2009

Craig and I worked together on most of our assignments, but on this particular one, I had started out solo. Everything had gone perfectly until the day we were scheduled to make the bust. The sun was slowly setting and I was confident that everything would go smoothly. I had managed to get enough evidence to set up a bust of a group of five drug dealers in Greensboro. They were all pretty big players, and we knew that getting them off the streets would be a giant step in cleaning up the neighborhood.

As Craig and I were being wired so our back-up would be in constant contact with us in case there was a problem, we went over our cover story. I was going to introduce Craig as a friend who was new in town and looking for some new connections. I thought I had gained the confidence of these guys to bring somebody else into the deal. What I didn't know until later was that one of the guys who'd been attending a couple of the recent parties had been Jayde's ex-boyfriend. He had gotten out of prison about a year before, but I hadn't recognized him. Unfortunately, he had known almost right away who I was.

I casually walked into the house with Craig to join the party and began introducing him. Suddenly, all hell broke loose. Scott, Jayde's ex-boyfriend came bursting out of the kitchen, where I assumed he'd been smoking crack, the drug of choice for most of the group that hung out in the house. Waving a gun in the air, he began screaming that I was a cop and that he was going to kill me. Before I could react, our back-up was pouring in through the doors, and Scott began firing wildly. As I drew my gun, I felt a sharp pain in my left shoulder and could feel a number of bullets slicing the air around my head. A number of our group tackled him, wrestling the gun away from him.

Ignoring the pain in my shoulder, I turned to look for Craig and found him lying on the floor in a pool of blood. I fell to my knees beside him and pulled open his jacket. His eyes fluttered open and I looked down into his ice blue eyes, as he struggled to breathe. Although we were both wearing Kevlar vests, a bullet had penetrated his and I assumed had gone right through. I pulled his vest open and covered the wound with my hand, putting pressure on it to try to stop the bleeding.

"Officer down! Get EMS here now!" I screamed. "Hang on honey. EMS will be here any minute," I pleaded, my eyes misting over.

"I love you. And Jess. Don't you ever forget that. Take care of her," he whispered.

"No. You take care of her, too. Don't you dare die on me, Craig. You can't die on me dammit. Jessika and I both need you. Hold on, honey. Oh God, please don't die on me!" I demanded.

"I love you Brie," he whispered again. As I started to plead with him to fight, he closed his eyes and his grip on my hand loosened.

"No!" I screamed, looking for a pulse and frantically began CPR. The EMS crew arrived then and I was pushed aside as they worked to revive Craig, getting him onto a stretcher and removed him from the scene. Standing, I looked around for the team holding Scott. Deliberately, I walked over to him.

"Do you realize you just shot and killed an officer of the law? That makes you a cop-killer. Or are you too strung out on crack that you don't know?" I asked.

"Course I know. But -- "

"Well, you want to know something else? You just took my husband from me, you bastard. And we have a twelve year old daughter at home. Would you like to be the one to explain to her why her Daddy's never coming home?"

"I'd rather tell her that her bitch of a mother isn't coming home. That bullet was meant for you, Karma. I barely hit you the first time. I've been waiting twelve and a half years to put it to you." I had started to walk away, but stopped as I realized what he'd said. I slowly turned back to him.

"What did you say?"

"You heard me, Karma. If it wasn't for you calling the cops, 'cause I'd beat up my old lady, I never woulda had to kill her. I've been rotting in jail, just waiting for the chance to kill you too, bitch. I woulda killed you that same night if I'd been thinking," he announced. I froze, absorbing what he had said. Most of the guys holding him had been friends with Craig when Jayde had been killed and had helped in the manhunt for Scott. My blood ran cold, as I realized that it was supposed to be me that had died, not Craig. I couldn't believe one person could harbor so much hate for one person as to wish them dead for over twelve years.

"You want us to take him outside now, Brianna? Or do you want to take care of him yourself?" James, Craig's best friend, asked.

I knew it was tearing him up inside to restrain himself and not kill Scott himself. Since I was the one in charge of the investigation, it was up to me when a suspect was removed from the scene.

Slowly, I shook my head, the tears streaming down my face. I was standing about half way across the room from them and picked up a gun that had dropped to the floor during the shootout.

Looking at it, I could easily see that it wasn't a standard-issue police weapon, but it did have a silencer on the end. Raising the gun and leveling it at Scott, I took a deep breath before speaking again.

"The only way he's leaving this room is in a body bag," I declared. "You've taken two innocent lives and ruined a dozen others. Now it's your turn to die. This one's for Jayde."

I fired the gun, hearing him scream as the bullet ripped through the zipper of his jeans. I heard the other officers groan as the front of his pants quickly turned red. Taking a deep breath, I winced as the pain intensified in my shoulder. I raised the gun further as he screamed more. Pulling the trigger again, his screams ceased instantly as I hit the center of his forehead. The men dropped him to the floor as the EMS crew returned to deal with any other casualties. I dropped the gun back on the floor and headed towards the door.

James accompanied me to the hospital where I had a bullet removed from my shoulder and left with stitches and bandages, my arm in a sling to restrict movement. Back at the station, James filled out the report as I stared numbly as a photo of me, Craig and Jessika. The picture had been taken at the beginning of the summer, right after school had let out for Jessika. James had everybody else sign the report who had been at the scene before bringing it to me. I signed it without bothering to read it, and James drove me home. Walking into the house, Craig's parents, who had stayed with Jessika for the night, met me in the front hall. They were shocked to see the sling, but I could tell they probably already sensed their son was dead.

"We heard on the news that an officer was killed, but they didn't release the name," his mother began, expectantly. I wished I could tell them that Craig was fine, and burst into tears, knowing I couldn't. They pulled me into their arms, careful of my shoulder. We walked into the den and sat down as my tears slowed and I was able to explain what had happened.

"It's all my fault," I moaned as the sun came up.

"No, Brianna. It's not your fault," his mother reprimanded.

"Yes, it is. I should've recognized Scott and called off the bust," I argued. Just then, Jessika burst into the room. At twelve, she was already quite tall and had Craig's same blonde hair and blue eyes.

"Where's Daddy? What happened to your arm, Mom?" she asked quietly. I put my good arm out to her and held her to me. She pulled away after a minute and repeated her questions.

"Well, honey. I got shot last night while I was at work," I began to explain, not knowing how to tell her about Craig.

"Where's Daddy though? He promised he'd spend today with us. When's he coming home?" she demanded.

"Jessika, honey, Daddy's not going to be able to spend the day with us. . . " I began.

"But he promised. He said he'd be here when I woke up and we'd go horseback riding. He promised!" she cried, stomping her foot.

I took her chin in my hand and forced her to look into my eyes.

"I know he promised, Jess. And I know he's never broken a promise to you before. And next weekend, we'll go horseback riding, just you and me. . . "

"But I want Daddy to come too!" she interrupted me impatiently. I took a deep breath before I continued.

"I need you to be a big girl for me right now, Jessika. Please let me finish. I don't like having to tell you this way, but I'm afraid I'm going to have to be very blunt with you. I have to tell you something that you're not going to like; you're probably not even going to understand it fully for a while. Daddy's not going to be coming home. Do you remember we told you yesterday that we were going to be arresting a bunch of men who were selling drugs? Well, one of those men shot me and he shot Daddy. Honey, Daddy was killed last night."

"No! I don't believe you! My Daddy isn't dead. He's coming home. He promised me he would!" She ran from the room and I heard the back door slam a minute later. I sighed and looked at Craig's parents. His mother placed her hand over mine, and squeezed gently.

"Give her some time to adjust to what you told her. She'll come back. She's young still; and it's probably going to be difficult for her to understand. After all, this is the first time she's had to deal with death," she explained.

"I know. I wasn't much younger than her when my grandmother died. It was difficult for me to understand why she wasn't gonna be waiting for me everyday when I got home from school. I wish there was some way I could make it easier for Jessika."

"Just do what you and Craig have been doing for her since she was born. Be here for her. She's gonna have questions. Answer them honestly; and don't treat her like a child. She's probably going to do a lot of growing up in the next few weeks," Craig's father joined in.

"But what if she asks me what happened to the creep that killed her father? I don't know if I'm ready for her to know that I took a man's life without even hesitating."

"You did what you felt you had to do. And that is something that you will have to decide when the time comes. But won't there be an inquiry into the man's death? After all, there were other officers present," he asked.

"There's already been a report filed by James and signed by the officers at the scene. Hell, I don't even know what it says. James filed it," I paused as I heard the back door open again. "Would you be able to take Jessika home with you for a couple hours? I'd like to sleep for a while before I go back to the station."

I had a meeting that afternoon to go over what happened. They agreed as Jessika came back into the room. Her face was tear-stained as she hesitantly approached me. I opened my arm to her and she jumped onto my lap, jarring my shoulder and sending shock-waves of pain though my arm. I winced as she buried her head on my shoulder, sobbing. When her tears slowed, she pulled away slightly, swiping at the tears on her cheeks.

"Jess, Grandma and Grandpa are going to take you to their house to spend the day, okay."

"But I want to stay with you!" she cried.

"Honey, I have to go back to the police station today for a meeting about what happened last night. And you know you can't go with me to that. But I'll come pick you up just as soon as my meeting's done," I explained gently.

"Promise?" she asked.

"I promise." After Jessika had left with her grandparents, I slowly walked upstairs to the bedroom Craig and I had shared. Laying down on his side of the bed, I hugged his pillow to my chest and cried until I was too exhausted to cry any further and fell into a dreamless sleep.

When I awoke, the clock read three in the afternoon. Reluctantly, I got up and walked into our bathroom, turning on the shower. As the water cascaded over me, I closed my eyes to try to ease the tension that was tying my body in knots. Instead of relaxing, I found myself reliving the shooting and seeing Craig motionless on the floor, surrounded by a pool of blood. Fighting tears, I quickly finished my shower and turned the water off.

Carefully drying off and trying not to hit my shoulder, I froze as I heard somebody walking around downstairs. I tied my robe and dashed back into the bedroom for my off-duty revolver. Clicking off the safety, I tiptoed to the door and looked out into the hall. I raised the gun as I heard footsteps ascending the stairs. Rounding the corner, James jumped seeing me with the gun.

"Geez, Brianna. Relax. It's just me. Don't shoot," he breathed.

"Dammit James! What are you doing creeping around the house? Trying to scare me out of my wits? Or get yourself killed?" I practically yelled, lowering the gun.

"I wasn't creeping. I came to pick you up for the meeting," he explained.

"Yeah, yeah. Take your ass back downstairs and make some coffee, why don't you. I don't know how old the shit is that's down there. I need to get dressed still."

Joining him in the kitchen a short time later, I poured myself a coffee and leaned against the counter, slowly meeting James' eyes. He looked like he hadn't slept much since he'd dropped me off that morning. We drank our coffee in silence and finally headed out to James' car to return to the police station. My truck, as well as Craig's car, was still in the parking lot there.

"So, how's Jess taking it?" James finally spoke.

"As well as can be expected. She didn't believe me at first. Craig promised her we'd go horseback riding today; he's never broken a promise to her. His parents took her home with them so I could get some sleep and come to the meeting."

Arriving at the police station, James pulled into his usually parking space and we headed into the building. The flags had been lowered to half-staff in honor of Craig. I paused as we passed Craig's car, slowly trailing my fingertips across the hood. James put his arm around me, guiding me towards the door.

Walking down the hall, the mood was somber, although the station was bustling with activity. I took my seat in the meeting room and somebody lightly patted my shoulder. Our department sergeant came through the door a few minutes later and began the meeting.

After briefing us on the charges being laid against the dealers arrested the night before, he gave out the next assignments. I was the only officer not given another assignment. Concluding the meeting, he asked to see me in his office. Silently, I followed him down the hall and sat as he closed his office door.

"I'm sure you noticed that I didn't assign anything to you. I'd like you to take some time off. Besides the time you're allotted for Craig's funeral. I know this isn't an easy time for you. Spend some time with your daughter. Take a vacation. Whatever. But I don't want to see you anywhere near this building for two weeks. And I want your shoulder completely healed before I put you back out on the street. Understand?"

I nodded silently, knowing it was pointless to argue with him. Even if I did come into work, he'd have me tied to a desk all day, doing paperwork until my shoulder was healed. Standing up to leave, I paused with my hand on the door.

"What about the funeral? What arrangements do I need to make?" I asked quietly; I had no idea about the first thing concerning funerals.

"None at all. The department has taken care of everything. The information should be on your desk by now. And there will be a car to pick up you and Jessika for the service. Get the information and go home."

Everybody watched me silently as I approached my desk. True to his word, the information promised to me by the sergeant was on top of my other paperwork. My gaze fell on the photo on my desk as James crossed the room to stand beside me.

"Do you want me to drive you home?" he asked as I ran my fingertips lightly across the frame. I shook my head.

"No. I have to go pick up Jessika from her grandparents. I think I should spend some time alone with my daughter. I have so many questions to answer for her."

"You've got my number if you need anything," James offered.

"Yeah. I think I'll be okay though. I'll see you at the funeral." I walked away without another word.

* * * * *

CHAPTER THIRTY

When I got to Craig's parents' house, Jessika burst out the door and wrapped her arms around me as I crossed the lawn. Walking into the house, I was surprised to find my parents among the large group filling the rooms. Also there to provide a shoulder to lean on were my best friends from back home, Maya and Paul. The living room was a sea of familiar faces and I briefed everyone on the funeral arrangements before taking Jessika home to change for the visitation.

The days flew by in a blur and before I knew it, there was a uniformed officer at my door, to take us to the service. I had chosen to wear my uniform, as the rest of our division would be instead of the traditional widow's black. Jessika was silent as we rode to the church and held my hand as she stared out the window. Following us, were my parents in a car with Maya and Paul, as well as Craig's parents. The church was overflowing with uniforms from surrounding communities as well as our own department.

I barely heard the service, or the condolences expressed by our fellow officers, families and friends. Instead, I reflected on my life with Craig. I had assumed he would always be there; I had never taken the time to consider what life would be like without him. Numbly, I returned to the house after the graveside service. I was soon joined by my parents and Craig's. Before I knew it, I had a full house offering condolences, from co-workers to old friends and family, sharing their memories of Craig. Overwhelmed by the show of love and support by so many people, I quietly slipped out of the house. In our backyard, Craig had built a pond one summer, complete with a fountain and a bridge large enough to accommodate a bench for two.

We had spent countless summer nights, sitting on the bench, looking up at the stars and planning our future together. Never once had either of us brought up the possibility of one of us having to continue on without the other. The sun was almost below the horizon as I sat and the lights Craig had installed threw a soft glow across the water. Hearing footsteps a short time later, I turned to see James coming down the walk.

He had been Craig's best friend for as long as I had known him, standing up as Craig's best man at our wedding and was also Jessika's godfather. He eased himself slowly down next to me, taking my hand.

Reluctantly, I met his eyes and could see his pain reflected mine. They had been like brothers and I knew Craig's death was as hard on James as it was on me.

"Everybody's starting to leave. You might want to come back up to the house now. Unless you'd rather stay out here. I'm sure they understand you need some time alone."

"Yeah, I think I'd rather be alone right now. I have a lot of things to think about. I'll be back in a little while."

"Okay. I'll come out again before I leave, if you're not back in before then." He stood and looked down at me for a minute before returning to the house. Once everybody else had left, except for our immediate families and close friends, I returned to the house to begin the chore of cleaning up. With help from those remaining, the clean-up took no time at all and I was soon bidding good-night to the last of my guests.

Two days later, my parents flew home after making me promise to call if I needed anything. Paul and Maya left the next day, and I was alone with Jessika. I had allowed her to take the week off school so we could spend some time together and she could see her grandparents. We had also spent a lot of time together, just the two of us, and Jessika had dozens of questions for me to answer.

Sunday afternoon, as we sat watching the Sprint Cup race, I was contemplating what I was going to do. Without Craig, I had no real desire to continue working for the department. Jessika had been an avid fan of racing since Craig and I had first introduced her to the sport, and had easily talked us into taking her to the races in Charlotte.

Craig had bought me an old Mustang that we had built up to run at the local short track and she had whole-heartedly come out with us every weekend when we took the car out, cheering me on from behind my pit. James and a number of our friends from the police station had volunteered to serve as my pit crew and we had a great time, whether we took a trophy home or not. Eventually, we had bought another car, retiring the Mustang to the junk yard when it was too beat up to run any longer.

Jessika's squeals of delight brought my attention back to the television. After a minute, I figured out the reason for her happiness; her favorite driver had just taken the lead. The announcers broke away from the battle for the top spot to update viewers on the latest news.

"And finally, we're saddened to announce that Matthew Thompson has decided to put the Reed Motorsports team up for sale. Now, I talked to Matthew at great length earlier this week and he told me that since Daytona's shooting and subsequent retirement, his heart just hasn't been in the sport. If you might recall, Matthew and Daytona assumed ownership of the team after the death of Chad Reed, the original owner."

"That's a shame. It will prove to be interesting who will purchase the team. I hate to see Matthew leave the sport, but I can understand his decision to leave," the co-anchor replied. "And now, back to the battle for the lead, which has heated up considerably."

When the race was over, Jessika headed up to her room to finish her homework. Her homeroom teacher had dropped everything off Friday afternoon, so she wouldn't fall too far behind in her classes. She had spent all day Saturday in her room, her head bent over her books. At nine-thirty Sunday night, I made her put the books away and get ready for bed.

"You've got school in the morning and I'm sure your teachers will understand why you don't have all the assignments complete."

After changing into her pyjamas and brushing her teeth, Jessika quietly walked into my room as I tried to read a book. Silently, she climbed onto the bed, resting her head on my shoulder. This had been our nightly routine since she had learned to walk. However, she hadn't done it in quite a while, although I wasn't too surprised that she'd started doing it again after Craig's death. Setting the book on the nightstand, I stood up to walk her back to her room. Tucked into her bed, I sat on the edge and lightly brushed her hair out of her eyes. Suddenly sitting up, she threw her arms around me, hugging me tightly.

"I love you Mama," she whispered.

"I love you too, Jessika," I answered. After a long moment, she laid back down and quietly closed her eyes. Without another word, I stood up and walked to the door, turning out the light before pulling the door, leaving it slightly ajar. Jessika had been having nightmares lately and I had gotten into the habit of leaving our doors open, so I could hear her if she cried out in the night. I hadn't been sleeping well myself, dreaming about Craig's death over and over again. The dream would vary from time to time; sometimes, I would dream of my own death, rather than Craig's. Once the dream came each night, I gave up all attempts at sleeping and would quietly venture downstairs and look through all our old photo albums, thinking of our time together.

* * * * *

CHAPTER THIRTY-ONE

Over the next week, I spent my days sitting at the edge of our backyard pond, wondering what direction I should take. I hoped to somehow find the answer in the sunlight reflecting off the water. I had lost all interest in continuing my career as a police officer, but was at a loss as to what to do next. A conversation with Maya Thursday night gave me some direction and Friday morning saw me hitting the interstate to Mooresville once Jessika had been dropped off at school.

The drive passed quickly to Mooresville, where many of the Sprint Cup teams were housed. Pulling into a parking space at my destination, I was in awe at the size of the facility. Walking into the lobby, I introduced myself to the receptionist, who led me upstairs, showing me into the office of the team owner. He was seated behind a massive oak desk and stood to greet me, leaning across the desk to shake my hand before motioning for me to sit.

Within an hour, we had worked out the terms of transferring the team to me and I had secured a sizeable loan from my bank. Confident I had made the right decision and after arranging to meet again the following Tuesday to sign the paperwork, I returned to Greensboro.

My first stop was the police department. I was greeted warmly by my co-workers, but avoided all conversation as I headed straight to the sergeant's office. He waved me in as he concluded his telephone conversation.

"You know, I expected to see you in here sooner, bugging me to let you come back to work. How's the shoulder doing?" he began. I looked out the window, then down at my hands before answering.

"The shoulder's doing okay, I guess. It's still a little sore, but the doctor said it's gonna take at least a month to six weeks before it's fully healed and I'm gonna have to go through some therapy before I can get full use of it again."

"So, I suppose you're here either to ask for another month off, or to bug me to put you back out on the streets before your doctor approves it. I hate to say this, but we don't need you right now. We've been able to take care of things pretty well in your absence," he replied. "You know you're one of the best here, but we can manage for a while without you. Go ahead and take all the time you need to heal. Your job will still be here waiting for you whenever you're ready and able to come back."

"Actually, sir, I'm not here to find out about coming back. The past two weeks have allowed me a lot of time to think," I paused, unsure of how he was going to react.

Looking up at him, I could see how confused he was. Without another word, I placed my service revolver, badge and letter of resignation on his blotter. He picked up the letter, which I had written the night before, and read it silently.

"Are you absolutely positive about this?" he asked, after re-folding the letter and setting it back down on his desk, next to my gun.

I nodded silently, as I walked back over the window, looking down at the parking lot. Craig's car was still parked in his usual spot. Nobody had thought to move it yet.

"Craig's death really woke me up to my own mortality. I have a daughter at home to think about. I don't want her to be wondering every time I leave for work if I'm going to come home at the end of the day. Or if she's gonna hear on the news that her mother's been shot and killed. I can't put my daughter through that again. And you and I both know I can't take a desk job. If I'm a cop, I need to be out on the street. But I can't do that either. I think it's time for me to move on," I explained.

"So, what are you going to do? Do you know yet?"

"Actually, yes. I just came from a meeting in Mooresville. I'm buying Reed Motorsports," I revealed.

"You're buying a stock car team? What do you know about racing? Anything?" he seemed shocked, to say the least, at my revelation.

"As a matter of fact, I've always had a somewhat abnormal interest in auto racing. At least abnormal for a woman. But I think I could do just as well as Daytona Hudson, and it's her team I'm buying. Her husband's going to stay on as an advisor to me until I get the hang of things."

"Didn't she get shot and almost killed about two months back?"

"Yeah. Some deranged fan broke into her house and shot her and her bodyguard. I guess she'd been stalked by this psycho for a number of years. She was part owner with her husband, Matthew Thompson. He's selling the team now. He'd rather get out now, and spend some time with her and their daughter. I guess she's a few years younger than Jessika. He's taken Daytona's retirement pretty hard."

"And you want to run this team. What are you going to do for a driver?"

"You're looking at her."

"You're gonna drive a race car? You're getting out of law enforcement because of the danger, but you're gonna jump into a race car. Racing is probably just as dangerous as being a cop, you know."

"Actually, racing is a lot safer than most people think. I've seen cars virtually disintegrate after hitting the wall, and the driver walked away. And I'll be able to spend a lot more time with Jessika."

"Well, then. I guess your mind's made up already. There's no chance I can talk you out of this decision? I suppose the only thing I can do now is wish you luck. When do you move to Mooresville?"

"Probably not until December. I don't officially assume ownership of the team until the checkered flag falls in Homestead in November. And I haven't told Jessika about my decision. You're the first person I've told. I'll be telling Jess tonight when she gets home from school."

"Well, congratulations. And good luck. I hope you'll keep in touch with us. You know you were one of my best officers. You're gonna be missed around here."

"Thanks. But you're not making this very easy for me to leave. Of course I'll be in touch. I'll clean out my desk now. And Craig's while I'm here."

"Are you sure that's a good idea? I mean, I can have somebody else do it and drop everything off to you."

"No. I can do it. It's time I started taking care of things like that. I haven't started packing up his things from the house yet. Starting here is probably the best bet." I stood up and he walked me to the door.

Retrieving a few boxes from the storage room, nobody questioned when I cleared out Craig's desk, although I did receive a few sympathetic glances. It wasn't until I turned to my desk that the questions started and soon my desk was surrounded by my former fellow officers. It was James who asked first why I was packing up my desk.

"Because I'm done guys. I can't keep going like this. I've got to think about Jessika now. She just lost her father. I don't want her to wonder when she's gonna lose her mother too. I've just lost my drive. My heart's not in the badge anymore. I can carry the badge and the gun, but they don't mean anything to me anymore."

"I can't believe you're quitting," one of the other guys spoke up. "I thought you woulda been here forever."

"One thing I learned from Craig's death is that nothing is forever. Except death. I'm not quitting. I'm retiring and moving on. It's time for me; eventually it'll be time for all of you too. You just haven't realized it yet. There'll be a time someday when each and every one of you decide that you've had enough."

"So what are you gonna do?" James asked.

"I'm pursuing my other dreams. I'm moving to Mooresville to run a stock car team," I smiled shyly.

"No shit? You're buying a stock car team? Got a driver yet?" Jeff, one of the younger guys, asked. My smile widened as I looked at James.

"You're kidding, right?" James asked. "I'm misreading your smile, aren't I? You're not really gonna drive, are you? Oh my God, you are."

"But you're a woman," Jeff spoke up.

"Thanks for noticing, Jeff. But I already knew what I am. And as of mid-November, I'm going to be a woman race car driver."

"But women don't drive race cars," he protested.

"Excuse me? What do you think I've been doing at the track here every weekend? What was Daytona Hudson? A figment of our imaginations?" I asked, dumbfounded that Jeff would make a remark like that. I thought he had been open to the idea of women taking on any career.

"Well, no. But. . ." he stammered

"But nothing, buddy. I know she can do it. And so do you. Because we've all seen her do it on a smaller scale," James defended me.

"I'm sorry, Brianna. I guess I just wasn't thinking," Jeff hung his head, sheepishly. I finished packing up my desk as we discussed my career change. They helped me carry the boxes out to my truck, since my left arm was still immobile. Loading everything into the back of my truck, Jeff pointed out Craig's car.

"What are you gonna do about the Mustang?" he asked.

"I don't know yet. Probably sell it. Or park it in my new garage when I move and hold on to it until Jessika's old enough to drive it. I haven't really thought about it yet. Hell, packing up his desk was the first move I made to packing up anything of Craig's. I'm just not ready to deal with packing up our entire life together yet. For now, I'm gonna leave it parked right where it is. I'll get it towed to the house later in the week."

Heading home a short time later, I stopped at the grocery store to pick up a few things to make Jessika's favorite dinner. Everything was ready when she was dropped off after school, and she rushed into the house, bursting into the kitchen as I read the newspaper. She skidded to a stop in front of me, pausing before hugging me. I had noticed she had become more careful about hugging me, so as not to hurt my shoulder.

"Hi honey. How was school?" I asked as she sank down into the chair across from me.

"Good. We had a test in History today, but I think I aced it."

"Did you study for it last night?" I asked, narrowing my eyes at her. I knew she'd been glued to the television for most of the night. And she knew the consequences for not studying for tests.

"Relax, Mom. It was a surprise quiz. Nobody coulda studied for it. So you can't take away the tv," she explained, sticking her tongue out at me.

"Well, go wash up. Dinner's ready."

"What are we having? It smells good."

"You'll find out when it's on the table. Now, go." Returning to the table, she squealed, seeing her favorites. Sitting down, she looked at me expectantly.

"What's the occasion?"

"Nothing special. I just thought you might like it," I replied. "And I have something I want to talk to you about."

"What?"

"Well, how would you feel about travelling, oh, 38 weekends a year, and spending part of the winter in Daytona Beach?"

"Sounds cool. Why?"

"Even better, how would you like to spend almost every weekend hanging out with Doug Madison?"

"I'd love to. But how would I be able to do that? Wait a minute. Travelling every weekend, spending every weekend hanging out with Doug and winters in Daytona Beach. . . Do you mean? Did you buy Daytona's old team?" I nodded as she screamed, running around to my side of the table, throwing her arms around my neck, mindless of my shoulder.

"So, does that mean you're agreeable to moving to Mooresville to go racing with me?" I asked.

"Of course. When do we leave?" I motioned for her to return to her chair before I answered.

"Well, there is the matter of you finishing your semester here. I don't want to pull you out of classes midway through. And I don't officially take ownership of the team until after the last race in Homestead. So we've got a little over a month to find a house and get everything moved. But you might be able to stay with your grandparents while you finish the semester. I'll call them tomorrow and talk to them about it. I've got a lot of work to do with the team too and organizing it. I don't know who's gonna stay and who's gonna leave. After all, their team is being sold. Some of the guys may not want to stay. So I'm gonna have to hire some new guys. I already know I have to look for a new crew chief. I met him today and Brian told me he's leaving the team. He won't stay without Matthew and Daytona there."

"This is so cool. I can't wait to tell my friends."

"That's another thing, Jessika. You're gonna be leaving a lot of close friends behind here. You're gonna have to make new ones at your new school. Are you gonna be okay with that?"

"Of course. Don't worry about me, Mom. It's gonna be cool. I can't believe it. My mom, a race car driver. Have you told Grandma and Grandpa yet?"

"Not yet. I want to wait until everything's been taken care of. I have to drive back to Mooresville on Tuesday to take care of the final paperwork. And I thought that maybe next weekend, we could go there together and start looking for houses. Do you think you can keep it a secret until after we buy a house?"

"Of course," Jessika nodded.

We decided to spend the weekend packing up Craig's things and finished up late Sunday night. I kept a few of his things as mementos, shirts and whatnot and gave a few items to Jessika. I would be donating most of his clothes to the local shelter.

Tucking Jessika into bed, I began to wonder if I was doing the right thing in moving to Mooresville. Although I had wanted to drive a race car professionally for as long as I could remember, I didn't want to completely disrupt her life. Leaving her room, I quietly slipped out the back door and walked down to our pond, hoping to clear my mind of any doubts I had about my decision.

* * * * *

CHAPTER THIRTY-TWO

Finalizing the sale on Tuesday of the team to me, Matthew gave me a tour of the shop, introducing me to the employees, and provided a brief history. We also discussed my previous experience in a race car and what I was going to do with the team. I explained to him that I was going to move the team down to the Nationwide level for at least a year to get some experience on the big tracks before I brought it back up to the Sprint level.

Returning to his office, he handed me a list of names. Covering almost half the page, I glanced over it quickly, recognizing some of the names as employees he had just introduced me to.

"I take it these are the team members who have given their notice?" I met his eyes again.

"I'm afraid so. I've talked to all of them, and tried to convince them to stay, but what can you say when you're leaving yourself? I can't exactly ask these guys to stay when I'm bailing. Most of these guys have been here from the start. I can understand them wanting to leave. But I'm sure you'll be able to find guys capable of replacing them. I can even recommend a few for you that I know have been looking for a new team to join."

"I'd appreciate that, Matthew. And I can understand you wanting to leave. I've actually done the same thing."

"How's that?"

"Well, you already know that I was a cop in Greensboro, and that I got shot when a bust went sour. What I haven't told you is that the night I was shot, so was my husband. Unfortunately, he didn't make it. He died at the scene. There was nothing that could be done to help him. After he died, I completely lost the interest and drive I used to have for my job. It was like my love for the job died with him. I want to be home when my daughter comes home from school every day. I don't want her to be worried every time I strap on the badge and gun that I might not be coming home at the end of the day. Right now, my daughter is my top priority; the sun is going to rise and set on her. I'm sure you understand where I'm coming from."

"Of course. Samantha took Daytona's shooting really hard. And I know she worries every time I leave them at the house that somebody's going to break in again. She's still having nightmares about Daytona being shot, but then, she was there and heard the entire thing, even though she didn't see it," he paused.

"Daytona shot and killed the other woman. That's gotta be rough, seeing somebody take another life. She's talked to me about it, but I know it's gonna take a long time before she gets through it."

"It is. I've seen it too many times, being a cop. And I've seen too many children witness their parent's murders. It's traumatic, to say the least. For the child, mostly. As a cop, you learn to condition yourself, so after a while, it doesn't affect you as much, but it still does to some degree. The worst part is knowing that each death could've been prevented. My best friend was killed twelve years ago by her boyfriend who was high on drugs. They'd had a history of him beating her up so badly that she couldn't work, couldn't even see hardly. I warned her repeatedly and tried to get her to call the police and press charges. This was while I was still in school, training. But she wouldn't listen until it was too late. He found her at my apartment one night, where she'd been hiding out from him after she finally decided to leave and press charges. He beat her to death, leaving the apartment only minutes before I got there, after she had called me hysterical because he knew where she was and had threatened her life. We managed to put him away, but when he got out of jail, he came looking for me, and ironically, he was the one who pulled the trigger and killed my husband."

"Wow. That's gotta be rough. Did he get put in prison for killing a police officer and I'm assuming attempted murder on your life?"

"No. He was killed that same night. It was a fluke. Everybody started shooting and somehow, he got hit. Twice." I shook my head slowly, looking down at my hands folded in my lap. Matthew regarded me silently for a moment before responding.

"It was your gun that the bullets came from, wasn't it?" I looked up at him, surprised.

"What would make you think that?"

"Because that's what I would've done. If I had been in the house, when that woman shot Daytona, I would've killed her if Daytona hadn't managed to do it."

"I'm not saying that it's right. But he killed my best friend and my husband. He left a twelve year old girl without her father. I reacted on instinct. If I hadn't shot him, one of the other officers would've done it, or beaten him to death in lock up. It was inevitable that he would die. I'm not proud of the fact that I so easily took another person's life, but sometimes circumstances dictate your actions. If you had killed your wife's attacker, your daughter would be without you in her life, because you would've been charged with murder and put in prison."

We sat silently considering out conversation for a few minutes before Matthew spoke again.

"I suppose you'll be looking for a house soon."

"As a matter of fact, I was going to bring Jessika on the weekend and we were going to look together. Do you have any suggestions?"

"Actually, there are a couple over near me that are up for sale right now that you might want to take a look at. They're spacious, but not too big. I'm not sure exactly what you want, but I'm sure you'll be able to find something around here. It's a great area to live in. And there are a lot of kids from racing families, so it shouldn't be too difficult for your daughter to make friends. Even though her mother's gonna be the new kid on the track, so to speak."

Matt took me home to meet Daytona and have her sign her part of the paperwork and I was thrilled to finally be able to meet her. When I'd worked at the bar, her sister had been the one there taking care of things most of the time. And I'd cheered for her every week when she was racing, not only being a woman on the track, but seeing as she was from the same hometown as me. When Matt brought me back to the shop, we stood in the parking lot talking for a few minutes before I headed back to Greensboro.

"I'd be happy to show you around on the weekend, if you like. Kind of help you get to know the area, show you the schools and all. I'm sure our daughters would get along well; they're not that far apart in age," he suggested.

"I'd like that. Where would you like to meet? Here?"

"Sounds good to me. Is noon okay for you?"

"That's fine. I'll see you then." I shook his hand and climbed into my car. Heading back to the interstate, I decided it would be best to tell Craig's parents of the move before the weekend. Arriving back in Greensboro, I called to invite them to dinner.

Their initial reaction was shock, until they realized that I was determined to see this through and saw how excited Jessika was about the move. Giving me their blessing, they agreed to take Jessika in once the arrangements were final and the house had been sold, until she could join me in Mooresville.

* * *

Meeting Matthew and his daughter went well, and by late Saturday afternoon, Jessika and I had decided on a house. It was directly behind Matthew's and close to the school that Jessika would be going to. It was also the same school that Samantha, Matthew's daughter, attended. I was happy that Jessika had made a friend so quickly. Most of what they talked about was Daytona and Craig.

Driving back home that night, Jessika was bursting with excitement at having found the house. Luckily, there had been a realtor available to work out the details. Interestingly enough, Matthew had seemed to know her well, and I soon surmised that he had already looked into the houses and had arranged for her to be there when we were.

The sale went through on Monday, the same day I arranged for a realtor to come out to list our house and put the for sale sign up on our front lawn. A key selling point of our house was the pond in the backyard and she felt that the house would sell quickly.

Tuesday, I went through the house, shooting pictures and video of the house and backyard, wanting more than just my memories. That night, I called my parents with the news, after Jessika had gone up to her room to do homework. They seemed happy for me and promised to fly down once I was settled in the new house.

Wednesday, I began packing up things we wouldn't need before the move, hoping to get the little things out of the way as soon as possible. We would be able to move in the first of November, and I knew what was left of October would pass quickly.

* * *

October 31

The day the moving truck arrived, James and a number of other officers showed up on my doorstep to help out. Packing the truck went quickly and before we knew it, the house was empty. I had already taken Jessika's things over to her grandparents' and sold off whatever we wouldn't need, like my old race car. James and I silently wandered through the empty rooms. The other officers had headed out to the backyard to sit by the pond and I'd called to order pizza for them to thank them for helping out.

"It's hard to believe I'm really moving out of here, James. When Craig and I moved in here, I never imagined leaving here, and certainly not without him. It's all so strange. I keep expecting him to come bursting through the door like he used to."

"I know, Brianna. There's been a dozen times when I've looked over at your desks, expecting to see you guys there, but they're still empty, exactly how you left them."

The doorbell rang then, with the pizza being delivered, sparing me from answering his statement. Taking the pizza out to the backyard, James grabbed a dozen cans of beer from the fridge and tossed each of the guys a can to start. The mood was sombre and finally, I had to speak up.

"Look guys. I'm only going to Mooresville. I'm still gonna be in the same state as y'all. It's not like I'm moving to the North Pole. It's only a two-hour drive. Y'all are gonna bring down my good mood. I'm kinda nervous about moving, but I'm real excited about starting my new career. Lighten up guys, okay. Otherwise, you're gonna make me cry. And I don't want to do that, a'ight?"

They began to cheer up then and before I knew it, they were leaving. I had to hit the road soon, and James was the last to leave, helping me clean up. Walking with me out to my truck, he hugged me.

"You be careful. Don't go getting yourself hurt on that race track, girl."

"Don't worry. I'll be fine. And you come down and see me and Jess once in a while, okay. You're her godfather. I don't expect you to disappear from her life just because we live in another part of the state. I'll be back in a couple days to pick up Craig's car. I've decided I'm gonna keep it for now. I'm just parking it in our new garage." Climbing into my truck, I waved with barely a backwards glance at the house, knowing if I stopped to think about it, I would only get emotional and cry.

Two days later, as I unpacked the kitchen, there was a knock on the back door.

"Hello? Anybody home? Welcome wagon!" I recognized Matthew's voice and waved at him to come in. He found me surrounded by boxes, trying to figure out where to put everything. I had more than enough cupboard and shelf space and was at a loss as to where I should put everything.

"This is a pleasant surprise," I said, shoving a number of pots and pans into a bottom cupboard and turning to face him.

"Well, I was driving by yesterday and saw the moving van unloading, so I thought by today you could use a friendly face. And I figured you wouldn't mind seeing something besides boxes. I also thought you might need some help unpacking."

"Thanks, but I've got most of it done. And whatever I don't get done, Jessika's gonna help me with on the weekend when she comes down. Right now, I just want to take a break. I've been avoiding taking breaks, since I've had nobody to talk to here. I think I should get a dog. Or a cat. Or a something. I still have another month or two before Jessika moves in. I didn't want to pull her out of her old school until the semester was done. It's gonna be pretty lonely here by myself until then."

"Before you know it, the race season will have started. And you won't have time to think about being lonely. In fact, you'll probably need to get a pet for Jessika, since she'll probably get lonely being here by herself, unless you're gonna take her with you to the shop."

"I was thinking about it. She really loves the sport. I'm sure I could find something for her to do, even if it's just organizing bolts."

"Well, you know. You could always make her your crew chief," Matthew laughed.

"Yeah. That'd work. There are crew chiefs that've been in the sport longer than she's been alive. Although if I get stuck for one, I might actually have to put her to work."

"Say, what are you doing tomorrow? Do you want to come by the shop and see what goes into preparing for a race?" he suddenly suggested.

"I can't. I'd love to, but I'm heading back to Greensboro for the day, and driving my husband's car back here. Maybe next week?"

"Yeah, next week'll work. It's the last race though. Are you gonna come to Homestead with us? I'll get you a team pass for the weekend, and Jessika if she wants to come."

"Sounds good."

"Great. I've got to get to the shop, but I'll talk to you in a couple days."

"Good luck this weekend," I called out. He waved before closing the door behind him. I watched him walking through the backyard as I picked up the phone to call Jessika to let her know. Hanging up from talking to her and assuring her that I would see her the next day, I decided to call Windsor. Looking through my Rolodex, I easily found the number I was looking for and hesitantly dialled.

"Hello?" a woman answered the phone. I almost hung up without saying a work, but swallowing my nervousness, I finally found my voice.

"Hello. Is Kyle there please?"

"Just a minute. Who is this anyways?" she demanded. I could tell she wasn't impressed with another woman calling and I assumed he'd gotten married since the last time we'd spoken.

"This is Brianna Lane. I'm an old friend of his from university."

"Hang on." I heard her set the phone down and sarcastically tell him who was on the other end.

"Hey, Brianna. What's up?" he cheerfully asked.

"Not much. I just called to see what you were up to these days. I haven't started a fight between you and your wife, have I?"

"No, I'm not married," he laughed. "Jennifer is my ex-girlfriend. She was just here to pick up her things and was just leaving."

"Oh. I'm sorry Kyle. If I've called at a bad time, I can call back later," I offered.

"No, I can talk to you now. How's Craig?" I took a deep breath before answering.

"Um, the best way I can describe him is. . . Dead. He was killed a month ago during a drug raid," I explained, sitting down in the living room.

"Geez, Brie. I'm so sorry. If I had known. . . "

"I know, Kyle. I know. But I'm dealing with it. Just taking things one day at a time."

"So, what are you doing now? Are you back to work yet?"

"Actually, no. That's part of why I called. I retired shortly after the shooting. I decided it was time for a career change."

"So what are you doing now?"

"Well, right at this exact minute, I'm taking a break from unpacking my new house in Mooresville. I bought a stock car team."

"No shit. Not Reed Racing? I heard it was up for sale."

"Yeah. I'm the proud new owner. But I have a problem."

"What might that be?"

"I need a crew chief. Half the team bailed on me. Nobody wants to stay on the team now that Daytona's had to retire and Matthew's retiring at the end of the season. So, I thought maybe you'd like the position."

"I don't know Brianna. This is all kinda sudden, you know."

"Take some time to think about it. I don't need to know right this minute. Just by Homestead, 'cause when the checkers fall, the team officially becomes mine."

"Okay, I'll think about it. Give me a couple days and I'll call you back. Is your number the same? No, I guess it wouldn't be if you've moved, now would it?" I gave him the new number before hanging up and returning to my unpacking.

I flew back to Greensboro early the next afternoon and spent some time with Jessika after I picked up Craig's car from the police station, before heading back to Mooresville.

When I returned from spending the day in Greensboro with Jessika, Kyle had left a message on my answering machine that he'd take the job and for me to call and let him know when he had to be in North Carolina.

I had him fly down for the race in Homestead, and picked him up from the airport and introduced him to Jessika and then to Matthew when we reached the race track. The announcement was made prior to the green flag that I'd be taking over the team at the end of the race and I was besieged with questions by the media. Everybody wanted to know where I was going to take the team and I answered everybody's questions the same way, 'I'm going to try to continue where Daytona left off.'

At the conclusion of the race, Matthew ceremoniously handed the keys to the shop over to me, wishing me luck, in front of a dozen television cameras. Brian also came over and shook my hand as well as Kyle's, wishing us both luck and offering to provide any advice or answers to whatever questions we might have. Along with Matthew, Brian was planning to stay on to help with the transition.

As we walked back in the door after the flight home, and I began showing Kyle around the house, I took my jacket off, realizing too late that my bandages were visible through my thin tee-shirt. I'd managed to ignore the pain, but it was still present, since I was forever ripping the wound open and causing it to bleed more.

"Brianna, what happened to your shoulder?" Kyle suddenly asked, gently pushing my shirt sleeve aside, exposing the bandage.

"It's nothing, really," I protested, pulling my sleeve back down. Silently, I wished Jessika had come back with us, instead of having to fly back to Greensboro.

"Bullshit. It's not nothing. Obviously, you've been hurt. What happened?"

"I got shot. Plain and simple. It was the night Craig was killed. The same guy that killed Craig, shot me, except both bullets were meant for me."

"How can you even think that? What happened?" he asked, his tone becoming gentler.

We settled in the living room and I began to relay the story of the night I was shot. When I was done, I was surprised to discover that my cheeks were wet as tears ran down them. Kyle moved over to sit next to me and put an arm around my shoulders, gently, to comfort me. Resting my head on his shoulder, I sighed quietly, feeling emotionally drained.

"I can't believe you've been through so much, practically by yourself. And having to help Jessika through it too. I wish you had called me. I would've come down sooner. You know that."

We talked well into the night, and the next morning we were both exhausted when we drove to the shop. I had offered to let Kyle stay in the guest room until he found a place of his own.

Walking into the shop in the morning, my receptionist, Kara, welcomed us and informed us that the remainder of the team was awaiting my arrival in the conference room. Kyle and I walked into a sea of smiling faces, obviously eager to begin work for their new boss. I gave them a brief speech before sending them to whatever work they had done before my arrival. That day, Kyle and I began interviewing mechanics to take the place of those who had resigned.

By the end of the day, we had hired enough to cover all positions and we turned to the task of learning who was who on the team as well as who performed what duties at the shop and the track. We also went over the books to find out what we needed to order in the way of parts and supplies. Matthew and Brian stopped by late in the afternoon to see how we were making out with the transition.

And so began my career as a NASCAR Nationwide Series driver and car owner.

* * * * *

CHAPTER THIRTY-THREE
June 2015

Finishing my story about how Jessika's father and I met and buying the race team after his death, I sent the girls up to Jessika's room and sat out on the patio, reflecting on the years gone passed. As I sat, I looked up to see Matthew walking through my backyard along the edge of the pool. Our backyards connected and we had spent many evenings sitting together, either on his patio or mine, talking into the early hours of the morning. He wordlessly sat down beside me, waiting for me to speak.

"You heard about Doug?" I finally asked, not knowing what else to say.

"Who hasn't? How is he? I didn't want to call the hospital."

"He seemed to be doing okay when we left last night. But it's gonna be a while before he drives again. I don't know what they're gonna do for a driver until he's able to return," I replied, looking at Matthew in the moonlight, wondering what had prompted him to come over tonight.

"When will he be coming home? Do you know?"

"Probably in a couple days, I imagine. Ricky should be able to tell you if you call. Or I can ask Mandy. She's upstairs with Jessika. She's talked to him a couple times a day since Sunday."

"How's Mandy holding up? I think this is the first time her Dad's been really hurt, and she's been old enough to understand. Most of the other injuries were just minor, like broken bones."

"She's doing okay. It was pretty rough on her seeing the crash. I called the house right after it happened and she was a mess. By the time she got to see Doug, she'd pulled herself together though," I explained. Just then, Mandy and Jessika burst out the door, interrupting us.

"Sorry, Mom. Didn't realize you had company. We'll come back out later. Hi, Mr Thompson," Jessika apologized.

"Hello, girls. It's nice to see you both again. Mandy, I hope you'll wish your father the best for me. Ask him to call me when he's home, please," he stood, turning to me. "Brianna, as always, it's been a pleasure talking to you. Good night."

"Good night, Matthew."

I watched as he slowly walked back across the yard to his own gate. When the gate was closed behind him and he had disappeared into the shadows surrounding his own house, I turned to Mandy and Jessika.

"So?" I asked.

"We wanted to play pool," Jessika answered.

"You know you don't need my permission. You could've gone down there by yourselves to play."

"Yeah. But we wanted you to play with us," Mandy announced.

"Okay. Let's go girls. Who's playing first?" I asked as the doorbell rang. "Now, who could that be?"

"Why don't you go answer the door while we go set up the table?" Jessika replied, grabbing Mandy's arm and practically dragged her down to the basement. Opening the front door, I was surprised to see Kyle standing on my front step.

"Why do I get the feeling my daughter has something to do with you being here?"

"Well, she did call and tell me you wanted to talk to me. That could be why," Kyle offered, stepping inside as I held the door open for him.

"But you wanna know something? I didn't ask her to. I don't want to talk to you; well, I don't have anything that I need to say to you that can't wait until morning, but since you're here, come on downstairs and help me beat my daughter," I led the way to the basement stairs as I spoke.

"Now, wait a minute, Brie. Beating her isn't the answer," he protested, taking my arm.

"Oh, it's not what you think. I can do it, but I can always use some help and Mandy's here still. Would you please stop looking at me like that? We were just about to play pool when you arrived. What? You didn't think I actually meant I was going to physically harm her, did you?" I laughed as I realized that was his exact thought.

Joining the girls, we were soon caught up in the game. Before we knew it, it was almost three o'clock in the morning. Jessika and Mandy were about to head up to bed, when I noticed Kyle trying to hide a yawn.

"You know, Kyle. You can stay here tonight if you want," I suggested, hearing Mandy and Jessika elbowing and whispering to each other as they walked up the stairs. I walked over and leaned on the pool table beside him.

"I don't think that would be a good idea, Brianna. Although I'm sure the girls would love to see me at the breakfast table in the morning."

"Yeah, I know. I apologize for their behaviour. I swear, they've made it their goal in life to hook us up. I'm sorry you have to be a victim of their matchmaking attempts."

"It's okay. It's kinda cute, actually. But I think Jessika's trying to tell you something."

"And what might that be? Besides the fact that she totally adores you and would probably love to have you as her step-father?"

"Well, I was thinking along the lines that she needs a father figure, but I wasn't necessarily thinking of me."

"Well, she has been. We've had a lot of long talks about it lately. She's determined to get us to fall in love with each other. I just don't know what to do about her."

"How about giving up?" I looked at Kyle in shock, realizing what he had said. I had always known there was some sort of attraction between us, and although I had tried to get him to notice me on more than just a friendly level when we'd first met, he had let me know in no uncertain terms that he wasn't interested in pursuing a relationship with me. Without another word, Kyle put an arm around my waist, pulling me to him. As he began to kiss me, I could hear Jessika and Mandy at the top of the stairs, but was too caught up in Kyle's kiss to reprimand them.

When he finally broke the kiss, I was light-headed and had to lean on him to avoid falling over. I didn't think my legs would support me. As he held me, I rested my head on his shoulder. I couldn't help but think about all the times we'd joked with each other at the university pub and the time he'd flat-out told me he wasn't interested. I had managed to put aside my feelings for him after that, and it wasn't long after that I had moved to North Carolina. Remembering his cold refusal of me years ago, I suddenly pulled away, walking over to sit across the room.

"What's wrong, Brianna?" Kyle asked quietly, coming to sit next to me.

"Please don't do this to me, Kyle. Don't play these games with me," I whispered, refusing to look at him.

"What are you talking about, Brianna?" he asked, putting a hand under my chin and gently turning my head to look into my eyes.

"We stopped playing these games twenty years ago. I'm not gonna start playing them again. I don't want a relationship with you. I can't have a relationship with you. We couldn't do it back then and I'm not gonna do it now," I explained.

"What do you mean; you don't want a relationship with me? Kiss me like you did and then make a statement like that. You're really confusing me, Brie."

"And what do you think you were doing to me back home, when we were at the university? Do you think you were so easy to figure out? I never knew from one day to the next how you were gonna react to me. One day, you flirt with me and make me think you're interested and the next you tell me you're not interested. You had me more confused than anybody ever did."

"But I didn't want a relationship back then. Oh hell, I did want a relationship with you but I knew you were leaving to come here. What would the point have been for us to get together if you were leaving? If you had been staying in Windsor, I would've started something with you. But then you moved here and met Craig," he answered quietly.

We talked for hours about his revelation, and before we knew it, the sun was coming up. I was exhausted and knew he was probably tired too, but we both knew we had to make an appearance at the shop for a couple hours. Heading back up to the kitchen, I made coffee for us, and we sat out on the patio, our conversation turning to the team. Finally, Kyle stood, stretching and we walked back into the house.

"I'll see you at the shop later. Try not to kill Jess and Mandy for what they did. You know they were only trying to help," he said, hugging me.

"Yeah, I'll spare their lives. For now," I laughed as I pulled away and we walked towards the front door. There, Kyle pulled me into his arms again, and lightly kissed me. I watched as he jogged out to his car and drove out of the driveway, heading home. Closing the front door, I slowly turned and headed upstairs to shower and change before heading to the shop myself.

* * * * *

CHAPTER THIRTY-FOUR

August 2015

The remainder of June passed quickly, turning into July and Doug returned home a little over a week after his accident. Matthew met with him and Ricky the day they returned home and offered to drive for him until he could get back in the car. The media had a field day with Matthew returning to the track, but he didn't let it affect his performance. Doug began his therapy as soon as he could, and Mandy moved back home to take care of him, but was still over to see Jessika every day. I was surprised that Jessika had chosen to forgive her so easily, but I knew she'd talk to me about it when she was ready.

As her birthday approached, I began planning a celebration for her, since she was turning eighteen. Kyle offered to help me with it and Jessika was happy to see that we were spending so much time together. We kept it a secret until the last minute, letting only Mandy and Doug know about it the day before, so they could help us surprise Jessika.

The party was scheduled for later in the day, and Jessika came with me to the shop in the morning, sitting in my office with me, while I took care of the mail and my messages. Just as I was about to finish up, Jessika took my attention away from it all, calling me over to the window where she'd been standing, watching the activity below. The guys on the team had put up a banner in the lobby wishing her a *'Happy Birthday Jessika'* and everybody had signed it, hanging balloons and streamers from each end.

"Hey, Mom. Come take a look at this," she called, motioning for me to join her. Worried that signals had been crossed and something for her party was being delivered to the shop, I rushed over to the window. My office looked out over the reception area. Imagine my shock at seeing Todd standing in the lobby, amid the next tour group scheduled to see the shop.

"Damn. What is he doing here?" I asked, as Kyle walked into my office.

"I thought we had a meeting today, Brie. Did you forget?" he asked, obviously thinking I was referring to him.

"Not you. Him," I answered, pointing down into the lobby. Kyle walked over to join us at the window, to see who I was pointing at.

"Who?"

"Todd! He's down there. Leaning on Kara's desk."

"So? He'll tour the shop, and while he's on the tour, we'll slip out and go to lunch. Unless you want to talk to him."

"Of course I don't want to talk to him. I don't even want to be in the same building at him. It's bad enough we have to be in the same state twice a year. And we live in the same country. Hell, I don't even want to be on the same planet as him."

"Well, I can have security show him the door, if you want," Kyle offered. I was prevented from answering when my phone rang. Picking up my cordless, I walked back to the window, knowing it was Kara. Looking back down on the reception area, I saw Todd leaning against her desk, obviously flirting with her.

"God, can he make it a little more obvious he's flirting?" I asked as I picked up the phone. "What does he want Kara?"

"How did you. . . " she asked, the surprise evident in her voice until she looked up at my office window. "Oh. Mr Berkley wants to meet with you."

"My schedule is full from now until the end of eternity, Kara."

"He says it's important."

"And I'm sure to him it is. Tell you what. Send him along with one of the tour groups and tell him I'll check my schedule and you'll let him know when he gets back to you after the tour."

"Okay, boss." I watched as Kara hung up the phone and relayed the information to Todd. He looked up at my window and I could tell he was upset at the offer, but reluctantly joined the tour group as it began its journey through the shop. Grabbing my purse and keys, I headed out of the office as soon as the group had disappeared into the shop area, Jessika and Kyle close behind. Running out the front door, I called over my shoulder to Kara that I would be gone for the rest of the day. Dropping Jessika off at Mandy's, I told her I'd see her later that afternoon and followed Kyle to confirm the final arrangements for Jessika's party.

* * *

Once everybody had assembled in the ballroom at Charlotte Motor Speedway, I called Mandy to get her to bring Jessika and Doug in. I had reserved the room for Jessika's birthday and they had decorated exactly how I had specified. I had invited all her close friends as well as a number of crew members from each team that she hung out with. Hundreds of balloons hung from the ceiling, scheduled to drop after she walked in. I had hired a band for the occasion, one of her favorite local bands, and they stood to one side of the enormous room, waiting for my signal to begin playing.

When they walked in and everybody yelled 'Surprise,' Jessika was genuinely shocked that we had gone to such great lengths for her birthday. I had also flown in both sets of grandparents that day, and had them driven directly to the speedway, so she wouldn't know they were in town. Both sets would be staying at the house for a week to spend some time with her as well. Luckily, the house had three spare bedrooms.

Once the initial shock had passed, Jessika made her way over to me to thank me.

"Hey, I didn't do this all by myself," I explained. "I did have help you know. What do you think Kyle and I have been doing all this time when we've been disappearing for hours on end?"

"You don't want me to answer that, Mom," Jessika laughed, throwing her arms around us both, before turning to rejoin her friends. The band had begun playing when she had walked in and soon the dance floor was filled with Jessika and her friends. We had arranged for a buffet-style dinner and everyone eventually wandered over to the tables. Just after I suggested to Jessika that she begin opening her gifts, I looked to the door as it opened, thinking it was a few latecomers. Jessika was standing behind the table that held most of her gifts and was ripping the first one open. I had been standing with my mother and she seemed as shocked as I was to see who did walk through the door. I head Jessika gasp as she looked up.

"What is he doing here?" my mother asked.

"I don't know Mom. He showed up at the shop earlier, but I managed to avoid him," I replied. "I have no idea how he found out where we'd be tonight, unless he managed to charm the information out of Kara." Just then, Kyle arrived at my side.

"I take it you've seen him?" Kyle asked, taking my hand. I nodded silently, surprised when he moved his arm to encircle my waist, protectively. We watched as Todd scanned the room, presumably for me. Finding me, he purposely strode over, oblivious to the activities around him. We were standing at one end of the room, in full view of all the party-goers. I didn't want to cause a scene, so I motioned for Jessika to continue with the evening and Mandy handed her another gift to open. Kyle pulled me closer as Todd stopped in front of us.

"Brianna, you're a very difficult woman to get a hold of," he began.

"I think that depends on your point of view, buddy," Kyle spoke up.

"I'm a very busy woman, Todd. If you didn't know, I do run my own race team. And I have a daughter to take care of," I replied, levelly.

"Looks to me like she's doing fine. I think she can take care of herself for ten minutes for me to talk to you. That is, if buddy here will let you go for ten minutes."

"The name's Kyle, buddy. And I happen to be Brie's -- "

"Yeah, I know. Crew chief. Thank I can talk to your boss in private for a minute?"

"I'm more than her crew chief, Todd. I happen to be her husband too," I looked at Kyle, shocked for a minute, but recovered quickly.

"Husband? I didn't know you'd remarried."

"We wanted to keep our relationship out of the public eye. It's not easy to have a relationship with anybody when you're constantly in the spotlight. But then it's not any of your business either," I replied.

"Well, either way, can I talk to you? I was hoping you'd stop so I could talk to you when you were in Michigan, but you seemed too intent on outrunning me."

"So you thought you'd just come down here and harass me here? Obviously you can't take a hint that I don't want to talk to you. Everything we ever needed to say to each other was said twenty years ago, when you broke up with me."

"No. There's something I want to say to you that I didn't get to say back then. I didn't know what to say then. Would you please give me a minute of your time?" Just then, Jessika came running over to join us.

"Jessika, please return to your guests," I said quietly.

"Sorry, Mom. I got something I want to say first," she turned to Todd. "Look, buddy, I know all about you. And I don't like you; I don't like the way you treated my mom when you were younger. And I happen to like my Mom with Kyle, so why don't you go screw yourself. Preferably not here, 'cause this is my party and you were not invited."

"Excuse me, little girl, but you don't know me. You only know what your mother told you about me. And I came here to talk to your mother, not you. So I will leave when I'm damn good and ready. Didn't your mother teach you any manners?"

"I will not have you talking to my daughter like that," I stormed. "I want you out of here now. I have nothing to say to you. And I don't think there's anything you could possibly say to me to make me want to listen. Anything you want to say to me, you should've said twenty years ago. Not waited until now. Because now it's just too damn late. I'm gonna ask you one more time. I want you to leave, or I'm going to have security forcibly remove you. And don't underestimate me; I will call security if I have to. That was your big mistake before, underestimating me."

"Fine. I'll go quietly. But don't underestimate me. I will talk to you before I leave, no matter what it takes. If I have to camp out front of your house twenty-four seven, until I get to talk to you, I will." That said, he turned and abruptly left. Once I had convinced Jessika to return to her guests, Kyle and I walked outside in his attempt to calm me down.

"Hey, don't let him get to you. Eventually, he'll give up and go home and be out of your life again."

"But what if he does what he said and camps out in front of the house?"

"Then we'll have him arrested for harassment, plain and simple."

"Yeah, but you told him we're married. Obviously, if he camps out, he's gonna know you lied," I reminded him.

"Not if I come stay at your place for a few days. I'll sleep in the spare bedroom downstairs, like when I first moved down here, that's all. Problem solved."

"Are you sure?" I asked, looking up at him.

"Positive. Jessika's staying at Mandy's tonight. I'm sure your parents and Craig's won't have a problem with it. After all, it's your house. They'll understand. What better time for me to move in?" I agreed and we headed back to the party.

An hour later, I followed Kyle to his apartment, before driving back to the house. My parents as well as Craig's already had a set of house keys to let themselves in later. I motioned for him to pull into the garage in my usual spot, so nobody watching from the street would see him bring his things into the house. As the garage door closed, Kyle climbed out of the car and pulled me into his arms. Laughing, I half-heartedly struggled to get out of his grasp, which he tightened the more I struggled.

"Kyle!"

"Hey, if I'm your husband, I think I deserve for you to act like a wife should," he laughed.

"Oh really? Does that include the nagging to take out the trash and complaining that you spend all your time with your friends and not enough time at home with me and your stepdaughter?" I joked.

"If that's what comes with the package, yes." I pulled back to look into his eyes, unsure if he was joking or not. Suddenly, he turned us around so he had me pinned against the driver's door of his car. With nowhere to go, I was helpless, knowing I could never use what I'd learned during my years on the police force to overpower him. Without another word, he leaned over and kissed me slowly and gently at first, then more insistently. Returning his kiss, I hesitantly wrapped my arms around his neck and allowed myself to be swept away by the moment.

When he finally broke the kiss, he looked into my eyes tenderly. Without another word, he took my hand and led me upstairs to my bedroom. Hesitantly, I followed him, knowing we had both waited for this moment for twenty years and not wanting to break the magical spell that seemed to have been cast.

* * *

Later that night, after we had made love with all the urgency and hunger of twenty years of bottled emotions, I had tried to talk to him, but he had silenced me with a kiss, choosing to hold me in his arms rather than talk about what had just happened and where it was going to lead. I had so many questions for him, but knew they would have to wait until he was ready.

We both drifted off to sleep in each other's arms, but I was soon awake again, having gotten accustomed to being alone at night. Quietly, I slipped out of bed and pulled on my silk robe. Walking to the window, I sat on the cushioned ledge, looking out over my front yard. I noticed that both rental cars were in the driveway, which meant that Jessika's grandparents had come in sometime during the evening. I just hoped it was sometime while Kyle and I had been asleep, to avoid having to explain to them why Kyle was spending the night in my bed.

Tucking my knees under my chin, I hugged my legs to my chest. It was times like this that I missed our backyard pond. I had been tempted to call a contractor to build a replica of the one in Greensboro, but had never gotten around to actually making the call. I had spent many nights looking out over the front yard since we had moved to Mooresville, or sitting out on the patio at the back of the house, thinking about whatever problems faced me. This time, I didn't want to go outside to sit on the patio, in case Kyle woke up before I could return to bed.

Hearing movement behind me, I turned to find Kyle merely rolling over. I gazed at him in the moonlight cascading through the windows. I had longed for a night like this with him for years and now that I had it, I wasn't so sure I wanted it. He had awakened so many emotions in me during the passed few weeks since the night we had played pool together and the first time we had kissed, but I wasn't quite sure how to handle those emotions.

Not finding the answers I had hoped for, I sighed and returned to bed, slipping between the sheets. Without waking, Kyle put his arm around me, pulling me closer. Rolling onto my side, I closed my eyes and soon fell asleep again.

When I woke in the morning, I thought at first that I had dreamt the entire evening with Kyle, until I heard the shower running in my bathroom. Minutes after the water turned off, Kyle emerged from the bathroom, with just a towel wrapped around his waist.

I was grateful that Jessika had chosen to stay at Mandy's the night before. I knew I wasn't ready to deal with the reaction when she found out Kyle had stayed in my bed last night. Self-consciously, I pulled the sheet closer to my chin as he leaned over to kiss me.

"Don't tell me you're gonna get shy on me now," he teased, tugging on the sheet playfully. I swatted his hand away and reached for my robe. Pulling it on, I climbed out of bed and stormed into the bathroom to shower. As I was about to turn the water on, there was a knock on the bathroom door. Pulling it open, I glared at him.

"Still not a morning person, huh? Do you want me to stick around to wait for you and we'll drive over to the shop together? Or would you rather be alone right now?"

"Don't bother waiting for me. I can drive to the shop by myself. If you don't mind, I'd like some time to myself today. And I don't think the entire team needs to know we spent the night together last night," I answered, looking down at my feet and noticing that the nail polish on my toe nails was fading. I made a mental note to fix them that evening.

"Okay, don't get yourself in a huff about it. I was just making an offer. See you at the shop." He walked away to dress, obviously offended about my remark about the team knowing about our spending the night together. I took a longer shower than normal, hoping he'd be gone by the time I was done. Slowly towelling myself dry, I checked myself out in the countertop-to-ceiling mirror covering the wall over the sink.

I still worked out regularly, almost religiously, and my body still held the same tone and definition it had before I'd gotten pregnant with Jessika. Pulling my robe back on in case Kyle was still around, I walked back into my bedroom to dress. Deciding on jeans and a team golf shirt, I quickly dressed and pulled my still-wet hair up into a clip, before walking downstairs to the kitchen.

I was surprised to find Kyle had made coffee before leaving, and had gone out to my garden and found the most perfect purple rose, my favorite, setting it in a vase of water next to the coffee pot. Instantly, I was ashamed of my attitude towards him and silently promised I would make it up to him somehow. Pouring myself a cup of coffee, I looked out over the backyard towards Matthew's house.

We'd be leaving for Michigan in another week and a half, and it was tentatively his last race as Doug's replacement. I had long since taken over the point's lead, since Doug was required to start each race to be eligible for his points. Matthew and I had spent many evenings talking since I had taken over the points lead, with him lending whatever advice he felt necessary.

Lingering a little too long over my coffee, I finally headed out to my truck, after pausing to smell the rose on the counter, and leaving a note for everybody that I would be at the shop if they needed me.

As I pulled out of the driveway, I noticed a car parked across the street with Todd sitting behind the wheel. Ignoring the car, and pretending I hadn't seen it, I calmly dialled the number of the shop. Kara immediately got Kyle on the line and I asked him if he had noticed the car.

"No, sorry. I wasn't really paying attention though. I had other things on my mind, if you catch my drift," he answered.

"Yeah, I know and we'll discuss it later when we get home. Look I'm not gonna come right to the shop today. I think I'm gonna take good ol' Todd on a nice tour of the city, maybe drive by the police department."

Hanging up the phone, I immediately dialled one of my friends from my Criminal Justice class who had signed on with the Mooresville Police Department after our graduation. Explaining my situation, I told him I'd be driving by the station in five minutes and for him to be waiting outside for me.

Slowing down to pick him up, I was grateful he was a plain clothes officer. I knew Todd wouldn't suspect that my passenger was a cop. As we drove, I described Todd and his car to Peter.

"Look, I just don't want any trouble from him. He's a part of my past and I'd prefer he stay there. I know it probably sounds crazy, but I was glad to have him out of my life all those years ago. Now, he's just gonna disrupt everything I've worked for. Do you understand where I'm coming from here?" I asked.

"I don't like the thought of this guy threatening to camp out in front of your house and then bingo, there he is this morning. I don't know about Michigan laws, but if he keeps it up, that's stalking or harassment here. Now, you used to be a cop. Why don't you just use that against him?"

"Because I want as little contact with him as possible. If I can get him out of this state without talking to him again, I will. The only problem I'm worried about is that we have to go to Michigan for the race and we leave in a week and a half. I don't know what he'll do in Michigan, if he's back there when we are. He may not know our schedule," I explained.

"Okay. Let me see what I can do. I'll give you a call later tonight at home. If I have to, I'll send a uniform over to sit in front of your house to intimidate him a little. Do you have somebody who can stay with you just in case he gets into the house?"

"Of course. My parents as well as Craig's are here for a week for Jessika's birthday. Even if I didn't, I'm still licensed to carry a piece in this state, and I still remember how to use it."

"Just be careful. I'll talk to you later," he said as I dropped him off back at the police station ten minutes later. Pulling away with a wave, I was still aware of Todd following me. Calling the shop again, I instructed Kara to have the loading dock door open for me to drive in when I got there. She sounded confused as she agreed and I assured her I would explain later.

"Oh, and Kara?" I added.

"Yeah, boss?"

"Don't ever release any personal information or schedule of any member of the team to anybody without my authorization, understood?" I didn't like the fact that she was so eager to give out information about anybody's whereabouts on the team.

"Yes, Miz Lane." Hanging up the phone without another word, I checked the rear view mirror, and confirmed that Todd was still right behind me. It was obvious he had never been a police officer. Otherwise he would've known not to follow somebody so closely. I chuckled as I thought I could give him a few pointers.

Arriving at the shop a short time later, I drove around to the back of the building, watching in the mirror as Todd pulled into a parking space out front. Driving right into the building, Kyle closed the loading dock door behind me.

Climbing out of the truck, Kyle took my arm and walked with me up to my office by way of the back stairwell. Walking to the window, I saw that Todd had come into the building and was leaning on Kara's desk.

"Guess I shoulda waited for you this morning," Kyle broke the silence.

"I don't think it would've made a difference. He still would've been there and followed us. But I talked to Peter a little while ago. He's gonna figure something out and call me tonight," I explained.

"Maybe we should stay at my place tonight," Kyle suggested.

"No. He's not going to scare me out of my own house. I spent almost two years being intimidated by him. I won't allow him to do it again," I turned and walked over to sit behind my desk.

Kyle stayed at the window and told me a few minutes later that Todd was leaving. Breathing a sigh of relief, I leaned over and turned on the stereo in my office. By mutual agreement, the entire building had the same country station piped through as was on my stereo. Turning to the days' paperwork and mail, Kyle joined me at the desk, sitting across from me, watching me silently. My thoughts were disrupted a few minutes later when I heard my name on the radio.

"This next song is an oldie and it's going out to Brianna Lane. Brianna, the guy that called this in says he really wants to talk to you. And he hopes this song still means something to you." I froze as I heard the opening chords of the song.

I tuned the rest out, turning down the music as I dialled the phone. Kyle looked at my quizzically as I waited for the phone to be answered.

"Bob? It's Brianna Lane. I'll make this short and sweet. I want you to play a song for me. Jo-Dee Messina's 'My Give a Damn's Busted.' It's for the guy that called in 'I Never Knew Love.' And for the record, this song has absolutely no meaning for me anymore. It hasn't for twenty years now and you can put that fact on the air if you want. Thanks Bob." I hung up the phone and looked across the desk at Kyle.

"Maybe you should talk to him. I don't like the fact that he's calling radio stations now, trying to get your attention," Kyle suggested.

"I have nothing to say to him."

"Hang on a minute. You don't have to spend the rest of your life with him. Give him ten minutes. Let him say what he came to say and what he came to say and then it's over. Obviously it's important that he talk to you," Kyle reasoned.

"Of course it is. Everything he ever had to say was important, according to him. Unfortunately for him, I don't think anything he has to say is worth listening to. Why do you think I should talk to him?"

"To get him out of our lives."

"Our lives?" I wasn't sure I had heard him correctly.

"Yeah. Our lives. I'm getting tired of him hanging around here, disrupting things."

"Are you a little jealous, Kyle? You don't think I'd actually go back to him, do you?"

"Well, the thought did cross my mind."

"Well, let it uncross your mind, 'cause there's no way in hell I'd go back to him." I was dumbfounded that Kyle would even think such a thing. I turned back to the mail as Kyle headed downstairs to check on the preparations of the car for the weekends' race at the second road course of the year.

* * * * *

156

CHAPTER THIRTY-FIVE
Watkins Glen, NY

Jessika had chosen to stay in North Carolina with her grandparents instead of coming with me to New York, and I felt confident that she would be fine there with them. I had managed to avoid Todd until we left for New York, and hoped that he would have returned to Michigan by the time we flew back home. I called Jessika after the drivers' meeting, before I had to head to the front stretch for driver introductions.

"Hi, Mom. How's everything going?"

"Good. Strange not having you here on the other end of the radio. How's your visit going with your grandparents? Everything okay at home?"

"Yeah. Everything's been fine. Why? You're not expecting Todd to try anything while you're gone, do you?"

"No, Jess. I'm sure he's already headed back to Michigan. But do me a favour. If you do see him hanging around the house, call Peter; his number's on my desk next to my phone. He already knows what's been going on and he said he'd be there in no time at all if we need him."

"Okay."

"Listen, they're calling for driver introductions, so I gotta run. I'll see you tonight, Jess."

"Good luck, Mom. I love you."

"I love you too, Jessika." I hung up the phone as Kyle walked into the hauler, and picked up my gloves and helmet.

We walked together to the front stretch, meeting up with Matthew and Doug along the way. Doug was not able to walk without crutches, so we slowed down to match his pace. Although Kyle and I had been sharing a hotel room, we had been careful about our public appearance, avoiding any lingering glances or touches when there was the possibility of being seen by any of the media. I had explained to Kyle that I didn't want our relationship to become a media event, and he had whole-heartedly agreed.

Climbing into my car after the conclusion of the national anthem, Kyle leaned in to lock my steering wheel in place. Surprised, I reached for my helmet. I had always taken care of the steering wheel myself. Before I could put on my helmet though, Kyle turned and gave me a quick kiss.

"Kyle!"

"Don't worry. Nobody saw that. Everybody's gonna know sooner or later anyway." I pulled my helmet on and waited patiently as he connected my radio and air lines. Tugging on my gloves, he caught my eye again, smiling at me. Giving him the thumbs up that I was ready, I smiled shyly at him before he straightened and put up my window net. When the call was made to fire our engines, I looked over to the car next to me, which was Matthew's. He gave me a slight wave as we began to roll down pit road. I knew he'd seen the exchange between me and Kyle and figured it would just be a matter of time before he gave me his opinion of our new relationship.

The race seemed short in comparison with those at the bigger, oval tracks, being only seventy-two laps. I managed to finish in the top ten, cushioning my points lead over my nearest competitor, who had fallen out of the race early after dropping his oil pan on one of the straightaways. After I had dealt with the media's questions and interviews, I retreated to the motorhome to relax while the crew loaded the car for the trip home. I had learned early that they didn't want my help after the race; they always sent me to sit and relax while they worked.

* * *

Heading home on the plane, Doug and Matthew had joined us, and we were soon discussing the outcome of the race. One of the rookie challengers had nudged Matthew to send him fish-tailing and passed him coming out of the last turn to take the checkered flag. It had been the rookie's first win and Matthew's best finish while he'd been substituting for Doug. I knew Matthew had been hoping for a win while he was back in the car, and reminded him he still had one race left. Doug praised him on finishing as well as he had, considering he'd been out of a race car for five years. Just before we landed, Kyle took my hand. I noticed the curious looks from Doug and Matthew.

"What?" I asked, looking at them both. Doug was the first to speak.

"I never said a word. Did you say something Matthew? No. Although now that you mention it, I suppose we can offer our advice, now can't we?"

"About what?" I asked defensively.

"Well, about that," he pointed at our hands. "I know you two have been trying to keep it out of the public eye, the relationship y'all got going on. But don't you think you could've told us? I mean, after all, we are all friends here, aren't we?" Doug replied.

"Yeah, well, it was all kinda sudden. To be perfectly honest, I'm still trying to get used to it," I answered.

"I don't think it's a good idea. No offence to either of you. But I really don't think you should turn a working relationship into an intimate one," Matthew offered.

"Why?" Kyle asked. "What's the difference between mine and Brie's relationship and yours and Daytona's? Besides the fact that you two got married."

"Brianna's your boss. You're her employee. How do you think the rest of the crew would react to the news you're sleeping with the boss?" Matthew asked.

"I don't care what the team thinks," I burst out. "When the time is right, we'll go public with the relationship."

"Now, let's not let our tempers get out of hand here. We're all friends. We just wanted to offer our advice. Personally, I think the two of you are great together. I'm just worried about if things don't work out between you both," Doug interrupted.

"Look. This is our relationship. We've been fighting it for twenty years. If it doesn't work, then so be it. I know it's not going to affect our friendship, or our business relationship," I stated.

"Fine. I trust you to know what you're doing," Doug replied.

"No you don't. If you did, you wouldn't have started your little lecture about mixing our business relationship with a sexual one," Kyle declared.

"Okay. Everybody just relax. We're not going to debate who's sleeping with who here. Let's just take into consideration what's been said and we'll take it from there. If things don't work out, we'll keep in mind what you both said," I announced. "Case closed. I, for one, don't want to hear another word on the subject."

The conversation turned to other events and we were soon back on the ground in Mooresville. Kyle and I drove back to the house, where we were warmly greeted by the houseful of guests. Jessika pulled me aside after we'd been home a few hours and it was apparent Kyle wasn't leaving.

"Mom, is Kyle spending the night?"

"Well, he is my husband. Where would you like your step-father to sleep? In the pool house?" I replied dramatically, rolling my eyes at her.

"What? When did this happen?" Jessika squealed.

"Shh. It's only temporary. Until we know Todd's back in Michigan. Kyle told him we were married to get him to stop harassing me. I guess he thought it would work," I explained.

"Cool."

"It's only temporary," I repeated. "Once we know for sure that Todd's safely back in Michigan, things will be going back to the way they were. I think."

"But you are dating, aren't you?"

"Yeah, I guess you could say that, although I think we're closer to married than dating right now," I answered with a laugh.

"Just keep it down tonight, okay. I've had a long day and I'd like to get some sleep. Besides, I don't think you want to disturb any of my grandparents. They might not be too open to the idea of Kyle spending the night," Jessika lectured, laughing.

"I'm a big girl, Jessika. And if they don't like the idea of me sleeping with somebody, I'll gladly provide them with the phone numbers of nearby hotels. Remember, this is my house. It's up to me who sleeps in my bed, not your grandparents. And would you please do me the favor of keeping the information to yourself of who spends the night in my bed?"

"Yeah, sure thing Mom. But I think you should make it permanent. If you're gonna live in sin, at least do it properly, and actually live together."

"Great. I'm getting advice on getting a man from an eighteen year old." I threw my hands up in mock desperation. We rejoined the group of elders in the living room then and they all praised me again on my top ten finish before heading up to bed. Jessika followed shortly after, leaving me and Kyle alone.

"We made Jessika's day," I began when we were alone.

"Why's that?" he asked absently.

"I told her about us. Well, first I told her what you told Todd and she totally freaked on me. She thought I was serious when I said we were married," I replied.

"So why don't we?"

"Why don't we what?"

"Get married."

"Are you serious? You're joking, right?" I asked, moving to sit on the edge of the couch so I could read the expression on his face.

"No. I'm not joking. I'm very serious. Is there something standing in the way of us getting married?"

"Besides the fact that we've just started seeing each other?"

"Brie, we've known each other for more than twenty years!"

"This is all so sudden. I need some time to think about it," I began, trying to find a reasonable explanation why we shouldn't get married.

"Fine. Take your time. I'll be here when you're ready. Now, why don't we go up to bed? It's been a long day. You must be exhausted." Turning out the lights along the way, we headed upstairs to my bedroom.

* * * * *

CHAPTER THIRTY-SIX

I decided to stay home from the shop on Monday, choosing instead to spend the day with Jessika's grandparents. After going with them to the airport, I dropped Jessika off at Mandy's before heading back home. I was looking forward to having some free time to myself, kicking off my shoes as I walked in the door. Changing into my bikini, I grabbed a towel and walked out to the pool.

Dropping the towel at one end, I dove into the cool water, and began swimming leisurely laps, allowing the tension that had built up in my body to slowly melt away. The day was quiet and I was surprised when I felt my arm being grabbed as I was about to begin another lap.

Pulling my arm free, I backed up far enough to see Todd standing on the deck at the edge of the deep end. Treading water, I propelled myself backward, safely out of his reach.

"I want you off my property," I demanded.

"Not until you listen to what I have to say," he countered.

"You have nothing to say that I care to hear," I said stonily.

"Please?" he asked quietly.

I debated it for a moment, then swam to the side away from Todd and hauled myself out of the water. Walking towards him, I watched as he blatantly inspected me from head to toe. I knew my bikini was revealing, but I also knew I had that to my advantage, since one of his complaints when we'd been together was that I wasn't interested in working out. And I knew I still had the strength and ability to defend myself if I needed to. Standing at the side of the pool, I met Todd's eyes, almost daring him to try something. Still not taking my eyes off him, I sat down.

"I'd offer you a seat, or a cold drink, but you're not staying that long, and I'm not that hospitable towards you any longer. You have ten minutes. Then I want you off my property and out of my life for good. Otherwise, I'm calling the police and having you arrested for trespassing and harassment. Am I understood?"

"Why are you being so cold to me, Brianna? You used to love me."

"Used to, being the key words. I used to do a lot of things. I used to think your opinion was worth something to me. I used to value your opinion. I used to trust you. I used to be very self-conscious because of you. I used to have a very low self-image. Because of you. But here I am, taking up your ten minutes."

"Look, I know I made some mistakes. But I want you to know that I never stopped loving you. Even when I was with Virginia, I still loved you. But I knew I'd screwed up, and I was afraid of how you'd react to me coming back into your life, asking you to take me back. I know you were angry with me. And you had every right to be. I admit, I originally came down here to ask you to forgive me and give me another chance, but when what's-his-name announced that you were married, I knew you'd never even consider it. But I still wanted to ask for your forgiveness, and hopefully, we can be friends."

"I heard that story already. Remember? *'Give me some time to get over the bad parts of our relationship and then we can try being friends.'* I gave you time. I tried calling you to talk to you. But as I recall, you never called back. You didn't even have the balls to break up with me to my face, waiting instead for me to call you at work. Couldn't you have even been big enough to face me when you and Virginia announced your engagement to Elaine? Which, by the way, you had great timing for that, what would've been our second anniversary. What took me so long to understand was if you loved me, how could you be so cruel as to blatantly lie to me?

"You cheated on me. With her. After promising me that she would never come between us. You broke up with me for no apparent reason. Hell, you gave everybody a different story about why we broke up. I don't think you even knew why you were doing it, except to be able to screw her with a clear conscience. And to bring her into our bed before I even had a chance to move my things out. That was downright cold.

"But you know what I finally figured out? I came to the conclusion that you never really loved me. All those cards, with all the pretty poems for our anniversaries and Valentine's Day, the Doug Stone song; I never knew love til I was loved by you. That was all a load of shit; all of it was just words. You never meant any of it. I'm sure you bought the cards because the poems in them sounded convincing. And the song was just beautiful, for someone who was in love. You were in love with the idea of being in love, but I don't think you knew what love was. You don't try to completely change somebody you claim to love and that's exactly what you were doing to me.

"Nothing I ever did was good enough for you. Nothing. I gave you my heart, my body and my soul. I trusted you completely. I trusted that you would never hurt me, never lie to me, and never leave me for another woman. But you ripped my heart out and shredded it into a million pieces. You hurt me more than anybody had ever hurt me before. How could you even think for a second that I would want to give you another chance? Leaving me was the best thing you could have ever done for me.

"You hurt me deeply, but I got over the pain, the anger, the self-doubt, with time. And you will never have the control over me that you had before. Nobody will. You will never hurt me like you did before. I will never give you that opportunity. You will never make me laugh, never make me cry, and most importantly, never make me feel bad about myself again. You no longer have any control over me, my body or my emotions."

I was interrupted as I heard Kyle come through the patio doors.

"Brie, do you want me to call the police?" he asked. I stood up before answering.

"I don't think that will be necessary, dear. Todd was just leaving. I'm afraid your ten minutes are up. So if you will excuse me, I'd like to go back to my swim that you so rudely interrupted."

Wordlessly, Todd walked away and minutes later we heard his car start and pull out of the driveway. Kyle rushed to my side and held me to him, as I tried to slow my breathing. I had been afraid Todd would do something that would force me to use one of my old police techniques to subdue him and get him to co-operate.

Walking into the house, Kyle sat me down in the den, holding me as I relaxed. Finally, I was able to ask him how he knew to come to the house. His response surprised me.

"Matthew called the shop and told me. I guess he saw you were home and was going to come over to talk to you when you were done your swim, but he saw Todd come around the corner of the house. Since he'd seen him at Jessika's party, he knew who he was and immediately called me. Of course it only took me a couple minutes to get here. I drove a little faster than normal, hoping nothing would happen before I got here. I forget sometimes though, that you can probably take care of yourself better than I can."

"But I don't need you to take care of me, Kyle," I protested.

"I know. But I want to. I want to be able to take care of you and Jessika. I want to marry you Brie." I stood up and walked across the room to the patio doors. Kyle silently followed me and stood behind me, lightly placing his hands on my arms. I felt so confused about what I should do. I cared deeply for Kyle, but I wasn't sure if I wanted to get married again. Turning to face him, I looked into his eyes.

"I don't know Kyle. I don't know if I'm ready to get married again."

"Do you love me?" he asked. I hesitated before responding. I hadn't expected him to ask that.

"Yes," I whispered, nodding.

"Then what's the problem? I love you. You say you love me too. So there's nothing stopping us from getting married. We've been acting like husband and wife for the past week. Why don't we make it official?" he reasoned.

"It's not that easy, Kyle. I have Jessika to think about," I began.

"I can tell you right now. Jessika would be thrilled to see you remarried. And I think she likes me. I mean, she has been trying to set us up for a while now," Kyle interrupted.

"What about the publicity our wedding would generate? We're already in the spotlight enough as it is. Think about what it would be like if we were to get married. Every time we have an argument, the media would tell the public we're getting a divorce," I countered.

"I don't care what the public or the media thinks. You're stalling, trying to think of reasons why we shouldn't get married. If you don't want to marry me, just say so."

"Kyle, it's not that I don't want to marry you --"

"Then, what is it?"

"I'm afraid to," I whispered.

"Why? What are you afraid of?"

"Todd left me for Virginia --"

"I'm not Todd," Kyle interrupted. "You should know by now, that Todd and I are nothing alike."

"Yeah, I know you're nothing like Todd. When I met Craig, I thought I'd finally found the fairy tale prince. That'd he'd be there forever. I never stopped to think about him getting killed. But he did," I tried to explain.

"But Craig was a cop. It comes with the territory. You expect that you're gonna get shot, and you know it's a possibility that you're going to get killed. You know that. You've been shot before. You knew the dangers of the job. I don't know if you've noticed or not though, but I'm not a cop. I'm your crew chief."

"But something could still happen to you. Don't you see what I'm getting at here?"

"No, I don't. You lost me somewhere along there."

"Every man I let myself get close to, and fall in love with, somehow leaves. Todd left me for Virginia and Craig was killed. There's a reason why Todd left me and Craig was killed. It's fate. I'm not supposed to be happy. I'm meant to be alone for the rest of my life."

"That's not true, Brie. Think of it this way. Todd and Craig came into your life for different reasons. Your relationship with Todd made you stronger emotionally. You had happiness with Craig; you had Jess together. But you were meant to be with me. Fate determined twenty years ago that we were meant to be together. Just not twenty years ago. That's why we met."

"Then why didn't we get together twenty years ago?" I demanded.

"Because if we had, you wouldn't have had Jessika when you did. And you wouldn't be driving a race car for the championship right now. Trust me. Everything happens for a reason."

We were both silent as I considered what Kyle had said. Our discussion was halted temporarily as Jessika and Mandy burst through the front door. I could hear them laughing and joking as they came through the house. They stopped just inside the den as they noticed Kyle and I standing near the patio doors.

"Are we interrupting something?" Jessika asked.

"Not exactly. Kyle and I were just having a discussion," I replied.

"Oh. Well, Mandy and I just came for a swim. Are you going to join us, or are you done?" Jessika asked, as they walked across the room.

"I'll be back out in a minute, girls. Just let me send Kyle back to the shop," I turned to Kyle again. "We'll finish our discussion later, after you get home."

"I'm going to hold you to that Brie. You're not getting out of this so easily," Kyle took my hand, leading me to the front door.

As I held the door open for him, he leaned down and kissed me deeply before jogging out to his car. I watched as he drove away and headed down the street. Sighing as I closed the door, I slowly walked back out to the pool. The girls were sitting on the edge of the pool at the far end when I returned to the back yard. Diving back into the water, I quickly reached them and pulled myself up next to Jessika.

"So, what was the discussion about?" she asked.

"Oh, nothing really. Kyle just wants to get married," I replied casually.

"It's about damn time. So when's the big day?"

"I don't know. I haven't given him a definite answer yet. That's why we're going to finish the discussion tonight when he gets home."

"Why haven't you given him an answer yet? I think you two make an awesome couple. You've already proven that. You haven't even had a fight yet. You don't even fight at work. I'd really like to have Kyle as my step-dad, you know," Jessika offered her opinion.

"I know. I guess I'm just afraid of making that commitment again. I almost made it with Todd when we were together and look how that turned out. Then I met and married your father, and he was killed. I guess I'm worried that if I make a commitment to Kyle, something will happen to mess that up too," I explained.

"But Kyle isn't Todd. And Daddy died doing what he loved. I don't think he'd want you to stay single for the rest of your life when you've got love staring you in the face. Face it, Mom. You and Kyle were meant to be together," Jessika reasoned.

"Did you and Kyle practice your speeches together? He said almost the exact same thing to me right before you came in. So I guess I should say yes when he comes home, eh?"

"Only if you really want to marry him. You do love him, don't you? If you love him, marry him, dammit."

"Well, if we do get married, it won't be until after the season ends. Now that we've got that dealt with, I thought you two came to swim. Get in the pool then. I had my swim rudely interrupted earlier by Todd. I plan on finishing it now."

I dove back into the water and was joined seconds later by Jessika and Mandy. We spent the remainder of the afternoon doing laps and relaxing by the edge of the pool as we discussed when and where they thought the wedding should be. When Jessika and Mandy left to return to Mandy's for the night, I showered and dressed before returning to the kitchen to begin dinner for me and Kyle.

* * * * *

CHAPTER THIRTY SEVEN

"Where'd Jess and Mandy go?" Kyle asked when he returned home.

"They decided to go back to Mandy's. We have the house to ourselves tonight," I explained, not looking up from the newspaper I was reading. I felt him sit down next to me on the couch, and dropped the paper into my lap, turning to look at him.

"So, did you have a fun afternoon with the girls?"

"Yeah. We talked about when and where our wedding should be. The girls have quite a few good ideas. I think we should have them help us with the planning," I answered with a smile.

"Our wedding? You mean you're saying yes? I don't believe it. Here I thought it was gonna take me forever to convince you. What made you decide?"

"Besides the fact that we're in love? What more reason do I need?" I asked.

"None at all. Just the fact that you decided to say yes is enough for me." Kyle followed me into the kitchen and helped me set the table for dinner. As we ate, we discussed the wedding further and tossed ideas back and forth about when and where. I wanted to wait until after the end of the season, but Kyle was determined to have the ceremony as soon as possible.

"What's the matter? Are you worried I'll change my mind if you don't get me to the altar before the end of the month?" I laughed as we cleared the table and headed into my office. As Kyle sat on the couch, I pulled out a notepad from my desk to jot down our ideas. Joining him on the couch, he put an arm around my shoulders, pulling me closer.

"No. I'm just eager to make you my wife and give you my name," Kyle replied.

"Now wait a minute. I think we'd better discuss that too," I interrupted.

"What?"

"Me. Taking your name," I answered.

"What about it? What's wrong with it?"

"There's nothing wrong with your name. I'm just not gonna take it," I explained quietly.

"Why not?"

"Because I started out my racing career as Brianna Lane. And that's how it's gonna stay. I'm not changing my name five years into my career."

"So hyphenate it. Or go back to your maiden name."

"Why don't I just hyphenate all three? Then I can be Brianna Hawthorne-Lane-James. Try signing that as an autograph. Try saying that as a commentator. Please try to understand Kyle. Yes, on paper, I will be Brianna James. But out on the track, I want to remain Brianna Lane. If I hadn't been married to Craig, I would I be Brianna Hawthorne on the track. It has nothing to do with you. I just don't want to change my name on the track. I don't know if you've noticed or not, but you work for Reed Motorsports. Why didn't I change the name to Lane Racing or Lane Motorsports? Because people recognize the Reed Motorsports logo, just like people recognize Brianna Lane," I explained.

"Okay. I get it now. I think I can understand. I guess I shouldn't complain. At least I'm getting you to the altar, or wherever we get married." We discussed where we could possibly have the ceremony and Kyle suggested we get married at one of the tracks prior to a race.

"That's a little unconventional, don't you think? I mean, exchange our rings and vows than then turn around and have me climb into the car and run five hundred miles. And we'd have to get permission from the track president first, plus find a minister to perform the ceremony," I reasoned.

"That'll be easy enough. How many track owners wouldn't love the publicity of having a wedding on the front stretch? And I'm sure whoever does the pre-race prayers would be willing to perform the wedding ceremony for us. And just think, whoever we invite, that can't make the wedding will still be able to see the highlights of it on the evening news. Or during the telecast of the race itself," Kyle replied. "So, I guess the big question now would be, when do we do it? How about we compromise? You want it after the season is done, and I want it before the end of the season. Why don't we do it in Homestead? Then, after the race, we can have the reception and celebrate the championship at the same time. Merge the two celebrations into one."

"I suppose that's a possibility. But, and this is a big but, I have to win the championship before we can celebrate that I won it. I may be leading in the points now, but a lot can change in the last ten races during the Chase. We have to be realistic about this."

"So we'll invite everybody for the wedding and reception and celebrate our championship too. Problem solved. I have faith in you. I know we'll have the Cup in our offices. And that you'll be making the big speech in Las Vegas."

We continued our discussion of the wedding plans and agreed on most things. Finally, as the evening wore on, I decided it might be a good idea to call our families to let them know of our decision. Kyle called his parents first and we were warmly congratulated, promising to fly them down for the ceremony.

When I called my parents, my mother's first question was what Craig's parents thought of the idea of me remarrying. Explaining that I hadn't broke the news to them yet, I told her they were next on my list of people to call.

"How does Jessika feel about you getting married again?"

"She loves Kyle. She's been trying to get us together since he came down here when I bought the team. She's practically bouncing off the walls, helping us plan it," I explained. "Besides, I thought y'all liked Kyle."

"We do, Brie. Really, we are happy for you. It's just so sudden," my mother reasoned.

"Not really. I mean we've known each other for twenty years. And Kyle's been my crew chief for five now. That's five years of being together day in and day out. It's not like we're complete strangers."

"Well, congratulations to both of you. We'll see you later in the week when you come up here." I hung up from talking to my parents and dialled Craig's. They expressed their congratulations to us, and gave us their blessings, promising to attend the wedding. After all the phone calls were made to tell our families and close friends about our decision, I was exhausted and we stretched out together on the couch in the den. Resting my head on Kyle's chest as he turned on the television and flipped through the channels, I soon fell asleep listening to his heartbeat. When I awoke, the only illumination in the room came from the muted television. I raised my head to find Kyle asleep too. Leaning up and kissing him lightly, he slowly woke and wrapped his arms around me, kissing me deeply.

"Let's go upstairs," I said as I pulled myself out of his grasp and stood up next to the couch. Standing, Kyle turned off the television and took my hand, walking with me up to the bedroom.

* * *

The next morning, Kyle was up and out of the house before I woke up, leaving a note on the pillow that he'd see me at the shop later. As I showered, I thought back over the past, hoping I was making the right decision agreeing to marry Kyle. I knew I'd always love Craig, and there were still days when I missed him and wished the past could be changed somehow, but I also believed that everything happens for a reason, and I knew if things were meant to be with Kyle, then everything would work out.

When I got to the shop, everybody was busy getting the cars ready to load into the hauler, as well as a backup, just in case there were problems with practice and qualifying. If something happened to both cars we were taking with us, the team always had another backup, loaded into the spare hauler, ready to drive to any track on a moment's notice.

As I sat behind my desk, going through the day's mail, Kara phoned up to me that somebody was here to see me. Fearing it was Todd again, I walked over to the window. I looked down on the lobby to see James standing beside Kara's desk. It had been the better part of a year since I'd last seen him, and I waved for him to come up to the office. I raced out the door, and met him at the stairs. Hugging me tightly, I laughed as he lifted me off the floor.

"What are you doing here? Wow, it's so great to see you, James. Jess is gonna be so excited to see you. How long can you stay?"

"Well, I came to see you and Jess, of course. Why else would I come clear across the state? You look great. We've been watching the races every week to see how you've been doing. Everybody back at the precinct is so proud of you, you know. And I can stay indefinitely. I retired last week."

"Retired? You? Wow. What brought that on? Come into my office and have a seat so we can catch up." Leading him into my office, we sat on the couch by the window to talk.

"Well, it just hasn't been the same without you and Craig there. And I've been thinking about it for a while now. Woke up one day last week and said to myself that it was time to go. Went in to work and handed in my badge and gun and then just hung out at home for a few days trying to figure out what I was gonna do with myself now. Finally decided I'd drive out here and see how my two girls were doing. You look great you know. I gotta ask though, what's going on with you and Doug? You two a couple or something?"

"Me and Doug? No. We're just friends. Why would you ask me that?"

"Well, we all saw how you jumped out of your car last time y'all raced in Michigan when he crashed. We couldn't figure out why you'd do that, and risk losing all those points if you weren't dating him."

"No. I just reacted. I think I would've done the same thing no matter who it was, if I was running right behind them and saw the way that crash happened. That was scary. Freaked me out for a week; kept dreaming about it at night, seeing it over and over again in my mind. I was definitely glad that he was okay. Actually, he'll be back in the car to race in another couple weeks. He's been testing and practicing getting in and out of the car the past week or so. And his daughter and Jess are pretty good friends."

"So what's going on with you these days? Everything going okay with you and Jessika?"

"Yep, things are great. Hang on; let me give her a call. She's gonna want to see you. I know she's missed you." Picking up the phone, I called Jess' cell phone.

"Hey Jess. You busy today?"

"Nope. Not really. Why? Everything okay Mom?"

"Yeah, hun. Everything's great. I'm just wondering if you could come by the shop sometime today. I have a surprise here for you."

"A surprise? For me? What is it?"

"Well, if I tell you, it won't be much of a surprise now, will it? Just swing by the shop when you get a chance. Okay?"

"Okay, Mom. I'll be there in a little while."

Hanging up, I turned back to James.

"So, you'll stay at my place while you're in town, right? I've got lots of room, and a couple spare bedrooms. Actually, they all just cleared out again yesterday. I had all of Jess' grandparents here for her birthday and they all just left to go home yesterday."

"That'd be great. I have her present in my car too. Wish I could've been here for her party. How did it go?"

"Great. Had an uninvited guest show up, but once we got rid of him, the party went off without a hitch."

"Uninvited guest? What happened?" Relating the story to James, his brow furrowed as I told him about Todd showing up at the house and shop repeatedly.

"Well, why didn't you kick his ass? We both know you could have," James asked as I finished.

"Didn't want to waste the energy. As far as I know, he's gone now. Haven't seen him since yesterday when he left the house after I told him off. So hopefully, I won't have any more problems with him now. And if I do, I'll just have him charged with harassment."

Just then, we were interrupted by a knock on my office door.

"Mom? You busy?" Jessika poked her head around the door.

"Come on in, Jess." James and I both stood up as Jessika pushed the door open further and walked into the office.

"James!" Jess flew across the office and into his arms, hugging him as she laughed.

"Well, I can see everybody's happy to see me. I'm glad I decided to drive over today," James said as he set her back down.

"How long are you staying?" Jessika asked.

"As long as you want me to," he replied. "I'm retired now, so I've got lots of time."

"Cool. Mom invite you to stay at the house?"

"Of course. Oh, and I have something in my car for you. Wait here and I'll go get it." James walked out of the office as Jess turned and grinned at me.

"This is so cool. Did you know he was coming?" she asked me.

"Nope. I was just as surprised to see him as you were."

A few minutes later, James returned with a small box, handing it to Jessika. Ripping open the package, she pulled out a framed picture of Craig in his uniform.

"I hope you don't mind. I had this picture from when we graduated, so I had a copy made and framed for you."

"It's awesome. Thanks so much James." Jessika threw her arms around him, hugging him again as she held the picture frame.

"You know, while we're reliving the past, there's something I've been thinking about for a while now, trying to figure out the right time to do this, and I think that time is now," I said, walking over to my desk. Pulling out a set of keys, I handed them to Jessika.

"Are these? You're giving me Daddy's car?" Jessika asked, looking shocked.

"Yep. I think you're responsible enough to drive it. I've just been waiting for the right time to give it to you."

"Oh Mom. This is amazing. Thank you so much. I promise I'll be so careful with the car. I wondered why you've been hanging onto it for so long." Jessika hugged me and James again, before heading out of the office, with the promise to see us later that night back at home.

Returning to my desk, James talked to me while I finished going through the mail and we caught up on things that had been going on the past little while. Except for my engagement. That I wasn't so sure how to announce to him. Shortly after, there was a knock on the door, and Kyle walked into my office, stopping when he saw James.

"Well, hello James. Long time, no see. How've ya been?" he asked.

"Hi Kyle. Still working for Brie, eh? Good to see you." James shook Kyle's hand as Kyle took a seat beside him.

"Yeah. Don't think she's gonna get rid of me anytime soon. I signed up for the long haul. Doing the lifetime commitment contract here."

"Oh? Is that just cuz you're old friends? Don't want to leave her for something better?" James laughed.

"Actually, I don't think there is anything better than Brianna out there for me. Not only is she a great boss, and an awesome race car driver, but she owns my heart and soul too," Kyle looked from me to James and back again. "Wait a minute. You haven't told him yet, have you?"

"Told me what?" James asked.

"No, Kyle. I haven't told him yet," I sighed. "James. Kyle and I are getting married."

"You're what? When did this happen?" he asked me.

"Yesterday. The day before. The last couple days have really been a blur. It's been crazy here, between Todd showing up, Jessika's birthday, everything. I was gonna tell you, really I was."

"Well. As long as you're happy, I'm happy for you, Brianna. You know that. I've always supported your decisions. Congratulations." James shook Kyle's hand, smiling at us both. "So when's the big day?"

"We're still working on that. Kyle's determined it's going to be as soon as possible, and I'm trying to convince him to wait until the season's done. Right now, we're looking at doing it during the pre-race stuff in Homestead. If we can get the track to agree with it," I explained.

"How's Jess taken the news?"

"Great. She was actually the one who got us together, and convinced me that this was the right decision. She loves Kyle, and they've gotten along great since we moved here and Kyle joined the team."

"Well, that's a good thing. You know we all just want to see you happy."

The conversation turned to the upcoming race in Michigan, and the points standings. We still had four races left, including Michigan, until the official Chase for the Sprint Cup began, when my points lead would be cut dramatically for the last ten races of the season.

We knew that as long as I was leading the points, and had enough good finishes, in the top five or ten, I still had a good chance to win the Cup.

We decided to head out for lunch and I let Kara know as we were leaving that I wasn't sure when we'd be back that afternoon. Pulling out of the parking lot, James pointed out the flashing lights of an ambulance, police and fire crew down the road. Heading down that way, since it was the only way out of the complex, I wondered what might have happened to call out so many emergency vehicles. As we got closer, I noticed a motorcycle mangled and wedged under the front bumper of a large pick up truck.

"Hey Brie. That's one of our guys," Kyle exclaimed, pointing at the gurney being loaded into the back of the ambulance. Pulling to a stop, I jumped out of my truck and ran over to the ambulance. Sure enough, it was Joe, one of my main mechanics, and my race day gas man. He was unconscious and the EMT loading him into the ambulance looked over at me.

"Do you know him?" he asked.

"Yeah. He's one of my mechanics," I replied. "What happened?"

"Dunno yet. I guess somebody wasn't paying attention somewhere. The driver of the truck is still talking to the police over there," he pointed over to one of the police cars parked across the road. Kyle and James joined us then.

"Anything we can do?" Kyle asked.

"You can call his family. He's pretty banged up here. At least a broken leg. Probably a concussion too. Gonna take him to Mooresville Met so you can let his family know to meet him there," the EMT explained.

Kyle climbed into the back of the ambulance to ride with Joe to the hospital while James and I headed back to my truck to follow the ambulance. Calling Joe's family while I drove, I explained to his wife what had happened, as much as I knew.

"Do you want me to come pick you up? Or are you okay to drive to the hospital?" I asked.

"I'll be okay to drive. I'll meet you there," Jane replied. Hanging up, I dialled the shop to let Kara know I probably wouldn't be returning to the shop that afternoon and why. Pulling into the hospital parking lot, my phone rang.

"Mom! What happened to Joe? Is he okay? I just talked to Kara," Jess asked as I answered the phone.

"He had an accident on his motorcycle. That's all I really know Jess. I'm just getting to the hospital now. I have to find out from the doctors what happened. Or from the police if they come here. Otherwise I'll give Peter a call later and see what he can find out for me. I'll call you back as soon as I know something."

"Okay Mom. Have you called Jane yet? Is she on her way?"

"Yeah. I called her. She's on her way. I expect she should be here soon."

"Okay. I'll be at Mandy's."

"Okay Jess. I'll call you as soon as I know what's going on." Hanging up the phone again, James and I headed into the hospital to meet Kyle and find out what was going on.

"They've taken him right in for x-rays to find out what his injuries are," Kyle explained as he put his arm around me. A few minutes later, Jane came through the doors and headed straight to me. I could tell she'd been crying, and I pulled her close as Kyle and James stepped back a bit to give her some space.

"What happened Brianna?" she cried.

"I don't know exactly Jane. I'm waiting to hear from the doctors or for the police to show up to let me know. All I know is he was hit by a pick up truck. I don't know where it came from or what exactly happened. They were already loading him into the ambulance when we got there. He's been here for about twenty minutes now, so hopefully we'll have some answers soon."

Just then two police officers walked through the doors, looking around. Seeing the four of us standing together, they walked over to us.

"Are you Joe's wife?" one asked, looking at Jane.

"Yes. I am. Can you tell me what happened?" she asked.

"The driver of the pick up truck says your husband came out of nowhere and he had no where to go. He was coming out of one of the other race shop parking lots, and turned right in front of Joe. Have you been in to see him yet?" Jane shook her head.

"I just got here a couple minutes ago. As far as I know, he's still in having x-rays done. How badly do you think he was hurt? You saw him."

"Well, I know he's at least got a broken leg. The EMT said maybe a concussion too."

"But he would've been wearing his helmet. He never drove the bike without a helmet on. You know that Brianna," Jane explained.

"Even with a helmet on, he could still get a concussion, Jane. It just depends on how he hit the ground. The helmet would've protected him, to some degree, but not completely. It just made the injuries less severe than they would've been without the helmet on," I replied. Jane nodded silently as she listened to what I said. I didn't have to tell her what might've happened if he hadn't been wearing the helmet.

"What are we gonna do Brianna? If he's off work. . . " she trailed off.

"I'll take care of it. Don't worry, Jane. Joe's still a part of this team. And he'll still be able to work at the shop, even if he can't travel to the races. And whatever time he needs off to heal whatever injuries he does have, I'll take care of it. Trust me."

She was due to deliver their first baby any time, and had been planning on taking at least six months off work after the baby was born. I had already told Joe he could modify his hours at the shop and if needed, he could fly out race day to join the team to be able to stay home as much as possible with Jane and the baby. Leading her over to some chairs, the four of us sat down while the police went to find out what they could about Joe's injuries. Shortly after, a doctor came out to talk to us. After introducing himself, he explained the injuries.

"Well, your husband is a very lucky man. The main injury is a broken leg. We're going to be setting it shortly. He's got a few cuts and scrapes and he'll probably end up with quite a bit of bruising. And he's got a slight concussion, but it could've been much worse. I'll have a nurse let you know when you can see him. We'll be admitting him though so we can keep an eye on the concussion, at least for the night."

He shook hands with all of us before he headed back to take care of setting Joe's leg. Jane stood up and started pacing in the waiting room while Kyle put his arm around me. Watching her pace, I noticed every few steps Jane would slow down and wince. I stood up suddenly and walked over to her.

"Jane, when is your baby due?" I asked, holding her arm.

"Not for another two weeks," she replied, breathing in sharply.

"I think you're gonna have this baby today, hun. Did you take any prenatal classes?"

"Yeah, Joe and I took them. I can't have this baby if he's in with a broken leg and a concussion."

"Well, I think this baby has other plans," I smiled. "Don't worry. I'll stay with you if you're okay with that."

Jane nodded as another pain hit.

"Okay, we need to time these pains now and see how far apart they are. Then we'll figure out when we need to get you upstairs to the maternity floor."

We kept walking, pacing across the waiting room and back, slowing down as another pain hit, and I timed them at five minutes apart.

"They usually say to go to the hospital at two minutes apart. At least that's what my doctor told me when I was pregnant with Jessika. Since we're already here, we can wait down here until they're two minutes apart, and then we'll head upstairs. Do you have your hospital bag in your car?" Jane nodded, handing me her keys.

I tossed them to Kyle and sent him out to get her bag. Just as he returned, another pain hit, harder and faster than the last. Jane had to hold on to me for support as she struggled to breath. The nurse had been watching us, and motioned for us to head upstairs.

The four of us headed to the elevator and reached the maternity floor as another pain hit.

"Okay, breathe Jane. Come on. You can do this," I encouraged her as we stepped off the elevator.

After the nurses had her settled in a room, Kyle and James headed back downstairs to wait for news on Joe while I sat with Jane and coached her through her labor.

Two hours later, I met Kyle and James in the hallway with the news that Jane and Joe's baby had been born just minutes before, a healthy baby boy. And Kyle had news that Joe had been moved to a room and was resting comfortably after having his leg set and put in a cast. I returned to the delivery room to give Jane the good news.

"When can I see him?" she asked.

"Just as soon as the nurses here will let you go downstairs to see him. I'm sure they want to finish up with you here first," I replied. "You just had a baby don't forget. They're not gonna let you go running off anywhere, no matter how easy your delivery was." I squeezed her hand and headed back out to the hallway to wait with Kyle and James while the nurses finished up and moved Jane to a private room.

When the nurses gave the okay, we settled Jane into a wheelchair with the baby wrapped in her arms to take them downstairs to see Joe. Walking into the room, Jane started to cry seeing Joe bandaged and propped up in the hospital bed. I put out my arms to hold the baby while Kyle helped Jane out of the wheelchair so she could hug her husband. Once her tears had slowed, she turned back to me, to take the baby to hand him to Joe.

"He's early. Is everything okay?" Joe asked, looking worried as he pulled back the blanket to look at his new son.

"Everything's fine, Joe. Your little guy just decided he didn't want to wait any longer to make his entrance into the world. The nurses said he's very healthy. And you'll all get to go home together in a day or two," I explained. "Listen, why don't we leave you three alone for a little while, and we'll come back to take Jane and the baby back upstairs after you have some time together."

Jane stood up and gave me a hug.

"Thank you so much for all your help Brianna. I don't think I could've gotten through this without you."

"Hey, it was nothing, really. I was glad I could help you out. Now, you two get some rest and spend some time getting to know your new baby. We'll see you in an hour or so," I replied, heading towards the door with Kyle and James.

"So much for going for lunch," Kyle said as we waited for the elevator to head downstairs.

"Yeah, why don't we just grab a coffee or something downstairs and we'll just go for dinner after we get Jane back up to her room," I suggested. They both agreed and we headed to the coffee shop.

An hour and a half later, after calling Jessika to let her know how things had turned out, we headed back up to return Jane to her room before we headed out. I'd made plans with Jessika to meet back at home for the four of us to have dinner together. I dropped Kyle and James back at the shop for them to both pick up their cars and then met them back at home a short time later. Jessika already had dinner started, and we sat out by the pool while we ate.

"So, Jess. Now that you're done school, what are your plans?" James asked as I cleared the dishes and took them into the kitchen.

"I haven't really decided yet. I was thinking I might like to get into public relations, specializing in motorsports marketing, obviously. Mom's pr guy is great and has been teaching me a bit about the business and it looks like something I'd like to do. But then I've been Mom's spotter for a couple years now. I know I can't do just that as a career but Mom said that when I figure out what I want to do, she'll support my decision, no matter what. I know I want to do something involved with racing, it's just a matter of narrowing it down to one specific aspect of the sport," Jessika explained.

"Good idea. You think you'd want to be your mom's pr rep?" James asked.

"Sure. Why not? She's my best friend. I've been her spotter long enough. I think we work pretty well together. And she's great with the media. Everybody loves her. Jake says she's awesome to do pr for; he was Daytona and Matt's pr rep you know. And he says she's as good to work for as Daytona and Matt were."

"Yeah, your mom is pretty great," James agreed.

"So, what happened with Joe today?" Jessika changed the subject. After I relayed the story, of his crash, his injuries and the baby being born, Jessika had another question.

"So what are you going to do for a gas man until Joe comes back to work? Obviously he's gonna be off for a while. NASCAR won't let him cross the wall with the cast on his leg."

"I really don't know. We've never had to find a back up in all these years. I was thinking of asking Matt what his thoughts are on the subject. I mean, he was in the sport long enough. He should have some idea of what to do. We don't have a backup on the team yet. Although we probably should train back ups for all the pit spots, eh? Joe will be able to work in the shop without a problem, once he's back up on his feet. I told him to take as much time as he needs to recuperate and get his injuries healed before he comes back to the shop, and then I'll have him on limited shop duties, so he doesn't overwork himself when he comes back. So I don't need another mechanic, just another gasman until he can start travelling to the track again and he gets his cast off and can cross the wall again."

"What about James?" Jessika suggested.

"Me? What about me?" James sat up, looking at us both.

"Well, I don't know. I hadn't really thought about it Jess," I looked at James. "Do you think you can handle a gas can?"

"I suppose I could try."

"Good. I'll set up a practice tomorrow at the shop for you to train with the team and see how you do. Then we leave for Michigan Thursday morning for the weekend," I explained.

Shortly after, Mark showed up to swim with Jessika, followed soon after by Mandy and Jonathon. Kyle headed back to the shop to check how things had gone during the afternoon, taking James with him to show him around. With some time to myself, I headed through the backyard, and over to Matthew's patio to see if he was around to talk for a while.

I could see him at the kitchen sink as I crossed the patio and knocked on the door, waving at him as he looked up and motioned for me to join him. Grabbing a towel, I started drying the dishes he'd been washing and putting them away.

"How have you been Brianna?" Matthew asked. "Any more problems with your ex?"

"Nope. I think those problems are behind me now. I told him yesterday when he showed up that I didn't want to have anything to do with him, that it was too late for him to make amends, since I'm happy with my life now. Thank you, by the way. I heard you called Kyle to come home when you saw Todd was there."

"Don't mention it. Would've done the same thing for anybody."

"Well, I appreciate it. I think he probably would've stayed longer if Kyle hadn't shown up when he did."

"So, what brings you over tonight? I noticed you had company over earlier."

"Yeah, that was Craig's best friend, and Jessika's godfather. He just retired last week, so he drove over to see us for a couple days. Think he might be sticking around for a while though. Joe had an accident on his motorcycle today."

"Yeah. I heard about that on the news tonight. How is he doing?" Matthew asked shutting the water off as he finished up the last dish.

"Well, he's got a broken leg and a slight concussion, plus some cuts and bruises. He's gonna be off for a few weeks. And he's got a new baby at home too. His wife went into labor at the hospital this afternoon while we were waiting for the doctors to set his leg and check out his other injuries."

"Wow. Sounds like quite a busy day y'all had," Matthew laughed. "I guess you'll have to let your backup gas man know he's up for the next couple months now."

"Actually, I hadn't thought I'd need any backups, so we didn't have anybody at the shop train for the spot. But James crewed for me when I was running the local track back in Greensboro. So he's gonna train with the team tomorrow morning and see how well he works with them, and go to Michigan with us. Then when we get back from Michigan, I'm gonna get started with training anybody else at the shop that wants to be on backup for the other spots. I think I can talk James into staying on until Joe's able to come back."

"Good idea. Why don't we go sit out on the patio now? Thanks for helping me out with these dishes. Sam's gone to her grandparents for a few days, so it's been pretty quiet here without her. Daytona's been quietly working in the office since Sam left. I get the feeling she's finally working on another book."

"I can imagine. I remember how quiet the house was when I first moved and Jess stayed back in Greensboro with Craig's parents. Or when she goes to stay with my parents. It's just way too quiet without her in the house. I don't know what I'm going to do when she finally decides she's had enough of living with me and wants to be on her own. Although then I'll have Kyle there too now won't I?"

Matthew handed me a bottle of beer and we headed out to sit on the patio, hearing the four in my backyard playing in the pool on the other side of the fence. Sitting down at the patio table, Matthew looked at me as he took a long drink from his bottle.

"You know, you remind me a lot of Daytona. I told her that when I first met you and was telling her about you wanting to buy the team."

"I do?" I blushed. "That's a good thing, right?"

"Yep. You've got the same determination she had when she was driving. You want to succeed and do your best on the track. But you've got a good heart too. I've seen how you take care of your team, and make sure they've got everything they need, whether it's equipment to make the cars better, or time off to be with their families. I bet you would've been sending Joe home for a while to be with his wife and new baby, even if he hadn't been in that accident today. And you'll make sure they're not hurting financially while he's off too, aren't you?"

"Wow. You're pretty good. I'm flattered that you would compare me to Daytona. And you're right. I had already planned on giving him time off to be with the baby. And I told them both today that he doesn't have to worry about his job or losing wages while he's off. A happy crew is a successful crew, right?"

"You're right. Just make sure you have a happy driver too. You are happy, aren't you?"

"Very. I mean, who wouldn't be? I'm sitting at the top of the points standings, with four races to go until the Chase. I know it's gonna cut my lead a lot when we finally get to the Chase, but having the lead going in is a great thing. Increases my chances of taking that Cup home at the end of the year. I've got a great team and we all work well together. My daughter is thinking about going into public relations to take over from Jake when he retires. My crew chief wants to marry me and I've got a great mentor that I learn from each and every time I talk to him."

"Hold up. What's this about your crew chief? You do mean Kyle, right? This is new, isn't it?"

"Yeah. Kyle proposed yesterday. We're planning on making it official before the race in Homestead."

"Wow. Well, congratulations. Now, back to you and Daytona being so much alike. You never noticed it before? I mean, you're both from the same city, same kind of background and all," Matthew continued.

"Yeah. I guess we are kinda alike. We both took the same course in college but she was ten years ahead of me. Except she got out of town right after school and actually did something with her education. I stuck around for a couple years and ended up not using my journalism education. She was successful at everything she did before she made it into the Nationwide Series. I went back to school and changed careers before I got into racing. I did work at her bar for a while during my last year of college though and then for a while after I graduated."

"Did you really? I didn't know that."

"Yep. Was an awesome time too. Daytona and Torie were great to work for. I guess that's where I learned how to treat my staff. By how they treated us at the bar. I mean, I didn't get to see Daytona often, just the odd time she was in town and stopped by the bar to check things out. But she was still a great boss all the same. I guess she was kinda my inspiration to get into racing. I knew that if she could do it, with all the struggles she had to go through to get to where she did, I could follow in her footsteps and make it too. And you've been a great mentor since I bought the team from you. I don't think I'd be even half as successful as I am without the advice you've given me over the years. And the few times I've gotten to sit down with Daytona and pick her brain too."

"I could see your drive and potential when you walked through the door that first day I met you. I knew you'd be a success, just like Daytona was. Although you know Daytona and I didn't get along at all when we first met, or when she first joined the team. She just knew exactly which buttons to push to get me fired up. Man, she drove me crazy those first couple years. But let me tell ya, when I realized I was in love with her, I knew I wanted to spend the rest of my life with her, no matter how crazy she made me," Matthew laughed.

"I think as women in the sport, we have to have that drive and determination. Otherwise, what's the point of going out there? Granted, Daytona made it a little easier for women to get into the sport, but those boys are still pretty tough on me, and don't give me any breaks out there. We're all the same once we pull the helmets on and strap into the car. And I don't expect them to give me any breaks, or make it easy on me. I didn't get into the sport, thinking it was gonna be a walk in the park. I like the competition and the challenge of going out there and beating forty-two men every week. Or trying to anyway," I replied.

"So you plan on sticking around for a while?" Matt asked.

"Hell, yeah! I'm thinking in another couple years, I'm gonna field a Nationwide team and start looking for another woman to take over where Daytona and I have already conquered. There've been a few women who've been around, but haven't had the drive or equipment to stick it out. Daytona and I were lucky enough to have both. And I owe everything I have to you. If you hadn't taken a chance on me, and agreed to let me buy the team when you were selling it, I definitely wouldn't be where I am today."

"You know, equipment will only take you so far. You can have the best equipment on the track, but if you don't have the heart or soul to drive it, you'll never get anywhere. I took a chance on you, cuz I could see a little bit of Daytona in you. And every once in a while, I look at you, and you'll say or do something, and I swear it's Daytona and I have to look again and make sure it's really you and not her. I know the media has compared you to her a lot, and they're all right. You're more like her than you realize. I'm gonna have to pull out some of our old home movies sometime to show you. Then you'll see it. And what she was like before the shooting."

"Yeah? I'd really like to see them sometime. But right now, I should probably head back to my side of the fence. Sounds like the kids are done in the pool. And Kyle and James should be back from the shop soon. They'll be wondering what happened to me. Thanks for the beer and the talk." Matt stood with me and hugged me before I turned to walk back across the yard.

"You're very welcome and you know you're welcome on this side of the fence any time. I'm always here if you need advice or just to talk."

I headed back through the yard and saw that Jessika, Mandy, Mark and Jonathon were sitting by the pool still, wrapped up in towels. Jessika stood up as I came across the patio.

"Hey, Mom. We were just talking about going downstairs and playing pool. You want to join us?"

"I'll be down in a little while. You kids go ahead."

"Okay. Maybe when Kyle and James get back, you can partner up with one of them to play against me and Mark?"

"Sounds good. Better go get warmed up then, cuz you know you'll get your butts kicked once we get down there," I laughed as the four headed into the house and downstairs.

Settling into one of the deck chairs, I rested my head on the back, looking up at the darkening sky as stars began twinkling in the darkness. Closing my eyes, I drifted off, feeling the summer breeze on my skin.

Suddenly, I felt fingertips brush my cheek, and a feather light kiss on my forehead, like Craig used to do in the mornings before the alarm would go off. Bolting upright, I looked around, but realized I was still alone. Breathing deeply, I could almost smell his cologne. Had I dreamt the touch? I'd dreamt about him many times in the past few years, and every once in a while, it felt like he was still with me, but never felt quite that real.

I was interrupted from thinking about it any more when Kyle and James came through the house and onto the patio, talking about the shop and the upcoming race.

"Hey Brie. What're you doing sitting out here all by yourself? Where's everybody else? We saw all the cars in the driveway," Kyle asked kissing me on the cheek as he sat down with me.

"They're all downstairs playing pool. They've challenged us to beat them when you got back."

"Really? Well now. I guess Jess forgot the last time we all played together and we kicked her butt eh?"

"Yeah, they forget so quickly you know," I laughed.

"Well, I guess it's time for a reminder, right?" Kyle replied, taking my hand. "You know, this hand is pretty naked. Don't you think so James?"

"Yep. I was just thinking the same thing. You'd never know she was engaged to be married." Suddenly, Kyle was down on one knee on the patio, beside my chair. Holding out a ring box, he looked up at me.

"I wanted to do this the right way. Brianna, will you do me the honor of becoming my wife?" He opened up the ring box, showing me the diamond inside.

"Of course. Oh my God. Kyle, this ring is beautiful! I can't believe you went out and got a ring."

"Well, I wanted to give it to you when I proposed. I didn't exactly plan on just throwing the proposal out there yesterday. I've been thinking about it for a while now and I wanted to do it properly," Kyle replied, taking the ring out of the box and slipping it on my finger. Looking at it sparkling in the moonlight, I smiled down at Kyle. Standing up, he pulled me up with him and kissed me deeply.

"So I guess it's official now?" James asked, stepping forward to hug me.

"Yep. Now to just get her to the altar," Kyle laughed.

"Well, I'll leave you two to argue about that detail," James replied. "I think I'm gonna head to bed. I know I'm gonna have an early start tomorrow and a long day with my training. I'll see you two tomorrow."

"Good night James. And thank you for taking over the spot on such short notice. You know I appreciate it."

"Hey, don't thank me until you see if I can do the job or not. I know how tough pit stops can be and that I'm gonna be under pressure to perform. Good night."

James headed into the house, leaving me and Kyle alone outside.

"So you really like the ring Brie?" he asked, looking into my eyes.

"Yes. It's beautiful Kyle. I love it," I replied, touching his cheek lightly.

"Good. I was so worried it wasn't gonna be big enough, but Jess said you wouldn't care how big it was."

"She's right. I don't care how big it is. Hell, I didn't even expect a ring. I'm happy enough just knowing I'm going to be marrying you. I don't need a fancy rock on my hand to show it."

"I know. But I wanted to make it official, you know? It just doesn't seem real without the ring." I nodded, smiling as Kyle explained himself.

"Well, I think we should take a cue from James and head to bed. I don't know about you, but I'm exhausted."

Taking my hand, Kyle walked upstairs with me, turning out the lights along the way, but leaving one or two on for Jessika when she came upstairs. I called down to her that we were taking a rain check on the pool game, and not to stay up too late playing.

"Good night Mom! Good night Kyle! Love you! See you in the morning!" she called up to me.

About an hour later, I heard cars start up in the driveway and listened to the front door closing and Jessika walking up the stairs to her room. Finally, I fell asleep and dreamt of Craig again.

* * * * *

CHAPTER THIRTY-EIGHT

The next day's pit stop training went well with James as the gas man. After a few initial mix ups, he quickly got the hang of the routine and the pit times were as fast as with Joe in the spot. I'd called first thing in the morning to arrange for a uniform for James and was told it would be ready and delivered to the shop the next morning before we left for Michigan.

After the practice, I posted a notice up on our message board that all positions would be available for training after we returned from Michigan to have backups trained in case they were needed in the future. James and Kyle met me in my office after the training to discuss how it went.

"He's pretty good out there Brie. I think he'll be able to handle himself fine come race day," Kyle explained.

"Good. How do you think you did James?" I turned to him.

"Pretty good. I know I screwed up a bit the first couple times; I was nervous getting started, but once I got into the rhythm of things, I think I did a lot better. Now, if I can do that during a race, that's another story."

"If you can do it here, you can do it at the race. I have no doubts about that," I replied. "Now, are you willing to stay on until Joe can come back? I'm still going to train a backup, but I'd rather keep you on until Joe returns, if you're willing to, and then whoever gets trained as a backup will be your backup until Joe returns and then will become his backup when he's ready to come back to the track."

"Sure. I'll stay on as long as you need me to," James replied.

"Cool. I appreciate you helping out."

"You know I'll help ya out whatever way I can Brie. What are friends for?" James laughed.

"True. You always were there to help me out whenever I needed it," I replied.

I turned the conversation to Kyle then and began discussing with him who he thought would work well as backups in any of the pit jobs. After we made a list of who would work in each spot, we headed downstairs to watch the final preparations of getting the cars loaded into the hauler so they could head out to Michigan.

It was a twelve hour trip for the haulers, but I always made sure they left early for each track to give them plenty of time to get rest along the way. I didn't want any of my crew over worked or over tired.

Once the cars were loaded up and the hauler safely on its way, we headed back home to pack for our flight the next morning.

* * *

The next afternoon when we arrived in Michigan, I had an interview scheduled at the track with the network covering the race. Kyle headed to get the car unloaded from the hauler with the rest of the team, while Jessika and I headed over to the media building for the interview. We met up with Doug and Matt on their way over to the media building, since they were going to be getting interviewed after me about the change back to Doug driving the following weekend.

Just before the interview was done, the reporter pointed to my left hand.

"This is something new, Brianna. Do you have something you want to tell us?" he asked.

"Yep. I was hoping to have my other half here when I made the announcement, but Kyle and I will be getting married by the end of the season," I replied.

"Kyle being Kyle James, your crew chief? Right?"

"The very same. We've been together for awhile now, and he proposed the other day. We both figured it was about time."

"Well, congratulations. I hope you'll let us know when the big day is so we can send a camera crew to get some footage."

"Actually, we're hoping to do it at one of the tracks before the end of the season, if we can get all the details worked out with whatever track we decide on. So you'll definitely get your footage."

"Great. Have a great race this weekend."

"Thanks." I stood up when they motioned that the camera was off and removed my microphone, handing it over to the assistant. Standing off to one side, I watched as Doug and Matt began their interview, before heading back to the garage to check on how the crew was doing with getting the car set up for the first practice session.

"How'd the interview go?" Kyle kissed me on the cheek as I joined them.

"Good. They noticed my ring and asked about it at the end of the interview, so the official announcement has been made."

"No backing out now, you know," Kyle pointed out.

"You think I was going to back out?" I asked.

"You never know. I know you're set in your ways, and it's gonna be a change having me around twenty-four-seven."

"Compared to now, when you're around oh…. Twenty-three-seven?" I laughed.

"True. I guess we are together a lot already, aren't we?" he replied.

"Yeah. Good thing we get along, eh? So, you think we've got a shot at the pole?" I asked, changing the subject. "I'm definitely finishing the race this time around. Not gonna be like last time we were here. I need those points this time."

"Good. I think we've got a fast enough car. This is the same car we brought up last time, so as long as you can run 'er well, I think you can definitely put this baby on the pole."

"Great. It's a good car. I'm gonna go get changed so I can get some practice laps in and test it out. I know you had to fix the body where I parked it on the wall last time around," I laughed.

"Yeah. No parking it on the wall this time, okay? We're finishing this race if I have to get out there and push it around the track for four hundred miles," Kyle joked.

"Well, hopefully it won't come down to that," I replied. I headed to the hauler to change into my drivers' uniform and was met by a throng of media asking questions about my engagement to Kyle.

"I'll take care of this Mom," Jessika said, motioning for me to head into the hauler to get changed as she turned to the media. When I returned a few minutes later, Jessika was alone again, having answered the questions and sent the media on their way.

"Wow. That was quick. Guess you're a quick study under Jake, eh? You think you're ready to take on the job full time now?" I asked, looking around.

"Nope. Not yet. But soon enough, I'm sure. I'm happy enough being your spotter for now, Mom. You'll have to find a new spotter before I can change jobs, and I don't think Jake's going to be leaving anytime soon."

"True. But whenever you're ready, just let me know. I'm sure Jake will be more than happy to step back a bit and let you take the reins for a while. I know he's been thinking for a while about retiring, but doesn't want to leave me without a competent rep."

"Yeah, well. I still have lots to learn," Jessika reasoned.

"Not really. You've seen everything that goes on. You can probably run the whole team as well as I can. And you'll have all the contacts that Jake has. He'll just pass his whole office on to you when the time comes."

"That's a lot of responsibility for an eighteen year old, though. Don't ya think, Mom?" Jess asked me.

"Not really. You're awfully mature for your age. You've been more mature than all your friends for a long time now. I know I asked you to grow up a lot faster than you should have. You did a lot of growing up in a short amount of time after your Dad died. I think you can handle anything that's thrown your way."

"Yeah. I did grow up pretty fast after Dad died, didn't I? But you know what? I wouldn't trade the past couple years for anything. Well, except for having Daddy back with us, but we have no control over that. I'm happy with my life. With our life. I'm so glad we had the chance to do this. And I'm looking forward to many more years of this. As long as you're racing, I want to be here, beside you. Whether it's as your spotter, or your pr rep. Whatever you want me to do, you know I'll do it."

"You've always done whatever I've wanted you to do though. Isn't there something you want to do for you? You don't have to be involved in racing if you don't want to, you know."

"But this is where I want to be, Mom. I can't imagine my life any other way. I want to be involved in racing. I'm more like you than you think Mom. Racing's in my blood too, not just yours," she stressed.

"Okay. But anytime you want to pack it in, you just let me know, okay? I'll support your decision, no matter what career path you want to follow," I explained to her.

"No worries, Mom. I plan on sticking around here for a long time. I signed up for the lifetime commitment, just like you and Kyle did."

Our conversation was halted then as we reached the garage and I turned to Kyle and the crew to discuss the car. When the announcement was made that the track was open for practice, I climbed into the car, put my helmet on and strapped in as Kyle attached the radio and air lines. As he double-checked the safety belts, I attached the steering wheel and tested the radio. Once everything was ready, Kyle secured the safety net and I fired the engine to head out to pit road and onto the track.

After running a couple laps, I passed Matt as he was coming out onto the track. I slowed down, waiting for him to get up to speed, so we could run together. When we were both back up to speed, we took turns running out front so see how our cars each worked leading another car. The radio was quiet except for Kyle giving me lap times, and only a couple other cars were on the track with us, according to Kyle.

When we pulled back into the garage, Matt, Doug and Ricky came over to talk to us, and compare notes on the lap times. They were all pretty close, and we all agreed we were happy with how the practice run had gone. Once Matt had agreed to take over for Doug while Doug recuperated from his injuries, our two teams are started sharing information on how to get the cars to run a bit quicker at each track.

Even though I drove a Ford, and Doug's team was Chevy, most of the things we were doing to the cars were the same, and Doug had offered whatever we needed to be a contender for the championship. He had known once he was going to be off for so long, that his team wouldn't have a chance, with Matt having to substitute for Doug for so long, and was more than willing to help us out whatever way he could.

Wanting to save the cars for qualifying and the race, we covered them both and I headed back to the hauler to change back into my street clothes before we headed to the hotel for the afternoon. Hanging out by the pool and relaxing, Matt and Doug soon joined me and Kyle, as we watched our two teams having a spirited beach volleyball game on the court beside the pool.

"Hey Brie, would you ever consider combining our two teams?" Doug suddenly asked.

"Hell, no. Unless you're planning on switching sides and coming over to the Ford camp," I laughed. "Because you know I'll never leave Ford and go to Chevy."

"Yeah, I guess I forgot that part. I was just thinking that since you're the top team, and I would've had the top team if I hadn't crashed back in June. If we combined our resources and our talents, we'd be a force to be reckoned with next year, don't ya think?" he asked.

"I think you're crazy to even think of suggesting we combine our teams. I'm quite happy running a one woman show, thanks. Why would I want to complicate things by bringing you into my shop?" I answered.

"What's the matter? Don't think you could handle having me around all the time? Would I be too much of a distraction for you?" Doug joked.

"Um, no. I don't think so," I shot back, holding up my hand for him to see my ring.

"Oh. Wow. Nice rock. You gonna wear that while you race?"

"Of course. I don't plan on taking it off. I wore it during practice today and didn't have any problems. It fits under my gloves alright."

"Well, good for you. Congratulations. It's safe to assume it's Kyle you're getting hitched to?"

"Yeah. I finally convinced her to make it official," Kyle answered.

"So, when's the big day?" Doug asked.

"Sometime before the end of the season. Right now, we're looking at right before Homestead. Gonna see if we can talk the track into letting us work it into the pre-race activities," I replied.

"Well, now. That should be interesting. I bet the network will love that to add to their footage."

"I'm sure they will too. We're not really looking for the publicity, but we figured since we're both in the spotlight each and every week, why not let the fans share in our day. And I'm not one for doing things the old-fashioned way."

"I'm sure they'll love that. Especially with you being at the top of the points now."

"Yeah, we're planning on celebrating the wedding and championship after the race. Combine it all into one big party," Kyle spoke up again.

"Little cocky, don't ya think? To assume you're gonna have the championship? A lot can happen in the next fourteen races you know."

"Hey! Have some faith eh?" I burst out. "You think I'm not capable of taking the Cup this year? I know you lost it to Daytona when she got her last Cup. So don't even try telling me you don't think I can do it cuz I'm a woman. I know you better than that."

"Did I say that? No. I'm just saying, a lot can happen between now and then. There are eleven guys behind you who're just as hungry to have that Cup as you are."

"That's where you're wrong, Doug. NOBODY wants the Cup as much as I do. I WILL have that trophy in my shop at the end of the season. I have no doubt about it whatsoever. So you'd better get used to calling me the Sprint Cup Champion," I replied.

"I know I have no doubts at all about whether or not you can do it," Matthew spoke up. "I already told you I see the same drive in you that Daytona had. And I think you'll make a great champion. One to make our sport proud. I wish you'd been around a few years ago when we were looking for a new driver to replace Wayne when he retired."

"Don't suppose you'd like to make a friendly wager on the Cup, would you?" Doug leaned on the table towards me.

"And what're the stakes?" I countered.

"Let's see. If you do win the Cup, I'll come sweep your shop floors once a week for a month. And if you don't win it, you have to come sweep mine," Doug offered.

"That's it? That's all you're willing to give up?" I asked. "I say, WHEN I win the Cup, you come sweep my floors for six months, plus wash my truck."

"Okay. You're on. But same thing, if you lose, it's MY floors and my vehicle," Doug agreed.

"Deal." We shook on it as Kyle laughed and Matt shook his head at us.

* * * * *

CHAPTER THIRTY-NINE

Friday afternoon's qualifying run went well and Matt and I would both be starting from the second row, with me on the inside, slightly faster than his run. After we parked the cars back in the garage and covered them, as per NASCAR's impound rules, I changed back into my street clothes and headed out for a public appearance at one of the area Ford dealerships. My show car had already been set up by the time Jessika and I got there, and the line up was through the showroom and out the doors into the parking lot. Sitting down at the table the dealership had set up, I got down to signing autographs right away and taking pictures with the fans.

Four hours later, I had signed the last autograph and had the last picture taken. I had only been scheduled to be there for two hours, but I had always held true to the belief that the fans made my job possible and whenever I could, I always stayed at my public appearances until all the fans had had a chance to meet with me.

During the short drive back to the hotel, Jessika and I talked about a few of the fans that we had met during the appearance.

"Don't you ever worry about being so close to the fans, Mom?" Jessika asked. "I mean, what if you meet one that's not quite right in the head?"

"Being close to the fans is part of the job honey. You know that. You've been by my side from the start. And you of all people should know I can handle it if something out of the ordinary happens."

"Yeah, but what about a crazy like was stalking Daytona? I bet she never thought about that happening."

"Well, Daytona was being stalked for quite a while when she was shot. She knew there was a danger. That woman was pretty much the exception though. You know not all fans are like that. You've seen that most fans are pretty down to earth. Even if they do get a little over-excited meeting their favorite driver. I mean, look at some of the girls that Doug meets. How crazy do some of them go when he's around?"

"It's just something about meeting somebody famous and we've all got to get used to the fact that being stock car drivers, we become famous when we get a hot streak going. If you look back over the years of the sport, I think you'll see that some fans do some pretty outrageous things to get noticed, but for the most part, they're pretty sane and safe."

"Are you worried at all about Todd showing up again?"

"Nope. And even if he does, I can handle it."

"I think everybody today was really nice. I mean, they all waited so long for you to get there, and those people that were near the end, I think they were really happy that you stuck around to make sure they got their stuff autographed and got pictures with you. Not every driver does that. I've heard a couple other pr reps saying that if their driver's scheduled for an hour or two hours, that's the time they stay. They don't stick around to make sure everybody gets taken care of like you do."

"Well, every driver's different, right? That's one of the things that Matthew told me about when him and Daytona went to public appearances. She always made sure they stayed until the last fan had been met. And it only makes sense. I mean, when you think about it, the fans are the ones who support us week in and week out. They buy the tickets, show their support by buying the merchandise, the tee-shirts and ball caps, the die cast cars, posters, you name it, they buy it. Some of them drive pretty far to go to the races; it's only fair to return the support and show how much we appreciate them being our fans. If I didn't stick around to make sure the last fan gets met, do you think they'd still be a fan next week? Or next month? Probably not. They'd move on to another driver who's more accessible. You'll notice when Jake books my appearances, he always makes sure if there's two on the same day, there's more than enough time for one to run over an hour or two. Or they're close enough that if a fan doesn't get to one, they might get to the other one. He started that with Daytona, and when I met with him when I first bought the team, I told him I was planning on running things the same way she did."

"You're right. I heard a few people when I was walking around today, that were near the end of the line. They were commenting that there's other drivers that don't stick around, but they knew they were going to get to meet you, 'cause they've heard that you stay until the last fan has been met. They thought that was really cool of you to do that."

"Well, you watch next time there's an appearance where there's a bunch of us, and you'll see how the other drivers are during their meet and greets. Everybody handles it differently. I meet with as many as I possibly can. And others sign a few quick autographs and then they're gone. Look at the time I spend at the fence with the fans, compared to some of the other drivers. How many times have I had to run 'cause I've stayed too long with the fans and I'm running late to practice?"

"True. You're an inspiration, Mom. I hope there'll be other drivers that come along that are even half as good as you. I think you're a great role model for so many other women out there. Just like Daytona was."

"I hope so. Even if it's not inspiring women to drive race cars, but to chase their dreams, no matter what they are. That's what I did. I chased a dream buying the team from Matthew. I didn't know what the hell I was doing; I just acted on impulse really. But I knew I had a dream that I wanted to go after and I needed to do something as far away from law enforcement as I possibly could, to try to stop thinking about everything that happened the night your Dad died. I didn't know when I bought the team if I was making the biggest mistake of my life; or if I was gonna make it as a car owner and a driver. But I knew that I had to chase the dream. Otherwise, I wasn't being true to myself. And you see how that's turned out so far."

"Yeah. I think it's turned out great so far. You're an awesome role model, Mom. So, when you decide to retire, are you going to put another woman in your car? Or go with a male driver?"

"Depends on who's out there, and what talent I see. I think in another year or two, I might start a Nationwide team and see if I can find another woman driver to put in the car to get ready for Sprint. There've been some great women drivers in the truck series too, which a lot of drivers have used to get some experience on the tracks and some seat time, before they've moved to the Cup Series. But I'll take a look around the local tracks too and see who's out there. I'd love to see more women in the sport, but only when they're ready. You've seen how tough it can be. How much time do I spend at the gym or doing some sort of training? It's not an easy job to have, and there are some guys that have a hard time sometimes. Watch the drivers after a race like the Coke 600 every May. That's our longest race still. Or after a race in Vegas or Phoenix. Seeing how hot it is outside, think of how hot it is inside the cars. It takes a lot to get through a race when it's that hot."

We arrived back at the hotel then and our conversation was interrupted as I parked the car and Kyle came out to meet us.

"We were starting to wonder what had happened to you," he said, kissing me lightly as I got out of the car.

"They were lined up out the doors and into the parking lot when we got there. You know I always stay until everybody's been through the line. When have I ever gotten out of an appearance in the allotted time?" I asked.

"True. Always in demand. Guess I just have to get used to the fact that I'm going to be married to the most popular woman in the world."

"Well, I wouldn't say the most popular," I laughed. "I'm sure there must be one or two women out there that are most popular than me. How's everything going here? The team all back from the track?"

"Yep. They're all hanging out by the pool, waiting for you so we can go for dinner."

"Well, y'all didn't have to wait for us. You know that. Jess and I would've just grabbed something when we got back here if y'all had already eaten."

"How often do we not wait for you? It's no big deal. I mean, if you'd been four or five hours late, yeah, we would've gone ahead without you. But they all agreed they could wait a little while for you. We're a team, remember? What don't we do as a team?" Kyle laughed.

"True. But next time, just go ahead without me." We went into the hotel and rounded up the team to go next door for dinner. Over dinner, Jess sat at the other end of the table with Mark, while I sat between Kyle and James and relayed the conversation Jess and I had had on the drive back.

"She's right you know," James said when I was finished.

"About what?" I asked.

"Everything," James laughed. "You being an inspiration. And a role model. I'd bet there's hundreds of little girls out there who watch the races and want to be just like you."

"You know, when I was younger, my role model was Teresa Earnhardt. I mean, she ran a multi-million dollar organization and was successful. How many girls look up to her? Hell, she's still one of the most successful car owners around. She doesn't drive, but she runs one hell of an operation. But if I had to pick one driver that I looked up to growing up, I'd definitely have to say Shirley Muldowney. I mean, she didn't drive a stock car, but she was pretty successful as a driver when I was really young. She went through a lot to become successful as a drag racer. And of course, I admired Daytona when she was racing. She went to hell and back with some of the shit she had to put up with from other drivers. Matthew's told me about some of the stuff that you wouldn't normally hear about, shit that went on in the garage and behind the scenes. But she didn't take any crap from anybody. Matthew's even told me about some of the stuff he put her through before they finally got together and I can't believe they not only ended up getting along, but got married and had a baby together. Let me tell ya, she had a lot of shit dumped on her, and she fought back and didn't take any of it from anybody."

"Sounds like another woman we all know and love," Kyle said.

"What? Me? Yeah, I guess I don't take any shit from anybody either, do I?" I laughed.

"Exactly. But that's just part of what makes you, well, you," James agreed. "You've always been one to say it like it is, shoot from the hip, so to speak, and somehow not come across as a bitch either."

"No? You don't think I'm a bitch?" I laughed.

"Nope. Never. Not even when I've had you pointing a gun at my head. I never once thought you were a bitch."

"Hold it!" Kyle butted in. "Do I want to know why you had a gun pointed at his head?" He turned to me.

"Geez, you had to bring that up, didn't you James?"

"Sorry." James laughed, shaking his head.

"Yes, I pointed a gun at him. And I probably would've shot him too, if it'd been the middle of the night and dark. He's just lucky it was the middle of the day and I was still woozy from the drugs they gave me at the hospital to stitch me up after they took the bullet out of my shoulder."

"I showed up at the house to drive her into the precinct for a meeting the day after Craig was killed. She was in the shower when I got there, but I didn't know it. I'd been calling her name and not getting an answer, so I'd headed upstairs to see if she was still sleeping. Got to the top of the stairs and there she was, gun pointed at me, ready to shoot. And considering I knew how good a shot she was, I was definitely worried. I'm just glad she realized it was me before she pulled the trigger. I wouldn't be here otherwise. Man, you shoulda seen the shot she got off. . . "

"Enough, James. Please. I don't want that brought up right now please," I stopped him, knowing where the story was going.

"She's told me enough of that night, that I think I know where you're going," Kyle put his arm around me, pulling me closer to him.

"You're right. Now's not the time for that trip down memory lane," James agreed. "So, what's the plan for the rest of the weekend? I know the race is Sunday. But what happens all day tomorrow with the cars being impounded?"

"The Nationwide cars run tomorrow and we have the day off," I explained. "I've got an interview in the morning, and I have another public appearance to go to in the afternoon. While I do that, the team will either go to the track to hang out and watch the race, or they'll hit the gym, see the sights, stuff like that. It's a pretty quiet day for us, well for the crew anyway. I still have a busy day tomorrow, which I don't mind. After all, it is the fans that make the sport as popular as it is. So, what you do tomorrow is up to you. If you want to go to the track and hang out to watch the race, go ahead. If you wanna check out the area, that's your choice. I'm sure the guys'll all discuss it over breakfast of what they're all gonna do. And I can tell you, you'll be more than welcome to tag along with any of them, no matter where they're going. They're pretty good with taking in strays, and making you feel welcome on the team. And since you might be with us for a few races, if you're okay with that, you'd better get used to hanging out with these guys. Unless you'd rather tag along to my interview and appearance," I offered.

"I think I'll check things out in the morning and see what the other guys are gonna be doing," James replied.

"Okey dokey. Your choice. I'll be leaving here between six thirty and seven, so if you're gonna go with me, just meet me in the lobby by then." Shortly after dinner, I headed up to the room to get some sleep. My interview was scheduled for nine the next morning, and I had an hour and a half drive to get to it, so I had my alarm set for six to make sure I had plenty of time to get ready and get to the interview.

When Kyle crawled into bed later that night, I woke up briefly as he pulled me into his arms, then fell back to sleep as he held me close to him. I had gotten used to him sharing my bed and seemed to sleep better when he was there at night. He had yet to give up his apartment, since he had another couple months on the lease, and occasionally spent a night there.

* * * * *

CHAPTER FORTY

When the alarm went off the next morning, Kyle held me tighter, kissing the back of my shoulder.

"You don't have to get up already, do you?" he asked quietly.

"Unfortunately, yes I do," I groaned. "I can't be late for the interview this morning and I have an hour and a half drive to get there don't forget. You could come with me to this one you know."

"No thanks. I'll stay here and hang out with the rest of the crew. You know I don't do interviews and public appearances."

"Yeah. I know that. Better get used to the fact that your wife is a hot item on the NASCAR circuit. The interviews are just gonna increase the better I run, and the longer I hold the points lead. And as the championship crew chief, there's gonna come a time when there's requests for you to be interviewed," I pointed out to him.

"Well, we'll see about that. And we'll deal with that when the time comes. I know I've got one of the most popular drivers right here. I'm not complaining. I know how important the fans are. Just make sure that after we're married, we get some sort of honeymoon away from the fans, the tracks and the interviews. I want some quiet time with my wife before we retire."

"Who said anything about retiring? I'm not retiring any time soon," I laughed.

"Yeah, everybody knows that. Now, you'd better go start getting ready, or I'm gonna keep you here all day and you'll never make it to your interview."

After a quick shower, getting dressed and doing my makeup, I gave Kyle a quick kiss before I headed out the door and downstairs. Coming out of the elevator just before seven, I didn't see James around and assumed he'd chosen to hang around with the rest of the team.

The drive to Southfield and my interview was quiet at that time of day, and passed quickly. I would be getting interviewed by one of the local news channels, followed by a public appearance at the nearby Ford dealership. Walking into the news studio, I was greeted by the receptionist and directed to the studio where the interview would be taking place.

The reporter was already there, going over notes, while he talked to the station manager. Seeing me walk in, he greeted me warmly and invited me to sit across from him.

"Well, it's a pleasure to meet you Brianna. Thank you for agreeing to the interview," he began, shaking my hand.

"It's great to meet you too, Pat. And I'm happy to be here."

"So, just a quick overview of what we're going to do here. I'll start out asking you about your current season, explaining that you're leading the points, the only woman to do so since Daytona Hudson. Then I'd like to ask you a few questions about your background, and then we'll wrap up with your future plans. Sound good?"

"Sure."

"Okay. So as soon as the cameramen are all ready to go and the lighting is set up, we'll get started. Do you need anything before we start? Tea? Coffee? Water?"

"Water would be great, please." Pat motioned to somebody to bring me water as the station manager called that everything was set to start, whenever we were ready. The cameras started rolling and the interview began.

"Welcome Brianna Lane. You're currently leading the NASCAR Sprint Cup points, the first woman to do that since Daytona Hudson won her last championship. With the start of the Chase for the Sprint Cup only four races away, are you feeling any pressure from the other drivers out there that are after the same goal as you?"

"Well Pat, to be honest, the other drivers out there aren't after exactly the same goal as I am. I'm going out there to become the second woman to win the championship. None of them can say the same thing. But yes, there is a lot of pressure out there. Being a woman in the sport doesn't make much of a difference. When it comes right down to it, there's forty-two other drivers who want to have the chance to take that trophy home at the end of the year. Unfortunately only twelve of us will have the chance to compete for it, with the way NASCAR has set up the championship chase. And only one will be lucky enough to claim the big prize when it's all said and done."

"True. Very true. Now, you are not only the driver, but the car owner as well. You actually bought Reed Motorsports from Daytona Hudson and Matthew Thompson, to begin your career. I know you've been racing against Matthew for a couple months now. Has he given you any advice on how to run the team, or pointers on how to run at different tracks?"

"Oh yes. Matt's been a wealth of knowledge from the time I took over the team. He pretty much taught me everything I know about running my own NASCAR team. He took the time to show me what it takes for the day to day running of the shop, and travelled with the team for the first little while to talk me through getting around the tracks, how to handle being in the draft, taking over a spot, fighting for the lead, you name it. He talked me through my first win when I was still running the Nationwide series.

"Even now, he still gives me advice whenever I ask for it. I certainly value his opinion, and his advice. I don't think I'd be where I am today without his guidance. And Daytona's as well. I've had the opportunity to talk with her a number of times, since we share a back fence and she's been great for sharing her advice with me."

"Now, you were pretty much an unknown before you bought the team from Matthew and started running the Nationwide Series."

"Yes. I had only run at the local track in Greensboro before buying the team. But I'd had the dream of being a professional stock car driver from the time I was fifteen. I just didn't have the chance to start racing until I was older."

"So what led up to you buying the team? Did you just wake up one day and say 'hey I want to buy a stock car team'?"

"In a sense, yes. It did kind of work out that way. When I was in Greensboro, I was at a crossroads in my life. I didn't feel that I could continue in the career I had been in and I needed a change. And it just so happened that right around the same time was when the announcement was made that the Reed Motorsports organization was going to be put up for sale. So I made a phone call, met with Matthew and got all the details worked out. Resigned from my job and moved to Mooresville to take over the team."

"So, going back to your previous career. What was it and why did you decide you couldn't continue with it? I think I read somewhere that you were an undercover police officer. Is that right?"

"Yes. I was an undercover police officer for about 9 years, almost ten. And racing at the local track on my off weekends."

"So then what made you decide you didn't want to do that anymore? I mean, I read that you were part of the drug squad, weren't you? So you were helping to clean up the streets and get drug dealers put in prison and cutting off some of the drug trade. Why would you decide to give all that up?"

"My husband was killed during the last drug raid I had been involved in. I think losing your partner to such a senseless crime would turn pretty much the most dedicated officer off the profession. And we had a young daughter together to consider as well. We had never brought our work home with us, and here I had to explain to her why her father was killed. So I chose to switch to a career where she could be with me whenever she wasn't in school. And she's been by my side for every race I've run. She's been my spotter for three years now, and she's already begun training to become my pr rep somewhere down the road."

"And what does the future hold for Reed Motorsports? You never changed the name after you took over the team. Why's that? Will you be looking for another woman driver to take over when you retire from driving? Do you have a plan for how long you're going to drive?"

"I do have a plan. But I don't think any of us really knows what the future holds. We only know what we want the future to hold for us. Obviously, I want the team to continue to be a success, but then I've never heard a driver or car owner say, 'yeah, I want next year to suck, and end up at the bottom of the barrel when it's all said and done.'

"Somewhere down the road, I'll be looking into fielding a full time Nationwide team again. Hopefully with another female driver. I know there's a number of them in the feeder series' that have quite a bit of potential, with the proper guidance and equipment. But I'm not going to be looking into that for another couple years still. Right now, as a team, we're happy running just one car. And I chose to keep the name and logo the same, with Matthew and Daytona's blessings, because the name and logo are something that everybody involved in NASCAR recognizes. I was showing up with an established team, just with a new driver and owner. Half of my crew now are the same guys Matthew and Daytona had on their crews."

"Well, thank you for taking the time to come today. Good luck this weekend. We'll be watching for you in Victory Lane on Sunday. And good luck with the rest of the season and the Chase."

"Thank you for having me." The lights went out on the camera and I stood to shake Pat's hand again, thanking him again for the good wishes.

After signing autographs for a number of the production crew there, I headed back out to my rental car and the Ford dealership for my next appearance. Getting there early, I could see quite a crowd had already gathered, lined up out the door of the dealership and into the lot. Parking in a reserved space near the door, I was joined by the general manager of the dealership and he walked me into the showroom.

"You're early," he pointed out.

"Yeah. My interview didn't take as long as we had anticipated. But I can start early with this one. You have everything set up already?"

"Yep. As per your pr rep's request. We've got you all set up beside your show car here. We started the line on the opposite side of the car, so anybody wanting pictures with you and the car can get a good picture," he explained. "Your pr rep said he'd be here in time for you to start, so if you want to wait for him, that's fine. You're not scheduled to start for another half an hour. If you want to sit in one of the offices to wait, you're more than welcome to."

"Actually, I really don't mind starting early. Weren't there any other Ford drivers scheduled to be here today too?" I asked, walking towards my show car. The crowd had finally noticed I'd arrived and was buzzing with talk. I could see camera flashes going off every couple seconds and turned to the crowd to wave.

"There was one other, Eddie Ibsen, but he hasn't arrived yet. But yeah, if you want to get started, you're more than welcome to," he ushered me over to the table and chair they'd set up for me.

I had followed Daytona's lead with requesting a higher table and chair to be set up for autograph sessions to make things easier for fans. I had a box of photo cards in the back seat of my car and sent one of the salesmen out to retrieve it for me while I got settled in the chair. He placed it on the table as I greeted the first fan. It was a little girl, about nine years old.

"Hi there! What's your name?" I asked, sliding off the chair to bend down to talk to her.

"Jessica," she shyly replied.

"What a pretty name. You know, I have a daughter whose name is Jessika too," I took her hand as she smiled up at me. Looking up at her mom, we smiled as the picture was taken.

"Can I have your autograph?" Jessica asked.

"You sure can sweetie," I answered, standing to pull a card out of the box to sign. Handing it back to her, she looked down at it, reading what I had written.

"Follow your dreams?" she read out loud.

"Yep. If I didn't follow mine, I wouldn't be here right now, meeting you," I revealed.

"So I could be a race car driver just like you?" she asked.

"If that's what you want to do, I don't see why not," I answered. "But first, you have to grow a little bit more, and finish school. You're a little too young to drive a car like mine, but if you start out with something small, like a go-kart, you can work your way up to the Sprint cars. You get some experience in the smaller stuff and give me a call in about nine or ten years, okay?"

"Okay!" she grinned up at me.

"She just loves watching you race," her mom explained. "So we knew we just had to come today to see you here, so she could meet you."

"Well, I'm glad you could come. Thanks so much!" I replied.

They moved on and I greeted the next fan. Almost an hour into the appearance, the other Ford driver finally arrived to join me. He strutted in, shaking hands with fans along the way until he reached my side.

"I see you started early. What's the problem? You couldn't be bothered waiting for me?" he demanded.

"Wait for you? Who the hell do you think you are?" I replied quietly. "Maybe if you'd show up on time once in a while. You were supposed to be here an hour ago. But I guess it boosts your ego to force people to wait for you. Too bad I'm not gonna cater to your fragile ego."

"Whatever. I get here when I get here. You better learn that. And remember that you don't start an appearance without me," he shot back. I held up my hand to let the next fan know to wait before they approached the table.

"I'll be damned if I'm gonna hold up a public appearance just cuz you think you're some sort of hot shit. Cut the diva act Eddie. It may work with your fans, but it ain't gonna fly with me," I told him, standing to face him.

We were about the same height, but choosing to wear heels to the interview and appearance at the dealership, I stood a few inches taller than he, causing him to have to look up at me when he talked.

Matt had told me about him, when I had first started racing. His father, Evon had been responsible for Daytona's wreck during her first Winston Cup race when she'd filled in for Matt in Atlanta. He'd had his NASCAR licence revoked after officials determined he'd wrecked her purposely, causing her to be temporarily paralyzed for a number of months.

Eddie had come into the Sprint Series just before I had bought the team, driving a car for his father. Even though Evon hadn't been permitted to drive or step on any racing property, he was still able to field a team, joining up with Ryan Renaud, the other driver barred from racing for the same incident.

"Where the hell do you get off? I've been around this sport longer than you have. You've been here, what? All of five minutes and you're gonna tell me how to run an appearance?" he spat.

"Screw off Eddie. You really think the fans want to see you acting childish like this? You need to grow up before you end up like your father," I calmly replied.

"You bitch! You think just cuz you buy Daytona's team, you have the right to push people around? You'd better watch your ass," he threatened. I raised my eyebrows, looking him in the eye.

"Are you threatening me, Eddie?" I asked.

"Just warning you, that's all. Take it however you want, but watch your ass," he repeated.

"Don't you dare threaten me, Ibsen. I can kick your ass any day of the week," I warned.

"Bring it on bitch. Any time you think you can," he shot back, stepping forward. Holding my ground, I refused to be intimidated by him.

"Okay! So, here we've got both Ford drivers here now," the dealership manager stepped up to us. "How about we get back to signing some autographs here? I think we can save the discussion for later, right?"

I could see he looked worried we were going to come to blows right there in the middle of the showroom floor.

"You know, I don't need to put up with this shit. Y'all are gonna tell me how I should act? This Daytona-wannabe may be leading in points, but there's no way I'm gonna have some rookie tell me what to do," Eddie sneered. "You know what? I'm done here. And you can be sure there is no way in Hell I'll ever be at another appearance with you." Eddie turned to walk away. A couple of the fans booed as they saw him walking towards the door.

"Hey Eddie! What's the matter? Can't ya share the spotlight with a woman? Or you just ashamed that she's beating your ass in the points?" I heard a voice call out from the crowd. Eddie spun back to face the fans lined up in the showroom.

"Who said that?" he demanded, walking back a few steps towards the crowd. There was an even mix it seemed, between his fans and mine, looking at the shirts and hats in the crowd.

"I did," one man stepped forward. He was wearing an Eddie Ibsen shirt and wearing one of the sponsor hats.

"You got a problem?" Eddie asked.

"Yeah. Actually I do. I thought you were a cool guy, but now I see you're a douchenozzle just like your father," the man pulled off his shirt and hat and tossed them at Eddie's feet. "I can't believe I actually paid for this crap and drove here to get a picture with you and your autograph today. You should go home. Go cry to Daddy that a woman put you in your place."

Eddie sputtered for a minute, trying to think of something to say in response. Coming up empty, he turned and stormed out of the dealership. The crowd cheered and clapped as the door started to close behind him. Turning back to the line-up, I motioned the next fan forward, apologizing for the delay.

"Hey, no problem for me. I thought that was a great show. Just goes to show what kind of guy he really is. Can tell he learned a lot from his Daddy. Too bad his Daddy didn't teach him not to mess with a woman," the fan laughed, handing me a hat to sign.

"Well, thanks for coming," I replied, signing the hat before I returned it. Looking up, I noticed a number of Eddie's fans had removed their hats and were looking around.

"You know," I called out. "If any of you are Eddie Ibsen fans, and came only to see him, I won't be offended if you feel it necessary to leave, seeing as he's not participating now." Nobody looked like they were heading for the door.

"Hey Brianna? Would you mind if we switched over to your team?" one of his fans shouted over to me.

"Heck no I don't mind! Tell you what," I offered. "How many of you are coming to the race on Sunday?" I paused as almost everybody in the crowd held up their hands. "Okay, for anybody here who decides they want to switch, if you're willing to give up your Eddie tee shirt, bring it to my souvenir trailer anytime this weekend and trade it in for a fifteen percent discount off any merchandise from my trailer."

"What are you gonna do with all his old shirts?" somebody asked.

"Well, I can always use some new shop rags," I laughed. "And that's about all they're good for. That and maybe starting a campfire." The crowd laughed with me and the mood was lightened quickly.

An hour later, the crowd was still quite large and looked to be growing. The dealership manager had gotten somebody to take down the banner with Eddie's name and picture on it, and had his show car driver pack the car up and move it off the lot. He came over to me as I had a picture taken with a group.

"Everything okay?" I asked, signing another autograph.

"Yeah. I just wanted to check on you and see if there's anything that you need. Something to drink? You want to take a break for lunch or something?" he asked. "You've been signing for quite a while now."

"Can I get a bottle of water please? Other than that, I'm good. I'll take a break when the crowd has cleared," I replied.

"Sure. No problem. Listen, I just want to thank you for not leaving when all that happened with Eddie. I don't know what I would've done if both drivers would've stormed out."

"Well, one thing about me, I don't leave when there are still fans left waiting for an autograph. Like you saw, these fans are what keep us in business really. It'll be interesting to see how many people that are here today actually show up to trade in their shirts this weekend. If I acted like Eddie did, I wouldn't have the fans I have. And it just goes to show, you treat the fans like crap and they're gonna switch to another driver," I explained. "That's one thing I learned from Matt and Daytona. You treat the fans with respect, and they're gonna keep supporting you."

"True. Well, I'll let you get back to your fans now."

A short time later, my cell phone started ringing. From the ringtone, I knew it was Kyle. Picking it up while I continued to sign, I answered it.

"Hey babe. What's up?" I asked.

"Just wanted to check on things and see how you're doing," Kyle answered.

"Doing good. Don't let me forget I've gotta go see Joyce today when I get to the track," I replied.

"Joyce? Why? Everything okay?"

"Yeah. I'll explain it all when I see you. I'll meet you at the track later. I'm probably gonna be later than expected getting back. There's still quite a crowd here."

"Well, considering there's two drivers there signing, I'm not surprised the crowd's pretty large. I think Eddie's probably got all his dad's fans cheering for him now."

"Yeah. I don't think that's happening much," I laughed. "Eddie left without even signing one autograph. But I'll tell you about it when I get to the track."

"Okay. I'll let you get back to your fans then," Kyle answered. "Love you."

"Love you too. I'll see you in a couple hours," I hung up the phone, turning back to the fans again.

* * *

When the last autograph was finally signed and the last picture taken, the dealership manager came over to thank me again for staying.

"I'm always happy to get some time with the fans. It's nice to see such a good crowd came out today. Thanks so much for having me here today. And I want to apologize for what happened with Eddie. I really didn't think he'd act like that just because I started the appearance without him. I've really never had another appearance with just him before, so I didn't know what he's like. I mean, I know he's a spoiled brat, but I really didn't expect that attitude from him."

"Not a problem, Brianna. At least now I know for next time, not to bother requesting he be here for an appearance. I'm going to be letting the guys at Ford know what happened. I don't think I've ever seen another driver act like that before," the manager pointed out.

"Well, it was my pleasure to be here today. I look forward to coming back again another time," I shook his hand before heading out to my car. The drive back to the track passed quickly and soon I was on the highway that passed the entrance to the track infield. There wasn't a lot of traffic on the road, since the Nationwide cars were in the middle of running. There had only been a couple other cars in front and behind me since I'd turned onto US 12.

Hearing another car speeding up behind me, I looked in my rear view mirror in time to see the other car right on my back bumper. The windshield was tinted, and I couldn't see the other driver. Wondering what they were thinking, I pulled over slightly towards the shoulder of the road. There were ditches on either side of the highway, and I knew I didn't want to end up stuck in one of them. Hoping the other driver would speed passed when I gave them room, I put my hand out the window to wave them by as I inched as far onto the shoulder of the road as I dared. The other driver started honking the horn and drove up beside me, pushing my car closer to the edge of the road.

"Go passed already dammit!" I muttered, checking the shoulder to see how much room I had left. Suddenly, the other driver sped up again, and inched closer to my, pushing my car into the ditch. Hitting the soft shoulder, my car tipped and rolled onto the passenger side as I watched the other car speed off.

Taking a deep breath, I slowly undid my seatbelt and rolled my window down the rest of the way, before I took the key out of the ignition. I figured it would be easier to climb out the window, than trying to fight to open the door. Pulling off my shoes, I shifted in my seat, leaning down to grab my purse. Tucking my shoes into my purse, I climbed out the window to sit on the side of the car. Phoning the rental company to report the accident, the rental agent told me she'd send out a tow truck and a replacement rental for me for the remainder of the weekend, asking if I needed an ambulance as well.

"No. I'm not hurt at all," I replied as another car pulled up on the shoulder of the road behind me. I was surprised to see Todd climb out of the car. Knowing it hadn't been him that had pushed me into the ditch, unless he'd had another car hidden somewhere nearby, I wondered who it had been.

"Brianna! Are you okay?" he called to me as he ran up to my car.

"I'm fine. What the hell are you doing here? Following me?" I demanded as I hung up the phone.

"Good thing I was following you. I saw the way that other car was tailing you, so I called the state police. I'm sure they'll have somebody here soon," he replied.

"Well, you've done your good deed for the day. You're free to leave now. I don't need you hanging around me."

"I'm sure the police will want my statement when they arrive, since I saw the whole thing happen," he explained.

"Oh goody. I feel so freakin' privileged to have to sit here with you until the police arrive," I remarked.

Just then, I could hear the sirens of approaching emergency vehicles. Looking up the road, I could see a state police car as well as an ambulance. They pulled onto the side of the road in front of where I'd rolled the car and the paramedics jumped out as the state trooper climbed out of his car, assessing the situation.

"Are you hurt ma'am?" he asked me, tipping his hat at me.

"No. I'm fine," I replied.

"Are you the witness that called in the crash?" he asked Todd.

"Yep. I was on my way to the track when I saw the way the car behind Brianna was trying to ram her rear bumper. That's why I called it in. I was close enough to get the licence number of the car, so hopefully that'll help y'all," he offered.

"We have an officer looking into it. The vehicle you reported was a rental, so we'll have to find out from the rental company who it's registered to," the officer explained. "If you'd come with me sir, I'll take your statement so you can be on your way. If you were on your way to the track, I don't want to hold you up."

The paramedics stood by as I climbed down from the side of the car and put my shoes back on. Walking over to the ambulance, I sat on the back so they could give me a quick on-site exam before sending me on my way.

"Ma'am? Do you have somebody who can come pick you up?" one of them asked.

"Yeah. I can call somebody from my crew to come get me I suppose. It'll probably be a while before the replacement rental gets here with the tow truck," I replied. After a quick exam, the paramedics packed up their equipment as I saw Todd finishing up with the state trooper. They both walked together over to the ambulance as I stood up again.

"Ma'am? I have a few questions to ask you," the trooper began.

"Brianna? I'll wait and drive you to the track if you want," Todd offered.

"No thanks Todd. I'll wait for the tow truck if I have to," I replied, turning back to the state trooper. "What questions do you have for me?"

He motioned Todd to head back to his car and waited until he was on his way before he turned back to me.

"Sorry. I just didn't want him to influence your answers."

"No problem. I think I could've answered them with him here. I know the drill. But I'm glad you sent him on his way all the same," I answered, walking back to his car with him.

"So. Do you have any idea who was driving the car that hit you?" he asked.

"None at all. The windshield was tinted, so I couldn't really see who was behind the wheel. I honestly couldn't tell you even if it was a man or a woman," I offered.

"Have you had any problems with anybody the past little while?"

"Nope. Not that I can think of," I answered. "I figured it was just somebody who was in a hurry to get passed me. I mean, I moved over as far as I could and waved them by. That's when they pulled up beside me and pushed me into the ditch."

"Okay. Well, let me give you a lift to the track and as soon as we know anything, I'll let you know. Can I make a suggestion to you though? Don't go anywhere alone until we know who pushed you into the ditch today," he led me around to the passenger side of the car and opened the door for me. Getting into the car, I pulled my seatbelt across me and secured it as he walked around the front of the car and slid behind the wheel.

Arriving at the track, we were waved through the tunnel entrance and he drove directly to the team parking lot. Getting out, I thanked him for the ride.

"Listen, just to be on the safe side, I'm gonna walk you to wherever you've gotta be, okay?" he put his hat back on and stayed by my side until we got to the garage. When Kyle saw us, he rushed over.

"Brie? Are you okay? What's going on?" he asked.

"I'm okay. I just had a little accident on the way here," I held up my hand as he started to protest. "Really Kyle. I'm okay. Somebody ran me off the road into a ditch. That's why I got a ride the rest of the way here. The rental company is sending out a tow truck and another rental for me. So if there's anybody you can spare to go wait for the new car, the other one's about two miles down US 12."

"Yeah. No problem." He called two of our crewmembers over, told them what he wanted and sent them on their way to drive out to wait for the tow truck.

"Well, now that I've seen you safely to the track, I see you're in good hands here, so I'll be on my way. Like I said, I'll let you know as soon as we know who it was," the state trooper shook my hand, turning to leave. Just then, his radio crackled with his supervisor calling him. "I'm at MIS right now, sir. I just finished dropping Brianna Lane off here."

"Well, take a look around the parking lot and see what you can find. We found out the other car was rented by ER Racing out of Mooresville. I'm guessing you'll find the car somewhere there. I'm sending out more officers to help with the search if you need them."

"That'd be great. There's a heckuva lot of cars out here boss," he chuckled, looking around. Kyle and I had started walking back towards the parking lot with him.

"ER Racing?" Kyle asked. "Isn't that Eddie?"

"Yeah. I thought he would've been back here by now. He left the dealership almost right after he got there. He should've been back here before I even left," I replied.

"You know this guy?" the trooper asked. "You have problems with him before? Why didn't you mention that when I asked you at the crash site?"

"I didn't even think of it, to be honest. I mean, we had an argument this morning, but I just passed it off as Eddie being a spoiled brat, not that he had any real problem with me," I explained.

"Where would I find this Eddie?"

"If I had to guess, I'd say either in his hauler, or in the team motorhome," I replied. "I can show you where they are."

"I want to see the car first. Think you could show me where he might've parked?"

"Yeah. That's not a problem," I walked into the team parking area and we began walking up and down the aisles, scanning for the car. "There it is!" I pointed across the hood of one of the cars, towards the one I had been run off the road by. Going over to it, I bent down looking at the passenger side. Kyle and the state trooper quickly joined me. The trooper radioed in as we looked at the scrapes and paint transfer on the door.

"Yep. This definitely matches the vehicle description," he was telling his boss. "I might need some back-up bringing this guy in. I've got the vehicle, but not the driver here."

"There he is," Kyle pointed out. Looking up, I saw Eddie walking towards the garage with his crew chief. The state trooper followed them and called out to Eddie. They turned and Eddie looked shocked to see me standing beside his car.

"Sir? I'm going to need you to come with me," the trooper began.

"What for?" Eddie demanded.

"Well, I have some questions for you regarding your rental vehicle."

"My rental? Why? It's right there," Eddie pointed towards his car.

"Yes. I know that, sir. That's why I have some questions for you. If you'd step over here please," the trooper took his arm and guided him back to the car.

"Holy crap! What the hell happened to my car?" Eddie yelled when he got close enough. "Did you do this Brianna?"

"Cut the crap Eddie. We know you ran me off the road," I replied.

"Ran you off the road? How'd I do that when I've been here since I left the dealership this morning," Eddie argued.

"Do you have somebody who can verify that you were here and what time you got back to the track?" the trooper asked.

"Sure. You can ask my crew chief here. I've been with him the whole time," Eddie motioned towards his crew chief.

"Sir? Can you verify that Mr Ibsen was here when he says?"

"Huh? Oh yeah. Of course. He's been here for a while now," his crew chief replied, staring wide-eyed at the side of the car.

"Well then, can you tell me who else might've been driving your car roughly forty-five minutes ago?"

"Nobody is supposed to be driving my car," Eddie pointed out. "Are you telling me somebody stole my car and ran Brianna off the road? Somebody's trying to make me look bad."

"Well, we're going to have to impound your vehicle sir. And there'll be an officer here to take your fingerprints, just to eliminate them in case there's more than one set in the vehicle. I'm sure you'll understand that if you don't know anything about the incident with Miz Lane on US 12."

"Oh yeah, sure. No problem. I'll give you my fingerprints. I hope you catch whoever did that. Man, that must've been scary eh Brianna?" Eddie turned to me. I saw the smirk on his face as the state trooper turned to take a closer look at the side of Eddie's car. Disgusted, I turned away and walked towards the motorhome parking area as another state trooper arrived. Kyle took my hand as we walked, asking me what had happened at the dealership. Recapping the story, I finished just as we arrived at the motorhome. Doug and Matt were sitting between mine and Doug's and heard the end of the story.

"I told you that punk was just like his father," Doug said to Matt, shaking his head. "I don't get it though. He wasn't racing when Evon wrecked Daytona. So what's he got against Brianna?"

"Besides the fact that I bought her team and I'm not going to take any shit from him?" I asked. "Like you said, he's just like his father. If Evon felt threatened by Daytona, then it stands to reason that Eddie would feel threatened by me. Add to the mix the fact that I'm leading the points right now. He hasn't gotten any wins yet, and I have, so I've got the extra ten bonus points coming when the Chase starts, which will leave him further behind."

"Yeah, but most of the guys are used to you being around, just like they got used to Daytona being a competitor. You'd think he'd get off his high-horse and accept the fact that you're not going anywhere," Doug argued.

"But if he's as much like his father, you never know what he might try on the track. I mean, if he did run me off the road, what do you think he's gonna do given the chance on the track? All because I told him to stop acting like a diva," I pointed out.

"Speak of the devil," Matt nodded towards the walkway. Turning, I saw Eddie storming over to us.

"What the hell is your problem?" he shouted at me.

"What are you talking about?" I asked.

"You told that cop I ran you off the road? He said he could arrest me right now if he wanted to. Just cuz you're pissed about an argument at the dealership? What's the matter? Did all the fans leave after I did?" he kept shouting.

"Piss off Eddie. I didn't tell the cop anything. Somebody driving behind you saw the whole thing and called the police. It was whoever was behind you that reported what happened. And if your car has all the evidence that matches up to the scrapes on the drivers' side of my car, and your prints are all over the interior, what conclusion do you think they're gonna come up with? You really think that story's gonna fly that somebody must've stolen your car, ran me off the road and then returned your car to the parking lot just to make you look bad? Give me a break." I turned to walk into the motorhome.

"You bitch!" Eddie lunged at me, catching me off-guard in a chokehold. Matt and Kyle both jumped forward to intervene, but before they could reach me, I'd managed to flip Eddie over me onto his back on the concrete in front of me. Knocking the wind out of him, he looked up at me, gasping for air. Putting my foot on his chest, digging my heel in slightly, I looked down at him.

"I told you before, I'll kick your ass any day of the week Eddie. Don't underestimate me. And don't fuck with me. Now get the hell away from me." I moved my foot off his chest as his crew chief came running over.

"What the hell happened over here?" he shouted.

"Keep your driver away from me. Next time, I won't be so gentle on him," I warned.

"Holy crap Brianna!" Matt exclaimed as Eddie was led away by his crew chief. Doug still looked shocked, sitting in his chair.

"What's the matter Doug? Cat got your tongue?" I laughed.

"You flipped him right over you! He's gotta have at least fifty pounds on you! And you're wearing high heels!"

"Doug? Did you somehow miss the fact I was a cop in Greensboro? I do know a little about self-defense you know. I've taken down guys bigger than Eddie. It probably would've been easier if I wasn't in heels, but hey sometimes you gotta do what you gotta do," I explained, finally kicking off my shoes to stand barefoot as Kyle stood beside me, shaking his head.

"Yeah. You're more like Daytona than I even thought," Matt pointed out. "She would've done the same thing."

"Well, what was I supposed to do? Let him choke me until one of you pulled him off me?" I laughed. "I would've been the one on the ground then. I'm just faster than you guys, that's all. Guess instinct just kicked in when he grabbed me."

"You do realize that's just gonna piss him off even more, don't you? Too bad nobody got that on tape to air on the news tonight," Matt joked.

"Hey. If he wants a rematch, I'm more than willing to go a second round," I laughed as I saw the state trooper approaching. As he got closer, I could see he had some paperwork in his hands.

"Hey Brianna? You got a minute?" he asked.

"Sure thing. What's up?" I asked. "You missed the excitement you know. Eddie was just here."

"Really? What did he have to say?" After I repeated the story, the trooper shook his head.

"Man. That boy's a whole lotta stupid, ain't he? Didn't anybody warn him who he was up against?" he paused when he saw the shocked look on my face. "Yeah, I know you used to be a cop. That's why I came over here now. We managed to lift some pretty good prints off the interior of Eddie's vehicle. I was hoping you'd take a look at them."

"Sure. But why do you want me to look at them?" I took the paper and a couple plastic cards he held out to me.

"Well, I figure you should see the evidence before I take it down and file my report. I know it's not normal protocol to let somebody not involved in the investigation see the evidence, but I figured we can make an exception here, considering your background."

I held the plastic cards against the fingerprint card that Eddie had submitted. They were a perfect match. I looked at the state trooper.

"They were perfectly aligned at three and nine. Exactly where you'd grip the steering wheel if you're running at a high rate of speed. We found a couple partials, that all look like they match up too, and nothing smudged where you'd think somebody else might've held the wheel," he explained.

"So I guess it's safe to say Eddie lied about where he was when the accident happened," I replied.

"Yep. And his crew chief covering for him too. That's obstruction of justice, but you know that already," the trooper agreed. "We're just waiting for the warrant to arrive for his arrest and the prisoner transport van. Then we'll take him into custody and have him charged with reckless driving, and leaving the scene of an accident. And we'll charge the crew chief with obstruction. I'll make sure they ask to deny bail. Just to make sure he doesn't try to retaliate on the track tomorrow during the race. I remember what happened when his father got into it with Daytona years ago."

"Well, I don't know about anybody else, but I wanna see him get cuffed," Doug stood up. "Why don't we head over to the garage to watch the big show?" Matt and Doug started walking towards the garage, as Kyle and I walked a little distance behind with the state trooper.

"Listen, I want to thank you for all your help today," I started.

"Just doing my job, ma'am," he paused. "Besides, maybe I'm a little biased but I happen to be a fan of yours. I never liked him from the first race he ran. Guess his name was working against him. I didn't like what his Daddy did to Daytona. It's true sometimes you know that the apple don't fall far from the tree."

When we got back to the garage, we were met by another state trooper who handed over a sheet of paper. Looking it over, my escort nodded and handed it back, looking around for Eddie. I could see a couple reporters and camera crews standing off to one side, and I walked over to Doug and Matt.

"Do either of you have anything to do with the circus over there?" I asked, nodding towards the media.

They both looked at me, feigning innocence.

"Yeah, I know it was one of you. Y'all just gotta dig the knife in deeper, don't you? Like it's not gonna sting enough for him to get arrested, but for it to make the evening news too? You are sneaky." I laughed with them, seeing Eddie walking towards his garage stall with his crew chief.

"Edward Ibsen?" one of the troopers asked. Eddie paused and turned to walk towards us.

"Is there something else I can help you with?" he asked. "I already submitted my fingerprints and my statement about where I was when Brianna had her accident. My crew chief verified I was here. What else do you need from me?" He stopped in front of the troopers. I could see Doug motioning to the media to start filming.

"Edward Ibsen. You are under arrest for reckless driving, as well as leaving the scene of an accident. If I could have you charged with stupidity, I'd do it too. Please put your hands behind your back," the trooper continued reading Eddie his rights as he handcuffed him. As he and his crew chief were both loaded into the back of the prisoner transport van, Eddie looked out at me.

"I'm gonna get you for this Lane! This isn't over you know!" he shouted as the cameras continued to roll. I shook my head, turning to walk back to the motorhome.

"Brianna! Can you tell us what that was all about?" one of the reporters called out. I paused before answering.

"You'll have to get your information from the state police. I'm sure they'll provide whatever you need to know," I replied, as I started walking again. Kyle, Doug and Matt walked with me and we returned to the motorhomes, sitting out in the sun to talk about the next day's upcoming race.

* * * * *

CHAPTER FORTY-ONE

Sunday morning, Doug and Matt joined us for breakfast in our motorhome, bringing with them the local paper. Eddie's arrest had been shown on the late news Saturday night and we found a small section about it in the article highlighting the cars to watch during the race.

"Boy is Evon gonna be pissed when he finds out Eddie got arrested," Matt pointed out as I set the paper down.

"I'm sure he's found out by now. If he watched the news last night, unless Eddie called him to try to get him bailed out of jail last night," Doug replied.

"It'll be interesting to see how NASCAR handles it," Kyle added.

When we went to the drivers' meeting later in the morning, Dave addressed the room after he went through any rules changes and reminding us of the mandatory pit road speed for the days' race.

"Now, I know most of you have either seen last night's news or read the paper this morning. And I'm sure you all want to know what's going on with Eddie's car after the unfortunate incident yesterday. We will be pulling his entry for today and his car will not be permitted to join the starting grid, whether he returns to the track today or not. I don't think I have to remind any of you that behaviour such as his will not be tolerated, in the garage or anywhere that NASCAR is involved. Whether you're at the track, at a public appearance or out on your own, you still need to remember you're public figures and your actions reflect on the sport. So if anybody else has any inclination to repeat Eddie's performance yesterday, keep in mind the consequences he's gotten. Now, I'll see y'all out on pit road for pre-race activities later on. Have a safe race everybody," Dave closed the meeting and the room quickly emptied.

Emerging back out in the sunshine, we were immediately approached by a large group of the media, all shouting out questions at us.

"Brianna! Can we get a quote about what happened yesterday with Eddie?"

"Brianna! What's the next step regarding the accident you and Eddie were involved in?" I held up my hand to silence them. When they were all quiet again, I finally spoke.

"I'm only going to make a brief statement here, and then I hope y'all can let this rest. Yes, I was involved in an accident yesterday involving my personal rental vehicle. Yes, I was run off the road on my way here. The evidence collected by the state police was what prompted them to arrest Eddie. I didn't see the driver of the other vehicle, so I can only go by what evidence the state police told me they'd collected. As far as Eddie's arrest is concerned, I can't comment on that. Anything regarding his arrest or any charges that may or may not be laid against him, you'll have to contact the Michigan State Police for a statement or his team owner. Thank you," I turned to walk away.

"Brianna? Do you think this has anything to do with you buying Daytona's old team and the feud between Daytona and Evon years ago? Could this be payback for Evon being barred from NASCAR?" somebody called out.

"I can't really comment on what prompted this incident. Whether it has something to do with Evon and Daytona, I really wouldn't know. That feud if you want to call it that, happened long before I ever came into the sport. Right now, I'd like to go get ready to run a good race today."

Smiling, I turned and walked away, surrounded by Kyle, Matt and Doug. When Jake arrived that morning, we headed over to the souvenir trailer while Kyle headed to the garage to get the team started setting up the pit.

I slipped in the back door of the souvenir trailer and greeted Joyce. I usually tried to make an appearance at the souvenir trailer at least once during the weekend to sign autographs and meet with the fans that were in attendance.

"Brianna! You have got to see the number of trade-ins we've gotten this weekend!" she exclaimed.

"There've been a lot?" I asked, surprised. I hadn't thought the fans would really take me up on the offer to trade in their shirts. But it was pleasant surprise, knowing I'd made a few new fans over the weekend.

"I've filled four garbage bags so far, and just started a fifth," she replied, pointing at the bags stacked in the storage space. "What are you going to do with them all?"

"Make sure they get sent into the track before the end of the race so they can get loaded into the hauler to go back to the shop. I told the crowd I was gonna use them as shop rags and that's what I intend to do," I laughed.

"Brianna! Will you sign my shirt?" somebody in the crowd called out.

"I sure will," I replied, turning to grab a pen to sign with.

"Brianna! Brianna's here! Come on! Let's get a picture!" The crowd around the trailer quickly grew as word spread that I was there. After signing autographs and helping to run the trailer for an hour, I waved to the crowd and thanked them for their good wishes.

"Thanks everybody! Enjoy the race!" I called out.

"Good luck Brianna!" most of them yelled back as I slipped out the door and climbed back into the golf cart with Jake.

Getting back to the motorhome, I headed inside to get ready for the race. Once I was changed into my firesuit, I met Doug and Matt between our motorhomes and began the walk to pit road for pre-race activities.

"How'd it go at the trailer?" Matt asked.

"Great. Joyce has got half a dozen bags of Eddie's shirts that his fans traded in for one of mine. So I shouldn't have to buy shop rags for a while," I laughed.

"You're seriously gonna use his shirts as shop rags?" Doug asked.

"Why not? That's about all they're good for," I replied.

When we got to pit road, pre-race activities were set to begin and we got into line for the driver introductions. Kyle stood with me, letting me know the car had passed inspection without a problem and was sitting out on the starting grid, my helmet and gloves on the seat. He would be walking down the grid to wait by the car while I took my trip around the track after driver introductions.

When my name was called, I jogged up the steps and waved to the crowd. The cheers escalated and I smiled as I shook hands with the various dignitaries there.

Matt was waiting for me at our designated truck and climbed up beside me before letting the driver know we were ready. As we headed out onto the track, Matt turned to me.

"Hard to believe it's my last race already. I gotta say, it's been a fun ride the past two months. I never realized until I got back in the car just how much I missed driving."

"Getting that itch to come back full-time?" I joked.

"Daytona would probably kill me if I said I wanted to come back to racing. But I'm happy being home with her and Sam. It's nice to be able to enjoy my family instead of missing so much. I know watching the races at home is nothing like actually being here, but it's nice to just sit back and relax, knowing I don't have to worry about if the car's fast enough, if we've got the supplies we need, if the car's gonna pass inspection. It's nice being a spectator now," he explained.

"Well, it's been an awesome experience running against you the past two months. I'm glad Doug asked you to fill in for him," I replied. "You know you taught me a lot when I bought the team from you and Daytona, but I think I've learned so much more being able to race against you every week too."

"You know, I was thinking about what Doug said before about the two of you combining teams," Matt paused.

"You should know I'll never leave Ford. As long as they're still willing to partner with me, I'm sticking with them. So unless you can convince Doug to switch from Chevy, I don't think we'll ever have a partnership at all," I pointed out.

"Well, that's what I was thinking. I'll have a talk with him and see if I can lead him down the right path to switching teams," Matt laughed. "If you're willing to join forces with him, professionally speaking, that is."

"It's worth thinking about, I suppose. I mean, we've done awesome the past two months working together, even if we are on opposing teams. And it'd be nice to have a teammate out there on the track. I like that NASCAR mandated the four-car rule for these bigger multi-car teams. I know it's a lot harder for us little guys to get a break anywhere when there are teams that all four drivers and teams are swapping information. But with the new car they brought in, it's nice to be on a more level playing field with the bigger teams."

When we made it back around to pit road, Matt and I hopped down from the back of the truck and walked together to our cars near the front of the starting grid. Doug and Kyle were waiting there for us. During the national anthem, the four of us stood together, while our teams were lined up in our pit stalls. We had chosen our pits together so we could hopefully work together during the race and pit stops.

Going through the routine of fastening the safety belts and pulling on my helmet, I focussed on clearing my mind of any outside distractions before the green flag. As Kyle hooked up my radio and the air lines, I secured my steering wheel and pulled my gloves on. When the grand marshal made the announcement to start our engines, Kyle locked the window net into place and headed over to our pit stall to take his place on the pit box.

"Okay Brie. We've got four hundred miles here. The lights are out on the pace car, so green next time by. You've got a great car under you, so take care of it, and don't use it all up at the beginning," I heard Kyle's voice coming through the radio as I warmed the tires along the back stretch.

"Let's do this," I replied, watching the leader ahead of me. When the green flag flew, Matt quickly tucked his car in behind me and we worked together to try to pass the two lead cars. Working together, we easily passed the leaders and pulled away from the rest of the field in a four-car draft. It didn't take long for a caution to fly as one of the rookie drivers spun and tagged the wall on the backstretch.

"We've only got twenty laps on the tires, Brie. You want to come in for fresh ones?" Kyle asked as I passed under the yellow flag.

"No. I think we're good. Unless we run over some debris on the back. I'll watch out for it though. Let's hold off as long as possible. I kinda like the view out here. I don't wanna give up the lead yet," I laughed.

"Ten four. It's your call," he replied.

Taking the green flag once the track was clear again, Matt and I pulled away from the rest of the field. When the next caution came out, and we were finally ready to make pit stops, I radioed to Kyle.

"Four tires and gas. Y'all know the drill. Everything's perfect."

"You heard the lady," Kyle replied. "Okay, pits are open so next time by, come on in, Brie."

Waving to Matt, I dropped down to the apron of the track, closely followed by Matt's Chevy. Matching our pit times, we headed back out to the track.

"You've got one car slow in Turn Two Mom. You'll have to go high to pass," Jessika informed me.

"Thanks Jess. I see it." Travelling up the banking to pass the other car, I watched in my mirror as Matt followed me. With about a car and a half-length between us, there was just enough room for the other car to slide between us. Suddenly, the other car veered up the track, cutting between me and Matt and catching my rear bumper. Spinning my car, I turned into the spin to try to minimize any damage and hopefully keep the car off the wall.

"What the hell?" I thought, getting the car back under control.

"Mom! Are you okay?" I heard Jessika asking.

"Yeah. I'm gonna have to come back in to get that fender looked at," I replied. "Kyle, get ready. I'm coming in."

"Got it. We'll be ready. Hopefully the fender's not rubbing too badly and you can get back through the field."

Coming to a stop in my pit stall, the crew surrounded the fender, pulling it away from the tire to keep it from rubbing and cutting down the tire. The last thing I needed was to have a tire blow at race speeds.

"Okay Brie. You're good to go. There's not too much damage. You're gonna have to work to get back up front though," Kyle told me.

"Hey, I've never backed down from a good challenge. You want to go see if that rookie's got something to say for himself?"

"Already got somebody on it Brie," Kyle replied.

Losing a lap in the pits, I slowly worked my way back up through the field until I was behind the leader again. With any luck, when the next caution came out, I'd get NASCAR's free pass and get my lap back. I didn't want to have to work my way back through the field a second time, but I knew that would be a lot easier than trying to pass the leader and make up my lap the hard way.

When the checkered flag flew at the end of the race, I'd managed to work my way back up to fifth. Matt was in front of me in fourth. After I finished my post-race interviews, I headed back to the motorhome to shower and change before we headed back to the airport for the flight home.

Once we were in the air and headed home, Matt turned to Doug.

"So, Doug. I gotta ask you something," Matt began.

"If you're hoping to talk me into another couple races in my car, you can forget about it. I can't wait to climb back into the car and strap in for a race," Doug laughed.

"No, actually I'm quite happy to fade back into retirement and enjoy spending time with my family instead of rushing off to another race," Matt replied. "What I was going to ask was how much in love with Chevy are you? I mean, are you open to the idea of switching teams at the end of the season?"

"What are you talking about?" Doug asked. "You're not driving or owning a team anymore. Or are you thinking about coming back as an owner next season? Is that what this is about?"

"Nope. I'm not coming back. Just trying to be a negotiator here," Matt laughed. "If you're willing to switch to Ford next year, I think I might have a really good teammate for you to work with."

"You mean Brianna? We've already been working together this season. What's the difference if I switch to Ford?"

"Well, we were thinking if you two consolidate your two teams, you could both be contenders for the Chase next year."

"I would've been a factor this year if I hadn't had my wreck back in June," Doug argued.

"That's true. But think about how well the two teams have been running when you've been sharing information the past eight races. And think about how well you'd run for an entire season under the Ford banner," Matt pointed out.

"You really think merging the two teams is gonna work?" Kyle asked.

"Why not? You look at all these other two and three car teams that are running. The last single car team to win a Cup was Wayne Davis. And look how long ago that was. It was before his team was bought by me and Daytona. I think it's great that you guys have a chance to lead the Chase for the Cup this year. And I'm really holding out that Brianna is gonna be the one making the big speech this year, but I also know how much easier it is to run as a two-car team."

"Well, I'd be willing to think about it, if Brianna's open to it," Doug replied, looking to me.

"I'd be willing to consider it," I added.

"Well, good then. Why don't you both think about it for the next week, and then sit down and discuss it seriously in the next couple weeks?" Matt offered.

"Yeah, like we don't have enough to think about and plan in the coming weeks," Kyle laughed.

"I don't know what you're worried about," I said. "Jess and I are the ones doing most of the wedding planning. All you have to do is show up."

"True. But you know if there's anything you want me to do, all you have to do is say the word," Kyle agreed.

"So, speaking of the wedding. Have you two finally settled on a date?" Doug asked.

"Yeah. I think so. We're aiming for the day before the Homestead race. If I can get the track to work us into the schedule," I revealed. "I think we should be able to take care of it before the Nationwide race. Which reminds me, I need to come over and see Daytona sometime soon. Matt, do you think she'd mind if I stopped in sometime this week?"

"I don't see why not," Matt replied. "She said before you were welcome to stop by anytime. I think you know the way through the yard."

"Thanks. Let her know for me that I'll be stopping by one day this week then, please," I asked.

"No problem."

When our flight landed in Mooresville, the teams scattered to their cars and headed off to their homes as Kyle and I headed home, dropping Matt off along the way. Jessika had offered to drive Doug home so she could spend some time with Mandy before she came home. Mandy had finally decided on a major to apply to university and was going to be heading off to Raleigh in another week to get settled. Jessika had planned that she'd take a year off before she applied to the University of North Carolina in Charlotte.

Having the house to ourselves, Kyle and I made dinner together and headed out to the patio to watch the sunset as we ate and talked about our wedding plans. It seemed every spare minute was spent discussing the wedding. As Kyle stood up to take the dishes back into the house, I looked up to see Matt walking with Daytona through the back gate connecting our two yards. Standing up to meet them halfway, Daytona surprised me with a hug.

"I hear you're getting married," she smiled.

"Yeah. Kyle finally convinced me it was time to move on," I revealed. We sat together beside the pool as Matt excused himself and headed into the house to join Kyle.

"Matt said you wanted to talk to me?" she asked.

"I was going to come by and see you sometime this week. It didn't need to be tonight," I laughed.

"Well, it's been a while since I've been out visiting. Usually everybody comes to me, and I decided it's time I start getting out again," Daytona explained.

"I'm glad you said that. Because that's one of the things I wanted to talk to you about," I hesitated. "Obviously, you know Kyle and I are getting married. I don't know if Matt mentioned to you that we're planning the wedding for November in Homestead."

"He briefly mentioned it. Something about doing it on Saturday before the Nationwide race."

"Yep. And seeing as you've been such an inspiration in my life, I was wondering," I paused.

"What?"

"Well, I was wondering if you'd possible come to Homestead for the wedding?" I asked.

"Come to Homestead?" Daytona looked shocked.

"I'll understand if you say no, really I will. But just think about it. I'd love it if you'd agree to be my matron of honor."

"Oh! Wow. I don't know Brianna. I mean, I hardly ever leave the house anymore. And to show up at the track on one of the biggest weekends of the year, and for your wedding, I don't know if I'm ready for that yet," she revealed.

"Promise me you'll think about it. I've still got three month, so we've got lots of time. I just figured you were such an inspiration to me when I was getting into the sport. If it weren't for you, I literally wouldn't be where I am today. You taught me that a woman can be a race car driver and can succeed," I explained.

"I can't make you any promises, but I will think about it," Daytona replied with a smile.

"Thank you! That's all I ask is that you consider it," I exclaimed.

"Now. What's this I hear you're thinking about merging teams with Doug Madison?" she demanded.

"Actually, it was your husband's idea, not mine. I mean, Doug had brought it up once before and I thought he was joking. And then Matt started talking about it before the race today. I hadn't really given it any serious thought, since we're driving for opposing manufacturers. But Matt seems to think it's a good idea. And you know I've always valued any of the advice either of you have given me. I don't think I'd be leading the points right now if it wasn't for all the help I've gotten from you both over the past few years."

"Well, if you do decide to combine your teams, I hope it all works out for you. I know Doug's a great driver. And he'll work with you, instead of against you, especially as your teammate. I was really surprised when I saw you jumping over the wall to help him out when he crashed back in June. I don't know if I would've done that myself. But then, I have done things in my life that I'd never expected I'd have to do," Daytona trailed off.

"You mean like shooting somebody to save your own life?" I asked.

"Like shooting somebody to save my own life. And to protect my daughter. Who knows what that crazy bitch would've done if I hadn't shot her. I did what I had to do to protect what was mine. And if I had to do it all over again, I would. Of course, I'd make sure I shot her while she was ranting, instead of waiting until she started pulling the trigger. It'd be nice to not have been forced into retirement the way I was," Daytona shook her head.

"We all do what we have to do in life. You know that I know what it's like to take somebody's life. It's eerie how similar our lives are in some ways. I mean, we both lost somebody very close to us in senseless crimes. We both killed to save our own lives. Aside from both being amazing women stock car drivers, that is," I laughed.

"You know about Rick?" she asked.

"Yeah. I heard about the shooting. I used to always read the paper online from home. So that's how I heard about it. And I remember seeing him at the bar once in a while after it first opened before I moved down here."

"That was a rough time for me, you know. Right after he died. If it hadn't been for Matt, I never would've made it through those months. I mean, he saved me from myself. I started drinking heavily after Rick's death. I just didn't want to feel anything. I did whatever I could to just numb myself. And then after I knocked myself silly one night and ended up in the hospital, Matt finally got through to me that I was still living and needed to move on with my life. I think that's when I realized how much I loved Matt."

"I remember when you first starting racing, all we ever heard about was the fighting. I was so surprised when you guys announced you were getting married," I laughed.

"Yeah. I think that threw everybody for a loop. That's gotta be the last thing anybody ever imagined would happen to us. Most people were probably taking bets on which one of us would run the other one over and when," Daytona laughed with me. "But I've gotta admit, he's the best thing to happen to me. I don't think I would've made it through the time after Rick's death without Matt beside me. He was so supportive, and so patient, just waiting for me to figure out I was in love with him."

"Almost like a fairy tale come true, eh?" I asked.

"Almost. Just with more drama than your normal fairy tale," Daytona agreed. "I know if I had stayed with Drew instead of finally coming to my senses, I wouldn't be as happy as I've been with Matt. Kinda like if Craig hadn't died when he did, what would you be doing now?"

"I'd still be working undercover probably. Trying to clean up the streets and get rid of the drug dealers. We managed to get a few off the street with that last bust, but for every one you lock up, there's three more waiting to take their place. I certainly wouldn't be here today," I explained.

"Exactly. Who knows what life holds for any of us, but you know at the end of the day, you do what you have to, what's best for you, your family and your future. I'm so glad you were the one to take over the team after I got shot and Matt decided to retire. You've taken the team exactly where I would have. Right back into the Chase. I had hoped to keep racing until Sam was ready to get in the seat, and be able to be the first mother-daughter team. But I'm glad I'm still here to be able to watch her grow up and fall in love, get married someday and have children of her own. What about your daughter? Does she have any interest in taking over the ride when you retire?"

"Nope. I mean, she absolutely loves the sport. And she loves being at the track with me every week. But she's leaning more towards taking over the public relations in another couple years. Jake's been great with teaching her what he does on a day-to-day basis, and she's picked up pretty easily on what his job is. So whenever he's ready to retire, we'll have somebody to replace him with. Until then though, she's happy being my spotter."

"I'm glad she decided to do something involved in racing. Sam's leaning towards other things right now. She loves watching the races every week, and used to love going to the track with us, but after I got shot, she withdrew into herself for a while and it took a long time before she finally came out of her shell again. Lately she's been talking about going into teaching. But she's got a long time until she's gotta make a decision. And she knows that no matter what she decides to do, Matt and I will support her every step of the way."

Just then, Matt and Kyle joined us.

"How's everything going out here?" Matt asked.

"Great. Just getting to know each other a bit more," Daytona replied. "You know, I never realized until now that I didn't really know much about Brianna. Just the little bits and pieces of information that you passed along to me. I wish you'd gotten me out of the house and over here sooner."

"Well, I knew you'd be over here when you were ready," Matt pointed out. "We all know nobody can force you to do something you don't want to do."

"True," Daytona laughed.

"Well, I should get you back home so our neighbors can get some rest. We've all had a pretty busy day today," Matt stood and held out his hand to Daytona.

"Thanks for coming by tonight. It was really great to talk to you," I said as they headed towards the back gate.

"I'm glad I came tonight. I'll think about what you asked me and I'll let you know soon, okay?"

"Take your time. Like I said, I've got three months to get everything all planned out. No rush. Have a great night you two," I waved at them.

Kyle and I watched as they made their way through their back yard to the patio doors. When Matt closed and locked the door behind them, Kyle put his arm around me, holding me close.

"So? How was your visit with the great Daytona Hudson?"

"It was great. She's so awesome. I really wish I could've had the chance to race against her. I hope now that she's come over once, she'll start coming out more often. I asked her to be matron of honor for me when we get married."

"Really? What did she say?" Kyle asked.

"She said she's gonna think about it. You know she hasn't been to the track since before she was shot. And aside from going to doctors' appointments and the occasional outing with Matt, she doesn't leave the house. I really hope she agrees to come to Homestead with us. It'd be awesome to have her at the track just once. Especially if we win the Championship this year."

"You mean when we win," Kyle pointed out.

"No guarantees you know. I'm glad you're being optimistic about this, but you never know. Anything can happen in the next few races. It just takes one or two bad days, and we're done. But for us to win the Championship, me being the second woman to do it, with the first woman champ in my pits that day, that would just be perfect."

*****

CHAPTER FORTY-TWO

When the Chase for the Sprint Cup officially began in New Hampshire, my points lead was cut as the top twelve in points were reset as per NASCAR's rules. I had an extra thirty points added for the three wins I'd gotten through the first twenty-six races. Starting the race in Loudon, I would be second in points, since my next-closest competitor had won one more race than I had.

Walking through the pits before qualifying, I paused to take a few pictures with fans and sign some autographs. Kyle was waiting at the car when I arrived, as the crew made some last minute adjustments.

"Everything okay?" I asked, leaning on the car.

"Yeah. We thought we had an oil leak, but it seems to be fine now," Kyle explained. "We're good to go here. It's all up to you now."

"No pressure," I laughed.

"Hey, I know you can handle it. You're the best woman out there," Kyle joked.

"Hmmm… last I checked, the only woman out there," I shot back, looking across the garage. I saw Eddie walking into his garage stall with his crew chief, to prepare for his qualifying run. Eddie had returned to the track the weekend after his arrest, with stern warnings from Dave that he would be watched closely to make sure he didn't display any aggressive moves towards me on the track. Luckily, he hadn't run anywhere near me during the races since his arrest, but I knew there was a chance we'd end up somewhere close together sometime in the next ten races.

The representative from Ford had called me after Eddie's arrest to discuss with me what had happened. After hearing my side of the story, he assured me he would seriously consider whether or not to renew the sponsorship Ford had with Evon's team for the following year. I knew Eddie wasn't happy with how things had turned out since then, and he'd fallen further back in points, seeing as he hadn't won any races yet this season. I wasn't worried about him hurting me on or off the track, but I did wonder just how deep his hatred ran.

Trying to push thoughts of Eddie out of my mind, I walked around to the front of the car to take a look under the hood before the team closed it back up and secured the hood pins.

"So it's all good now?" I asked.

"Yep. No leak. Was just a little drip from over-filling it I think," Kyle assured me.

"Cool. It'd be nice to have a good run this weekend to catch up those extra points."

"You'll be great out there," Kyle put his arm around me.

"I hope so," I slowly climbed into the car and took a few minutes to focus myself before I turned to securing the safety belts. Once my belts were secure and Kyle had hooked up the radio to my helmet, I fired the engine to prepare to back out and head to the track. I heard another engine rumble shortly before mine and assumed the majority of the teams around me were getting ready to line up as well. Kyle locked my window net into place and walked along beside the car as I slowly backed out.

Watching my crew member directing me in the rear-view mirror, I turned the wheel to angle the car out before switching to first gear. I waved to Kyle as he walked back into the garage stall to retrieve his radio before he headed to pit road to wait beside the car for my qualifying run. Most of my crew had gone ahead to watch the cars ahead of me during their qualifying runs to see how the competition was doing. As I neared Eddie's garage stall, a flash of colour drew my attention.

Before I could react though, Eddie had backed into the side of my car, crumpling the drivers' door in towards my seat. Switching to a higher gear, I tried to drive the car forward, but Eddie continued to back up, pushing my car into the corner of the garage opposite ours. I could hear him revving the engine higher, attempting to push the car further into the wall, damaging both sides. Looking out the drivers' window, into Eddie's car I could see he hadn't even put his helmet on. Seeing the hatred in his eyes, I quickly unfastened my safety belts and hit the kill switch on my engine before I scrambled out of the seat over the roll bars to the opposite side of the car and I pulled my helmet off. I thought briefly about trying to squeeze through the window, but worried that I would get pinned between the car and the garage wall.

Finally, I could see a number of NASCAR officials surrounding our cars, and could hear them yelling to Eddie to shut off the engine on his car. One official reached through the opening in the window net and hit the kill switch before Eddie's crew arrived and began pushing his car away from mine.

"Brianna! Are you okay?" I could hear Kyle yelling.

"What the hell happened here?" Dave yelled as he arrived on the scene.

Crawling back across the roll bars into my seat, I dropped the window net and slowly climbed out of my mangled Ford and onto the rear deck lid of Eddie's car before climbing down and putting my feet on the ground again. Looking at the damage from Eddie's car, I shook my head in amazement.

"I can't believe he totalled my car in the middle of the garage," I exclaimed as Kyle put his arm around me.

"Are you okay?" he asked again.

"Yeah, I'm fine. The car took all the beating. Dammit. What the hell is his problem?" I looked around.

Eddie had finally climbed from his car, smirking as he looked over at me. My crew returned from pit road then, presumably having heard about the commotion on their radio, and began looking over the car from all angles to check out the damage. I knew we'd have to pull out the back up before I could qualify. I waved them over and gave them their instructions before I turned back to where Eddie was standing arguing with Dave. Walking over to join them, I could hear Eddie claiming innocence.

"Honest man, I didn't see her there. I dropped my gloves and when I bent down to pick them up, I musta hit the gas and next thing I knew y'all were yelling at me to shut the car down. I didn't realize I'd hit her until y'all told me," he explained.

"You lying son of a bitch!" I interrupted. "You knew damn well you'd hit me. I watched you looking in your mirror while you tried to drive my car through the garage wall. You knew exactly what you were doing."

"No way Brianna. I learned my lesson after Michigan. I wouldn't try to hurt you on or off the track. I know I fucked up back there, but I swear, I wouldn't try that shit again," he protested.

"Fuck you. You've been waiting and waiting for this chance. You're a fucking coward just like your father," I calmly replied.

"You bitch! Don't you dare talk about my father! You don't even know him! He'd be a champion ten times over if it hadn't been for that bitch you replaced. He was the best driver to ever run these tracks and you fucking well know it!" Eddie yelled, moving to confront me.

I could see his fists clenching and had the feeling if I pushed him, he would take a swing at me. Dave stood off to one side, watching and waiting to intervene if needed. I knew he'd let Eddie blow off some steam before requesting he go to the NASCAR trailer for a formal review of the incident.

"I know your father, just as well as I know you. Maybe I never raced against him, but I know him well enough just the same. And he was a coward, trying to kill a competitor, just because he couldn't measure up to Daytona. And you're a coward just like him for trying to make sure I don't make the race," I poked my finger into his chest to emphasize my point.

I could see out of the corner of my eye as Eddie brought his fist up towards my face. Seconds before he would've hit me, I reacted and grabbed his fist and forced him to his knees. Watching him wince, I heard a number of crew members around us begin to laugh. Looking into his eyes, I bent close to his face.

"If you ever try to hit me again, I am going to make you very sorry you ever decided to fuck with me little boy," I promised, squeezing his hand tighter. He had fairly small hands, for a man, and I could easily wrap my hand around his.

"Bitch! Let me go!" he yelled. "I'm gonna kill you!"

"You really think so?" I asked. "Good luck. I guess you never read my bio. I could kick your ass blindfolded, and you think you can hurt me? Think again douchenozzle. Have you forgotten Michigan already?"

I released his hand and gave him a shove away from me as Dave stepped forward.

"Are you gonna let her get away with that Dave?" Eddie whined as he stood up again. "She assaulted me! I've got witnesses!" I looked around and saw that every crew member in the area had turned their backs to us.

"Really? What witnesses Eddie?" I laughed. "Looks to me like nobody saw anything except you, me and Dave."

"She's got a point Eddie," Dave agreed. "And from where I was standing, you swung first which means Brianna was defending herself when she blocked your punch. So if you're done with your little temper tantrum, I want you and your crew chief in the NASCAR trailer. Now."

The tow truck arrived then to pull my car away from the garage wall and take it back to where my hauler was parked. I could see that my crew had unloaded my back up car already and was slowly pushing it towards our garage stall to check it over before I took it out to qualify. Once it was parked, the crew met my mangled car back at the hauler to take a closer look before they loaded it up for the return trip home. Kyle held my hand as we walked the hundred or so feet back to the garage stall I had backed out of just a few minutes before.

"Are you sure you're okay?" Kyle asked, looking at me closely.

"Yeah, I'm fine. I just can't believe he actually wrecked my car in the garage. I guess maybe he figured since he never gets close to me on the track, this was his best bet for trying to hurt me," I replied.

While Kyle and my crew checked over the backup car and prepared it for qualifying, I walked over to the hauler to retrieve my helmet from my primary car.

Doug was walking out of his hauler as I reached into my damaged car. Shaking his head, he circled my car, checking out the damage from all angles.

"Geez, Brie. What the hell happened? I've never seen damage quite like this," Doug exclaimed, whistling as he joined me on the drivers' side.

"You like it? I didn't even make it out of the garage. Surprised you didn't hear about it. But I'm sure there'll be highlights on ESPN tonight though." I tucked my gloves into my helmet and we began the walk back to the garage.

"Seriously. What happened? How did you do that in the garage? Wrap your car around a light pole?" Doug joked.

"I wish." Just then, we were passed by Eddie's crew pushing his car back to their team hauler.

"Hey guys! You switching to your back up too? Hope it's not an epidemic today!" Doug called out.

"Yeah, real funny. Like you don't know Eddie's been parked for the weekend," one of the crew replied.

"Parked? What the hell?" Doug paused as he caught sight of the rear of Eddie's car. The entire rear deck lid and wing had been forced up and buckled, crumpling like a sheet of paper. Doug stopped walking and put his hand on my arm, stopping me.

"The damage to your car; was that from Eddie?" he asked, the shock evident in his voice.

"Hey! You catch on pretty quick!" I joked. "There might be hope for you yet."

"No really. Come on, Brie. No joke. Did Eddie do that?" Doug looked closely at my face.

"Yeah. That was all Eddie," I explained. "Drivers' side is from his car. The other side is from where he tried to make me part of the garage wall." I continued walking.

"Holy shit Brie! Are you okay?" Doug caught up to me.

"I'm fine. Luckily NASCAR stopped him before he flattened me. And the car actually held up pretty well, considering," I assured him.

"Damn. I guess he really is a lot like his father. I don't get it though. Evon's beef was with Daytona. Why is Eddie doing this crap to you?" Doug asked as we reached my car.

"No idea. But if you figure it out, be sure to let me know, okay?" I turned to Kyle after setting my helmet on the roof of my car. "Are we good to go?"

"Yep. She's all set. Dunno if she'll be as fast as the primary but at least this one's raceable," Kyle replied.

"Good. It sucks to have to use the backup car and I know I have to go to the end of the line for missing my original qualifying slot. But let's see what we can do with the cards we've been dealt," I started to climb into my car.

"Are you sure you're okay?" Kyle asked. "Do you want to get checked out by infield care before you hit the track?"

"No, I'm good. Like I keep saying, the car took all the brunt of Eddie's rage," I settled myself into the seat and began the ritual of securing my safety belts again. Doug leaned down and put his hand on my shoulder.

"Good luck out there kiddo. I'll see you after qualifying." I nodded and focussed myself on all the details of qualifying. Once my belts were securely fastened and the air and radio hooked up, I fired the engine and motioned to Kyle that I was ready to go.

Getting out to pit road, I took my place at the end of the line and waited for my turn. After a final check that everything was in place and the safety belts were tight, I closed my eyes to clear my head of all outside distractions. Breathing deeply, I tuned myself into the car, hearing the rumble of the engine as it idled.

"Go get 'em babe."

My eyes flashed open and I looked over to Kyle. He had moved to stand on the pit wall. I keyed the button for the radio.

"What did you say?" I asked. Kyle turned towards my car.

"What?" he looked confused. "Radio's been quiet."

"Are you sure? I could've swore. . . " I trailed off.

"Positive. Maybe you're getting an overlap from another team," he offered.

"Yeah. Maybe." I knew otherwise though. *'Go get 'em babe'* had always been Craig's last words to me before every race I'd run in Greensboro.

Shaking my head to clear the memories, I saw the NASCAR official in front of me motioning that I could head out onto the track. Putting the car in gear, I slowly made my way down pit road. By the time I'd completed my warm up lap, I had my car up to full speed and felt confident as the green flag flew to officially start my qualifying attempt.

Two laps later, my crew erupted on cheers on my radio and I could see them celebrating on pit road. I knew the run was good; I just didn't know how good. Silently, I completed the cool down lap and dropped off the banking to coast down pit road. There, I was surrounded by my crew as well as the media.

When I finally brought the car to a stop and shut down the engine, Kyle dropped the window net and flashed a grin at me. He released the safety belts as I tucked my gloves into my helmet and hung it from the roll bars. Climbing out of the car, I jumped as the crowd erupted in cheers again.

"I take it that was a good run," I looked at Kyle.

"Good? Honey, you rocked it!" he exclaimed. "Not only did you get the pole, but you shattered the track record!"

"What? Seriously?" I was shocked as the news sunk in. Kyle nodded before hugging me. The media closed in then and I turned to address their questions.

* * *

Later that night as we relaxed together on the couch in the motorhome, I sat quietly with my back against his Kyle's chest, reflecting on the days' events. I was still in shock, although thrilled, that I had managed to get the pole with our back up car.

"Hey! Is everything okay?" Kyle asked.

"Sorry. What did you say?" I sat up to look at him, feeling guilty that I was too pre-occupied to pay attention to him.

"What's going on? You've been a million miles away since qualifying," he pointed out.

"I know. I guess it's just been a crazy day," I shook my head.

Kyle turned me back around and pulled off my shirt to start massaging my shoulders. I sighed as he worked on the knots I didn't realize I had.

"I think it's time for you to slow down and take a break," he said.

"You know as well as I do that I can't do that," I replied. "The Chase is just starting. And if we're going to win it, or at least be a factor at the end, we can't afford to slow down now."

"Okay. You're right there. But maybe cut back on your appearances. Focus on track time and the Chase," Kyle suggested.

"I'll sit down with Jake when we get home and see what we can do. You know I won't cancel any appearances, but I can get him to limit the number each week," I agreed.

"You know, I was thinking. Maybe it was good thing, what happened with Eddie today. I mean, that was an amazing run you had. I don't know that the primary car would've done the same thing."

"Well, I'm not about to thank him if that's what you're hinting at," I replied.

"I wouldn't even dream of asking you to do that," Kyle laughed.

"Good. Cuz I don't think Eddie wrecking our primary had anything to do with that run."

"Well, the backup is a backup for a reason. It's usually not as good as the primary. Unless we somehow go them mixed up. But I don't think so."

"No, they didn't get mixed up. But I think I had a little help out there today."

"What do you mean?" Kyle paused the massage, resting his hands on my lower back.

"This is gonna sound crazy but remember before I went out to qualify? I thought you'd said something and you suggested it was another team?"

"Yeah. What about it? You know we get frequency overlap sometimes. It's nothing new."

"It wasn't another team that I heard," I began. "It was a specific phrase that Craig used to say before every race back in Greensboro."

"Are you sure?" Kyle asked.

"Positive. It was part of our pre-race ritual. And I know I heard it today. It was as clear as you and I are talking now. And nobody else ever knew what he'd say to me once I was belted in to the car."

"So, you're telling me we're being haunted by the ghost of your dead husband?" Kyle asked.

"No. I don't think that's it at all," I laughed. "I think it was just his way of letting me know he's still watching over me. Keeping an eye on things and helping out where he can."

"Well, as long as I don't have to worry about shit flying around the room, or lights flashing on and off, or any of that other weird shit, I guess I can live with him helping put the car on the pole. Might be a good idea to keep that between us though. I don't think NASCAR has a rule about that," he joked.

"Yeah, I can just see that in the rule book and NASCAR trying to enforce it," I laughed, leaning back into Kyle's arms.

Pulling my hair to one side, Kyle began lightly kissing my neck as he unbuttoned my jeans. As he slid the zipper down, there was a knock at the door.

I groaned as I sat up, picking my shirt up off the floor. Slipping the shirt back on, I realized it was inside out as I opened the door.

"Uh, Brianna," Doug stammered, looking at my shirt and then past me to Kyle. "Sorry. I just stopped by to chat and hang out. I'll um, . . . I'll just see you tomorrow." He turned and walked away.

"Doug! Wait!" I called after him, but he continued walking without looking back.

"I wonder what that was all about," Kyle joined me at the door. "Do you want to go after him?"

"I'm sure if it was something important, he would've stayed," I replied, shaking my head as I closed and locked the door.

"Well, if you're not going to go see what he wanted, where were we? Oh yeah, this was off," Kyle pulled my shirt off again and picked me up to carry me into the bedroom.

* * * * *

CHAPTER FORTY-THREE

Sunday morning, I caught up to Doug as we headed to the drivers' meeting. Looking at him, I could tell right away he was hung over. Knowing he didn't usually drink the night before a race, I knew something was bothering him.

I looped my arm through his and handed him a bottle of water, smiling up at him.

"Hey sunshine," I began. "Did you get the plate number of the truck that hit you?"

"Funny," he replied. "Thanks."

"What the hell happened to you last night?" I asked. "If you wanted to talk, you could've stayed to talk you know."

"Naw, I could see I'd interrupted something. Figured it was better if I didn't stick around. Think I mighta had one or two more Buds than necessary though." Doug winced as we took our seats in the meeting room.

"You never drink the night before a race though," I pointed out. "Is everything okay?"

"Yeah. Just peachy," he replied sullenly.

"Bullshit. I'm not stupid Doug. I can tell something's bothering you. What is it?" I pushed.

"Nothing. Just let it go, okay?" he snapped, before standing up and walking away. Kyle joined me as I watched Doug sit down across the room.

"Damn, Brie. What'd you say to him now?" Kyle asked.

"Just tried finding out what he wanted last night. Something's bothering him, but he snapped when I asked what it was," I explained.

"I'm sure he'll tell you what it is when he's ready to talk. Maybe he struck out at the bar last night. You know how he likes to pick up every weekend," Kyle offered.

"Yeah, maybe," I replied absently, turning my attention to the front of the room as Dave called the meeting to order.

* * *

After the meeting Doug quickly left and disappeared before I could talk to him. I decided to wait for him to come to me if he wanted to talk and headed back to the motorhome to get ready for the race.

Jessika was waiting there and sat on the bed to talk while I changed into my firesuit.

"Everything okay sweetie?" I asked as I slipped my arms into the sleeves.

"Yeah," she paused.

"I know that tone. What is it?" I sat down beside her to put on my shoes.

"I don't know. Okay, it's Mark," she revealed.

"Did you have a fight?"

"No. That's the thing. We've never had an argument. I mean, we hang out all the time, but you know he's never actually asked me out. He's never kissed me even. He doesn't even hold my hand. It's like we're just buddies."

"Hmmm. Maybe he's shy about asking you out? And he knows what you went through with Jonathon. It's possible he's just giving you some time to heal from all that."

"Yeah, I guess so. Hey listen. I saw Doug before you came back. He was mumbling something to himself. Any idea what's up with him?"

"No idea. He wasn't very talkative when I saw him today. I know I've never seen him quite like that though. But I'm sure when he's ready to talk, he'll come see me. Or not. Maybe he's just having a bad weekend," I offered.

"He qualified pretty good though," Jess pointed out.

"I think it's personal issues, not professional," I suggested.

"Oh. Okay. Then I'm sure it's not anything I can help him with."

"Probably not. Are you ready?" I stood up and headed for the door, with Jessika close behind.

I signed a few autographs while she ducked into the hauler to get her radio and extra battery. Looking up as I handed back the last hat, I caught Doug watching me from the back of his hauler.

"Hey Doug!" one of the girls I'd signed for called out to him. "Can we get a picture of you and Brianna?"

"You sure can darlin'," Doug turned on the charm and smile as he joined us. "Who's gonna take the picture though?"

"I can," Jessika offered as she came back out of the hauler. Taking the offered camera, Jessika backed up as we all squeezed in together. After snapping a couple pictures, she handed the camera back and the fans headed off to get more autographs.

"I'm gonna head across the track now to beat the crowd, okay?"

"No problem sweetie. I'll see you after the race," I hugged her.

"Okay. Good luck. See you later Doug." I watched as she headed off. As she disappeared into the crowd, I turned back to find Doug standing right behind me.

"Listen Brie. I'm sorry about earlier," he began. "I was a real ass to you and I shouldn't have been."

"Hey, we've all had crappy days before. I know I've had my share. Are we good now?"

"I hope so."

"Good. You know if you ever want to talk, I'm here," I put my hand on his arm.

"No worries. It's nothing really. Let's just forget about it, okay?"

Kyle and Ricky joined us then for the walk to pit road for pre-race activities. Having the pole meant I would be last for driver introductions and had time for a couple interviews.

As I expected, I was asked about the incident with Eddie in the garage. I had sat down with Dave and NASCAR officials after qualifying and we had agreed that it would be best to discuss as little as possible with the media regarding the incident.

"I'm sorry. I would prefer to concentrate on today's race and the Chase for the Championship. I hope you can respect that and not dwell on an incident that has no bearing on the Chase," I recited each time I was asked.

Finally my name was called for driver introductions and I took my turn across the stage before climbing into the back of the truck for the customary parade lap. Returning to pit road, I jumped down from the truck and made my way through the crowd to the front row where Kyle waited beside my car. My crew was already lined up in the pit stall beside my car, waiting for the national anthem.

Kyle held my hand as the national anthem was sung and the crew lined up for high-fives after the jet fly-over. The crew headed back over the wall to get ready for the start of the race as I climbed into the car and started my own pre-race ritual. Before I pulled my helmet on, Kyle leaned in and kissed me deeply. He smiled as he pulled back from the kiss.

"Time to kick ass, right?" he handed me my helmet.

"Yep," I pulled my helmet on and fastened it as he hooked up the air and radio.

As the grand marshal was introduced, Kyle locked my window net in place. The crowd cheered as the forty-three engines roared to life and Kyle smiled to me before heading over to the pit stall.

"Okay boys. This is what we worked all year for. We've got an awesome start for the Chase. Let's try to keep our pit stops smooth, just like we've practiced. And I'll do my best to keep the car together," I encouraged my team as I followed the pace car around the track.

"You heard the boss. No room for mistakes here. Keep your eyes on the prize and let's stay out of trouble," Kyle added.

As we crossed the start-finish line, I watched as the lights went out on the roof of the pace car, indicating the last parade lap.

"Hey Jess. How are you doing upstairs?" I asked as we headed into Turn One.

"Doing good. Lots of sunshine. No clouds in sight. The view is awesome from up here. How's the view from your seat?"

"Could be better," I joked. "But I expect that'll change in the next sixty seconds or so."

"Well, just remember you've got forty-two hungry men behind you," Kyle reminded me.

"And they're gonna stay hungry if I have any say," I replied, checking my mirrors as we drove down the backstretch.

"Start's been waved off," Kyle said suddenly.

"Car in the wall on the back stretch coming out of Two," Jessika explained as the lights began flashing again on the pace car.

"Who the hell crashes on the parade laps?"

"One of the rookies," Jessika replied. "Looks like he bounced off the inside car and into the wall."

"Any damage to the other car? Who was it?" I asked.

"Doesn't look too bad from what I can see. It was Doug. He's on pit road now getting the car checked out."

"Damn, he must be pissed," I said. "Oh I see the car in the wall now. What a crappy way to get the day started."

"Guess we've got a few laps while they clean up. Any debris on the track over there?" Kyle asked.

"Doesn't look like it. He did a pretty good job of keeping it on the wall. Shouldn't take too long once the wrecker gets over here and hooks him up," I explained.

"He's out of the car, and walking around," Jessika said. "Emergency and safety crews are on scene now."

"Doug's heading back out onto the track now. Doesn't look like it'll take too long to get the race started now," Kyle added.

"Good. All this riding around behind the pace car is getting boring," I laughed.

Once the safety crew had cleared the crashed race car and Doug had taken his place in line, we prepared again for the green flag.

"Okay Brie. It's the real deal this time now. No screwing around. Just take it easy out there and don't use up the car all at once. Let's kick ass today. Green, green, green." I smoothly pushed the gas pedal down to pull out in front as the cars behind me fell back staying side by side.

The first fifty laps were uneventful as the cars behind me slowly worked themselves into a single file line. Occasionally, a faster car would pull out of line and pass a handful of cars.

"Doug's in the wall. Got a couple other cars involved on the front. Caution's out," Jessika radioed.

"Damn," I replied. "Okay. Let's use this caution to fill the tank and get four fresh tires. The car feels good, so no changes."

"Okay boys. Let's get four stickers on the wall. Pits should be open next time around," Kyle instructed the crew. "Y'all know the drill."

I followed the pace car around the track and through the wreckage on the front stretch. I could see Doug out of his car, checking out the damage. Shaking his head, he slowly walked over to the ambulance for the mandatory ride to the infield care center.

When pit road opened, I led the field off the banking and slowly travelled down pit road, watching for the giant palm tree on the Daytona's pit board. I watched as the team sprang into action. Checking the mirrors as first the right, then left, side tires were changed, I saw most of the other teams were going for four tires as well.

As soon as the car dropped back down, I headed out of the pit and onto the track. A couple other cars had passed by and I assumed they had only changed two tires, compared with our four.

"Okay Mom. You're fourth in line and NASCAR's stopping the field on the backstretch to get the cars out of the way," Jessika informed me.

"Thanks Jess. Any word on Doug yet? I noticed he was limping when he walked to the ambulance."

"No idea, Brie," Kyle replied. "I'm sure he'll be watching the race from his motorhome once he gets checked out and changes though."

"Well, one good thing about him being done, I've got a clear exit from pitting now." I pulled the car to a stop on the backstretch alongside the other cars and hoped the red flag wouldn't be a long one.

From where I sat, I could see the medical helicopter lift off from the helipad and head towards the hospital.

"Jess?"

"Yeah, Mom?"

"How's it looking on the front now?"

"Almost done," she explained. "They're just cleaning up the speedy-dry now."

"Yep, NASCAR says we're good to go now. Pace car should be leading y'all off any minute now," Kyle added.

"It's about damn time."

"Come on Brie. You know they've gotta make sure the track is clean to keep it safe," Kyle reminded me.

"I know. But that doesn't make sitting here any easier. Maybe we should see if we can rig up an MP3 player to the radio. Either that or y'all need to start entertaining me during red flags," I joked.

"Okay. Next red flag, we'll figure out some amusement for you," Kyle laughed as the cars ahead of me followed the pace car down the backstretch and into Turn Three. Weaving back and forth to heat the tires, I tightened the safety belts and adjusted the mirror.

"Here we go. Green next time by," Jessika told me.

"Okay Brie. Re-starting fourth, no need to storm the leader right away. Just stick close to the front three and we'll get the lead back in no time at all."

"No problem." As we headed through Turn Four, I closed in on the rear bumper of the third place car to draft as the green flag waved.

Suddenly, the car ahead of me slowed and I ran into the back bumper.

"Dammit! What the hell was he doing?" I yelled into the radio as he picked up speed and moved to catch up to the two lead cars.

"Breathe Brie. Caution's out. Bring it in and we'll take a look at it," Kyle tried to calm me.

I brought the car into the pits and the team surrounded the front as soon as the car came to a stop.

"Well?" I asked as I motioned to Kyle to find out the damage.

"It doesn't look too bad. We'll just have to keep an eye on your water temp. But it's just cosmetic by the looks of it," Kyle explained as the crew moved aside for me to leave the pit.

"Somebody better let that fucker know I'm not taking his shit. He's not in the Chase; he'd better stay outta my way."

"Brie," Kyle cautioned.

"Don't!" I fired back. "He pulls a stunt like that again, he's gonna end up in the wall."

"Just let it go Brie. The car is fine and I know you can make it back to the front. It's still early. We'll deal with him later," Kyle reminded me. "No point in pissing of the officials, right?"

"Kyle?"

"Yeah babe?"

"Don't talk to me right now. If we lose the Chase because of that asshole," I left the sentence unfinished.

"But I was just. . ." Kyle began before I interrupted.

"I know. But I don't wanna hear it."

Re-starting so far back increased the chances of losing a lap or getting caught in a wreck. I knew the car had been fast enough while I led the first fifty laps, but I didn't know how well it would run at race speeds with the nose wadded up like it was.

Leaving plenty of room between me and the car ahead, I silently worked my way through the gears as the green flag flew again. Waiting until I'd crossed under the flag, I steadily began passing the slower cars.

Twenty laps of caution-free racing later, I had managed to work my way back to inside the top twenty.

"Good work Mom," Jess radioed. "You're showing seventeenth. Lap times are faster than the leader right now."

"Good. So it shouldn't take too long for me to get back to the front and kick some ass." I pointed out. There was a minute's pause before Jess spoke again.

"Just keep in mind the nose damage. You might not run as well in clean air as you did at the start." I knew Kyle had to have sent her a message to have her remind me.

"Thanks Kyle," I addressed him. "I'd actually forgotten about that and thought the wrinkled hood was a new feature."

I continued working my way through the field and Jess let me know when I'd cracked the top ten. By the time the caution flag waved again, I was back on the rear bumper of the third place car.

Giving him a nudge to let him know I was there, I waved as I saw him check his mirror.

"Pits are open next time by. How ya doing out there Brie?" James asked.

"Good. Just four tires and gas. Maybe rip some tape off the grille to open it up a little. Water temp's gone up a little but nothing to worry about yet," I replied, wondering why it was James asking how things were and not Kyle.

"Okay. We'll be ready for you," James let me know.

Following the first three cars onto pit road, I was pitted the farthest down and watched as each one ahead of me pulled into their spots.

When I came to a stop in my pit and the crew went to work, I noticed Kyle wasn't standing on the pit box watching the pit stop. Looking around, I didn't see him anywhere in the pit. Heading out onto the track, I'd managed to hold on to the fourth spot.

"Where the hell did Kyle go?" I asked once I was back in line.

"He left," was James' reply.

"Are you fucking kidding me?"

"Said if you weren't gonna let him do his job properly, he wasn't gonna do it at all," James explained.

"I don't fucking believe this!" I exploded, hitting the steering wheel.

"Look. We're at the halfway point now," James reasoned. "We can make it the rest of the race without him if we have to. Focus on the race and you can sort it out later."

"James is right Mom. We can make the next hundred and fifty laps without him. And we'll figure out the rest of the season later," Jess added.

"Rest of the season?" I asked. "Are you telling me he quit? Completely?"

"Yeah. Sorry Mom."

"Un-fucking-believable!" I yelled at no one in particular.

"Mom. Lights are out on the pace car."

"Thanks Jess." I took a couple deep breaths, trying to re-focus on the race and the restart.

As the pace car headed onto pit road and the leader took the green flag, I moved down to a lower groove to avoid running into the back of the third place car again. I wasn't taking any chances of him pulling the same stunt as last time.

As I pulled my car even with his, he drove down into the side before moving back up the track. Pushing the gas pedal down as far as I dared, I pulled slightly ahead. Watching in my mirror, I saw as he hit the right rear fender to send my car into a spin. Unable to reverse the spin, I braced myself for the impact with the wall, and could hear Jess on the radio.

The hard hit knocked the breath out of me and the car bounced off the wall and into the oncoming traffic. I watched as the cars scattered around me as I slowly spun. Just as I thought it was over, another car came through the smoke hitting the rear corner and sending my car spinning again, igniting the gas tank.

I dropped the window net and released the safety belts as my flaming car spun down onto the grass. The inside of the car was quickly filling with smoke as I brought it to a stop.

Scrambling from my battered Ford, I ran across the grass before finally pulling off my helmet and HANS device and dropping them to the ground. Coughing from the smoke I'd inhaled, I dropped to my knees as the safety crew reached me.

"Brianna? Are you hurt anywhere?" One of the crew bent down beside me. I shook my head, taking deep breaths to try to clear my lungs. It hurt to breathe too deeply and I assumed it was from the safety belts holding me tightly in the seat as I bounced the car around.

"Let's get you to infield care and get you checked out anyway. Are you okay to stand?" He picked up my helmet and HANS device.

I nodded and slowly stood up, turning to wave at the crowd. I smiled as they erupted in cheers and walked over to climb into the back of the ambulance. One of the EMS techs handed me an oxygen mask as the ambulance slowly made its way around the track.

"Normal breaths, okay Brianna?" he instructed me. I nodded in acknowledgement as I tried to regulate my breathing. The trip to the infield care center was short and I emerged from the ambulance into James' waiting arms.

"Jess is on her way. That looked like some wild ride out there."

"Not quite how I wanted to finish the weekend," I smiled weakly. "But hey, it's just the perfect finish to my shitty weekend, right?"

"Hey. Shake it off and we'll kick ass next weekend," James walked me into the infield medical center.

"Okay Brianna. Let's take a quick look at you and make sure your car's the only thing you broke." The on-site doctor smiled, pointing to an exam table.

Sitting down, I winced as I unzipped the top half of my firesuit. Pain shot through me as I pulled my arms out and I tried not to scream.

"Okay. Where's it hurt?" the doctor asked, stepping forward.

"Right here," I indicated the lower half of my ribcage on the left side.

"Can you lift your shirt for me?"

Pulling up the left side of my shirt, the doctor carefully felt along my ribs, finding two fractured. I clenched my teeth, breathing shallowly and James moved to take my hand.

"Looks like you've got at least two fractured. I'm gonna send you to the hospital for x-rays and to get you taped up." The doctor pulled my shirt back down and James helped me down from the table.

"Thanks Doc. Do I have time to go change first?" I asked, leaning on James.

"Nope. Straight to the helicopter. I'm sure you can get somebody to bring your clothes to the hospital." The doctor led us out to the waiting helicopter. My crew was standing off to one side.

"I'm okay guys. Just a couple banged up ribs," I assured them. "Load up the hauler and we'll meet you at the airport for the flight home."

"Got it boss." The crew headed back to pack up.

"Mark?" I stopped him before he got too far.

"Take care of Jess for me. Ask her to bring my bag and drive her to the hospital to pick me up," I instructed him.

"Okay boss."

"And Mark?" I put my hand on his arm before he walked away.

"Yeah, boss?"

"Do you want to date my daughter?" I looked him in the eye.

"Umm. . . Yes ma'am," he stammered, blushing and looking down.

"Then ask her out already," I laughed.

"Oh. Okay." He smiled brightly as I shook my head.

"Come on boss lady. Now that you've scared the crap out of the poor boy, it's time to get you to the hospital and get you fixed up." James took my arm to help me into the helicopter.

When we arrived at the hospital, James headed to the waiting room while I was taken for x-rays. A nurse helped me remove my shirt while I waited my turn. Sitting in my bra with the top half of my firesuit tied at my waist, the nurse filled in the necessary paperwork. Handing me the clipboard to sign the various forms, I could see her eyeing the scar on my shoulder.

"What's the scar from?" she finally asked.

"Gunshot. Five years ago," I replied simply.

"How does a race car driver get shot?"

"You could ask Daytona Hudson that one. I was a cop when I got shot," I explained.

"Oh. Okay." My name was called then and I slowly stood and walked into the x-ray room.

Once the x-rays had been taken, the nurse led me to a cubicle to wait for a doctor. Focussing on a spot on the floor, I steadied my breathing to try to relieve some of the pain.

"Whatcha in for?" A familiar voice interrupted my thoughts. I looked up to see Doug peeking around the edge of the privacy curtain.

"Ran a stop sign," I joked. "Think they'll throw the book at me?" Doug walked over to sit beside me, whistling as he looked down.

"Damn girl. Looks like they threw a whole library at you. Is that all from today?"

"Yep." I looked down at the bruising that was quickly forming. "Guess you didn't get to see the fun."

"Saw the replay. We were just heading out of here to go to the airport. So I figured I'd hang out til you got here. In case you need a ride to the airport. Ricky met me here with the car." Doug took my hand.

"Thanks buddy," I smiled. "So what'd you end up with? I saw you limping to the ambulance."

"Just twisted my knee a little. They say I'll be back to normal in a week or so," he paused. "Or as normal as I can be."

"Don't make me laugh. It hurts too much." I gently held my side.

"I could kiss it better for you." Doug looked at me, lightly running his fingers across the bruising. I jumped at his touch and winced as the pain shot through me.

The doctor walked in then, carrying my x-rays. Clipping them up and flipping on the light, he pulled a pen out of his pocket and pointed out the fractures.

"Okay. So we've got two left side ribs fractured here," he began. "So we'll tape them up and give you something for the pain before we send you back on your way."

"Whatever." I shook my head. "Child's play compared to the rest of my day."

"That good huh? I hate to see how bad the rest of your day has been." The doctor brought over what he needed to set the ribs.

"I'm glad I'm not your car owner or on your crew, considering the mess you've made of TWO cars this weekend," Doug joked, standing to stretch.

"Two cars? In one weekend? Man, how pissed is the boss gonna be?" The doctor paused to look up at me.

"Oh geez. She's such a bitch when I wreck her cars. Add to the fact I made her crew chief quit today," I replied, trying to keep a straight face.

"What? Kyle quit? Are you serious?" Doug looked stunned. "What happened to the lifetime contract?"

"Well, maybe she'll go easy on you, knowing you got hurt," the doctor offered.

"Yeah. I'll try to go easy on myself, knowing I'm hurt," I laughed. The doctor looked from me to Doug.

"She IS the car owner," Doug explained, pointing to me.

"Oh. Cool." The doctor resumed taping my ribs.

"So tell me what happened with Kyle," Doug leaned on the exam table.

"I don't wanna talk about it right now, Doug." I closed my eyes.

"Okay. I wondered why James came to the hospital with you."

"Doug. Let it go. I may be hurt but you know I can still kick your ass." I opened my eyes and stared him down.

"Feisty. You know I like that," Doug joked, winking at me.

"Okay. You're all set." The doctor cut the tape and stood up. "I'll have the nurse bring you in something for the pain and then you can head out. But no more driving today and take it easy so those ribs can heal."

I gave him a mock salute before he left the room, shaking his head. The nurse came in a few minutes later, carrying a small cup with two pills in it and a glass of water.

"Demerol for the pain," she explained, handing me the cups.

"Awesome. Can I get some to go too?" I laughed.

"They won't eliminate the pain completely. But at least they'll numb it so you can get around." She handed me a small bottle that held four more pills. "Two more before bed if you need them. Then two in the morning. Anything more you'll need to see your doctor for a prescription."

"Thanks." I slipped the bottle into a pocket of my firesuit as I stood up.

"You might want to put your shirt back on before you head down the hall and out into the world," Doug suggested.

"Good idea." I carefully pulled my shirt back on and followed the nurse to the waiting room.

Jess was sitting between James and Mark, her head on Mark's shoulder as he held her hand. She jumped to her feet as Doug and I walked into the room.

"Mom! James told me you've got broken ribs," she looked at me closely.

"Yep. And some awesome bruises I'll show you on the plane." I turned to Doug. "I'll see you at the airport?"

"Yep. Ricky and I will be there," he leaned over to give me a kiss on the cheek. "Take it easy on the ride over."

"Thanks," I replied. "You too."

The six of us walked out together to head to our rental cars and then to the airport. Closing my eyes, I rested my head on the seat back, pushing down the pain and emotions of the day.

"Mom?"

"Yeah, sweetie?"

"I sent Kyle a message while we were waiting for you. He's waiting at the plane with the rest of the team."

"Whatever." I waved my hand, not worried about what he was doing. James held my hand the rest of the way to the airport and helped me out of the car when Mark pulled up at the curb.

Jessika and Mark met us at the car rental desk after he'd returned it to the lot as I paid the bill, and we walked together to the departure gate.

Doug and Ricky joined us a short time later and a quick head-count confirmed the team was all present and accounted for. Walking onto the plane, James pulled Kyle aside.

"Give her some space dude," I heard him say. "You both need some time to cool off. Deal with the shit from today when you get home. She's in a lot of pain right now."

Kyle nodded and headed towards the back of the plane. Lowering myself into a seat, James and Doug took the seats on either side of me as the rest of the team quietly prepared for take-off.

I noticed Jess and Mark across the aisle, still holding hands. Mark caught me looking and winked, mouthing a 'thank you' to me. I nodded back to him and smiled, silently hoping it would work out.

Once we were in the air and at cruising altitude headed home, I carefully stood up to address the team.

"Well boys and girls. I know this isn't quite the start we wanted for the Chase today. And I hate to think how much of a hit we took in the points today. We're gonna have to work all that much harder to catch up. I know we had some crazy shit happen today, hell this whole weekend. But if we all stick together and work together, we can get through it. I'm sorry I fucked up today. But if you guys will stick with me, I'll do everything I can to get us to the big table in Las Vegas." I looked around at my team all looking back at me.

"You know we're not going anywhere boss," Mark stood up. "Not any of us. We're in it to win it, through thick and thin." He looked pointedly at Kyle. There was a chorus of 'Hell yeah' and 'damn straight' from my team. I looked at Kyle but he refused to look at me.

"Okay then. Now that we've got that settled. Get some rest. We've got our work cut out for us over the next nine weeks." I carefully turned around and sat back down. James patted my knee.

"Great speech boss. You know these guys aren't gonna bail on you just because of one crappy weekend. I know they're all happy working for you. They don't wanna go anywhere else," James assured me. I looked at him, my thoughts unspoken. "Even Kyle. You know as well as I do he's crazy about you. He's not leaving you. Not personally and not professionally. He just needs some time to cool off and put things into perspective."

"We'll see." I put my head on his shoulder and closed my eyes to relax during the rest of the flight home.

* * * * *

CHAPTER FORTY-FOUR

When we landed, James collected our bags and we headed towards the parking lot. The team surrounded me as a crowd of fans approached. As flash bulbs went off around us, Doug came up behind me and spoke quietly.

"You okay to do this?"

"Probably not. But I'm gonna do it anyway." I smiled up at him. James stayed close to my side as I tapped the crew to let the fans through.

As the crowd pushed closer, James and Doug both held up a hand to stop them.

"Give her a little space please," James said firmly.

"Sorry folks. Just a little banged up from today. Don't mind signing autographs or doing pictures; I just need a little breathing room today." I held out my hand for a hat as Jess handed me one of her collection of Sharpie markers.

Once the crowd had dispersed, we continued on our way to the parking lot. As the team headed to their cars, I watched Mark walk Jess to her Mustang and open the door for her. She smiled and nodded as he spoke quietly to her. I turned away as he leaned down to kiss her, and carefully settled myself in the passenger seat of James' truck for the drive home.

Pulling into the driveway beside Kyle's car, James shut the engine off as Kyle opened the door for me and held out his hand to help me out. I slowly slid out of the seat and moved aside for Kyle to close the door as James got out bags and led the way into the house.

"I'll take your bag upstairs for you," James said, heading toward the stairs.

"Hang on James. I need a change of clothes first. Don't really wanna hang out in my firesuit all night." I held out my hand for the bag. Setting it on the kitchen counter, James opened it and waiting for me to pull out a pair of pants and a shirt.

As he left the room and headed upstairs, I kicked my shoes off and Kyle stepped forward to loosen my firesuit.

"I can do this myself, you know," I said quietly.

"I know you can. But it'll hurt less if you let me help you. I'm sure bending with two freshly cracked ribs isn't easy."

Kyle knelt to slowly pull my firesuit off and help me put my pants on. As he pulled them up, he gently kissed my hipbone and moved to pass his lips across the bruises peeking out from under the tape before standing up again.

I closed my eyes as he stood and cupped my face in his hands.

"Look at me," he said quietly. I looked into his eyes and opened my mouth to speak, but he quickly put a finger to my lips.

"Shut up. I get to talk now," he paused. "I'm sorry I was such an ass today. I shouldn't have left the track when I did. You just frustrate me so damn much sometimes when I was only trying to help you. I don't want to quit. Not the team and not you. I know how much the championship means to you. And I know the next nine weeks are gonna be crazy stressful. So if you'll still have me, I'm here."

"I'm sorry too. I never should've yelled at you like that. I just needed to vent and you weren't letting me do that. And I love you so much. I thought my whole world was falling apart when Jess told me you'd quit. The championship means nothing to me, if I can't share it with you."

Kyle leaned in and kissed me deeply as the tears spilled down my cheeks. I whimpered as he pulled me close. He stopped suddenly and pulled back.

"Shit. I'm sorry. I forgot the ribs for a minute. Did they give you anything for the pain?"

"Yeah. A couple Demerol, but they only take the edge off. The pain's till pretty strong," I explained, pulling the bottle out of the pocket of my firesuit. Setting the bottle on the counter, I walked over to the closet by the garage door to hang up my firesuit.

"I'm gonna get you some ice to put on them and we'll go hang out in the family room and watch movies or something. Are you hungry?" Kyle opened the freezer.

"Yeah. Let's just order pizza or something." I took the ice pack from him and handed him the phone. Following me into the family room, Kyle watched as I tried to get comfortable on the couch. Surrounding my left side with pillows, I put my feet up on the coffee table and set the ice pack across my broken ribs.

Kyle went back into the kitchen and I could hear him ordering the pizza and getting drinks before he returned to the family room to sit beside me.

Flipping through the channels, I found the sports highlights and stopped as I heard the announcer re-capping the race. Watching as they showed the clip of my crash, I gasped. Kyle put his arm around me.

"Wow. It didn't seem that bad when it was happening. I didn't even realize the wheels came off the ground with that last hit." I rested my head on Kyle's shoulder.

"It always looks worse than we think it is. The important thing is you got out and walked away. We'll repair the cars, your ribs will heal and we'll keep going."

I closed my eyes as Kyle took the remote from me and started looking for something else to watch.

A short time later, the doorbell rang and I sat up to let Kyle answer the door. I heard him call upstairs to James and the two of them joined me in the family room.

"I wonder where Jess got to," Kyle wondered out loud as he handed me a slice of pizza.

"I'm guessing she went out with Mark when we left the airport. They were looking pretty cozy during the flight home," I explained.

"Oh. Okay. Seems strange she didn't call to let you know though." Kyle looked at me.

"She's an adult now. She knows I trust her to make her own decisions. She's in love, I think. And I'm sure she figured we needed some time to talk anyway."

"And on that note, I'm going to head out of here for a little while." James stood up, grabbing a couple slices of pizza and heading towards the door.

"James. You don't need to run off," I pointed out.

"I know. Some of the guys were going to play pool and have a few beers. Told them I'd probably stop by," James explained.

"Okay. See you later then." I waved to him.

After we'd eaten and the leftover pizza was in the fridge, Kyle carefully pulled me into his arms. Closing my eyes, it didn't take long before I fell asleep, feeling Kyle's arms around me.

When I woke up, Kyle was still holding me close. I sat up and he lightly rubbed my back.

"Are you okay Brie?" he asked. Taking a couple deep breaths, I nodded and leaned back into his arms.

"Just had a bad dream, I guess."

"Wanna talk about it?"

"Was just dreaming about the crash," I explained.

"You probably will for a while. It's getting late. We should probably head to bed. Think you'll be able to sleep now?"

"Yeah. Just let me take a couple more pills for the pain." Kyle helped me stand before turning off the television. The phone rang as I was swallowing the pills. Kyle answered it and listened for a minute.

"Okay Jess. I'll let her know," he paused. "Yeah. I'm just putting her to bed now. We'll see you in the morning then." Kyle hung up the phone and turned to me.

"Everything okay?" I asked.

"Yep. She's with Mark. They went out for dinner and now they're gonna hang out at his place and watch movies. She said she won't be out late though."

I nodded and slowly made my way up the stairs to the bedroom. Kyle pulled the blankets back as I carefully undressed.

"You okay?" he asked as he pulled his shirt over his head and tossed it on the chair by the closet.

"Yeah. Just waiting for the pills to start working." I sat down on the bed and watched him strip down before he laid down beside me.

"Maybe you should go to the doctor tomorrow and get something stronger," he suggested.

"You know I have to be careful what I take, especially when I'm driving," I reminded him.

"Oh yeah," he paused. "Hey you know what really sucks about you being hurt after our first big fight?"

"What's that?" I slowly laid down beside him.

"No make-up sex." He pretended to pout.

"Hmm, guess we'll just have to get creative to work around my injuries," I giggled.

"I don't want to hurt you though. As much as I want you right now, I can wait until you're healed. We'll just have to make up for it later." Kyle pulled the blankets over us and turned off the bedside light.

Rolling onto my right side, I curled up beside Kyle. He carefully draped his arm across my hip to hold me close as I fell asleep.

* * *

By the time we got to the shop late the next morning, the hauler had returned and the crew had unloaded the cars and begun stripping the damaged sheet metal. I watched them work for a while before I headed up to my office to check my mail and take care of business.

When a knock on my office door interrupted me, I called out without looking up from my computer screen.

"Come in!"

"Are you busy?" Matthew poked his head in the door. Looking up from the computer, I smiled.

"You know I always have time for you." I started to stand.

"Don't get up. We saw Kyle downstairs and he told us about your ribs." Matthew motioned for me to sit down.

"We? Us?" I asked, looking passed him to the open doorway.

To my surprise, Daytona stepped into the doorway and into my office, smiling. Standing up again as Matthew closed the door, I walked around the desk to hug them both.

"What an awesome surprise!" I exclaimed. "Come sit down. What brings you here?" Daytona and I sat on the couch by the window while Matt turned a chair to face us.

"Well, I figured if I'm gonna be your matron of honor, I need to start venturing out of the house a little more. And in all honesty, I really miss this place," Daytona explained with a smile.

"Seriously? You'll do it?" I asked, looking back and forth between the two of them.

"Yep. I would love to," Daytona replied. "You know I never got to go to my sister's wedding, so if you don't mind me adopting you as my little sister, I'd be honored to stand up with you."

"You do realize we're doing it in Miami before the Nationwide race, right?" I reminded her.

"Yep. Matt and I were thinking we might try sneaking into a couple races before then. Just to test the waters so to speak and see how well I handle the crowds."

"Well, just let me know when you want to go and I'll make sure everything is set up for you and you can fly in and out with us. Kyle and I will stay at the motel with the team so you can have the safety and privacy of the motorhome."

"You don't have to do that," Daytona protested.

"I know I don't have to. I want to do it," I assured her. Just then, the phone rang and I looked down into the reception area. Doug was standing in the lobby. I knocked on the window to get his and Kara's attention. When they looked up, I motioned for him to come up.

"So how are you feeling?" Matt asked.

"We saw that crash yesterday," Daytona added. "Was it as bad as it looked?"

"Two cracked ribs and some nasty bruising, that's all," I explained, pulling up the one side of my shirt to show the bruising that wasn't covered by the tape.

"Ouch. I certainly don't miss the broken bones and injuries," Daytona said. "Now what's going on with Eddie? We heard something on the news about him wrecking your primary car before qualifying."

"Yeah. Apparently he's been pissed ever since Michigan when I kicked his ass and he got arrested for running me off US-12."

"You'd better watch yourself with him," Matt warned as my door opened again.

"I hope you're not warning her about me," Doug laughed as he walked into my office.

"Oh, we already did that," Daytona joked as Doug leaned down to kiss her on the cheek.

"Don't get up," he told me as he leaned down to me before turning to shake Matt's hand. Pulling the other chair around, Doug lowered himself to sit.

"So what brings you here?" I asked.

"Just wanted to see how you're feeling today," Doug replied.

"You drove all the way over here when you could've picked up the phone?" I laughed.

"Well, I knew you couldn't lie to me if I'm looking at you," Doug explained.

"Uh huh." I shook my head.

"So? How are you doing?"

"Sore. But functioning. I've got a team to run here. Shouldn't you be up to your ass in paperwork and business stuff too?"

"Nope. That is what I have a team manager for," Doug shook his head. "Drew takes care of all that stuff for me. I just show up and look good. Sign a few checks once in a while."

"Lazy bastard," I laughed.

"Hey, it just means I can worry less about the business end of things and concentrate more on the car," Doug pointed out. "You should try it."

"Whatever. You do it your way; I'll run my team my way."

"Actually, that's the other reason why I wanted to stop by to see you."

"What's that?" I asked.

"Well, I was thinking about what Matt said before. About combining our two teams."

"I told you before: I won't switch to Chevy. I'm locked into a contract with Ford for another five years and I wouldn't change even if I could," I pointed out.

"I know. And I've heard the rumors that Ford's pulling their support for Eddie after all the crap he's pulled this year. My contract with Chevy is up for renewal this year. So I might be convinced to cross the street, so to speak."

"Well, damn. As shitty as the weekend was, this week is starting out pretty damn interesting," I shook my head, amazed.

"I think we could make it work, you know. I mean, this was a two and three horse stable before, when Matt and Daytona were running the show. So I know you have plenty of room for me and my guys. I've got all my own equipment and we've already seen that our two teams work well together," Doug explained.

"I suppose it is a possibility. Just a matter of figuring out the logistics," I looked at Daytona.

"Hey! Don't look at me. I'm just an innocent bystander here," she laughed. "But I think it would be a smart move. Both of you have championship-quality teams. You could both benefit from a merge."

"It would be just a merge, wouldn't it?" I asked Doug. "Nobody buying anybody right? Just combining the two teams and resources to be more competitive?"

"Yep. Listen, why don't we try it out on a trial basis? We'll start whenever you want, until the end of next season. And then, or at any time, if it's not working, I'll pack up my toys and take my boys back across town. Otherwise, we'll keep going one year at a time," Doug offered.

"Well, this isn't a two person decision. At least not in this shop. This is going to affect two teams so I think we should probably get their input too," I pointed out. "I'm not going to bring another team in here if my guys aren't gonna be able to play nice. Hanging out at the track together is one thing."

"But crowding the sandbox is a whole different story," Daytona added.

"Exactly," I agreed.

"So full team meeting. Before, after or during race weekend?"

"Probably best to do it before to get it out of the way so we can focus on getting ready for the weekend. Can you spare an hour tomorrow or Wednesday to bring your crew here?" I asked.

"I don't see why not," Doug replied. "Tomorrow is good for me. We're pretty much ready to go for the weekend. And if it goes well, I'll leave some of my guys here to help you get your shit together for the weekend."

"Sounds good to me. I don't want these guys getting burnt out, but that was my favorite car Eddie wrecked this week. I wanted to be able to run it again."

"Cool." Doug stood up, returning the chair to its spot. "I'm gonna head back to the shop and let the guys know about tomorrow. I'll see you about one." After he left, Matthew looked at Daytona.

"Are you ready to go too?"

"Yeah." She looked at me. "I'm sure you've got a ton of stuff to do that we interrupted." They both stood.

"You know how it is. Never-ending paperwork. Mail to answer," I laughed as I stood to walk out with them. "Thanks for coming by. And thank you Daytona for agreeing to come to Miami."

I walked downstairs with them and hugged them both before heading to find Kyle to fill him in on the events of the last half hour.

* * *

The next afternoon, we closed down the shop for an hour to have the joint team meeting. Doug left most of the talking to me and I explained what Doug and I had discussed.

"Now obviously this is a decision that affects each and every one of you. So we wanted to be able to address any questions or concerns you might have and include y'all in the final decision."

"Who would be our boss if you combine the two teams?"

"Both of us. This will be an equal partnership. I'm not buying into Doug's team and he's not buying into mine. It's a simple fact of merging the two teams and resources and housing everybody under one roof," I explained.

"Exactly," Doug added. "When you look at how both teams have run this year; we would've made the Chase again to defend our championship if it hadn't been for my wreck in June. And Brie's still in the hunt. So we figure if we join forces for next year, we will be the top team to beat next year."

"Well, if y'all have already made the decision, why involve us?" one of Doug's body men asked.

"The final decision hasn't been made yet. Over here, a decision this big gets team input. If y'all come over here, we have team meetings every Monday afternoon to re-cap the weekend and gear up for the next race. When we prepare for next weekend, we factor in everything. You name it, we look at it."

I walked around the room as I spoke.

"And we wanted to let you guys have a say in this because when you look around the room, these are the guys you're gonna see and have to work with day after day. But if y'all can't or won't work together, there's no point in taking this any further than just kicking the idea around," Doug explained.

"That's right. Doug and I can only do so much to have this work. We need you guys for this idea to succeed."

"When would all this happen? Like are we moving today or do we wait until the end of the season?" Drew finally spoke up.

"We were thinking we'd do it in stages. Obviously, we're still racing under the Chevy banner these last nine races. So basic ops will have to stay across town til we get home from Homestead. But if you guys are willing to try this experiment, I'm gonna move a handful of you over here as of today. You'll be helping Brie's guys get ready for this weekend. We'll share our information and set-ups. Everything."

"We want to make the transition as smooth and seamless as possible for you guys. So if there's anything you need, just let us know," I offered.

"What about offices? And how will this affect me?" Drew asked.

"I was thinking you could have your old office back if you want it. I never hired a new team manager to replace you. I do all that stuff myself. Ricky, you'll be sharing an office with Kyle, like Brian and Darryl did when Matt and Daytona were here. And Doug can take Matt's old office."

Doug's team looked around the room. After a minute's silence, Drew stood up.

"Well, what are we waiting for? Time's a-wasting. Let's get to work."

I looked at my team.

"Are you guys good with this?"

"Hell, yeah. Let's do it," Joe spoke for the team. He'd returned to light shop duty the week before.

Doug instructed the crew members he wanted to stay behind and sent the rest back to his shop. My crew headed back to their respective areas with whatever added staff there was from Doug's team. Drew, Doug and I headed to the conference room with Kyle and Ricky.

"So that went pretty well," Doug said as the five of us sat down around the conference table.

"Okay. So now comes the real fun. Working things out to merge the two teams. We'll have to go through all our procedures and routines to see what works best and what needs to be changed." I turned to Drew. "You've been here before, when Matt and Daytona bought the team you and Wayne were with. Do you have any suggestions to make this easy and painless?"

"Well, I think both teams are run pretty much similar. See, the stuff I did here is the same stuff I do for Doug. I know you're a hands-on team owner like Daytona was. Her and I worked closely running this place after Wayne retired. And I know Matt taught you her way of doing things when you bought the team."

"Well, I wanted the transition to be easy when I came in. I knew the guys who were staying would appreciate the stability. And having no experience running a Nationwide team, I figured it would be easier for me to learn the ropes if I didn't turn the whole operation upside down."

"So I guess if I'm staying on with the team my concern is: what is it exactly that you want me to do? Do you want me to continue running just Doug's side of things? Or am I going to be managing the two teams?"

"I hadn't really thought about it Drew. I've always taken care of all the business stuff myself, partly to learn everything I could about running a team and partly because I had no idea what to look for in a team manager. But it would make sense to have you taking care of both teams."

"Daytona and I used to have a meeting every other week or so, to go over everything."

"Sounds good. When we get the computer system expanded to include you guys, you'll see we have a universal schedule. All meetings, races and really anything of importance goes on it. Well, you'd already know that. It's just an upgraded version of the system that was here before."

"So getting ready for this weekend, Ricky, I'm gonna get you to bring over all our specs from last years' race so Brianna's car can get set up. This is a race we won in the Chase last year, so hopefully our set up will help. You've got the manpower now to get that car ready. Do you have any extra body panels made up?" I shook my head.

"We could take them off one of the back-ups," Kyle suggested.

"Too much work," Doug replied. "I have a bunch of extra side panels ready to go. I've got one group of guys where that's all they do. They make up the extra panels and we store them til we need them. I'll get them to bring some over."

"Great. Thanks. Kyle can you let the body crew know? Then they just have to make sure the front and back ends are ready. Or concentrate their efforts on Wreck Two."

"I'm on it." Kyle and Ricky both stood and headed out of the room.

"I'm gonna head back and take care of whatever's left to be done for this weekend," Drew stood, leaving Doug and I alone in the conference room.

"So are you really sure about this Brie?" Doug looked closely at me as I sat back in my chair.

"Sure. Why wouldn't I be? If I wasn't one hundred percent sure, I would've told you I needed to think about it, not invited your team in here."

"Okay. I just wanted to double-check."

"No, it's good. I was actually tossing around the idea of adding a Nationwide or truck team in the next year or so. So, you coming on board makes sense. And if this works out, we can grow the team together."

"Sounds like a great idea to me. I think it'll all work out for all of us."

"I hope so. Only time will tell though, I suppose."

"Well listen. I promised Mandy I'd come see her today, so I'd better get moving to get there."

"Okay. Tell her I said hello. Hey, I know it's still two months away, but why don't you and Mandy come for Thanksgiving?" I offered as we walked out of the conference room.

"Thanks. I'll let you know." Doug left me at my office door and headed downstairs.

* * * * *

CHAPTER FORTY-FIVE

Talladega – October

The next couple races were fairly routine but we slowly gained ground on the points leader. By the time we arrived in Talladega at the beginning of October, we had moved back into the second spot in points.

Our two teams had merged smoothly and it was a common sight as crew members passed back and forth between the Ford and Chevy garages and our two team stalls. Using Doug's set-ups as our starting points, we were competitive and finishing in the top five every week. Rolling the primary car out of the hauler, the team was quietly optimistic about the weekend.

I watched as they slowly rolled the car through the garage to our assigned stall. Once everything was in place, Kyle released the hood pins and the team went to work double-checking that everything was set up properly. James had continued to fill Joe's place on the road crew. Although Joe's cast had been removed and the doctor had cleared him to resume normal activities, they had discussed it and Joe had asked James to stay on for the rest of the season.

Hooking up the laptop on the toolbox, I opened the program that compared my previous years' set up to Doug's before checking the weather report for the coming days. The year before the weekend had been hot and dry. I shook my head as I read the weather forecast.

"What's up Brie?" Matt asked as he and Daytona joined me at the computer. I pointed to the screen as I answered.

"We've got rain coming tomorrow. Says seventy percent chance. What are the odds it holds off until after we qualify?"

"Slim to none?" Daytona laughed. "But look at it this way. If it's rained out, you'll be starting second."

"Yeah. But on a green track. I've never run well here when the track starts out green," I pointed out.

"So we'll adapt. And you'll have a retired champion on your pit box Sunday talking you through it," she countered, putting her arm around me.

"Wow. You're just diving right in, aren't you?" I laughed. "I mean, just coming to the track this weekend is a huge step for you, I know. But to choose to sit in the pits too. I bow to your determination."

"It's not determination. Stupidity maybe. Pure lunacy possibly. But not determination," Daytona joked.

"Well, whatever it is, I'm glad you're here. Sitting on the pit box or not, it means a lot to me that you came this weekend." Daytona looked around as the garage steadily filled with the other teams. Public access would not begin for another three hours.

Matt had walked over to talk to Kyle and the crew, but I could see he was keeping a close eye on Daytona.

"Will you take a walk with me?" Daytona asked, taking my hand. "Before the crowd gets here?"

"Sure. Where do you want to go?" I wondered.

"Just around the garage and out to the pits. We won't go for a long time; just long enough for me to put my feet on pit road," Daytona explained.

"Yeah. We can do that. You want to bring Matt or one of the guys?"

"We don't need them. I saw the footage of you taking Eddie down in Michigan," Daytona assured me.

"Okay." I turned to Kyle and Matt. "Hey! We're gonna take a walk. We won't be gone long."

"You want one of us to come with you?" Kyle called back.

"Nope. It's GIRL stuff," Daytona answered, pulling me towards the open garage door. I looked over my shoulder to see Kyle motioning for James to keep an eye on us as Matt watched us walk away.

Slowly walking through the garage area, a number of crew members from other teams and NASCAR officials said hello to me as we walked by. I noticed most of them barely gave Daytona more than a passing glance. She was wearing a baseball cap with her hair pulled back and dark sunglasses to cover the few scars that were still visible from the shooting.

"Have I been gone from the sport that long?" Daytona asked.

"Nope. Just nobody expects you to be here. And you're pretty well hidden under the cap and shades. I can leak it to the media that you're here if you want," I joked.

"Thanks. But it's kinda nice to just be a face in the crowd for now. I'm sure once the media gets here, I won't be quite so anonymous anymore."

Dave met up with us then and looked closely at Daytona, the shock obvious on his face.

"Well, aren't you a sight for sore eyes. How are you? What brings you to the track?" Dave hugged her tightly.

"I'm good. And just wanted to see how my old team is running."

"Are you staying for the whole weekend? Come by and see me later so we can catch up and have coffee. I've gotta run to a meeting, but it's great to have you here." Dave kissed us both on the cheek before he rushed off.

"That man needs to slow down soon," Daytona watched as Dave headed off and caught up to a group of tech inspectors. I saw that James had stopped at Doug's garage stall and hoped Daytona wouldn't notice him watching us while he talked to Doug's crew.

I looped my arm through hers and guided her through the crowd of crew members coming from the Goodyear tire trucks. Silently, we walked onto pit road and Daytona stopped to take a slow look around.

"Seems like so long ago I was climbing into my car to run my first race here," Daytona looked at me. "But it's almost like it was just yesterday too. Know what I mean?"

I nodded silently as we turned to walk down pit road.

"I used to love coming here. It was one of my favorite tracks to run. Just the sheer size of the place. And knowing every lap held the chance of a big wreck. Being able to actually finish a race here was something to celebrate. It really feels good to be here. Damn I miss being a part of the action, but it's good to be here."

When we returned to the garage, Matt and Daytona headed to the motorhome to avoid the crowds that would soon be passing through. They planned to watch practice from the roof of the hauler later in the afternoon.

"Everything okay?" Kyle asked after they were gone.

"Yeah. We just took a walk out to pit road," I explained. "Man, I wish I could've been able to race against her. Just once."

"There'd be something to see. I remember how competitive she was. Put the two of you together on the track and the rest of us would never have a chance," Doug said, joining us. "It's nice to see her back at the track though."

"Yeah. Maybe we can get her out more often," I commented.

"Hopefully if this weekend goes well, she'll come to more races," Kyle replied.

"That would be cool," Doug agreed, looking at his watch. "Well, I've gotta head out for a while. See you guys at practice."

Doug walked off in the direction of the reserved parking area as Kyle and I returned to the hauler. Once we were alone, Kyle pulled me into his arms.

"You know, I've got a really good feeling about this weekend," he said.

"Yeah? Not worried about us getting caught up in The Big One?" I asked.

"Nope. Gonna run up front all weekend."

"I hope you're right." I rested my head on his shoulder, lightly kissing his neck.

"Hmm. I didn't bring you in here for that, but hey, now that I think of it. . ." Kyle said with a laugh, pinning me against one of the parts cupboards.

"Didn't bring me in here for what?" I asked innocently, looking up at him.

"Like you don't know," Kyle replied, leaning down and kissing me deeply. We were interrupted as the door opened.

"Sorry guys," Dave apologized. "I was hoping Daytona was in here."

"She's in the motorhome with Matthew," I explained.

"Okay. Thanks." Dave waved and backed out the door.

"So, where were we?" I asked, grabbing the front of Kyle's shirt and pulling him close again. Just then, my phone began to ring and I groaned. Looking at the display, I frowned.

"What is it?" Kyle looked at the phone.

"Blocked number," I answered.

"Let it go to voice mail then," Kyle took the phone from me and switched the ringer off before setting it on the counter. He slid his hands under my shirt, lightly resting them on the tape that still covered my healing ribs and I giggled.

"Hey! That tickles!"

"Good. At least it doesn't hurt so much when I touch you now," he replied as the door opened and James walked in.

"Come on you two. Save it for later," he laughed, shaking his head. "There's work to be done you know."

"Yeah, yeah." I pretended to wave him away as more of the crew came through the door.

"It's starting to look pretty nasty out there," Drew said.

"Has the rain started yet?" I asked, looking towards the door.

"Nope. But it's looking pretty dark off to the south. Won't be long before it reaches us," Drew explained. "I had the crew closing everything up and covering the car. Nothing really to do to it til you can get out to practice and try out the set-up."

"Let's go through the previous years while we wait out the rain," I instructed. "Find a set-up that works for a green track and cooler temp. That way we know what our options are when the rain stops."

"I'm on it boss," Dean, my car chief turned to one of the laptops we had set up in the hauler.

The rest of the crew headed to the front of the hauler and it wasn't long before the sounds of a card game drifted back to us.

The rain fell most of the day and by late afternoon, NASCAR had cancelled the days practice sessions. Disappointed, we headed to the hotel.

* * * * *

CHAPTER FORTY-SIX

By the time race day arrived, everybody in the garage was frustrated. Practice as well as qualifying had been cancelled due to the rain. Every time it stopped long enough for NASCAR to send out the track drying crew, the track would be half dried and the rain would pour down again.

The officials had also had to re-schedule the truck and Nationwide Series' races to the only open weekend left in the schedule. Sunday brought clear skies and above-normal temperatures for October in Alabama.

Heading to pit road for the pre-race activities, I was joined by Matthew and Daytona. They had kept a low profile during the weekend, choosing to remain out of sight in the motorhome until Sunday.

As we made our way down pit road to the stage, we were stopped by a large group of reporters. They had been asking questions all weekend after learning that Kyle and I were staying at the hotel with the crew instead of at the track.

"Daytona! What brings you to the track this weekend?"

"Are you returning to team ownership?"

"Will you be returning to competition?"

I took her hand and squeezed it lightly as I smiled at her.

"Want me to handle this?" I asked her. She shook her head and took a deep breath. Smiling, she addressed the reporters.

"Brianna asked me to be her guest, and I came to show my support for my old team. I AM still the primary sponsor too, you know. I haven't even thought about starting a new team, but maybe Brianna and I will come up with a joint venture for next year. And no, as much as I would love to come back to driving, that's not an option for me now. If you'll excuse us, we're on our way to join the rest of the field for introductions. Thank you." Daytona stepped forward then, parting the crowd and ending the interview.

"Awesome! Are you sure you've been staying at home for the last five years?" I smiled at her.

"Some habits never fade," she explained. "Just like riding a bike."

We joined the rest of the crowd watching the band finishing up on stage. Driver introductions would be next. With qualifying rained out and the field being set by points, I would be starting on the outside pole and introduced to the crowd second-last.

When I saw James making his way through the crowd, I lifted my left arm to wave to him. He looked worried and I wondered what was wrong. I realized he was looking passed me and turned to find out what was behind me.

As I turned, somebody ran into me, and I felt a fist connect with my left side. Steadying myself, I heard James yell and saw it was Eddie that had run into me. The crowd of drivers and crew chiefs moved aside as James grabbed Eddie and wrestled him to the ground.

Trying to catch my breath, I walked the few feet to where James had Eddie pinned down, one knee digging into his back and his arms pulled behind him. As Eddie struggled to free himself, I bent down beside them.

"Let me go you asshole," Eddie spat.

"When are you finally gonna get it through your thick skull?" James asked. "You know every time you screw with Brianna, you get your ass thrown out of the track."

"You think your daddy's proud of what you've been doing?" I leaned close to him. "Or is he the one telling you to pull this shit?"

Track security arrived then with Dave close behind. James stood up, pulling Eddie with him and passed him off to two security officers. Dave looked at the group of us.

"What the hell happened here?" he finally asked.

"He ran into Brianna pretty hard sir," James spoke up first. "Looked like it was intentional too. Are you okay Brie?"

"Yeah. He kinda knocked the wind outta me and my ribs are a little sore. But I'll survive." I didn't mention him punching me.

"Eddie? What do you have to say for yourself this time?" Dave turned to him.

"Nothing." Eddie glared at me.

"So what do you want me to do with you this time? You've been parked twice now for your stunts. Didn't I warn you last time that this needed to stop? Do you need me to suspend you for the rest of the season?" Dave asked as Eddie's name was called for introductions.

"Dave. Let him race," I spoke up.

"Take him across the stage. You two don't leave his side til he's belted into his car. When the race is done, bring him to the NASCAR trailer," Dave instructed the uniformed men. As they led him to the stage, Dave turned back to me.

"You and I both know he's got the talent behind the wheel. He just makes stupid decisions outside the car," I explained.

"You're right. I just wish he'd figure that out soon. I want you to get your ribs checked out before you get in your car today. And we'll be paying close attention to Eddie on the track today." I nodded as Dave walked away and waited for my name to be called to take my turn across the stage. James stayed close to me until I was in the back of the truck for my trip around the track.

Once I climbed out of the truck, Doug stopped me as I passed his car on my way to the front row.

"Are you okay?" he asked. "Everybody's talking about what Eddie did."

"Geez. He ran into me. Nothing's broken. He just got stupid. I'm fine," I assured him.

"Okay. Well, good luck today. I'll get up front just as soon as I can."

"I'll be watching for ya." I continued on my way and found Kyle anxiously looking down pit road.

"I was starting to worry," he said, looking at me.

"Sorry. Doug stopped me to ask about Eddie."

"Yeah. James told me what went on during driver introductions. What's this you asked Dave to let Eddie race today? They should be tossing him out on his ass."

"Look. I'm fine. He didn't really hurt me as much as he probably thought he might. And he knows NASCAR isn't gonna let him get away with anything on the track. Dave will have a talk with him after the race."

"But what if he does something out on the track? You could get seriously hurt out there," Kyle argued.

"That's what I have a spotter for. Please don't worry so much." I hugged him as my crew lined up to wait for the national anthem.

Once I was settled in the seat and had the safety belts tightly fastened, I took Kyle's hand. I knew he would continue to worry.

"It's gonna be great, okay? We're not gonna have any problems today. Not with the car and not with Eddie," I tried to reassure him, hoping I was right.

"Okay." He took a deep breath. "I'll try not to worry. Kick ass out there today."

I nodded and pulled on my helmet to finish preparing for the start of the race.

Once all forty-three engines had roared to life and the field had followed the pace car out onto the track, I shifted in my seat to find a more comfortable spot.

"Hey Brianna. How ya doin' out there?" Daytona asked.

"Doing okay. How are you doing?"

"Feeling pretty good. Now, NASCAR is throwing a competition caution at lap thirty, since nobody got to practice this weekend. I know you're familiar with the procedure so just take it easy the first thirty laps. Treat the laps like practice and we'll figure out what changes we might have to make."

"Got it. Lights are out and I'm ready." I tightened the belts one last time and kept an eye on the flag stand for the green.

As the green flag waved, the pole sitter pulled ahead of me. I quickly pulled my Ford into line behind him and checked my mirror. The rest of the field was still running two-wide as Jamie and I drove away from them.

"Hey Jess. Ask Jamie's spotter if he'll let me by to get my point for leading a lap."

"Sure Mom." A minute later, I saw him looking back at me in his mirror and put his hand up to wave.

"Jess?"

"He wants to know what it's worth to you."

"Are you kidding me?" I radioed back to her.

"Well, that was his first answer. Then he said if you want the lead, go ahead and take it from him. But he's not gonna just pull over and give it to you," she replied. "Said it's one point that he's not willing to give up."

"Don't worry about it Brie. We'll get it at the caution," Kyle spoke. "How's the car feel?"

"Actually, it's better than I expected; this set up is perfect."

"Okay. So when we come in for the caution, we'll do two tires and gas. That'll save us time and get you back out faster."

"Sound good." I rode around the next fifteen laps following Jamie. I noticed he was running a little slower coming out of Turn Four and knew if there was a spot to take over the lead, that was it.

I stayed close to his bumper for the next lap and as soon as he slowed in the turn, I easily manoeuvred up the track and pulled ahead to pass him before we reached the start-finish line. Pulling down in front of him, I checked my mirror to see him shaking his head.

When the caution flag waved a few laps later, I slowed to let the pace car pull in front of me.

"Okay boys. Time to go to work. Two tires and gas. Any changes Brie?" Kyle asked.

"Nope. She's perfect. Just get me back out here first or close to it." I brought the car down onto pit road and watched the rest of the field follow me. The crew sprang into action as soon as I had the car stopped and quickly changed the right side tires while James filled the gas tank.

As I headed back out onto the track and took my place behind the pace car again, I radioed my crew.

"Awesome stop boys. Let's keep 'em short and sweet all day if we can. Where did Jamie come out?"

"About tenth. He made contact with the forty car leaving his pit. Right side's a little wrinkled but it doesn't look too bad," Jessika told me.

"Uh oh. I bet he's not too happy about that."

"And Doug's third. So he'll be up there to draft with you as soon as he gets past the second place car."

"Works for me. I know it's still early but it's feeling pretty good out here."

When the green flag waved again, Doug made quick work of passing the second place car and we hooked up to pull away from the tightly bunched field. Everybody behind us moved to run two and three-wide, fighting for the best spots.

"What a bunch of idiots," Jess commented. "Don't they all realize it's still early? Who wants to bet the Big One's gonna hit before halfway?"

"Hey maybe they'll smarten up and get in line before that happens," I offered.

"Yeah. I have a better chance of re-growing a sighted eye," Daytona laughed.

Somehow we managed to get through the next fifty laps without a caution. Two cars had gone to the garage with engine problems, but luckily hadn't blown them on the track.

"Okay Brie. Time to start thinking about coming in. You've got about a five lap window before we run out of gas," Kyle let me know.

"Got it. Let Doug know we're coming in four laps from now. Let's try to hold off as long as possible."

"Ten four."

Just as I checked my mirror, Jess' voice came through the radio. Looking past Doug, I could see the mess starting.

"Here we go!" Jess called. "Five. Ten. At least a dozen involved. Eddie's in the wall! Oh crap. Jamie's on his roof, sliding through the grass!"

"Okay Brie. Front stretch is a mess. Pace car is coming out. Slow down to let him catch you," Kyle pointed out.

"Here's that break we needed. Get four tires ready. I need a bottle of water and an ice pack too. It's getting damn hot out here," I replied.

"We'll be ready for you," Kyle answered. "Okay boys. You heard the boss. Four tires and gas."

"Mom. They're opening pit road right away to keep everybody off the front stretch while they clean up. And Jamie's out of his car walking around."

I followed the pace car down pit road and pulled into my pit stall with Doug right behind me. Taking the water bottle and ice pack that had been put through the window, I unzipped my firesuit as the crew went to work on changing the tires.

As soon as the jack dropped down and Kyle shouted for me to go, I pulled out of the pit stall and off pit road, beating the other cars racing to get out ahead of me.

"Good work boys. Another awesome stop," I praised them.

"Brie. They're holding everybody in Turn Four. NASCAR doesn't want y'all driving through the debris. The whole front stretch is a mess," Kyle replied.

"Okay. I see the pace car now." I slowed down and pulled to the top of the track to park my Ford and wait. From there, I could see the mess on the front stretch.

"Uh oh. This is gonna be interesting." I heard Jessika comment.

"What's up Jess?" I asked as I tucked the ice pack into my firesuit where my ribs were beginning to ache.

"The driver of the forty car just went over to Jamie to talk. Doesn't look like Jamie wants to have anything to do with him though. He keeps walking away."

I looked down to the front stretch just as Jamie turned around and walked back to the other driver. Tony was talking and pointing to Jamie and his car when Jamie suddenly raised his fist, punching the rookie squarely in the jaw.

"Holy crap! I think he just handed us the points lead on a silver platter," Kyle said quietly.

"Oh man. Dave's gonna be pissed. You know Jamie's gonna lose points and money for that. The footage will make the highlights tonight," I replied, trying not to get too excited about getting the points lead. NASCAR officials had repeatedly told us that any physical confrontations on the track or in the garage would be an automatic fifty points deduction.

"Better him than you," Daytona pointed out. I shook my head and laughed as I watched the track crew separating the two drivers.

Another crew came along, handing bottles of water to us while we waited for the mess to be cleaned up along the front stretch.

When the track was finally cleared and NASCAR gave the go-ahead, the thirty or so cars parked along the banking re-started our engines and followed the pace car around the track.

Once the green flag waved again, the field stayed single-file behind me and Doug. Every few laps a car would pull out of line to try to pass the car ahead. Most of the attempts were futile as half a dozen cars would end up passing on the outside.

Doug and I continued to dominate the race, swapping the lead every few laps. There were half a dozen more caution periods for wrecks and a handful of cars involved in the first big wreck managed to return to the track. Officials refused to approve Jamie's return to the track though, seeing as the roll cage on one side of the roof had been crushed.

When the white flag waved, Doug and I had pulled out to a fairly wide lead over the rest of the field. I knew Doug would be watching to take the lead on the last lap to win and I kept an eye on him in the mirror. To my surprise, he stayed behind me until the checkered flag waved. He finally drove up beside me as I slowed down on the back stretch and waved to me out his window.

As I completed the cool down lap, I spun the car around and waved to the crowd gathered at the fence, until I reached the entrance to pit road. Turning the car around, I made my way to Victory Lane were my crew waited.

Kyle handed me a bottle of water as soon as I had my helmet off and I drank half of it down before dumping the rest on my face and head to cool off.

"I need more ice," I told him as I unfastened the safety belts. He nodded and turned to send a crew member for another ice pack.

The reporter signalled me when I could climb out of the car and I carefully pulled myself out to stand on the edge of the window opening to spray my team with the bottle of Coca-Cola Kyle had handed me when I was done with the water. Kyle stepped forward and helped me from the car as the team cheered.

"Well Brianna. I know those broken ribs must feel a whole lot better with the excitement of this win," the reporter began.

"Oh man. I've been keeping ice on them all day after an incident during driver introductions, but this was an amazing day," I paused to take the new ice pack and unzip my firesuit.

"And you had a special guest in your pit today; what does it mean to you to have Daytona on your pit box?"

"It's awesome!" I motioned for Daytona to join me. "You know, every race I've won, I thank this woman for blazing a trail in the sport, but this win is even more special because Daytona was here for it. And of course, I have to thank my crew for giving me such a great car to drive today. And my sponsors, Daytona's Sports Bars, Ford, Goodyear."

"Thanks Brianna. Now, let's go to today's second place finisher, Brianna's teammate next year, Doug Madison."

I hugged Daytona and thanked her again before Kyle pulled me to him and kissed me. After we finished with the post-race pictures, Kyle and I changed before we headed to the media center for the mandatory post-race press conference. Still carrying an ice pack and a fresh bottle of water, I took my seat between Doug and the third place finisher.

"Great race today Brie." Doug leaned over to whisper in my ear.

"Thanks. I don't think I would've done it without your set-up." I smiled.

"Brianna! A lot of people heard about yet another pre-race incident with Eddie Ibsen today. Can you give us your version of what happened?"

"You know what? I would much rather talk about the race. I think y'all should know by now that I'm not gonna comment on anything that involves Eddie," I explained.

"You've taken over the points lead after Jamie and other drivers in the top five crashing. You were the only one in the top five in points that didn't have any problems on the track today," somebody called out.

"Was that a question? Sounded like a points recap," I laughed. "Guess I just got lucky today. I had an awesome car today, thanks to my crew and my new teammate here helping me out." I patted Dug on the shoulder and the reporters turned to the men for their comments.

Dave finally arrived and called an end to the press conference, announcing there would be a review of the various incidents and fines would be handed out accordingly.

Kyle put his arm around my waist as we walked to the car with Doug and Ricky to head to the airport for the flight home.

Boarding the plane, the team erupted in cheers and the party continued for the entire flight.

* * * * *

CHAPTER FORTY-SEVEN

Mooresville, NC

Monday morning, I made a detour on my way to the shop.

"Hello Miz Lane. What can I do for you this morning?" The receptionist greeted me with a smile.

"I'd like to see the boss if he's available," I replied.

"Do you have an appointment?"

"Now, you know I don't. But I'm sure if you want this team to keep running so you have a job to come to, you'll ring the boss and have him squeeze five minutes from his oh-so-busy schedule for me," I smiled sweetly, leaning on her desk as she picked up the phone and dialled.

"Sir? Brianna Lane is here to see you," she paused. "Yes, sir. I'll let her know." Hanging up the phone, she looked up at me.

"Don't even THINK about bullshitting me," I warned.

"No ma'am. He's on his way down," she informed me. I turned to look around the lobby. One wall held a trophy case and photographs.

"Well, Brianna Lane! What a pleasure to finally meet you! Please, come to my office where we can sit." He turned and let the way upstairs, holding the office door open for me. Sitting down, I looked around the small office.

"I'm sure you know why I've come here today," I began.

"Unfortunately, I do know this isn't a social call." He leaned back in his chair, looking intently at me. "I just finished talking to Dave actually. Trying to come up with some sort of solution that will benefit everybody."

"And? Did you find one?" I asked.

"There are a few different options. But until I come to a definite decision. Well, I'd rather keep the options quiet for now."

"Look," I stood up, planting my palms squarely on the desktop and looking him in the eye. "I don't give two fucks what options you've come up with. But get this straight and get it through to your fuckhead driver. I want this shit to stop. I AM NOT Daytona and I have NOTHING to do with YOU being banned from NASCAR."

"You ARE a spirited one, aren't you? I gotta say, I like that in a woman," Evon smiled at me.

"And I've really learned to respect and appreciate women race car drivers. Why don't you let me take you out sometime? We could have some fun together." He winked, running a hand up my arm.

"You disgusting pig!" I pulled my arm away. "If you ever touch me again, I'll break your hand. And if your son pulls one more stunt, I'll make sure he joins you on the lifetime ban list."

"Alright. Alright." Evon put his hands up in surrender. "I'm sorry. I should've known you'd never consider going out with me, not with my past. But I promise I will talk to my son today and make sure he knows to stop this silliness."

"Silliness? You call what he's been doing 'silliness'? This isn't silliness. It's stupidity and idiocy. And one way or another it's going to stop. Either you stop it or I will." I turned and walked out of the office, out of the shop and headed to meet with my own team.

* * *

After the meeting, I decided to take advantage of the unseasonably warm weather and drove home for a swim. Changing into a bikini and tying my hair back, I grabbed a towel and the phone and headed out to the pool. Setting the towel and phone on a chair, I slipped into the pool and began with slow, easy strokes. After a dozen or so laps, I rested, leaning my head back on the edge of the pool, my eyes closed and let the water hold me.

Hearing the patio door slide open and footsteps on the deck, I smiled.

"You know, it's a good thing we don't have a lot to do to get ready for this weekend. Are you going to join me for a swim?" I asked without looking behind me.

Suddenly two strong hands pushed me under the water. Struggling to break the surface, I clawed at the hands that were around my throat. Planting my feet firmly on the bottom, I pushed myself up and managed to break free. Trying to catch my breath, I focussed on Eddie at the edge of the pool, looking around.

"You won't find a weapon out here asshole." I moved to the edge of the pool away from him to climb out. I knew I had a better chance for survival out of the pool. As I stood, Eddie ran towards me and I braced for his hit, hoping to push him off balance and into the pool. He dragged me in with him and circled my throat, holding me under the surface again. I grabbed his thumbs and pulled them back enough to hurt and force him to loosen his hold so I could free myself. As I pushed myself away from him, I stood up. Regaining my footing and catching my breath, I barely saw the movement as Eddie punched me, knocking me backwards in the water.

Quickly swimming to the side, I pulled myself out, hearing Eddie splashing behind me. I wasn't quick enough though and Eddie grabbed my leg, pulling me off balance and I fell to the deck. I scrambled back to my feet as Eddie pulled himself out of the pool.

"You're dead bitch!" I heard him behind me as I ran into the house. Slipping on the tile in the kitchen, I headed towards the safety of my office. As I ran down the hall, Eddie caught me and I screamed as he tackled me, bringing me down on my left side. Rearing back, I hit him as hard as I could with the back of my head before twisting around to aim an elbow at his face.

Grabbing my arm, he flipped me over onto my back, digging a knee into my ribs. Trying not to scream in pain, I took a couple deep breaths. I knew I needed to calm down and think quickly to free myself from this madman.

"Let him think he's beat you," I heard Craig's voice in my head. I forced myself to stop struggling and relaxed my body.

"Come on Brie. I know you've got more fight left in you. Don't disappoint me." Eddie put more pressure on my ribs as he hit me again and I could feel my ribs cracking again. Screaming, I punched him in the side of the head, knocking him off balance enough to push him off me.

On my feet again, I ran into my office to my desk. Opening the bottom drawer, I pulled out my gun and clicked the safety off. Standing up, I spun around and raised the gun to shoulder level as Eddie burst through the door.

"That's not real," he said, stepping closer.

"No? Are you sure about that? Did you forget I was a cop before I moved to Mooresville?" I asked. "Take another step and you'll find out how real it is." I picked up the phone on my desk and dialled.

"This is Brianna Lane. I have an intruder in my house. I need a unit dispatched and if they're not here in five minutes, you'll need to send EMS too."

"Ma'am, I have a unit in the vicinity. I'm going to keep you on the line til they arrive." I could hear as the emergency dispatcher radioed the address and details before she came back to me. "A patrol car is on its way to you. Do you know where in your house the intruder is?"

"Standing right in front of me." I could hear the approaching sirens getting louder as Eddie started backing out of the room. I fired a shot into the doorframe beside his head and he dropped to the floor.

"Ma'am?" the dispatcher addressed me.

"Get off my floor fuckhead. If you take one more step towards the door, I will put a bullet in your ass," I warned him as he slowly stood up.

"Ma'am?"

"What?"

"Did you shoot him?" she asked.

"No. I shot my house. And yes, I do have a licence to carry a firearm. I'm a retired officer from Greensboro."

"Okay. The responding patrol car is in your driveway."

"Have them go around to the back. The patio door is open. We're through the kitchen and down the hall."

"I'm getting a report of another gentleman there, identifying himself as an officer with a key to your house."

"That'll be James. It's okay." I heard the front door open then and James calling my name.

"We're in the office!" I called out to him as I hung up the phone and lowered my gun. James led the way into my office and the two officers quickly handcuffed Eddie. James took the gun from me and re-engaged the safety before putting it away and turning to me.

"Are you okay, Brie?" he asked, lightly touching the tender bruises forming on my cheek from where Eddie had punched me.

"Yeah," I paused. "No. I think he might've re-fractured my ribs."

"Okay. I'm taking you to the hospital to get checked out. Go put some jeans on."

"We're gonna need a statement."

"Then I guess you'd better follow us to the hospital. You can get one while the doctors tape her up again."

By the time I returned downstairs, James had brought the phone back inside and locked the patio door. Eddie had been escorted to the waiting patrol car, and James was standing at the front door talking on his cell phone.

"Yeah. I'm gonna take her to the hospital now. She thinks the ribs might've been re-broken in the fight and she's got a couple bruises," he paused. "Hey, you forget she's a tough kick-ass chick. I'll let her tell you about it when you get home. Don't worry. I'll take good care of her."

James hung up and handed me my purse as we walked out the front door. Locking up, he led me to his truck and helped me into the passenger seat.

Getting behind the wheel and starting the engine, James chuckled and shook his head, before backing out of the driveway.

"What the hell is so funny about me being attacked by that fuckhead?"

"You know the dispatcher had your call patched through to the radio of the patrol car that responded, don't you?"

"So? What's your point?"

"We were standing in the driveway when you threatened to shoot Eddie in the ass," he paused, looking over at me. "I made them wait to go in, just hoping you WOULD shoot him."

I smiled and shook my head.

"You would do that wouldn't you? Wait a minute! Why the hell were you coming home anyway? Y'all were supposed to be practicing pit stops today." I looked over at him.

"You're gonna think I'm crazy if I tell you," James replied.

"No I won't. Just tell me."

"Craig told me you needed help." He glanced at me as my mouth hung open in shock. "See? I told you. You think I'm crazy. But I'm telling you; we were in the middle of a stop, and I swear I heard Craig's voice. Clear as a bell. Shit. I dropped the gas can. Thought he was right beside me."

"Seriously?"

"I'm serious Brie. So I took off like a bat outta hell to get home and got followed up the street by lights and siren."

"Holy crap." I looked out the windshield. The hospital was only another block away. I took a deep breath and finally spoke again as James helped me out of the truck.

"Craig was with me too. While I was fighting Eddie. There have been other times too."

We walked into the emergency room, followed by one of the uniformed officers. Luckily, the emergency room was empty and I was taken in for x-rays right away.

Once the x-rays were done, another officer had arrived; this one with a camera to document the bruising on my face and neck. The tape had been cut off for the x-rays and the second officer pointed to the bruising.

"Is that from the attack as well?" I looked down. Most of the bruising from the crash had turned an ugly yellow and begun to fade, but I could see darker bruising beginning to develop.

"Obviously not the older stuff. That's from a crash three weeks ago. But the darker ones are from today."

"How did your ribs get broken?"

"Originally? Or today? The original break came from a wreck in New Hampshire. Today's break is from Eddie sitting on me," I explained as the doctor walked in. While he tightly re-taped them, I gave my statement to the police.

"You're all set," the doctor said as he finished. "Try to take it easy this time."

I stood up and walked with James out towards the waiting room. A nurse stopped us before we walked through the door.

"You don't want to go out there," she warned. "It would be better if you went out through the front doors."

"Why?" James asked.

"My waiting room is packed with reporters. Photographers. Fans. It's crazy," she explained.

"Well the only way YOU are going to get rid of them is for ME to go out there," I replied. "If I sneak out a different door, they're here for the rest of the day."

I continued down the hall and through the door. As soon as I opened the door, the crowd jumped to attention, rushing towards me. With James beside me, the other officers took up spots in front of and behind me.

"Brianna! Can you tell us what happened?"

"Is it true you shot Eddie Ibsen?"

"Did you kill him in self-defense?"

I held up my hand for silence. The officer in front of me moved aside so I could answer the questions.

"I was attacked at my home this afternoon. The individual who attacked me is currently in police custody. No, I did NOT shoot Eddie or anybody else today. So, no I didn't kill Eddie in self-defense or otherwise. Thank you."

Stepping forward, I moved into the crowd, causing them to step aside to allow me to pass.

Back in James' truck, I signed the bottom of my statement so the police could return to Headquarters to file the official report. I rested my head on the back of the seat and closed my eyes as James drove out of the parking lot.

"Back home now?" James asked.

"Yeah. I just want to lay down with an ice pack and rest," I replied without opening my eyes.

When we arrived home, James sent me to the family room to relax while he got an ice pack from the freezer. Carefully setting it on my ribs, he sat on the floor in front of the couch and turned on the television, flipping through the channels.

"Is there anything decent on tv at this time of day?" he asked. Opening my eyes, I looked at him.

"You're asking ME about daytime tv listings? Do you have any idea when the last time was that I watched daytime television?" I laughed. "All the channels we have on the satellite, I'm sure you can find something."

"Yeah, I'm sure there's something on."

"Of course, there's always soap operas if you get really desperate for something to watch." James looked over at me, an eyebrow raised.

"Did you hit your head during the attack?" he laughed.

"Try the movie channels," I suggested, closing my eyes again. I fell asleep with James holding my hand.

When I woke up, James was replacing the ice pack and I could hear Kyle moving around in the kitchen.

"Good morning, sleepyhead. Did you have a nice nap?" James smiled as he sat on the edge of the couch. I nodded as I slowly moved to sit up.

"How long did I sleep?" I asked.

"Just over an hour. Long enough for the first ice pack to get nice and warm. Kyle's home too. Daytona called to find out how you're doing. Dave too."

"I'll call them back later."

"I already took care of it. I told them both you were taped up and resting. But that I'd have you call them tomorrow."

"You take such good care of me. All these years I've been retired and you've still got my back," I smiled as I stood up.

"I promised Craig the night I met you and he told me he was going to marry you that I'd take care of you if anything ever happened to him," James explained as we walked into the kitchen.

"Hey! You're awake! How're you feeling?" Kyle asked, gently putting his arms around me.

"Sore. Tired. Pissed off," I answered.

"All the news reports were saying you shot Eddie." Kyle looked closely at me.

"That's bullshit! I didn't shoot him. I fired a warning shot, that's all. I could've hit him if I'd wanted to," I paused. "Well, I DID want to. But I didn't do it. I'm sure he'll be milking it for all it's worth though. That I shot at him. And that I must be losing my skills since I missed him. I'm sure he doesn't realize I missed on purpose."

"Yeah. Well, at least you're okay. I mean, aside from some nasty bruises and whatnot," Kyle rubbed my back while he held me. When the door burst open a minute later, I jumped. Jessika rushed into the room, followed closely by Mark.

"Holy shit Mom! You're all over the news! Are you okay?" She threw her arms around me.

"Whoa! I'm fine," I assured her. "Now that you're here, let's all sit down and I'll explain what really happened."

"Dinner's ready," Kyle interrupted. "So why don't we all sit down and we can hear your story while we eat."

"Good idea." I led the way to the dining room while Kyle and James quickly set the table and brought the food in.

Once everybody was seated, I began re-telling the events of the afternoon. By the time I was done, Mark was staring wide-eyed at me while James chuckled beside me.

"So you didn't actually shoot Eddie?" Jessika asked.

"No. I only fired once. I could've. Lord knows I wanted to. But I didn't shoot him. The bullet is in the doorframe in my office. You can see for yourself," I told her.

"Jake and I will put out a press release tomorrow and put an official statement on the website."

"Thanks Jess. I'm sure it's gonna be on the news until after we get to the track. One good thing though; at least we're at home this week. I can hang out here until it's time to go to practice."

Changing the subject, I turned to Kyle to ask him about the set-up for the upcoming weekend.

* * * * *

CHAPTER FORTY-EIGHT

Keeping a low profile the rest of the week, I chose to work from home, answering mail and returning phone calls. The team email was set to come to my house as well as the shop so I could work from home occasionally.

Daytona had called me the morning after the attack. I answered the phone in my kitchen as I made my coffee.

"Look out your back window," she instructed me. Doing as she told me, I could see her standing on her patio as a tall muscular man strolled through her yard to our adjoining gate.

"What's going on Daytona? What's with the cop?" I could tell by the way he carried himself.

"I'm sending you Rick's old partner, Jon. He's retired now and does private security. He's one of the best and was part of my security team when I was being stalked," she explained as he made his way through my yard and around the pool to my patio door.

"I don't need a bodyguard," I told her as I unlocked the door to let him in. He closed the door, locking it and looked around the room.

"Yeah. I thought that too. And I fought against it for the longest time. Just try it out for the rest of the season. Jon and his guys will just be around when James can't be there and as an added back-up. I know you can take care of yourself, but until you're healed from Eddie's attack, you need extra protection," Daytona reasoned.

"Okay," I sighed. "I give up. I know you won't take no for an answer. So thank you for looking out for me. I appreciate it."

"Good. I'll be over later to see how you're getting along." She hung up then and waved before disappearing into her house. Shaking my head, I turned to face my new bodyguard.

Before I could say a word, Jon put his hands up.

"She told me you'd argue about this. And she wants me to tell you: Don't be such a stubborn bitch. Take the protection and don't fight it."

"Okay. I give up. I know her well enough to know once she gets something in her head she doesn't back down til she gets her way." I laughed. "Can I get you some coffee?"

"I'll get it myself. If I'm gonna be hanging around for a while, I'm gonna get to know you and your house pretty good." He turned to the cupboards. "Like two peas in a fucking pod. Are you sure you two aren't related?"

Once he had his coffee, I gave him a tour of the house before we sat in the office for me to get my work done.

James and Kyle both agreed it was a good idea to have the extra protection when they arrived home and heard the news.

* * *

When we arrived at the track Thursday afternoon for practice, I was surrounded by reporters hoping for another comment about the attack. Dave had called that morning to let me know NASCAR had suspended Eddie's licence for the remainder of the season.

"Please. I've already made an official statement about the events of Monday afternoon. I'm sure everybody involved would appreciate if y'all would let the matter rest so we can get on with our lives and try to get back to normal. Thank you."

I turned to the crew then as they prepared the car for me to take it out on the track.

"She's all set. Ready when you are," Kyle told me. "You feel up to running today?"

"I don't have much choice, do I?" I closed my eyes, breathing slowly. "I'll take it easy out there. I'm not gonna push myself any more than normal. But I have to be able to run the car Saturday. Just make sure we have lots of ice ready for me."

"Got it. Between now and Saturday, I'll make sure we've got a cooler just for ice for you."

Carefully climbing into the car, I settled myself into the seat as James held out an ice pack for me. After tucking it into my firesuit, I slowly fastened the safety belts. Once I was ready, I flipped the switches to start the engines, checked my mirrors to back out of the garage and headed out to the track.

Getting out onto the racing surface, I concentrated on how the car was running to be able to let Kyle know if anything needed to be adjusted.

I ran behind Jamie for a while until he waved me by to pull in front. As soon as I passed him though, and he had tucked his car in behind my rear bumper, my car became harder to handle. I moved up the track to run in a different groove, with the same results. I waved back at Jamie and headed to the garage. Pulling into the garage stall, I shut the engine off and took off my helmet, setting it on my lap.

"What's up Brie?" Kyle asked.

"She won't run in clean air. If I'm running behind somebody, it's perfect. But the second I passed Jamie, the car went squirrelly. She's a bitch to get to turn into the corners then the ass end breaks loose coming out of the turns. I won't be able to finish the race that way. Just those couple laps of wrestling her wore me out."

"Okay. We'll change things up a bit and get that corrected. Then when you're ready, you can head back out there."

I slowly climbed out of the car and walked with Jon back to the motorhome. Getting a fresh ice pack and a bottle of water, I tossed the already soft pack into the freezer and settled on the couch with Daytona's newest book. She had brought over one of the pre-release copies for me when they arrived. Less than an hour later, I could hear Doug outside shouting and went to the door to find out what the commotion was. Jon was close behind me and I gasped as I watched Doug swing at Ricky.

Jon stepped forward as Ricky tackled Doug to the ground. Putting my hand on his arm to stop him, I never took my eyes off the two men fighting between our motorhomes. With Doug pinned down and yelling, Ricky raised his fist.

"Ricky!" I warned him, stepping out of my motorhome. "Enough already. What the hell is the matter with the both of you?" I walked the couple feet over to them and looked down at them. Ricky stood up, shoving Doug away.

"Crazy bastard," Ricky shook his head. "The bitch left you and Mandy. Why the hell do you care what happened to her?"

"She was still my wife! Don't you dare talk to me about how I should feel!" Doug shouted, stepping forward.

Stepping between them, I put my hands on Doug's chest to stop him. I knew as mad as he was at Ricky, he wouldn't hurt me.

"Ricky, go hang out in my motorhome. Go work on the car. Take a walk. Just do something that's not here," I told him.

"Don't touch my fucking car!" Doug yelled. "I don't want him anywhere near any of my shit Brie."

"Fine. Ricky, can you go help Kyle with my car please? He'll let you know what we need." I turned to Jon. "I'm gonna be over here in Doug's motorhome for a little while. I'll let you know when I'm ready to head back to the garage."

He nodded and I gave Doug a shove towards his motorhome.

Inside, he leaned on the counter, his head hung down. Getting a bottle of water out of his fridge, I set it on the counter in front of him and gently put my hand on his shoulder.

"Doug?" I asked quietly. "What just happened out there?"

"She's dead," he replied dully.

"Who?" I moved my hand up to his face to make him look at me.

"Jenny. Mandy's mother."

"Oh baby. I'm sorry. But I thought you were divorced?"

Doug shook his head.

"I couldn't bring myself to have the papers filed. I guess I figured one day she'd change her mind and come back."

"Eighteen years is a long time to wait for her."

"Yeah. You'd think I would've accepted it after the first couple that she wasn't coming home to us."

"So what happened? How did you find out? When did it happen?" I asked.

"State troopers said she drove off the road and hit a tree. There was an empty bottle on the floor, so they figure she was drunk. Would you believe after all this time, she still had me listed as her in case of emergency contact?"

I put my arms around him and hugged him as he cried quietly.

"Just let it out. It's okay to grieve for her," I said. "Do you want me to call Mandy for you?"

"I don't know that she'll care. She never knew her mom except for through pictures and some old home movies I had from when we were first married."

"Well, it's better to hear it from you, or a friend, instead of hearing it on the evening news." I picked up his cell phone and dialled Mandy's number while he went to sit on the couch.

"Come on Jonathon. It's my Dad. I have to answer it," I heard her say. "Hi Daddy!"

"Mandy. It's Brianna," I began.

"Oh my God! What happened to my Dad?" she asked.

"Nothing. Your Dad is fine. He's right here with me," I explained.

"Oh. Okay. So what's up?"

"Mandy. It's about your Mom, honey."

"What about her? Did her finally darken the doorstep to mess with Dad some more?"

"No sweetie. The State Police notified your Dad a little while ago that she'd died in a car crash."

"Oh," she paused. "Well, okay. Thanks for letting me know. Maybe Dad'll move on now and find a woman who loves him. I'll come home for the funeral if he wants. Just let me know when it is." She hung up then and I looked at the phone for a minute, shaking my head, before I set it back on the counter and walked over to sit with Doug.

"I told you she wouldn't care."

"I'm sure she'll grieve in her own time. But she said she'll come home for the funeral to be with you."

"How do you grieve for someone you never knew? Miss something you've never had? Mandy was barely a week old when Jenny drove off. Left me alone with a newborn without even a backwards glance."

"I don't know Doug. But you know I'm here if you need anything. A shoulder to lean on. A friendly ear to listen. But I gotta draw the line before fighting. At least for the next six weeks. But I'll gladly offer up James or Jon if you need a good ass-kicking. They'd go easier on you than I would anyway."

Doug laughed and looked at me.

"Thanks. I will definitely take you up on that. Maybe the ass-kicking too. Oh man. What am I gonna do about Ricky?" He buried his face in his hands.

"I'll tell you what you're gonna do. You're gonna get off your ass. You're gonna swallow your pride and put aside that Texas-sized ego of yours. And you're gonna go apologize to your best friend."

"You think he's gonna wanna hear it?"

"He's your best friend Doug. You've been together a helluva long time. As long as you're willing to say it, I'm sure he'll listen. I'll even go with you. I'm sure Kyle's got my car changed by now so I can practice without worrying about smacking the wall." Standing up, I walked to the door. "Let's go."

Walking out the door, I stopped to get Jon from my motorhome on the way to the garage. When a group of reporters approached Doug, I stepped in front of him.

"I'm sorry. Doug and I are on our way onto the track to practice. Any questions you have you can field through Jake or Jessika for now. Otherwise there will be an official statement released tomorrow. Until then, I'm going to ask you all to please respect the privacy of Doug and his family at this difficult time." I took Doug's arm and led him through the garage to where Kyle and Ricky were leaning on my car.

"Okay boys. Playtime is over. Ricky. Go with Doug back to the Chevy garage. It's time for you both to kiss and make up. You were both acting like jackasses. Get over it. I don't have the energy to keep breaking up your fights." Both men stared at me.

"Damn. You're pretty pushy lady."

"Yep. And I could still kick both your asses. So be good little boys and do what you're told," I laughed as I waved them away before I turned to Kyle.

"She's all set. I think we got all the issues corrected."

"Good. You know I'd rather race instead of wreck. And I would've wrecked if I'd stayed out there."

I climbed into the seat and repeated my routine to get out onto the track. My car ran much better than the first time out and Doug and I drafted together for the rest of the practice session.

* * *

Doug qualified on the pole the next day with Jamie close behind him on the outside of the front row. Our changes during practice worked well for us, securing me a third place start right behind Doug.

Once qualifying was done, we took our crews out to celebrate. When we walked into Daytona's in Charlotte, the place was already packed. I had called ahead though and arranged for tables for our two teams.

Walking through the bar, Doug and I were stopped by fans for autographs and pictures. After we'd signed for a couple tables, I gave Doug a nudge towards our teams.

"Come on. We're all gonna be here for a while. I'm starving. We'll make the rounds to mingle after we eat," I explained as I kept him moving to the tables where our teams waited.

Taking a seat beside Kyle, I saw the waitress had already delivered pitchers of beer and pop to the team.

After we'd eaten, Doug headed out into the crowd while I stayed at the table with Kyle and James. Jon had gone home when we'd left the track, knowing James would be nearby the rest of the night. Kyle lightly rubbed my back as I kept a close watch on Doug making his way around the bar.

"Ricky told me about their fight today. And how you stepped between them. What the hell were you thinking?"

"I knew Doug wouldn't hit me. Besides, Jon was right there," I pointed out.

"So you should've let Jon break it up. You're not a cop anymore Brie."

"Really? Thanks for pointing that out. I must've forgotten that fact. Geez, Kyle. I was trying to be a friend. I wasn't acting as a cop when I got between them."

"Well, I still think you were crazy to get between them. You shoulda let them fight it out or had Jon break it up," Kyle argued.

"Thanks. I'll be sure to remember that for next time. Shall I ask your permission to go sign some autographs now too?" Standing, I walked away from the table to make my way around the bar.

Eventually I caught up to Doug and we had a few pictures taken together with fans. Between tables I put my hand on his arm and looked up at him.

"You doing okay?" I asked.

"Yeah. I'm fine," Doug looked away.

"Liar."

"Well, what the fuck do you expect? My wife died today. How should I be?" Doug burst out.

"Hey! I'm trying to help you here. I know what you're going through," I began before he interrupted.

"Do you really? How could you? With your perfect little life?" Doug argued. "How do you even begin to imagine the hell I'm going through?"

"You wanna know? You really wanna know? I held my husband while he died. It's MY fault Jessika's father was killed because I fucked up a drug bust. So don't you dare tell me I don't know what you're going through!" James walked up to us then, interrupting the argument.

"Brie? Are you just about ready to go?" he asked.

"Yeah. It's been a long day. I'm ready whenever you are." I turned back to Doug. "See you at the track tomorrow."

"What was that all about?" James asked once we were outside.

"Nothing. Just Doug blowing off steam. He's gonna have a rough couple days I think. You know this would probably be easier for him to get through if Mandy could actually understand. But I know she never knew her mother and I could tell when I called her today. She didn't care. I could've told her the dog ate her favorite shoes and gotten more of a reaction from her."

"Well, I'm sure Doug knows his friends are here for him when he needs them. I caught the end of the conversation though. Why are you still blaming yourself for Craig's death?"

"Because it was my fault. How many times do we have to have this conversation? I should've known who was involved. And I never should've taken Craig in that night. The whole fuck-up was mine. There's no denying it," I pointed out as we reached my truck where Kyle was waiting.

"No denying what?" Kyle asked.

"Nothing," James replied.

"No denying I fucked up the bust that killed Craig," I answered at the same time.

"Brie, we've talked about this before. There's no way you could've known. How many times did we go over everything that happened leading up to that night? Any one of us would've done it the same way. You know you did everything the right way."

"If I'd done everything the right way, we wouldn't be having this conversation. And Craig would still be alive. I know I fucked up. I live with that fact every damn day. So why do you keep telling me I did everything right? I killed Craig as sure as if I'd pulled the trigger myself!"

"Dammit Brie!" James exploded. "Craig knew the risks of the job. We all did. Have you forgotten he's the one who wanted to go in that night? If he'd had any doubts, any at all, he would've waited. You know that. You can't keep blaming yourself for something that was out of your control."

"Well, I'm sorry, but I AM going to blame myself. No matter how many times you tell me it wasn't my fault. I KNOW I should've handled it differently."

"Does beating yourself up about it make it any easier to deal with? Make you miss him any less?" James leaned forward to put a hand on my shoulder. "I miss him too. He was more than just my best friend. We were like brothers."

I bit my lip as I turned away. Looking out the window, I fought the tears that threatened to spill. We spend the rest of the ride home in silence.

* * * * *

CHAPTER FORTY-NINE

Saturday morning as planned, Jon was waiting for me in the driveway when I walked out the door to head to the track. Kyle and James had left a few minutes before to start preparing for the race.

He handed me a cup of coffee after I fastened my seatbelt and he pulled out of the driveway.

"Thanks. I can definitely use this today."

"Rough night? I remember Daytona used to get stressed during the final couple months of the season. Especially when her or Matt were in the Chase," Jon glanced at me as he stopped at the end of the block.

"Yeah. The Chase is part of the stress," I paused to sip my coffee.

"You're not worried about Eddie are you? They're holding him until his trial. The judge refused bail for him, citing past history. The judge isn't about to let him walk the streets, knowing he broke into your house and tried to kill you," Jon explained.

"Actually I'm not really worried about Eddie. I can't imagine he'd be stupid enough to come after me again so soon."

"So what else is on your mind? Doug?"

"Doug?" I sighed, shaking my head. "Not really. I mean, I know he's going through a rough time right now, with his wife dying. But aside from him being my friend and teammate, and he knows I'm here if he needs to talk, his stuff is the least of my worries right now."

"So? If it's not Eddie or Doug, what's bothering you? Everything okay with you and Kyle?"

"Yeah. Things are great, I think," I hesitated. "I guess you can probably relate better than most people. I'm still having issues with Craig's death. I suppose that's the easiest way to explain. I KNOW I could've – and should've – handled the bust differently that night. I live with the guilt of screwing up every day. But I've got James telling me how I did everything right. I don't see how that's possible if Craig died that night. Obviously I fucked up somewhere."

"So you want me to beat you up like you've been doing to yourself for six years? Tell you that you're right? You fucked up and it's a good thing you gave up your badge?" Jon asked.

"Sure. It would be a refreshing change instead of everybody kissing my ass as the grieving widow."

"How about I let you beat yourself up since you've been doing such a good job at it this long? And instead, I'll tell you what I learned. The pain of losing your partner, especially the way we did, that pain never goes away. Twenty years later, I still miss Rick. I still have nightmares and flashbacks of that night. I certainly wish things had played out differently and that Rick hadn't died. Being the one who survived that night, yeah, I definitely wonder why it was him that was hit. But I also believe everything happens for a reason. We may never know why something happens, especially something senseless like Rick or Craig being killed. But both their deaths set things in motion that otherwise might not have happened. You and I both know that," Jon replied.

"I'd still be a cop if Craig hadn't died," I offered. "At least I think so. It was his death that got me re-thinking my life and career choices. I didn't want to be a cop anymore. I mean, I suppose I could've stayed and kept working on cleaning up the street, but without him there, I just couldn't keep going."

"Exactly. And Daytona probably wouldn't have married Matt if Rick hadn't been killed. She would be with Rick and might've possibly moved back home. Which means I wouldn't be here either. I'd be enjoying a quiet retirement back in Windsor."

"Does it ever get any easier? I mean the pain is still as strong today was it was six years ago. I don't expect it to go away completely. But does it ever fade just a little? Do you ever close your eyes and NOT see it happening all over again?"

"Sure. But it takes time. You're right that it'll never completely go away. But over time it will get easier. I'll admit I still think about Rick at least once a day, sometimes more. We all still have days that are harder to get through, like the anniversary of his death. But whenever one of us has a rough day, we have the others to lean on. Just like you have Kyle and James to lean on."

"Kyle doesn't really get it though. He never met Craig. He moved down here after I bought the team from Daytona and Matt."

"Well, what about James? Or any of the other guys you were working with?"

"Every time James and I talk about it, he tells me I did everything right. And to stop beating myself up about it. I haven't seen the others since I moved here after Craig died. Whenever I go back, it's just to visit his grave and his parents; that's it," I explained.

"Well, James did have a bit more experience than you, didn't he?" Jon asked.

"Yeah. Probably ten years before I joined the department. Why?"

"Usually with that experience comes the ability to know where to place the blame of a fuck up. Tell me something. Do you honestly think James would be here today, helping out on your crew, if he thought you were the one to blame for Craig's death? Or is it possible that no amount of prep time would've prevented Craig being killed?"

Jon showed our team credentials and parking pass to the security guard at the track before being waved through.

"No. I don't think he blames me for Craig's death. He keeps telling me I did everything right. I'm grateful for all his help. But yeah, I wish he'd tell me I fucked up."

"But with all his experience, if he's saying you led the operation properly, followed all the procedures, don't you think you should listen to what he's saying? I haven't known him a long time, but from the few times I've talked to him, I know he's got a hell of a lot of respect for you. And if he thought you were to blame, he'd say so," Jon pointed out as he parked the car. I thought about what he'd said as we walked to the garage.

Kyle and the team was busily going over the car, doing all the race day checks to make sure everything was ready before the car would be taken through inspection.

"I suppose you're right. I never really looked at it that way," I agreed. "I know I'm always going to feel guilty, like I know there's something I could've done differently. But I can see what you're saying."

"Good. And you know I'm here if you ever need to talk about it," Jon reminded me.

"Thanks. I appreciate that."

"Hey Brie. Weather's looking perfect for today. Got a little break in the temps this afternoon. Still gonna be warm, but not as hot as the past couple days. And no clouds expected either," James joined us.

"That's good news. Should be a good day for us then. I'm gonna need ice at every stop though. You'll make sure there's a full cooler for me?" I reminded him.

"Of course. Jess and Mark are in the hauler making up the ice packs now," James told me.

"Cool. I'm gonna stop in there on my way to the motorhome. That's where I'll be if anybody needs me. Has anybody seen Doug yet this morning?" I looked around. My crew shook their heads.

"I'm sure he'll be here soon. If he's not already here. Hanging out in his motorhome maybe?" Kyle suggested.

"Probably. I'll leave you guys to finish up here. See you at the drivers meeting," I leaned over to kiss Kyle and was surprised when he walked away instead.

"Damn," I heard Jon say quietly as I shook my head. Taking my arm, he led me away, heading toward the hauler.

"What the hell was that? Did he really turn his back to me? He's never done that," I looked back as we walked away.

"Deal with it after. I spent enough race weekends with Daytona to know a typical race day routine. So I know you need to focus on your job for today and forget about everything else for a while. Right?"

"Yeah. I guess whatever the issue is, it'll still be there after the race. And we can deal with it then," I agreed as we walked into the hauler.

Jessika and Mark were quietly making up ice packs and stacking them in a small cooler. They both looked up as we walked in.

"Hey Mom. We're almost done here. I'm gonna put the ice packs in the freezer in the motorhome til closer to race time."

"Sounds good to me. I'm heading to the motorhome now to hang out til the drivers meeting."

"Okay. We'll be over there soon. The cooler's almost full now," Jess explained.

As Jon and I headed to the motorhome, I was stopped by fans for autographs and a couple pictures. Jon stayed close to my side until the last autograph had been signed and the last picture taken. I knew he was used to it after the years he'd spent protecting Daytona.

"You now, I never really understood this whole side of the sport. I mean, I get that you're famous and all over the television and newspapers every week. But I know from hanging around drivers as long as I have, you're all just like me or the average Joe. And yet, most fans will hang out somewhere for hours waiting to meet their favorite drivers."

"I think part of it is because we're all just like regular people. At least most of us are. We just have real cool jobs to go to every day. Hey! I'm still trying to get used to the idea that hundreds of people want my autograph every weekend."

"Yeah. I don't know if I'd ever get used to that. I guess that's why I like to stay in the background."

When we got to the motorhome, I knocked on the door to Doug's while Jon unlocked mine. Getting no answer, I crossed the short distance to where Jon held the door open and slowly climbed the few steps into my home away from home.

Getting a bottle of water from the fridge, I settled on the couch to watch the morning news. Tuning it out, I gazed out the window, wondering where Doug was. Normally on race day, he was up early, wandering around the garage and pits to mingle with the fans. I was surprised a short time later, when Mandy appeared and unlocked the door of Doug's motorhome. When she came back out a minute later and looked around, I could see she was worried.

"Brianna?" she called out. "Can you come over please?"

"I'll be right back," I said to Jon.

"Want me to come too?" he asked as I stood.

"No. If I need you, I'll let you know. She probably just wants to know if I know where Doug is." Walking outside, I crossed back over to Doug's motorhome. When I stepped inside. I was shocked to see Doug passed out on the couch surrounded by empty beer bottles.

"Are you fucking kidding me?" I shook my head. "Mandy, put on a pot of coffee please."

"Okay." Mandy quickly moved to the kitchen counter, looking for coffee. "There isn't any."

"There's a full pot in my motorhome. Go get it and bring it over then." I turned to Doug. "Doug? Hey! Time to get up. It's race day." I put my hand on his shoulder as I raised my voice.

"Fuck off and get out," he stood up and headed towards the bedroom. I could tell he was obviously still drunk.

"What did you say?" I asked as Mandy walked back in with the coffee.

"You heard me," he growled. "Fuck off and get out." He pointed towards the door.

"Daddy!" Mandy squeaked.

"Mandy. Go wait in my motorhome while I talk to your dad," I said firmly.

"But the coffee," she argued.

"I don't think your dad's ready for it," I explained, not taking my eyes off Doug. Once I heard the door close behind her, I stepped towards Doug. He'd stopped just outside the bedroom door.

"What part of get out don't you get? Or do you need me to put you out?" Doug demanded.

"I'm not leaving. And I don't believe you'd put your hands on me," I calmly replied, stopping him front of him. I could see a mixture of emotions flash across his face; pain, confusion and something else I couldn't quite read.

In a split second, he grabbed my shoulders and pinned my back against the wall before lowering his mouth to mine, kissing me forcefully. Breaking the kiss, I pushed him away from me as the door opened again. Jon appeared in the open doorway and looked around.

"Brie?" he asked, looking at us. "Everything okay?"

"Yeah," I turned to Doug. "Go sleep it off. I know you didn't mean what just happened here."

"You don't know even half of what you think you know. Now get out before I show you exactly what I mean." He turned and stumbled into the bedroom, slamming the door behind him. Looking at the closed door for a minute, I shook my head, wondering what he meant.

"Brie? Come on back to your motorhome. He doesn't want your help right now. Let him sleep it off. Talk to him when he's sober. No point in even trying to make sense of him now," Jon suggested.

"You're right," I agreed. "He's just gonna keep being an ass if I try talking to him now. And frankly, I don't give a shit if he sleeps through the race." I headed back to my motorhome where Mandy was pacing.

"Brianna? Is my dad okay?" she asked.

"I'm sure he will be. Once he sleeps off the binge from last night. When was the last time you talked to him?" I poured us each a cup of coffee and led her over to the couch to sit.

"Yesterday afternoon. He said he wanted to be alone after the funeral. I went back to the house to wait for him, but he never came home. I guess he came back here and got ripped," she explained.

"Funeral?" Jon asked. Mandy looked at each of us before answering.

"Dad just wanted something quiet. Just family and her friends. Said he didn't want y'all feeling sorry for him cuz he'd held on for so long waiting for her," She turned to me. "You know how he is. Dealing with shit on his own instead of asking for help."

"Yeah, I know. Listen, I don't think he'll be awake again much before the race. And even if he does wake up before the green, odds are he'll still be way too loaded to drive. Why don't you head back to the house? I'm gonna call Matt to hop in the car today." I picked up my cell phone and dialled Matt's number.

"Hey Brie. Daytona and I were just talking about you," Matt said as he answered the phone.

"You were? I don't suppose by any chance you're on your way to the track, are you?" I asked.

"As a matter of fact, we are. Did you need us to bring you something?"

"Just yourself. Ready to strap into a seat," I replied.

"Are you okay?" I could hear the concern in Matt's voice and smiled.

"What's going on?" I heard Daytona ask.

"I'm fine. It's Doug that needs a replacement. He's in the process of sleeping off a night-long binge," I explained. "There's no way Dave'll let him drive today."

"Crap. Yeah. I'll definitely do that for you. What a dumbass. What the hell was he thinking?"

"I have no idea. I'm gonna let Dave and the crew know. That way there's no surprises. I'll see you when you get here."

Hanging up the phone, Jon and I headed to the garage to let the crew know Matt would be driving. As we walked into the garage, I was stopped by part of the ESPN crew.

"Brianna? Do you have a comment about your crew chief moving to a new team for next year?"

Stopping in my tracks, I looked at Jon, and tried to cover my shock.

"Comment? No. I'll release a formal statement tomorrow through my rep." As they walked away, Jon leaned close to me.

"Do you think it's true? Or just a stupid rumour?"

"I don't know. But I sure as hell intend to find out right now." Heading to the garage stall, I walked straight up to the crew.

"Hey Brie. Car's all set. Any word from Doug yet? Somebody said they saw Mandy's car in the parking lot," James smiled as Jon and I joined them.

"Take a walk boys. I need to have a word with my crew chief please." I looked around at the guys. As they walked away, I pulled James aside. "Can you let Ricky know Matt's gonna be driving for Doug today?"

"Sure. Everything okay?" James asked quietly.

"We'll talk later," I replied.

"So what's up Brie? All of a sudden we can't talk in front of the team?" Kyle asked when we were alone. I leaned on the car and crossed my arms before I answered.

"When were you gonna tell me? Or were you just gonna wait til the media started asking for my comments about it?"

"What?" he asked.

"Don't give me that bullshit! You know damn well what I'm talking about. When were you gonna man up and tell me you were leaving?"

"I don't think this is really the time to talk about this."

"Is there a right time? I mean, come on. Changing teams doesn't just happen overnight. How long have you been thinking about this?"

"Not long. But the last couple days really made me realize I needed to do this. I wanted to tell you myself. Really I did."

"Are you fucking serious?" I couldn't believe what I was hearing.

"I'm gonna finish out the season with you. I'm not leaving you with only a handful of races left."

"Why bother waiting for the end of the season? You can pack up your shit and leave now. You don't want to be here; you got nothing keeping you here." I took my ring off and set it on the roof of the car. "Get an early start on getting to know your new team. We're done."

"I said I'd finish out the season," Kyle argued. "We don't have to end like this."

"Yeah. Apparently we do have to end like this. When I have to find out from ESPN that you've signed on with another team, that's . . . I don't even know what to say," I shook my head. "I'm going to Greensboro tomorrow so you can clear your stuff out of the house and the shop."

Turning away, I walked over to where Jon stood with the crew, waiting for me. I looked at each of them as they watched me.

"Anybody else wanna bail on me?" I asked. They all silently shook their heads. "Okay. So if the car's ready, let's get it out to inspection. I've got a drivers' meeting to get to. Somebody please call Drew and let him know I need him on the pit box today." The crew all jumped to get moving on their race day duties, as Jon and I headed to the drivers' meeting.

Matt, Daytona and Ricky were already there, holding extra seats for us. They looked around as Jon and I sat down.

"Where's Kyle?" Ricky asked as Drew slid into the empty seat beside me.

"Is it true?" Drew leaned over and asked.

"What?" I looked between the two men. "Kyle has decided to explore alternate employment options."

"Seriously?" Jamie turned around from his seat in front of me. A number of other drivers and crew chiefs around us stopped their conversations to look at me.

"Yes. It's true. ESPN broke the story today. Kyle is moving to another team, effective immediately," I paused. "And oh yeah, the wedding's off too."

Daytona stood up and waved Jon over to her now-empty seat to take the spot beside me.

"What the hell happened? When did it happen? Are you sure? Are you okay?" she fired questions at me.

"Geez. Slow down," I tried to laugh. "I'm not quite sure what happened. But Kyle's gone to another team. He said he'd finish out the season, but I told him he could leave effective five minutes ago. Yes, I'm sure. And yeah, I think I'm okay." Daytona took my hand.

"Sweetie. I'm so sorry. You know if you need anything. Hey! What are you gonna do for a crew chief for the rest of the season?"

"Well, I'm hoping Drew still remembers how to do the job and that he'll offer to lead us the rest of the way to the big table in Las Vegas," I looked at Drew.

"Hmmm. . . Well, gee. . . Another championship? I don't know Brie," Drew looked at me thoughtfully. "Oh alright. I'll do it." He laughed as I shook my head.

"Do you have any idea what team he's going to?" Ricky asked.

"Nope. I didn't ask and he didn't offer the information. I guess we'll find out soon enough. But does it really matter?"

"Well, maybe I'd like to go shopping for a better deal," he joked.

"Go ahead. Not my problem if you decide to change teams. Wanna come work for me?"

"Yeah. At least I know you'll show up sober for work," Ricky replied. "Well, I hope you will."

I turned my attention to the front of the room as Dave started the meeting. As he went over the usual race day reminders, I tuned him out, trying to figure out what had gone wrong with my relationship with Kyle. We had always had a great working relationship and we rarely argued at home or at work. The few arguments we'd had, were usually quickly resolved.

Daytona squeezed my hand as Dave dismissed the room. Standing, I looked around and noticed a few looks from the other drivers.

"If y'all are waiting for the hysterical meltdown, you can forget it. Ain't gonna happen here. Sorry."

"Come on Brie. Nobody's expecting you to get hysterical," somebody spoke up.

"Then stop looking at me like y'all don't know what the hell to do. I lost my crew chief to another team, obviously one of you. I really don't care who. It's not the end of the world. Shit happens. Big freakin' deal. Life goes on, right?" Putting my sunglasses on, I walked out of the room and headed back to the motorhome.

Matt and Daytona stopped to get his firesuit out of his car and met Jon and me at the motorhome while Drew and Ricky went to check on the cars. Jessika was in front of the computer and looked up as the four of us walked in.

"I assume you've heard the news?" I asked as I sat across from her.

"About Kyle? Yeah. He came to get his stuff a little while ago. So what happened?"

"Honestly, I really don't know. ESPN asked me for a comment. That was the first I heard of it. When I asked him, he confirmed the news. You know the usual lines for the press release. He's exploring alternate employment opportunities and we wish him the best in his future endeavours. Drew will be filling in as interim crew chief until we fill the position. And by mutual agreement, the wedding has been cancelled."

"Wow. You've had a pretty wild morning, eh?" Jess asked. "Mandy told me about Doug. And now all the crap with Kyle. Are you sure about the wedding?"

"Yeah. I'm sure," I nodded. "Talk about a crazy day. I just hope the craziness is over for the day."

"You should probably get ready for the race," Daytona interrupted.

"It's that time, eh?" I looked at my watch.

"I'll finish up this release while you're getting changed," Jessika said.

Once Matthew and I had both changed, the five of us walked together to the frontstretch. Jessika hugged me as we got to pit road.

"Good luck Mom. See you after the race. I love you."

"I love you too." Kissing her on the cheek, I squeezed her hand and smiled before she headed across the track.

* * *

Matt and Daytona stood with me and Drew during the national anthem before Daytona walked Matt to his car. Following NASCAR's rules, Matt would have to pull over and let the field pass him during the parade laps.

As we followed the pace car around the track, I focussed on clearing my mind of all the crap from the morning.

"Okay Brie. Time to go to work. Are you ready?" Drew asked.

"Getting there," I replied, pulling the safety belts just a little tighter.

"Just block out everything. Tune in to the car. Feel the steering wheel in your hands, the pedals under your feet. You know the drill," Drew reminded me. I took a couple deep breaths.

"Okay. Here we go boys. We've got a pretty good points lead, so let's protect it today. Quick, clean pit stops. Y'all know how this works. Lights are out; I'm ready to go."

The race was fairly uneventful, with the only cautions being for minor incidents, and I brought the car home with a third-place finish, padding my points lead.

Climbing out of the car, I praised the team and thanked Drew for taking over on such short notice. The team wanted to celebrate the finish after packing up. Sending them off to enjoy themselves, James and I headed home with Jon.

"You know you could've gone with the rest of the team," I told James as I unlocked the front door.

"I know I could've. But I'd rather hang out here with you," he explained.

"Well, I'm gonna go take a shower. Maybe we can sit out by the pool when I come back down." I headed upstairs to my room.

Once I'd stripped down and stepped under the running water, I finally let go of the emotions I'd bottled up all day: the pain of losing Kyle, my on-going guilt over Craig's death and the frustration of Doug's outburst.

Finally, my tears subsided and I moved to let the water massage my aching muscles before turning the water off.

Returning downstairs in shorts and a tee-shirt, I could hear James talking on the patio. Joining him, I was surprised to see Doug sitting across the table.

"Hey, Brie," he said quietly. "I heard you had a pretty good run today."

"Yeah. Even without my usual drafting partner out there," I replied, taking the beer James offered and sitting between the two men.

"Listen. I'm really sorry about that. Man, I fucked up pretty good there, didn't I? Thanks for getting Matt to run for me today."

"Well, I figured there was no point in your whole team suffering cuz you decided to be a jackass."

"I appreciate you looking out for me. And my guys."

"Hey! I didn't do it for you."

"Okay. I get it. I was a jackass and you're pissed at me. I'm sorry. Really, I am. Let me make it up to you. Maybe take you out to dinner. And Kyle too of course. Hey! Where is Kyle anyway? I didn't see his car when I drove up."

"I guess you didn't hear yet. Kyle's left the team. It's all over the news. He took a job with another team. I had to find out from ESPN this morning before the race. And I gave him back the ring. I figured if he couldn't be man enough to work out whatever the problem was and went looking for a different team to work for, he wasn't staying here at all. Everything's finished with us," I answered.

"No fucking way! You're kidding right?" Doug was obviously shocked.

"Nope. It's no joke. I guess everything kinda exploded today."

"But what happened? Crap, I never see the two of you fight," Doug paused. "It wasn't cuz of that stuff in the motorhome today, was it?"

"What? No! I think this was inevitable. I just don't know what happened to make him want to leave without talking about it first. Maybe I'll never know. I asked him to clear out his stuff tomorrow while I'm in Greensboro."

"You're going to Greensboro?" James asked. "Why?"

"Yeah. It was kind of a spur of the moment decision," I replied. "It's been a while since I've been. And I figured I was about due for a visit. Gonna take some flowers to Craig and go visit his parents. Maybe stop in at the department and see how things are there."

"Oh. Okay. Do you mind if I tag along? I mean, if you want to go by yourself, I get it," James asked.

"No. Sure. I don't mind. It's kinda boring making the drive alone. We can leave around ten maybe. Have lunch at that little diner we used to go to by the department."

"Sounds good to me," James said as he stood. "I'm gonna head to bed and leave the two of you to talk. See you in the morning." He kissed me on the top of the head before going into the house.

"So listen, I really appreciate you looking after my guys today. Man, I fucked up but good today didn't I? I was so out of line. I swear, that'll never happen again," Doug said.

"Really? And what part of today are you talking about?"

"All of it," Doug explained. "The drunkfest. My behaviour towards you. God, aside from Ricky, you're my best friend Brie. I don't want to lose your friendship because of today. I hope you can find a way to forgive me for kissing you like I did. I honestly don't know what possessed me to act like that."

"I'm going to assume all that shit in your motorhome was cuz of the booze. I'll let it go this time, but if it ever happens again -- "

"It won't. I promise. Scout's honor," Doug held his hands up.

"If it ever happens again," I continued. "Our partnership will be dissolved."

"Okay. Okay. It won't happen again," Doug paused and smiled. "Unless YOU want it to happen."

"I'm not kidding Doug. You'll be out of my shop so fast, your head'll spin," I warned.

"Got it. And I promise I'll behave from now on. I'm a changed man. You'll see."

"Yeah. We'll see." I tried to cover a yawn.

"Okay. You're tired, so I'm gonna take off and let you get some sleep. Have a safe drive tomorrow and I'll see you at the shop on Monday." Doug stood.

"I'll walk you out. Thanks for stopping by. I'm glad you did and we cleared the air between us before Monday. I don't want things to be weird between us," I said as we walked through the house to the front door.

"Yeah. So, um, see you Monday then?" Doug asked. He gave me a gentle hug as we reached the door.

"Of course." I held the door and watched him walk out to his car. Once he'd backed out of the driveway, I closed and locked the door, set the alarm and turned off the lights downstairs before I headed up to my bedroom.

* * * * *

CHAPTER FIFTY

Sunday morning, I woke up to voices downstairs. Pulling back the covers, I stood and walked quietly to the bedroom door to listen.

"Come on Kyle. She's still sleeping. Give it another hour or two and we'll be gone to Greensboro. You can clear your stuff out then like she asked. You know she doesn't want to see you." I heard James say.

"Seriously. Let me go up and talk to her James."

"What's it gonna accomplish? Nothing."

"She's had a day to cool off. I know she'll be willing to listen now."

Walking back across my room, I quickly threw on a pair of jeans and a tee-shirt and headed down the stairs.

"Brie! You're awake! I was hoping we could talk today!" Kyle exclaimed when he saw me.

"There's nothing to talk about. I said what I had to say yesterday. But since you're here, you can pack up your stuff. James and I are heading to Greensboro for the day."

I walked past him to put my shoes on at the front door.

"So you're not going to give me a chance to explain?" Kyle asked.

"What is there to explain? You weren't happy. You chose to leave instead of talking to me about whatever the issues were." I picked up my keys and purse. "There's boxes in the garage if you need them. Set the alarm when you leave please. And you can leave your keys at the shop."

"That's it? Set the alarm and leave your keys?"

"What do you want from me? You chose to leave! Do you expect some huge emotional good-bye? Cuz I'm all out of drama. I don't need or want it!" I burst out.

"You never really wanted to get married, did you?" Kyle asked. "You're still in love with Craig too much to love another man."

"That was low," I shook my head. "I can't believe you'd actually say that."

"But it's true, isn't it?" Kyle pushed.

"You don't have any idea what you're talking about," I turned and walked out the door.

Getting into my truck, I watched James say a few words before closing the door and walking down the driveway. Once he was in the truck, I started the engine and backed out of the driveway. I glanced over as he pulled out his cell phone and dialled.

"Hey. It's me. Listen, can you swing by and keep an eye on things?" he paused. "Yeah. About ten minutes ago. We just left to head to Greensboro, so we'll be gone most of the day." James smiled at me as he listened to the person at the other end. "That'd be perfect. I don't expect any problems but you never know. Can you send somebody to the shop too? . . . Great. Thanks bud. I appreciate that and I know Brie does too. I'll call you when we get back to town."

Hanging up, he looked at me.

"I'm assuming you're gonna fill me in," I said, pulling into a nearby coffee shop.

"Jon's gonna swing by the house and keep an eye on Kyle. Plus he's gonna send one of the boys to the shop. While they're there, they'll go over the security systems and make sure it's all good."

"Sounds good. I don't know about you, but I could really use a coffee."

"Yeah. I was just about to start a pot when Kyle showed up," James said as I parked the truck.

After a quick stop, we headed for Greensboro. We were both quiet for the first half hour of the drive, each absorbed in our own thoughts as the miles passed.

"So, Doug didn't stay long last night," James began.

"No. I was tired. Unlike him, I didn't get to sleep all day," I replied.

"Yeah. I still can't believe he did that. I mean, I can kinda understand where he was coming from. But to get that loaded the night before a race and pass out just hours before the green flag?" James shook his head.

"I know he's hurting right now, but yeah, that was some stupid crazy shit there," I agreed.

"So is it true?" James asked.

"Is what true?"

"That he kissed you."

"Who told you that?" I looked over at him in shock.

"Jon mentioned it. He didn't say he saw it happen. Just that it looked like it might've happened by the way you were standing when he opened the door. But from the look on your face, I can pretty much tell it did happen," James explained.

"Yeah. You know I'm not gonna lie to you. I don't know what the hell he was thinking. Of if he even WAS thinking. But I'm sure it was just the booze that made him do it. At least I hope so," I replied.

"Would you ever. . ." James trailed off.

"What? Hook up with Doug? Is that what you're trying to ask? Geez James. I've been single all of five minutes. You think I'm moving on that fast?"

"Damn Brie! I didn't mean right away. Slow down! I just meant when you're both ready."

"Yeah. I don't know about that James. I mean, Doug's a nice guy and all. But I just don't see the two of us as a couple."

"It's worked so far for Daytona and Matt," James pointed out.

"Totally different situation. You know, I got used to being alone the last six years. Yeah sure, Kyle was around and I dated casually but having Kyle move in was a huge adjustment for me."

"So is he right?" James asked.

"About what?"

"Not wanting to get married again. Still being in love with Craig." I thought about it for a couple minutes before answering.

"You know I'm always going to love Craig. And yeah, maybe more than I'll ever love another man," I shrugged my shoulders. "Getting married again? I don't know; I thought I was ready and I thought I loved Kyle. Maybe we were just moving too fast?"

"So give it some time. Maybe you both just need some time apart and him moving to a new team will help." James paused, looking out the window. "You know I just want you to be happy."

"I know. And I really don't mind being single. I guess we'll just have to wait and see what the future holds, right?"

"Exactly."

I turned my full attention back to the road and the rest of the drive passed quickly.

After a brief stop to buy flowers, I headed straight to the cemetery. Passing through the gates, I took a couple deep breaths and slowly followed the winding road to the section where Craig was buried. I'd made this trip hundreds of times before but it was difficult every time. Stopping the truck, I shut the engine off and closed my eyes.

"Brie?" James asked softly. "Are you sure you want to do this?"

"Yeah. It just never seems to be any easier when I come here. I still miss him so much."

"I know sweetie. But you know he's always with us."

"Yeah, I know. And sitting here isn't gonna make it any easier now, is it?"

"Probably not." As I got out of the truck, James reached into the backseat to bring the flowers. Walking slowly to Craig's grave, James put his arm around my shoulders, pulling me closer to him.

I knelt beside the grave, running my fingertips across the raised lettering of Craig's name, as James placed the flowers in front of the grave stone. James crouched down on the opposite side.

"Hey buddy. It's been a while since we talked, huh? Man, where does the time go? Last time I was here was right after I retired and was gonna go visit Brie and Jess for a few days. And wouldn't you know, I've been there ever since. You'd love it there man. Doesn't look like much has changed around town since I left. Guess some things never will change though. One thing that'll never change is that you're missed here. See you when I see you" James stood and stepped over to me. "I'm gonna take a walk to give you some time, okay?"

I nodded silently and he headed off. I knew both his parents and his wife were buried in the same cemetery but in another section.

"Well babe. Here I am again. Still missing you like crazy. God, I wish I could take back that night. From the first time I saw you, I knew. If I was gonna fall in love again, it was gonna be with you. I knew I wanted to spend the rest of my life with you. As scared as I was to let anybody into my heart again, I trusted you from that first moment. We were supposed to grow old together. And I had to go and fuck it up that night on the bust."

Burying my face in my hands, I cried for the second time in as many days. I didn't think the pain of Craig's death would ever fade. Silently, I wiped my tears and stood, slowly looking around.

"I wish you were here to share this championship with me. I know you're still here in a sense and keeping an eye on things, but it's not the same as you BEING here. I'm gonna go see your parents while I'm here and probably stop in at the department before I head back. But I'll be back after the season's finished. I love you babe. See ya later."

Turning, I slowly walked back to the truck and climbed behind the wheel, starting the engine again. Keeping an eye out for James, I cruised slowly through the cemetery. I found him kneeling about half way down a row on the other side of the cemetery. It was a fair-sized cemetery with gravestones of varying ages. Quite a few appeared to be fairly old.

Giving him time alone, I parked the truck and turned on the radio while I waited. I knew from Craig that both James' parents had died within months of each other and his wife had died shortly before I had moved to Greensboro. We had never talked about any of the deaths; Craig merely explained it was a difficult subject for either of them.

When James came back to the truck, I could see he'd been crying. Fastening his seatbelt, he glanced over at me with a forced smile.

"You wanna talk about it?" I asked quietly as I put the truck into gear.

"What? No. Not right now," James shook his head, wiping his face.

"Okay. Whatever," I paused, waiting for traffic to clear to pull out of the cemetery. "Thanks for coming with me today. I hate making the drive by myself, being alone with my thoughts."

"It's good to be back. But strange too. You know I've been hanging out at your place for a while now, and I really like Mooresville; I can see why you love it there. But THIS will always be home for me. Know what I mean?"

"Yep. I mean, I feel a strong connection here, and I don't think I'll ever leave Mooresville. But Windsor is always home for me," I agreed. "No matter how much time I spend away from there, it's always nice to go back, even for a day or two."

"You don't get there often, do you?" James asked.

"No. Not as often as I should. June and August when the series goes to MIS and then for a couple days at Christmas. It's just the way the schedule is, going thirty six weeks a year, plus all the extra appearances and commitments between races. Don't get me wrong, I love my job. I just wish I could see my family more often. Maybe I'll sneak away for a couple days before we go to Las Vegas and surprise everybody."

Turning into the driveway at Craig's parents' house, I waved to the neighbour out mowing the lawn. As I walked up the sidewalk, I heard the motor stop on the mower as he called out to me.

"Excuse me? Do you know the Lanes?" he asked as he walked across the lawn.

"I should hope so. I'm their daughter-in-law," I replied.

"I don't think so. They told me when we moved in that their son was killed years ago. Oh shit! I know who you are! You're that race car driver, aren't you? That's right. Now I remember, they did say he'd been married. Oh man! I can't believe I didn't know that. Geez, I'm sorry," he paused. "Are you here to check on the house or something? Cuz I've been taking real good care of it while they're gone."

"Gone?" James asked.

"Oh you didn't know? They went on a cruise. 'Bout two weeks now. Said they'd be gone three," he explained as he looked between the two of us.

"Well, I guess we'll come back another time then. Now that you mention it, I do remember getting that message," I sighed. "Thanks. Looks like you're doing a great job of taking care of things."

"Thank you ma'am. Good luck with that Chase, huh?"

"Thanks. Maybe I'll see you around when I come to visit next time. Have a nice day." James and walked back to the truck and headed towards the department.

"Well, that was interesting. Hey, you wanna go have lunch before we go to the department?" James suggested.

"Yeah. That sounds like a great idea." The diner was only a couple blocks from the department and a regular stop for both uniformed and plain-clothes officers. I recognized a few faces when we walked in, but noticed quite a few conversations stopped as I scanned the room.

"Hey. At the back. There's a booth there I'm sure we can join," James said as he waved to the men at the far end.

Walking through the crowd, I was aware of the stares, nudges and whispered comments. Ignoring them, I focussed on my breathing and made a straight path to the back of the room. Hugging Jeff and Shane as we joined them, the four of us sat down as the waitress brought two more menus.

"Can I get a Coke please?" I smiled at her.

"Pepsi okay?"

"Actually, no. How 'bout an iced tea instead please?" I laughed. "I'm not able to drink Pepsi."

"One iced tea then. And for you hun?" She turned to James. "The usual?"

"Yep. Thanks."

"Haven't seen you around lately. Somebody said you retired."

"It's true," James admitted.

"Well, we sure miss you around here." The waitress turned and headed to the counter for our drinks.

"So what are you doing back here? Thought we'd never see you again after you left," Jeff asked me.

"I've been back a few times, usually once a month, to visit Craig's grave and his parents. Hasn't been so much now that we're in the Chase, but we've had a crazy couple weeks, so I figured I was overdue for a road trip."

"Yeah. Shouldn't you be at the track now?" Shane asked.

"Nope. Race was last night. We finished third," I explained. "So I gave the crew the day off and James and I decided to make a run down the highway to see y'all. So what have you guys been up to since I left? Doesn't look like much has changed in six years."

"Nope. Pretty much the same. Got a few new dealers out there taking over as fast as we can put one group behind bars. You know how it is."

"Yeah, I certainly don't miss that," I shook my head as the waitress set our drinks on the table.

"Y'all ready to order?" she asked. Nodding, I handed her the menu and placed my order. Once she'd walked away, I could feel somebody standing over me. James looked up and shook his head. Turning I was confronted by a former classmate.

"So, what brings the famous Brianna Lane back to these parts? Shouldn't you be up in your fancy house lounging by the pool or getting your nails done or something?" the newcomer demanded.

"What the hell is your problem?" I asked.

"You. Dunno what the hell made you think you could just come waltzing in here. You don't belong here. You're not one of us anymore," he snarled.

"What the hell? Didn't realize this was a 'members only' club now. Did I miss the sign over the door? Did you guys have to flash a membership card when you walked in? I didn't see anybody checking id's at the door?" I looked at the guys at my table. They all chuckled and shook their heads.

"It's an unwritten rule. And everybody knows it. Except you apparently," he snarled as he leaned down and put his face inches from mine.

"Gee, I guess I missed that memo. I did get the one however, that you're still a fuckhead. So it's nice to see some things haven't changed since I left. Get lost Jay," I waved him away as the guys around me chuckled.

"Hey, at least I'm still a cop. I'm not the fuck up that ran out of town with my tail between my legs like you cuz I couldn't handle the real world. I knew from the beginning you'd never hack it as a cop. Get out and don't come back," he spat, straightening.

"YOU don't get to tell me what to do, Jay. I don't think you would've been able to handle it if YOUR partner had been killed. Or maybe you would've since you're such a cold bastard. I'd like to see how you could manage, returning to the job after your partner was killed right in front of you. Of course, you're such a macho asshole, you wouldn't care, would you?""

"At least I'm not responsible for a cop dying," he shot back.

"Okay. That's enough Jay. Get lost. You've had your say. We know you've got your issues, go see the department shrink and get your balls back in check," James stood up, giving Jay a nudge towards his own table.

"Gee that was fun," Jeff said as James returned to his seat. "What the hell is up with him? He's always been bitter towards you. He an ex or something?"

"Hell no!" I laughed. "I kicked his ass in every class through university and then again at the Academy. He's bitter that he got beat by a girl. And I refused to go out with him."

"Once an asshole, always an asshole," James said. "Are you okay Brie?"

"Yeah, I'm fine. I'm not gonna let a fuckhead like him bother me."

"He's always been a bad egg. I bet you everybody woulda cheered if you'd knocked him off his high horse," the waitress added as she brought our lunches.

"That's been done a time or two. It just never seems to stick," James smiled.

"That boy is all sorts of stupid. I don't know how he's managed to not get himself killed all these years."

"Just dumb luck," James pointed out.

"I suppose," she agreed. "Well, y'all enjoy your lunches. I'll be back to check on you in a while." The waitress walked away to check on her other tables as the four of us turned to our lunches and the conversations resumed around us.

As we ate, the guys fired questions at me about my life in Mooresville, the team, my season and the rumors about Kyle, and of course, how Jessika was doing.

Just as we were finishing up, a couple Homicide detectives stopped by the table.

"Hey Brianna. Just wanted to wish you luck on the rest of the season. And all that shit from Jay? Just ignore him; you're always welcome here."

"Thanks guys. I appreciate that," I smiled up at them.

"Well, good luck. See ya around."

They walked away, stopping briefly at Jay's table to say a few words before they walked out. A couple minutes later, he stood up, tossed some money on the table before he and his partner left.

"Well, we should probably get going," Jeff said, motioning for the bill. "It was awesome to see you again though. You know we miss you guys around here."

"Yeah? Maybe I'll try to make it back a little more often. Or at least stop in at the department when I do come to town," I replied as the waitress set the bill on our table.

"You make sure you don't be a stranger here either. You're always welcome here," she said to me.

"Thanks. I'll remember that and be sure to stop in when I'm in town." The four of us walked out to the parking lot together and I repeated my promise to visit again as we walked to my truck. Jeff and Shane headed across the parking lot to Jeff's car as I pulled out onto the road for the short drive to the department.

Walking into the Narcotics office, we were greeted warmly and surrounded by our former co-workers.

"Holy shit! Tell me you're here to ask for your badge back."

"Come on. You know I'd never be able to do undercover again boss. I've had my face all over the media the last six years," I laughed. "But if you want, I'll come back to do the high school tour during the off-season."

"Crap! You're right. But you know I'd hire you back here in a heartbeat. Damn we've missed you here," my old boss pointed out.

"So what're you doing here? Shouldn't you be at a race somewhere?"

"It was last night. We finished third. Been a while since I've visited Craig, so James and I decided to take a road trip on our day off. Won't get many more in the next month," I explained.

"Yeah. Right. You're the boss now. Don't you just work one or two days a week now?"

"I'm so sure! It's nothing like that," I shook my head. "Being the boss is a twenty-four seven job. I'm at the shop every day that we're home. I have to make sure the bills get paid, staff gets hired or fired, parts get ordered, cars get prepared and loaded up. I've got a great crew helping me, but overall, I'm responsible for everything that happens in the shop and at the track with my team. And now that I've got a partner, yeah, it's a little easier, cuz he brought with him a team manager who helps out with a lot of that stuff, but now Drew's working as my crew chief until we can hire a new one. So we work together to keep things running."

"She's a great boss too. All the guys love working for her. Hell, so do I," James agreed.

"You're working for her too? How'd that happen?"

"Just happened to be in the right place at the right time, I guess," James shrugged.

"One of her over-the-wall guys got hurt and she needed a replacement for him. It just happened to be the day I got there to visit, so I got tapped for the job. I'm just finishing out the season though. I don't think I'll be staying on next season cuz he'll be back to work full time by then. It's been fun though, getting to go to the different tracks every week. And I get to keep an eye on our star here. Can't seem to keep her out of trouble, but still keeping an eye on her."

"Yeah, we heard about the trouble you've been having. What's going on with that?" somebody asked.

"Oh, you mean Eddie? He's being held in custody until his trial. The judge decided he was a risk of offending again and a possible flight risk. They don't figure he'll be getting out for a while, considering the number of offences against him, and the fact that he attacked me in my own home. I've got plenty of protection though. Daytona sent me her security staff to travel with me. And I've got James at home with me," I explained.

"You think he'd try something again? We heard you shot at him when he attacked you at home."

"I did. I managed to get to my gun in my office and fired a warning shot. I missed him, obviously. But you never know. I mean, he had the balls to come into my house after repeated offences outside the house. So who knows how crazy the fucker is," I shook my head.

"So how's Jess doing? She must love you driving."

"She's great. She's working for the team now too. She's in her third season as my spotter and she's started training as my media rep the past couple months. Every press release that leaves my shop, and the web site updates, those are all hers."

"Cool. She doesn't want to drive?"

"No. Well, she hasn't said anything yet about wanting to. She seems happy working behind the scenes."

"Well, we should head back soon Brie. So we can check in with Jon before it gets too late."

"Yeah. Good idea."

"No way! You're not gonna leave already, are you? Y'all just got here."

"I'll be back. Probably not until after Miami. But I'll stop by next time I come to visit Craig."

"You're better stop here next time!"

"Have a safe drive home. And good luck with the racing thing."

"Thanks boss!" I laughed.

"You take good care of her James. Make sure she stays safe and both y'all come back to visit. Bring that fancy trophy with you too for us to see."

"Hey! She doesn't need me to take care of her. But she's got a whole crew just keeping her safe," James pointed out.

"And if I get the big trophy, I will bring it for y'all to see," I promised.

"Yeah. You'll have it. None of us have any doubts about that."

After saying our good-byes, James and I left the department and began the drive home.

* * *

Jon was waiting when we got back to the house and filled us in on his day.

"He was pretty good about clearing his stuff out. But he still wants to talk to you," he said of Kyle. "He was gonna wait around for you until I managed to convince him he'd be better off waiting and letting you make the decision of when to talk."

"There's nothing to talk about," I pointed out. "He maybe shoulda thought about talking before he went shopping for another team."

"Well, that's between the two of you. I'm not gonna tell you what you should or shouldn't do," Jon looked at his watch. "I should get back home though. I promised Katie I'd take her out tonight."

"Thanks for taking care of things today. I really appreciate you coming by," I said as I walked Jon to the door.

"All part of the job ma'am," he winked as he pretended to tip his hat towards me. I laughed and shook my head as he let himself out. Locking the door behind him, I returned to the kitchen where James had started making dinner.

"So are you gonna talk to him?" James asked as I took two bottles of beer from the fridge. Sitting down as I opened them and slid one across the counter to him, I thought about his question.

"What is there to talk about? He made the decision to go behind my back and look for another team to work for. He could've talked to me at any time. But he didn't. And I had to find out from ESPN that he was leaving."

"But only leaving the team," James pointed out. "He wasn't leaving you."

"Yeah. For now it was just the team. Obviously, if he wasn't happy working for me, the personal relationship wasn't going to work either," I explained.

"Well, maybe that's something you two need to sit down and discuss. I know you were great friends. And you were a great couple right up to the end. So maybe if you talk and look at it from each other's perspective, you can get passed this. And at least retain your friendship."

"You know, I really hope we can still be friends. But after everything that happened and the way I had to find out, I need a break and some time away from him before we can talk about what went on."

"So just let him know that. When we get to the track, tell him you're willing to talk and listen to what he has to say. But explain to him that you're hurting right now and you're not ready for that discussion yet," James suggested.

"That's a good idea," I agreed. "You know Craig and I never had these issues like this. If one of us had something to say, we just said it. There was never any worry about how the other would react."

"But Kyle's not Craig," James said quietly. "And I think that's one of the issues. You're not ready to let go and love another man yet. Which is okay. Trust me; I completely understand that. I don't know if I'll ever love another woman as much as I loved Anna. And she's been gone for twenty years almost."

"Craig told me you were high school sweethearts. And that you'd only been married a short time. But he didn't talk about her much."

"Yeah. The three of us all hung around together from the first day of school. I think I fell in love with her the second I saw her. I proposed right before our graduation ceremony, but we waited until we were finishing university before we finally got married. We were trying to get pregnant when we found out she was sick. The doctors told us the cancer had spread through so much of her body by the time they found it. They couldn't even pinpoint where it had started and it had progressed too far to treat it."

"That must've been so hard to go through," I said quietly.

"She didn't let it get her down though. Right up to the end, she said she wanted to live a normal life and enjoy every day to the fullest. And aside from tiring out easily, you couldn't even tell she was sick. She never let on to anybody when she was hurting. But when the end finally came, I had a hard time letting go. And I would never have made it without Craig there."

Standing up, I walked around the counter to where James was standing at the stove and put my arms around him. Hugging him from behind, I rested my head on his back and could feel him shaking as he cried. After a couple minutes, I felt him take a couple deep breaths and turn the stove off.

"Dinner's ready," he said quietly, reaching for plates. Letting him go, I went to the fridge for two more bottles of beer and set them on the counter as James set the now-filled plates on either side of the counter where we normally sat to eat when it wasn't a large group.

We kept the conversation light over dinner, talking about what the coming tracks were like and what I hoped the rest of the season would be. I headed to my office to check my mail after dinner. James joined me a short time later and sat across from me reading a book.

* * * * *

CHAPTER FIFTY-ONE
Atlanta, GA

Two weeks later when we arrived in Atlanta, I had extended my points lead with a solid top five finish in Martinsville. There had been numerous articles about Kyle leaving the team and Drew stepping up to fill the spot.

I was scheduled to appear at Daytona's in Atlanta and Coca-Cola Headquarters with the rest of the drivers in the Coca-Cola Racing "family" as well as one of the local morning shows.

"You're not over-booked are you Mom?" Jess asked as we drove with James and John from the airport to the track Thursday morning.

"No. There's plenty of time, Jess. The bar is this afternoon after practice. The morning show and Coca-Cola is tomorrow before qualifying. You did fine with the bookings. I won't be rushed to get anywhere and I can still focus on the car for the weekend," I explained, looking over my schedule for the coming days.

"What about the souvenir trailer? Do you want to do an hour on Saturday or Sunday?" Jess asked.

"Yeah. Let's do Saturday morning. Try to keep Sunday open so I can stay focussed on the race," I agreed.

"Okay. I'll get that set up for you," Jess replied as I made a note on my copy of the schedule.

When we arrived at the track, James headed to the garage to join Drew and the team while Jess went to the souvenir trailer to let them know the schedule for Saturday. Jon stayed with me while I went to the motorhome to get changed into my firesuit.

"So, how are things?" Jon asked once we were inside the motorhome.

"Good. Why?" I looked over at him as I set my bag on the counter.

"I haven't really seen you all week. So we haven't had much time to talk; just wondered how everything's been," he explained.

"Everything meaning what exactly?" I asked.

"You. Your ribs. Kyle. I can see how the race stuff is going. So what about everything not connected to racing?"

"I'm good. Ribs are healing. Kyle I don't know about. You'd have to ask him. I haven't seen him. I'm sure he's settling in nicely with his new team. But I'm not really worried about what he's doing either."

"Kevin said he saw you at the courthouse yesterday."

"Yeah. I wanted to be there to hear what Eddie had to say for himself."

"And what did you think about what he said?"

"That was quite a speech he gave. Blaming drugs and alcohol and projecting his anger and frustration at me because his dad couldn't drive anymore. Sounded like a lot of bullshit to me really."

"Well, some people can't, or won't, take responsibility for their own actions. I bet he figured the judge would send him to rehab and anger management and that would be the end of it," Jon pointed out.

"Yeah. He looked pretty surprised when the judge added jail time on top of the rehab and anger management. And you know Dave'll never let him race in any NASCAR-sanctioned event again. It's too bad cuz he is a talented driver once you look passed the ego. He's a lot like his father. Talented, but egotistical and chauvinistic."

"Guess he'll have to find a different career when he gets out of jail. Maybe Evon'll hire him on as a mechanic?"

"I doubt it. From what I heard, he doesn't know an oil pan from a frying pan," I said. "A couple of my guys were talking to his road crew. They say he's dumber than dirt when it comes to the car. He can drive the wheels off it but that's as far as it goes."

"Well, I'm sure he'll figure something out."

"Probably," I looked at my watch. "Crap. I'd better get changed. Practice is gonna start soon." Picking up my bag, I headed into the bedroom to change into my firesuit.

"So how're things with Doug?" Jon asked as I took off my street clothes.

"Fine. It's been great being able to use his information to set up the cars every week. I mean, even though it's Chevy versus Ford, everything is basically the same. Having the defending champion as my teammate is definitely helping with my bid for this year's Cup," I replied.

"Yeah, okay. But what about the personal stuff?" I stopped as I pulled my firesuit on and leaned over to look out the door.

"What personal stuff?" I asked.

"You know. You can't tell me you and Doug haven't hooked up."

"Actually, I CAN tell you that cuz it's true. Mine and Doug's relationship is strictly professional. We're teammates and yeah, friends, but really that's as far as it goes," I explained as I tied the sleeves of my firesuit around my waist and walked out of the bedroom.

"Seriously?" Jon looked skeptical.

"Seriously."

"So that kiss I interrupted a couple weeks ago?"

"Was one-sided and alcohol and grief-induced. Doug stopped by the house that night and we talked. He apologized for his behaviour and for crossing the line. And he's been a perfect gentleman since then. You can't honestly believe I'd hook up with Doug? Especially so soon after breaking up with Kyle and Doug's wife dying."

I took a bottle of water from the fridge and checked my watch again.

"Okay. Ready to go?"

"Yep." As we headed to the garage, Kyle caught up with us.

"Hey Brie. How're things going?" he asked.

"Good. How's the new team?"

"It's good. I guess you heard I'm working with a rookie, getting him ready for next year?"

"Nope. Hadn't heard that. Not the first time you've worked with a rookie though. Of course, last time you were a rookie too. Good luck with that."

"Thanks. Don't know that this rookie with be as good as the last one I worked with. But then you've always been in a class of your own."

"Well, good luck anyway. I really do hope things go well for you with this new team." I put my hand on his back.

"Listen, Brie. Do you think we could spend some time together this weekend? Away from the craziness of the track?"

I don't know Kyle. I mean, I've got a pretty hectic schedule. And trying to stay focussed on the Chase."

"Geez Brie. I'm not asking you to re-arrange your entire schedule for me. Or give up on the Chase. Just some time to hang out together like we used to before everything went to hell in a hand basket. You used to have time for me."

"And you used to be honest and come to me when there was a problem instead of slinking off behind my back to hide on another team," I shot back.

"You're never gonna forgive me for that, are you?" Kyle asked quietly.

"You know what? I don't care that you decided you didn't want to work with me anymore. Yeah, it hurt for a little while. But you know what bothered me the most? That you couldn't be honest with me and tell me you were looking somewhere else AND I had to find out from ESPN. Hell, you could've sent me an email if you didn't wanna tell me in person. Even a text woulda been better than getting the news from ESPN."

"You're right. I admit I fucked up there. And I really do wish I'd been the one to tell you. I was gonna tell you that night."

"Whatever. What's done is done. No sense in worrying about what woulda coulda shoulda been done. Like I said, good luck with the new team. I really do hope you're happy there and it all works out good for you." Turning away, I walked into the garage stall where the team surrounded me, preventing Kyle from continuing the conversation.

"Okay, Brie. We've got everything set. Car's ready to go whenever you are," Drew said.

"Weather looks good for the whole weekend. Sunny and warm," James added as I pulled my firesuit up. "Possibility of showers but only at night."

"Great. Let's get out there and get some practice laps in. Time to see what we've got here."

I climbed into the car as most of the crew headed out to pit road. After I fastened the safety belts and steering wheel, Drew handed me the HANS device while James held onto my helmet. Once everything was in place and secure, I flipped the switched to start the engine and pulled on my gloves.

Drew put up the safety net as James walked to the back of the car to direct me out of the garage stall. Once I got out to pit road, I picked up speed to get out onto the track.

"Okay Brie. Show me whatcha got," Drew's voice came through the radio as I shifted gears and pushed the car steadily up to racing speed.

"So far, so good."

"How's the new surface?" he asked. The track had been torn up and re-paved after the spring race.

"Smooth. Think we're gonna get some wicked fast speeds this weekend."

"Hey Mom. Doug and Jamie are coming out now. Kyle's rookie too," Jess informed me. "Track looks good from up here."

"Thanks Jess. Let me know where the boys are running once they get up to speed eh?"

"Sure thing Mom. So far the rookie's hanging low but Doug and Jamie are running about the same line as you, half a lap behind you."

"Hey Drew? I'm gonna slow down to let the boys catch up and try out the draft."

"No problem, boss." I eased my foot slightly off the gas and kept an eye on the mirror for the other two cars. It didn't take long before Doug was close behind and I pushed my car back up to near racing speeds.

With the three cars drafting together, Drew let me know the speeds were climbing. Waving to Doug, I dropped down to the lower racing groove to let them pass and tucked in behind Jamie.

"Let's see how fast Doug can pull this train for a while," I radioed Drew.

"Okay. Just keep an eye on your water temp. Don't want you over-heating during practice," Drew reminded me.

"If the temp starts to climb too much, I'll just drop back a bit to get some clean air," I replied.

"Hey Mom? The rookie's getting a little squirrelly in the turns. Think we're gonna have a mess out there soon," Jessika broke in.

"Uh oh. Guess Kyle's got his work cut out for him this weekend. Let's hope he doesn't make too big a mess," I said.

"I'm surprised Kyle hasn't brought him in to fix it."

"Probably seeing if the boy can correct it himself first," I suggested. I knew enough about the team to know that this new driver had been pretty successful in open-wheel cars.

"There's gonna be a few pissed off teams if he makes a mess of the track," Drew pointed out. "One thing to keep him out an extra lap or two to teach him. Just plain stupid to leave him out there to screw up somebody else's car."

"Guess we'll just have to wait and see. Don't forget, it's been a few years since he's worked with a rookie."

"But he knows what it's like to work with a vet who's been wrecked by a rookie," Drew commented. "How's your water temp looking?" I glanced down at my gauges.

"Climbing a little. I'm gonna drop back a little to get some clean air in," I slowed down to let Doug and Jamie pull away slightly. Once I had about a half dozen car-lengths between us, I resumed my normal speed.

"Okay Brie. Let's do a couple practice qualifying laps if you feel ready. Just to check your speeds. Then we can try some longer runs again. How's the car? Water temp back to normal yet?"

"Almost back to normal already. Guess I'll have to make sure I'm leading as much as possible on Sunday," I laughed. "Car feels pretty good though. Let's try the qualifying practice then park it. I don't wanna take any chances before qualifying and the race."

"Okay. Whenever you're ready, we'll start timing you."

"Give me one more lap to get passed the rookie. Once he's outta the way, I'll feel a lot better," I told Drew.

"Okie dokie. Just watch yourself when you pass him."

"Not a problem. As long as he stays low, I'll just pass him on the high side."

"He's still low Mom. And you're gaining on him pretty quick. Should be able to pass him in another turn or two."

"I see him Jess. See if you can talk to his spotter. Let him know I'm going outside and to have him stay low," I said.

"I'm on it," she replied.

"Just take your time Brie. There's no rush to pass him. It's just practice," Drew reminded me.

"I know. Just keeping an eye on him right now. He's having a hard time keeping his back end straight in the turns. Wiggling all through every turn. Thinking it'd be best if I pass him on a straight. Safest that way. Less chance of it getting away from him."

"Good idea. Do what feels right for you," Drew replied.

"Okay, Mom. His spotter says he'll stay low while you pass him. Says he's just trying to get used to the car and the track," Jess explained.

"That's good. Hopefully he figures it out soon or gets the hell off the track."

"I'm sure Kyle will bring him in soon. Seems strange that he wouldn't pull him off the track. Makes you wonder if he's even watching his driver," Jess said.

"Well, luckily it's not our problem; it's all on Kyle if his driver messes up out here cuz he's leaving him out here too long," I pointed out. "Okay. I'm just about ready to pass him."

I pulled even with him as we headed down the backstretch.

"Not quite clear yet. His front splitter's about even with your rear tire Mom," Jess let me know. "What the. . ." Jess broke off just as I felt contact with my rear fender. I pushed the accelerator further down to get passed him and felt a second hit, this one closer to my seat.

"Brie?" I heard Drew call.

"Tryin'," I radioed back letting off the gas as a third hit pushed my car up the track and into the outside wall.

"Are you okay Mom?" Jess asked as my car stopped.

"Yeah. I'm fine. Just pissed that I'm sitting on the wall here. Car was awesome. Sorry guys."

"Not your fault Brie. The wreckers are on their way to bring you back in. We'll take a look when you get here and see if we can fix it," Drew re-assured me. I released the window net as the emergency crew arrived.

"Are you okay Miz Lane?" one of the track workers asked me.

"Yeah. I'm fine. I'll take a walk to the infield care later," I replied, pulling my gloves and helmet off.

"Okay. I'll let them know you're going back with the car. Just make sure you do get there before you come back out."

I nodded as the tow trucks arrived to take the cars back to the garage.

Once the car was in front of our garage stall and dropped from the tow truck, I slowly climbed out.

Walking to the back of the car where the crew stood, we surveyed the bulk of the damage. The back end was wrinkled and pushed up about six inches from where it was supposed to be.

"So?" I asked, looking at Drew.

"It'd take most of the rest of the day to fix it. Probably better to unload the back-up and set it up," Drew looked at me.

"Okay. You know I trust you. If you want to get the switch made, I'm gonna head over to infield care for a quick check. As soon as you have the back-up ready, I'll get in some more practice," I replied, before heading towards the infield medical center with Jon by my side. As we got close, I could see Kyle talking to his driver outside the main doors.

"You wanna wait and come back?" Jon asked.

"No. I can't go back on the track til I've been cleared. Just gonna walk right by," I answered.

"Come on Kyle. It looked like an accident. What do you care anyway? You left the team and she dumped you," I heard his driver say.

"Are you fucking stupid? You and I both know that wasn't an accident. You don't intentionally wreck a competitor. Especially on your first weekend out here," Kyle pointed out to him as I stopped behind his driver.

"Whatever. So rookies aren't allowed to make mistakes now?"

"You might be a rookie in this series. But you can drive. Everybody here knows that. You're gonna apologize to Brianna for being an idiot. And you're gonna make sure it doesn't happen again. Got it?"

"Yeah, sure. I'll get right on it," he replied sarcastically, turning around and bumping into me.

"Hey! Watch it!" Jon warned.

"It's okay Jon. I think I can handle this kid. I've taken on bigger, tougher guys than him," I smiled, crossing my arms.

"So, I think you have something to say, don't you?" Jon asked.

"What? Oh yeah. Sorry Brie. I dunno what happened out there. Car just got away from me," he mumbled.

"Really?" I laughed. "So you didn't intentionally run me into the wall? Gee, that's not what it sounded like when I walked up just now."

"Whatever," he turned to Kyle. "I'm going to my motorhome. You can come let me know when the car is fixed to get back out on the track."

I shook my head as he walked away. Turning to walk into the medical center, Kyle put his hand on my arm to stop me.

"Listen, Brie. I really am sorry for all that. I had no idea he was gonna pull shit like that. If I had known, I never woulda sent him out while you were out there," Kyle apologized.

"Don't worry about it. If he's gonna be an ass, it'll happen anytime. Not a big deal. I can handle it," I assured him.

"I just don't want him trying to wreck your chase run," Kyle pointed out.

"Hey, look at some of the shit I've gone through this year. If it's meant to be, I'll win it. Remember? Everything happens for a reason," I paused. "I should get inside though if I wanna get back on the track today."

"Okay. I won't hold you up then. You got plans for dinner tonight?"

"I'll be at Daytona's. I've got an appearance there tonight," I told him.

"Maybe I can meet you there?" Kyle offered.

"Ummm, sure. I'm scheduled for two hours. Four to six tonight."

"Okay. I'll see you later then. I've gotta see about fixing a car." Kyle left as I headed into the medical center.

When I returned to the garage, the crew was just finishing checking the set-up of my back-up car.

"Everything okay, Brie?" Drew asked.

"Yep, It's all good. Cleared to run. Is the back-up all set to go?"

"Yeah. She's good. Identical to the primary. Just needs you in the seat," Drew replied.

"I'm ready."

"Should I call and have a second back-up readied to hit the highway?" Drew laughed.

"Geez, I hope we don't need another one. I think Kyle will probably hold his driver for a while. He apologized for what happened out there. And it sounds like they're fixing their car instead of pulling out their back-up," I explained.

"Okay. Well, let's get you out there and warmed up so we can get some practice qualifying laps done," Drew motioned the guys to head out to pit road while I climbed into the car. Going through the motions again, I was soon ready and fired the engine. As I backed out of the garage stall I noticed Kyle walk over to talk to Drew. The two men glanced at me and Drew nodded at whatever Kyle was saying. When Kyle walked away, Drew waved and motioned for me to head out to the track.

Pulling back out onto the track, I easily shifted through the gears and quickly brought the car up to speed. Drew gave me a couple laps to warm up the car.

"Okay Brie. How's the back-up?" he asked.

"Not bad," I radioed back. "Feels pretty good. Almost the same as the primary. Let's get some practice runs in to get an idea for tomorrow's qualifying."

"Whenever you're ready. You were right. Kyle's holding his driver til you're done out there. Just to make sure there are no other problems. Nice to see he's looking out for you, even if he's not part of the team anymore," Drew said.

"Yeah. Hopefully he can keep his driver in line come race day. Let's get this started so we can park and relax for the night."

"Okay. Ready when you are."

After a couple mock qualifying runs, I slowed the car and pulled off the track and into the garage. Shutting the engine down, I slowly pulled off the safety equipment and climbed out of the car.

"How's the speeds look?" I asked as Drew handed me the clipboard with the practice speeds. Quickly scanning the list, I was impressed.

"Looks good for tomorrow. As long as the weather holds. Of course, there's gonna be a lot of fast cars out there tomorrow."

"That's okay. We've got a good run there and an awesome car. It's the big show on Sunday that's important," I handed back the clipboard as the crew began the job of covering the car and putting the tools away. James packed up the laptops and headed to the hauler with my helmet and gloves.

"You gonna bring the boys out tonight?" I asked Drew as we headed towards the hauler.

"Yeah. Gonna have a quick meeting then take them back to the hotel to get them cleaned up before we meet you there," Drew replied.

"Sounds good. I'm gonna go shower and get to the bar. Don't wanna be late." Jon and I left Drew at the hauler and made our way to the motorhome.

Once I'd showered and dressed, Jon drove me the short distance to Daytona's in Atlanta. A good-sized crowd had already gathered and my show car was set up on display near the main entrance.

Jon drove around to the side of the building to park and we slipped in through the side patio entrance. Walking up to the bar, I was greeted warmly by the manager, Mike.

"Hi Brianna! It's great to have you here! Some of the crowd out there has been camped out since noon. Can I get you anything?"

"Hi! It's great to be here. If I could just get a cold Coke Zero, I'm gonna head outside and get started. If people have been here since noon, I'm not going to keep them waiting longer."

"Okay. I'll get that for you. And there's a couple boxes of postcards already out there for you with a package of Sharpie markers too."

"That's great. Thanks. Oh and my team will be coming later. Can you save a couple tables maybe on the patio for them?"

"Sure thing."

Jon walked with me outside. While I got settled, Jon opened the first box of postcards and set it on the bar stool beside me. Taking out a stack, I set them on the table and opened the box of Sharpies.

"Okay folks. We know you're been waiting a while now, so we're gonna get started. Please give a warm Daytona's welcome to Brianna Lane!" I heard a familiar voice announce through the bar's sound system. Looking at Jon and Mike, they were both grinning as the crowd cheered.

"Come on! Is that all you've got for NASCAR's points leader? Let me hear you make some noise!" Daytona yelled from the rooftop. Laughing, I waved to her and motioned for her to join me. Waving back, she disappeared from view as I turned to the crowd. Minutes later, she burst through the front door, igniting the crowd's excitement more.

"Why didn't you tell me you were coming? You could've flown down with us," I said, hugging her. "And where's Matt?"

"He's back at home with Sam. I flew down this morning with Kevin. It was a last minute thing to surprise you. And to see how things are going here," she explained as Kevin joined us.

Sitting down again, Daytona joined me at the table as we greeted the crowd.

As we signed autographs and posed for pictures, I noticed Jon and Kevin scanning the crowd.

"Are they watching for somebody in particular? Or just being extra vigilant?" I quietly asked Daytona. She glanced over her shoulder before she answered.

"Nope. Just typical crowd scanning. They'd probably do security checks on everybody if they could," she explained.

"I know you had a couple problems when you were driving, but aside from Eddie, things have been pretty good for me," I replied.

"Oh. I know. But that's what makes them good at what they do. If there's gonna be a problem, odds are they're gonna catch it and prevent it rather than having to deal with a bigger incident."

Drew and Jessika arrived just before five with the rest of the crew. I could tell right away that something was bothering her, but she smiled brightly as she joined us.

The rest of the crew stood for a while around the show car as some of the crowd took pictures.

"Everything okay Jess?" I asked.

"I'll tell you about it later, okay?" she replied. "It's just an email that I got for you during practice."

"Was it threatening? Do you need to tell Jon about it?"

"Oh no! Not like that Mom! It was just really sad. I printed it out for you. But I'll give it to you after you're done here," she assured me.

"Okay. But as soon as I'm done, I want to see it."

"Definitely." She looked around at the crowd. "Pretty good turn out today."

"Yeah. Mike said they started showing up at noon."

"Wow! That's awesome! Are you staying for the weekend Daytona?" Jess turned to her.

"I was thinking about it. If your Mom doesn't mind having me around," Daytona smiled.

"You know I love having you around! Especially when you get the crowd worked up like you did here. You can stay in the motorhome with me if you want. We'll send the boys next door to Doug's place," I laughed.

"Sounds good to me," Daytona smiled.

By six when my scheduled time was up, most of the waiting fans had gotten autographs and pictures. Jessika had taken Kevin's seat as he wandered along the crowd still lined around the parking lot.

"Mom? It's six now. Do you want me to get you anything?" Jess asked.

"No. I'm okay Jess. There aren't too many fans left in line, so I shouldn't be too much longer now. But you go ahead and join the rest of the crew," I told her.

"I'll wait for you. That way we can talk," she replied. "Oh! Kyle's here?"

"Yeah. He wanted to have dinner tonight. Guess he'll have to share me with you guys," I laughed.

"Hi Brie!" he said as he walked over, kissing me on the cheek.

"Hi. I'm almost done here. Hope you don't mind Jess and Daytona and the boys joining us."

"Of course I don't mind. I knew I'd have to share your time. Better than not getting any time with you at all."

"Okay. Drew and the guys are on the patio if you want to join them to wait for me," I offered.

"Umm, sure. As long as they don't mind," he replied hesitantly.

"I'm sure they won't," I assured him. "And I'll be in shortly."

Once I had signed the last autograph, it was almost seven. As I stood, I looked as Jessika.

"Okay. Talk to me. What's this email that has you so upset?"

"Do you remember meeting a little girl in Michigan in August?"

"Are you talking about Jessica? I remember her. She was so cute. Little blonde. About ten years old I think. Was with her mom. Why?" I smiled, thinking back to the day at the dealership when I'd met her.

"I got an email from her mom today."

"Obviously not a good one if it's upset you. What happened?"

"She's at St Jude's," Jessika began.

"The children's hospital? Don't they specialize in cancer treatment?" Daytona asked.

"That's the one. She's been there for about a month now. But the doctors are hopeful for a full recovery. Mom says little Jessica broke her leg and the hospital didn't like how the x-rays looked so they sent them to St Jude's for tests. That's where they found the cancer."

"Wow. That's awful. Do you have a number there so I can call her?" I asked.

"Yeah. It's all in the car. I figured you might want to, so I looked it up before I left the hotel."

"Good. Let's set up some sort of fundraising to help out the family too. Like a portion of souvenir sales goes towards her medical bills," I suggested as we joined the crew.

"I'm gonna have the bars do that too," Daytona added.

"Really? That'd be awesome!" Jess exclaimed.

"I'm gonna donate a portion of my winnings the next couple races too," I said.

"Contact Coke and Ford too," Daytona suggested. "Send out a press release to tell the media about her and St Judes."

"Let me talk to the mom first. She might not want her daughter all over the media while she's sick."

"Of course," Daytona agreed.

"I've got some free time Monday, so maybe I can fly up there for a couple hours to visit," I said as we sat down at the table with the rest of the crew.

"Fly where?" Drew asked.

"Michigan. To visit a sick little girl. I met her in August when we were there and Jess got an email from her mom today."

"Want some company?" James asked.

"Sure. That'd be great," I replied. The waitress arrived then and took our orders. After she walked away, I turned to Kyle.

"Any more problems with your driver today?"

"Surprisingly, no. Once we banged out the fenders and sent him back out somehow the car was perfect," Kyle replied, shaking his head.

"You didn't make any other changes?" Drew asked. "Jess said he was pretty loose in the turns."

"Nope. Told him we fixed all that though. But didn't touch anything except the body damage," Kyle explained. "Funny eh? Hopefully he behaves out there from now on. I'd hate to see him ruin your Cup run."

"I'm not worried about him. Like I said earlier, I've taken on bigger guys than him."

"Well, I warned him before he hit the track again. And I'll be reminding him Sunday before the race. Just 'cause I'm not with the team anymore doesn't mean I don't wanna see you win."

"Thanks Kyle. That's really nice of you," I replied sweetly.

The conversation turned to previous races.

"I bet you've got some great memories from here, Daytona," Jessika commented and Drew spit out his beer.

"You okay?" Daytona asked.

"Yeah. Fine. Just thinking about past races," Drew replied.

"I bet I know what one you're thinking about," she turned to Jessika. "This is the track where Evon and Ryan wrecked me pretty good. That's when we didn't know if I'd even walk again, let alone race."

"Oh. I think they mentioned that in the highlights when you retired."

"Probably. And it's usually shown in Atlanta history re-caps," Daytona pointed out.

"But you won here a bunch of times too, didn't you?"

"Yep. Got my first Cup win here a year after my wreck, when Matt won the Championship. That was the same year Chad died and I found out I was pregnant with Sam then. So it was a pretty emotional win."

"I remember that year pretty good," Drew added. "We finished third in points behind Matt and you. Was great when we merged the teams and we were all working together."

"Yeah. A lot has changed since then. Not just for us, but for the sport too. A lot of drivers didn't like the new car when NASCAR brought it in. But we didn't have any choice but to adjust and work with what we were given."

"And someday, maybe there'll be more women in the sport," I said.

"That would be great. But unfortunately, it's still hard for women to break into the sport. If you hadn't bought the team when you did, I really don't think there'd be another woman racing in the top series. Luckily, Matt said you reminded him of me. That's why he was willing to sell to you. He had five other offers but was waiting to make a decision. Then you walked into the shop and he said it was like looking at a younger version of me. He knew five minutes after meeting you that you were the perfect buyer for the team."

"Well, it's getting late," Drew stood. "I'd better get these boys back to the hotel."

"Yeah. I'd better get back to the track soon. I've got an early day tomorrow and a full morning before qualifying."

As we walked out to the parking lot, Kyle pulled me aside.

"Would you mind if I stop by the house one day this week?"

"It's gonna be pretty crazy this week with flying to Michigan on Monday," I shook my head. "Maybe sometime next week?"

"Yeah. Sure. Give me a call when you've got an idea of when's good for you." Giving me another kiss on the cheek, he headed to his car as Jon and I headed to my rental.

Daytona and Kevin followed us to the track. Once we got back to the infield and parked, Kevin got their bags from the trunk and the four of us walked the short distance to my motorhome. Doug and Jamie were sitting outside between the two motorhomes.

"Hey guys. Look who I found at my appearance today," I said as we walked up.

"Wow. Didn't think we'd see you again so soon," Jamie smiled.

"Want a beer? We've got a bunch on ice here," Doug offered, pulling two bottles of Bud out of the cooler and handing them to me and Daytona. Pulling two more out, he offered them to Jon and Kevin. When both men shook their heads, he put them back, looking at me.

Sitting down, I glanced up as Jon took the bags into the motorhome. Coming back out a minute later, he handed Kevin a bottle of Coke.

"You guys don't drink?" Jamie asked.

"Not while we're on duty," Jon explained.

"Are you ever off-duty?" Doug cracked open another beer for himself.

"Sure. But at the track we're always on duty, no matter what time it is," Jon explained.

"I don't see you at the shop much," Doug commented.

"Nope. I'm mostly around for appearances and travel. At home and the shop, Brianna has James to keep an eye on her," Jon replied.

"But Eddie's in jail, so why are you still around? No offence. I'm just surprised. I thought you were just supposed to be around to protect Brianna from Eddie," Jamie asked.

"That's true. But Daytona paid us through the end of the season. So we stay through the banquet," Jon revealed.

"Guess that makes sense," Doug said. "So are you staying for the weekend Daytona?"

"Yeah. Matt's gonna fly down tomorrow afternoon when Sam's done school."

"Cool. It's great to have you guys back at the track. Any chance you'll come back full-time?" Doug asked.

"I can't drive," Daytona reminded him.

"I know that. I meant as an owner. Even though you and Matt sold the team to Brianna, have you thought at all about starting another team?" Doug explained.

"Are you looking to sell?" Daytona laughed. "I thought you were happy with Brianna."

"Oh I am! I love being her teammate!" Doug exclaimed. "I wouldn't change that. Hope you feel the same Brie. Just would be nice to have you and Matt back at the track every week."

"Actually Matt and I have been kicking around the idea looking into it. Maybe just partial ownership," Daytona revealed. "But we haven't made a definite decision yet."

"I think that would be awesome," I said. "Of course, I get to see you anytime I want, sharing a property line."

"I think you two should run a team together," Jamie added. "There must be another female driver out there that's ready to benefit from what the two of you have accomplished."

"Yeah! I think that's a great idea!" Doug agreed. "Brie, weren't you thinking about adding a Nationwide team?"

"I was thinking about it. But I haven't really had a chance to check out the local tracks or anywhere really to see who's out there," I replied.

"Maybe after the season's done, we should sit down and talk about the possibilities? I know you've got a lot going on with the Chase. And Matt and I aren't in any rush. But it really does make sense," Daytona turned to me.

"Yeah. Maybe the four of us and Drew? I mean, with Doug and I being partners, so to speak," I replied.

"You want me involved?" Doug sounded surprised.

"Sure. Why wouldn't I? We're already partners and teammates, so it's make sense if I expand that you're part of this too."

"I guess so. But I was thinking more along the lines of a ladies only team. Owners, driver, crew chief. Hell, get the whole crew to be women," Doug said.

"I bet you'd love that, wouldn't you? Having an all-female crew out there every week," Daytona laughed.

"Sure. What guy wouldn't?" Doug shot back.

"Well, I think while you guys build Doug's fantasy team, I'm going to head to bed. Some of us have to actually be up early for commitments," I stood, handing the empty beer bottle back to Doug.

"I'll see you at Coke tomorrow?" Doug asked.

"Yeah. I've got the morning show first, but I'll see you after. Listen, can one of the guys crash with you tonight?"

"Sure, that's no problem. You know I'm more than happy to share my motorhome," Doug smiled.

Heading inside to bed, I quickly fell asleep.

* * *

Friday, I barely had a moment to myself, between the two appearances and qualifying. Both appearances passed quickly and uneventfully. Arriving back at the track, I headed straight to my motorhome to change into my firesuit.

Walking to pit road with Doug, he put his arm around my shoulders.

"You know, I was thinking about that whole conversation last night," he began.

"Yeah? You didn't hurt yourself, did you?" I laughed.

"What?" he looked confused before he chuckled. "Nope. Actually didn't. But seriously, this whole thing about us being partners. That's what I was thinking about."

"You're not changing your mind, are you?" I stopped walking.

"No! Not about the Cup partnership. That's working great so far. But what I mean is the whole Nationwide team expansion. I just think that's something for you and Daytona. I mean, if you have the ownership include Matt too, that's up to you guys, but I'm content with just the Cup agreement. I don't think I'm quite ready for more team ownership," Doug explained as I continued walking.

"Oh. Okay. If you don't want to be involved, that's cool. I just figured already being partners, you might want to be a part of this new team. You know if you change your mind, I'm sure we can work something out," I smiled.

"Well, don't you two look cute together," Kyle walked passed. I could hear the sarcasm in his voice as Doug dropped his arm.

"Hey man. We were just talking," Doug pointed out.

"Yeah. Whatever. Pretty cozy for just talking. Making plans for later I'm sure."

"Don't you have a rookie to babysit?" Drew joined us then. Shaking his head, Kyle stormed off, back in the direction of the garage.

"Wow. He's pretty bitter about the thought of you moving on, isn't he?" Doug asked.

"Geez. How the hell did that look like I'm moving on?"

"I've been asked a couple times if you two are more than just teammates," Drew offered.

"Are you kidding me? Who the hell is asking that?" I shook my head in disbelief.

"Couple drivers. Couple reporters," Drew replied.

"Even if we were more than just friends and teammates, it's not anybody's business."

"And anytime anybody asks, I tell them pretty much the same thing," Drew assured me.

"Doesn't anybody have anything better to do than gossip about who's doing what with who?" I looked around.

The first half dozen cars had already completed their qualifying laps. I was sitting twentieth and Doug twenty-fifth to take our turns. When the crews pushed our cars out to pit road, we joined them and I immediately climbed into the seat to prepare.

As Drew helped me secure the radio, he tapped on my helmet.

"What?" I asked.

"Don't worry about what people are saying. It's just like when Daytona was racing. There was a different rumor every week about her. Just gotta learn to ignore it all. Now, get out there, and show me what you've got," Drew directed me.

Nodding, I flipped the switches to start the engine as Drew put the window net up.

Once I rolled out onto the track, I put the conversation out of my mind and focussed on my laps, pushing the car as fast as it would go.

Completing the laps, I pulled back onto pit road and shut down the engine as the crew surrounded the car. Taking off my helmet and gloves, I hung them on the roll bars before climbing out of the car.

The crew pushed the car back to the garage as Drew handed me the stopwatch. Looking from the time to him, I was shocked. I knew my laps had been fast, but I didn't realize they were that fast. Checking the leaders on the scoring pylon confirmed I had captured the pole.

"No joke Brie. Faster than practice. That was one hell of a run out there," Drew assured me.

"Damn! But there's still two dozen cars left to qualify. And any one of them could run faster and knock me off the pole," I replied, unzipping the top of my firesuit and taking my arms out to cool off.

"True. But you just watch; a couple might come close, but nobody's gonna be faster than you."

"Did Doug finish his run yet?" I asked as Ricky joined us.

"Just. Should be back any time now. You've got a friend on the front row now," Ricky answered, motioning to the leader board.

When Doug re-joined us a few minutes later and saw he was sharing the front row with me, he hugged me, lifting me off the ground. Setting me back down, he kept one arm around me as a camera crew and reporter from ESPN approached.

"Can we interrupt with little get-together for an interview?"

"Sure," I nudged Doug to let me go and stepped back as Steve motioned the crew to start taping.

"So. Front row for Sunday's race. You've got a couple fast cars there. And forty hungry drivers lined up behind you. Think you'll be able to hold them off come Sunday?"

"Well, we've got a couple great cars and we're running on a wicked fast track. Guess we'll just have to wait and see what Sunday brings for us," I replied.

"So, can I ask, based on the display of affection when we walked over here: Is there any truth to the rumors running through the garage that this is more than a working relationship between you?"

"Whoa! So a hug makes us lovers? Really? Wow! Seriously, we're teammates and friends. That's it. Nothing more. So the answer would be no, there is absolutely NO truth to the rumors," I stated firmly.

"So there you have it, straight from Brianna. I'll let you get back to your team. Thanks for taking the time to chat."

Back in my motorhome, I took a quick shower and changed into jeans and a tee-shirt. Sitting on the couch, I picked up the email Jessika had printed out for me.

Double-checking the phone number she'd written at the top of the first page, I dialled as Jon stood to answer a knock at the door. Motioning to Doug walking in, I heard the switchboard operator answer.

"Jessica Bonde's room please," I requested, watching Doug sit across from me as Jon left. I handed Doug the email as the phone rang.

"Hello?" a tired voice answered after three rings.

"Mrs. Bonde?"

"Yes? Who is this?"

"Mrs Bonde; this is Brianna Lane. You sent me an email about Jessica," I began.

"Oh my God! Wow. I really didn't expect to hear from you. I mean, maybe an email back from your rep, but not a phone call," she replied, sounding shocked.

"Well, my rep is my daughter and something like this she knew I'd want to reply personally," I explained. "I'm not going to keep you long. I can hear how tired you are. But I wanted to call to let you know I did receive your email and if it's okay with you, I'd like to come see Jessica on Monday. If she's up for visitors, that is."

"Oh! She's sleeping now, but I know she'd love that! She's been having a rough time adjusting to the treatment and being here in the hospital. A visit from you might be perfect," she began to cry. "I'm sorry. We've all had a rough couple days here."

"No need to apologize. I can only imagine how difficult it's all been. Try to get some rest and I'll see you both on Monday."

"Thank you. And good luck on Sunday. Jessie and I will be watching the race here."

"Thanks. We got the pole today so hopefully we'll be up front most of the day."

"That's great! I'll have to let Jessie know when she wakes up. She'll be thrilled."

"I'd better let you go now. See you Monday," I said.

"Oh, yes. Okay. Monday. See you then." Hanging up, I saw Doug watching me closely.

"What's up?" I asked, setting down my phone.

"Nothing. Just wanted to see if you're coming out with us? Matt just got here so he and Daytona are just waiting for you. Unless you've got other plans."

"Yeah. Sounds good. The crew head out already?" I asked, standing to get my purse and shoes.

"Yeah. Drew and Ricky took them all back to the hotel," Doug replied.

Jon and Kevin were sitting outside as we walked out.

"Are you guys coming too?" I asked.

"Yeah. We'll meet you there," Jon answered as I locked the door. Walking to the parking lot, Daytona and Matt were leaning on his car.

During the drive and dinner, I noticed Doug watched me like he had been while I'd been on the phone. Choosing to ignore the stare, I focussed on the stories Matt and Daytona were telling about races they'd run in Atlanta.

Returning to the track, the rain started to fall and by the time we got to the motorhomes, we were soaked. Getting towels out of the closet, I handed them out to everybody to dry off a bit before I pulled dry clothes out of my bag in the bedroom to change.

While Matt and Daytona both changed, Doug ran across to his motorhome to change, returning a couple minutes later, his arms loaded with a case of Bud.

Turning on the television, I flipped through the channels and found a movie adapted from one of Daytona's books. Doug pulled me over to sit on the couch with him.

"Don't read anything into it Brie. I know we're just friends. I swear I'll behave," Doug said as I leaned back on his chest to watch the movie. Looking up as Matt and Daytona re-joined us, I caught Daytona trying to hide her smile.

They settled in on the other couch and I closed my eyes, relaxing after the hectic pace of the day. Falling asleep, I dreamt of the night Craig died. Replaying the events of that night, it all seemed so real, right down to the pain in my shoulder from where I'd been shot.

Waking, I sat up suddenly, breathing deeply to clear my head. Realizing the tv had been muted, I noticed the other couch was now vacant.

"You okay, Brie?" I jumped, hearing Doug's voice behind me.

"Yeah. I'm fine. How long did I sleep?"

"Over an hour. Matt and Daytona went over to my motorhome. Hope you don't mind me staying over here with you tonight. Jon and Kevin went with them," Doug explained.

"Yeah. Sure. That's fine," I replied absently, my mind still on my dream.

"Do you wanna talk about it?" Doug asked, lightly rubbing my back.

"What? No. It was nothing really. Nothing I haven't dreamt about before," I touched my shoulder, feeling the scar through my shirt.

"Do you dream about it often?" Doug moved to massage my shoulder.

"Not so much anymore. I used to dream about it every night. Then the dreams stopped for a while," I explained, picking up the remote.

As Doug slowly massaged my shoulders and worked his way down my back, I winced as he touched my still-healing ribs.

"Sorry. Forgot about the ribs. Do you want me to stop?"

"No. The massage feels great. Just a little sore where my ribs are healing. Bruises are still pretty nasty too," I replied.

"Okay. I'll avoid that spot then," Doug continued rubbing my back, lightly rubbing the bruising before moving to my lower back. Once he was done, he pulled me back to lean against his chest again as he lightly rubbed the front of my shoulder.

I'd found the classic movie channel and we watched an old Elvis movie while Doug gently held me. When I started to doze off again, Doug gave me a nudge.

"Hey! As much as I would love to hold you all night here while you sleep again, this isn't going to be too comfortable in another couple hours."

"Geez. I'm sorry. I didn't realize how tired I was. It's been a really long day," I apologized, sitting up.

"Hey! I'm not complaining. Just don't want us both to wake up sore tomorrow. Which couch pulls out to a bed?"

"This one. Why?" I asked, standing to stretch.

"Well, if you could toss me a pillow or two, I'll pull the bed out here," Doug stood, pulling the cushions off and setting them on the other couch as I put the empty beer bottles on the counter. By the time I'd gotten the extra pillows out of the linen closet, Doug had pulled the sofa bed out and straightened the sheets.

Tossing the pillows onto the bed, Doug grabbed my arm, stopping me from walking away. Looking up at him, I gasped as he plunged his hands into my hair.

"Relax," he laughed. "Knew I'd freak you out if I kissed you. Told you earlier I'd behave and I meant it. Just wanted to remind you I'm out here. I know you're used to having Jon out here. Hopefully I'm a suitable substitute for the night."

Hugging me gently, I relaxed, resting my head on his shoulder.

"Okay. You go to bed. Get some sleep and I'll see you in the morning," Doug let me go, giving me a playful nudge towards the bedroom.

"Yeah. Good night." Changing into a tee-shirt, I laid down, falling asleep almost right away. And dreamt about Craig's death again.

When I woke up screaming, Doug rushed into the room, followed shortly by Jon, his gun in hand.

"Brie? Are you okay?" Doug asked, looking around.

"Yeah. Was just a dream. Again. I'm okay. Geez, Jon. The gun isn't really necessary," I tried to laugh.

"Hey. The way you were screaming, I wasn't sure what I'd be walking into here. Better safe than sorry," he explained. "You're okay though?"

"Yeah. Go back next door to sleep," I assured him, standing to walk him back to the door. While I was up, I took a bottle of water from the fridge. Returning to the bedroom, Doug was still sitting on the edge of the bed.

"Are you sure you're okay? You scared the crap outta me the way you were screaming," he looked worried as I sat beside him.

"Yeah. Really, I'm fine. It was just a bad dream."

"Same one?"

"Yep." I nodded. "Would you feel better staying in here with me?"

Doug looked at me as I laid down again.

"Would you feel better?" he asked.

"Sure. I trust you to behave," I replied, patting the pillow beside me.

"Okay." He moved around to the other side of the bed to lay beside me, carefully putting a protective arm around me.

This time when I closed my eyes, I fell into a dreamless sleep.

* * *

Saturday was relatively quiet. After breakfast with Doug, Daytona and Matt, Jon and I headed to the souvenir trailer while Doug headed to a local Chevy dealership for an autograph session.

I was still at the souvenir trailer when Doug returned from the dealership and he joined me to sign for another hour. When the crowd finally thinned, we slipped out of the trailer and headed to the motorhomes to relax. Taking advantage of the still-warm weather, I changed into a bikini and climbed onto the roof of my motorhome.

Letting the sun warm my skin, I closed my eyes, thinking back to lazy summer afternoons with Craig, silently wishing he was still with me to celebrate my success. My trip down memory lane was interrupted by Doug's voice near my ear.

"My God. Those bruises are still pretty nasty, aren't they?" I jumped as he chuckled and moved to sit beside me. "Sorry. Thought you heard me coming up the ladder."

"Guess I was daydreaming. Good thing I have Jon at the bottom of the ladder to protect me from any crazy fans," I said as Doug stretched out beside me, propping himself on one elbow to look down at me. I watched from behind my sunglasses as his gaze slid down to my bruises, lightly touching them with his fingertips.

"Are these from the fight with Eddie?" he asked quietly.

"Yeah. Most of the bruising had faded from the original break when he attacked me. So I ended up with fresh ones on top of the old ones. Guess you could say I was lucky that he re-broke them in the same spot they'd been broken from the wreck," I explained.

"I'm just glad you were able to defend yourself and get away from him."

"I have no doubt he would've killed me given the chance."

"That would've really sucked," Doug said, looking so serious, I had to laugh.

"You're right. But if I survived being shot by a whacked-out drug addict, I sure as hell wasn't gonna let Eddie beat me," I assured him.

"This is from the night your husband was killed?" Doug traced the edge of the scar on my shoulder.

"Yep. I got hit twice in the chest too, but my vest stopped them. The vest didn't cover my shoulder thought. And it couldn't protect Craig. The junkie that shot us had two guns. The bullets went through his vest like he was naked. Nothing could've stopped them," I explained, blinking away the tears and grateful for my dark sunglasses.

"So how fast was that guy back out on the street?"

"He didn't get any jail time," I paused.

"What? He killed a cop and got away with it?" Doug exploded, shaking his head.

"No. He left in a body bag," I explained quietly.

"Oh. Wow. Good. So he can't hurt you or anybody else again," Doug placed the palm of his hand gently over my shoulder.

James joined us then and we both sat up. When Daytona and Matt returned to the track with bags of groceries, we all climbed down from the roof and I changed into shorts and a tank top before we all worked together to make dinner.

* * *

Sunday morning brought sunshine and blue skies. With Jon by my side, I went through my typical race day routine. We started with breakfast at the Ford VIP tent, greeting fans and Ford executives with the other Ford drivers. After breakfast and signing autographs, we headed to the morning services, where we met Doug, Daytona and Matthew.

Leaving the mandatory drivers' meeting, I was stopped by one of the reporters from the national network broadcasting the race and asked about my crash during practice.

"Obviously, it's disappointing to wreck such a great car. But my crew did an awesome job getting my back-up car ready to go. And luckily, it was good enough to get me the pole. I'm looking forward to having a great race today," I replied.

"Is it true that you're going to be teaming up with Daytona Hudson next year to field a Nationwide team?"

"We haven't made a definite decision yet. But when we do, and have all the details worked out, we will make a formal announcement. Until then, I have to say no comment," I smiled.

Ending the interview, Jon and I walked back to the motorhome so I could change into my firesuit. Walking to pit road, we passed Kyle, having a heated discussion with his driver.

Not wanting to get involved, I picked up my pace a little, hoping to avoid any confrontation whatsoever.

Once we reached pit road, we were joined by Doug, Daytona and Matthew again for the pre-race activities.

After driver introductions, Doug and I climbed into the back of the Ford pick-up for our parade laps around the track. Waving to the crowd, he kept looking down at me, smiling. As the truck pulled down onto pit road and stopped, Doug helped me down from the truck, and keeping his hand on my back, we walked the length of pit road to where our cars were lined up.

Standing between our two cars during the national anthems, our crew chiefs stood on either side of us and our crews lined up across our pit stalls.

As the national anthem ended and the jets flew overhead, Doug put his arms around me to hug me, whispering "Good luck" in my ear.

Climbing into my car, I carefully went through the motions of securing my safety belts before pulling on my helmet. Drew hooked up the radio and air hose as I locked my steering wheel in place.

Once the command was given, I flipped the switches to fire the engine, getting a thumbs up from Drew before he put the window net up and headed to pit road.

Following the pace car onto the track, I heard Drew's voice through the radio.

"Okay boss. You've got a kick-ass car there, so let's see you kick some ass today."

"That's right. You've got a points lead to protect," Daytona added.

"No problem," I replied.

"Let's go racing!" Jessika chimed in from the top of the spotters' stand.

When the green flag waved, Doug and I pulled away to an easy lead, running nose to tail, leaving the rest of the field to fight for the remaining positions among themselves. It didn't take long for us to catch the slower cars, among them Kyle's rookie. As we pulled to the outside to pass, I glanced over in time to see him turn the wheel, driving his car into the side of mine and pushing it up into the outside retaining wall.

"Mom?" I heard Jessika.

"I'm okay. I think we can still run." I was interrupted as another car ran into the rear of mine, crumpling the back end and looked into my mirror to see a ball of flame erupt outside my back window.

Dropping the window net with one hand, I removed the steering wheel and quickly released the safety belts and everything hooked into my helmet. Climbing out of the car, I looked around for the car that had run into the back of me as I pulled my helmet off.

Seeing it was Jamie, and the track was clear of any oncoming traffic, I ran across the track to where his car had come to rest in the grass. Tucking my gloves into my helmet, I dropped it on the grass and reached for his window net, releasing it as the safety crew reached us. Carefully pushing his tinted visor up, his head was resting against the seat, his eyes closed.

Placing my hand on his chest, I could feel it rise and fall as he breathed. As the safety crew surrounded the car, I moved aside to let them help Jamie. Picking up my helmet, I slowly walked to the ambulance, waving to the crowd.

A short time later, Jamie was conscious and alert, loaded onto a stretcher and riding in the back of the ambulance to get checked out at the infield medical center. After a quick physical revealed I was not hurt, I stopped to check on Jamie. The on-site doctor informed me he was being prepped to be air-lifted to the local hospital.

Leaving the care center, I was met by Jon, Drew and a group of reporters, all shouting questions.

"I'm fine. Was just in the wrong place at the wrong time. Hopefully we don't take too much of a hit in the points. But considering my nearest competition got taken out in the same wreck . . . The team here is sending him to the hospital for further tests and I hope it's not too serious. . . It sucks to be out of the race this early. My crew gave me an awesome car to drive today. But we'll be back next week."

Walking back to the motorhome, I told Drew to pack everything up. After a quick shower, I dressed in jeans and a tee-shirt, slipped on my running shoes and pulled my hair into a ponytail, covered by a ball cap, before heading to pit road to sit on Doug's pit box.

When the race was done, he had a fifth-place finish and once the crews had finished packing up, we headed to the airport for the flight home.

* * * * *

CHAPTER FIFTY-TWO

First thing Monday morning, James and I headed to the airport. Taking the bag out of the backseat that I'd put together for Jessica, I shut the door and turned around into Doug's arms.

"What the. . .?" I was shocked to see him.

"Hope you don't mind me tagging along today," Doug said, releasing me and taking the bag from my hand.

"Umm, no. I don't mind. Just surprised," I explained, locking the truck. As we walked towards the waiting plane, we were joined by Daytona and Matt.

"Hey kids! Can we come too?" Daytona called out as they walked up to us.

"Sure. Anybody else coming?" I looked around.

"Looks like it's just us," James replied as we reached the plane.

"Wow. Bigger crowd than I expected boss," the pilot greeted us, shaking hands with everybody. "I'll just need a couple minutes to change the passenger list before we can leave. Weather is clear all the way to Michigan."

Walking onto the plane, the five of us settled into our seats, fastening our seatbelts and waited for take-off. A few minutes later, the co-pilot secured the door, locking it and with a wave, returned to the cockpit.

"Okay folks. We've been given clearance to taxi out to the runway. So if y'all could make sure your seatbelts are securely fastened, we'll get this party started," the pilot announced.

The flight passed quickly and after landing and taxiing to the terminal, we headed to the car rental counter. Seeing the five of us, the rental agent smiled brightly.

"Welcome back! Would you like one of your usual rentals?" she asked.

"Yes, please. My passenger list grew at the last minute. So something roomy enough to fit the five of us would be great," I replied, handing her my credit card and drivers licence.

Reaching behind her for a set of keys, she set them on the counter as she typed the information into the computer.

"Okay. You're all set. First level of the parking structure. Red Ford Excursion in the first row. Enjoy your stay."

"Thanks." Taking the keys and tucking my id back into my purse, we slowly walked to the parking structure, easily finding the rental.

Handing the printed directions to James, I got behind the wheel as Doug, Daytona and Matthew got into the backseat.

Leaving the parking structure and following the signs to the freeway, James read the directions to me, and it didn't take long before I was pulling into the hospital parking lot.

Walking into the lobby, I stopped at the reception desk to find out Jessica's room number before we headed up in the elevator.

Reaching the floor she was on, I checked in at the nurses' station.

"Patients can't have too many visitors at once. Not even famous ones," the nurse informed us, frowning at the group of us.

"Would it be possible for us to visit with some of the other patients then? While Brianna and Doug visit with Jessica? Perhaps there's a common room we could go to?" Daytona asked.

"Sure. Common room is right there," the nurse pointed, before turning back to me. "And the patient you're looking for is at the far end of the hall, left side. But she's downstairs for treatment right now. Her mother is there now though."

"Thank you." Doug and I turned to walk down the hall as James, Matt and Daytona crossed to the common room. Doug took my hand, squeezing it gently as he smiled down at me.

Walking into the room, the lights were off but the sunlight streamed through the large windows. A lone figure sat by the window, her head resting in her hand. I recognized Jessica's mother immediately.

"Mrs. Bonde?" I asked quietly as Doug and I stood in the doorway. She jumped and looked up, startled. I could see she'd been crying.

"Oh! You came!" She stood, wiping her eyes as she crossed the room. When she got close enough, I hugged her gently.

"How are you doing?" I asked.

"Good. They took Jessie down a little while ago for her usual treatment. But she should be back soon. Oh! She'll be so thrilled to see you."

"Let's sit. You look exhausted," I led her back over to the window as Doug pulled another chair over. Sitting in front of her close enough that our knees were touching, I took her hands in mine as Doug sat on the arm of my chair. Looking closely at her, I waited for her to talk.

"I am. Just so tired," she paused, taking a deep breath. "I'm here all day. Everyday with Jessie. I go home most nights. But I can't sleep. Worried I'm gonna get a call."

"Where is Jessie's father? Is he helping at all?" I asked.

"He left when we got the news. Said he didn't sign on for a sick kid. I tried calling him at work a couple times. But he won't take my calls," she explained.

"Jessie's been asking for him but I can't tell her he left. I just keep telling her he's gone on business trips."

"You shouldn't have to lie to her. He should be here with you. Helping you," Doug said. I could sense his anger and glanced up at him.

"I know. But I don't know what else to do. He won't take my calls and he doesn't have any family for me to go to."

"Well, you have me. And I'm going to do whatever I can to help you. Daytona Hudson happens to be a friend along with being my sponsor and we're setting up a fund to cover the medical expenses. My daughter is putting together a press release to send out to the rest of my sponsors too," I explained.

"Oh no! Really, you don't have to do that!" she exclaimed.

"I know I don't have to. This is something I want to do," I assured her. "Doug, can you ask James to come in here for a minute please? I have a job for him to do for me."

"Sure. And I'm gonna go get us some coffee too. I'll be back shortly." After Doug walked out of the room, I took a notebook and pen from my purse, setting them on her lap.

"Kathy? I want you to write down your husband's name and the name and address of where he works. If you have a recent photo of him, I'm gonna need it too," I instructed her.

"Umm. Okay. I think I still have one in my purse," she replied, looking confused, but picked up the pen to write down the information. As she dug through her purse, pulling out a picture and handing it to me, James came into the room.

Ripping the page out of the notebook, I stood and met James at the door. Handing him the keys, picture and paper, I stepped out into the hall.

"I need you to take a drive for me. You'll find this guy here. I don't give a shit what song and dance he gives you, I want him brought back here," I explained.

"This the father? Man, Doug is pissed."

"Yeah. Mom says he walked after they got the news. Left her to deal with this alone."

"Got it. I'll be back just as soon as I can." I walked back into the room as James turned back towards the elevators.

"James is gonna go convince your husband to make some better choices in life," I explained. "And he'll be bringing him back with him."

Doug returned then with coffee for the three of us, and we sat quietly listening to Kathy talk about Jessica.

When the orderly pushed the wheelchair into the room, I was shocked at how tiny she looked. Her face lit up at seeing me and she lifted her arms towards me.

"Brianna!" she squealed, grinning from ear to ear.

"Hi Jessie. Hope you don't mind I came for a visit," I smiled at her as her wheelchair was brought over to us.

"I'm so happy to see you! And you brought friends!" she leaned close and lowered her voice almost to a whisper. "I saw Daytona and Matthew down the hall when we came off the elevator."

"You did? So I guess it wasn't much of a surprise to see me here, eh?" I laughed.

"Nope. But it's so cool that you're here. I was so mad yesterday after that stupid rookie made you crash. You should kick his butt for that," she suggested, crossing her arms in front of her.

The doctor came in then, and seeing the group of us, hesitated before clearing his throat.

"Mrs Bonde? Could I have a word please?"

"Sure. I'll be right back Jessie," she stood, leaning to kiss the top of her daughter's head before joining the doctor in the hall.

"Hey Jess? Do you want to come sit here with me for a little while? So your friend can take your wheelchair away," I offered.

She nodded excitedly and Doug moved to pick her up, gently transferring her from the wheelchair to my lap. As she settled in, I handed her the bag we'd brought.

"You brought me a present? Oh!" she giggled as she dug into the bag, pulling out the tee-shirt, teddy bear and poster I'd brought for her.

"When you feel better and can travel, I want you and your parents to come to a race okay?" I offered as she pulled the shirt over her head.

"That would be awesome!" She suddenly turned serious. "I don't think that'll happen though."

"Of course it will," I tried to sound optimistic as she shook her head.

"Nope. My doctor looked way too serious when he came in to talk to Mom. That's never a good sign. But thank you for the offer. And for the awesome gift." She rested her head on my shoulder and fell asleep in seconds.

"Do you think she could be right?" Doug asked, lightly stroking her cheek.

"God, I hope not! She's such a sweet little girl. None of these kids should be here. They should be at school. Playing with their friends. Enjoying life. Not fighting for their lives," I replied, trying to fight the tears.

Standing carefully, I slowly carried her over to tuck her into bed, much as I'd done with my own daughter at that age.

Leaning down, I lightly kissed her forehead, tucking the blankets around her and her new teddy bear. Straightening, Doug put his arms around me to hug me from behind and we both stood beside the bed, watching her sleep.

"It's so damned unfair!" I whispered, resting my head on Doug's shoulder.

"I know sweetie. Hopefully when her mom comes back from talking to the doctor, she has some good news," Doug said, holding me tighter and lightly kissed my temple.

When Kathy came back from talking to the doctor, she was crying and stood on the opposite side of the bed, looking down at her sleeping child.

"She always gets so tired after her treatments. She'll probably sleep for an hour or more now," she explained. Reaching over, I put my hand over hers as she stroked Jessie's forehead.

"Kathy? Do you want to talk about what the doctor said?" I asked quietly.

"She won't be going home. He said it's spreading too fast for them to treat it as aggressively as he'd like to. My baby's going to die and all I can do is sit here and watch it happen!" she sobbed. Doug let me go and I walked around the bed to hug the other woman. My heart was breaking for her, knowing there was nothing else I could do.

Doug quietly left the room and I knew the news was hard for him to deal with as well.

I was surprised a couple minutes later when James returned, bringing with him Jessie's father. Kathy looked up, obvious shock showing on her face when he came into the room.

"Kathy? There's a slip of paper in that bag there. It has my cell phone number, my home number and my personal email address on it. If you need anything at all – ANYTHING – I want you to call me, day or night." I let her know.

"Okay. Thank you so much for coming today. And for, well, everything. I know Jessie loved seeing you today."

"Are you going to be okay? I can stay longer if you need me to," I offered, glancing at James.

"No. I'll call you. Thank you again," she smiled weakly before I hugged her again.

Stepping back, I picked up my purse and watched as Jessie's father slowly made his way to his wife's side. Walking down the hall with James, we headed to the common room where we collected Doug, Daytona and Matt.

In the elevator, Doug pulled me into his arms, holding me tightly.

"Hello? Somebody want to clue us in on what the hell is going on?" Daytona asked.

"She's dying. The doctor told her mom it's spreading too fast," I explained, not bothering to lift my head off Doug's chest.

"Oh wow. That's so wrong!" Daytona started to cry and Matt held her to him.

"Did you have any problems with the father?" I asked James.

"Went pretty much as I expected it to," James replied. "Guy's an asshole. But he's gonna stick around now."

The entire trip home, we were all subdued, each absorbed in our own thoughts.

When the plane landed in Mooresville, Doug walked me to my truck and I handed James the keys. Hugging me again, Doug lightly kissed my forehead,

"See you at the shop tomorrow?" he asked.

"Yeah. Bright and early," I nodded as he opened the passenger door. James had already slid behind the wheel and started the engine.

Closing the door behind me, Doug waved and turned in the direction of his car as James pulled out of the parking lot and we silently drove home.

* * * * *

CHAPTER FIFTY-THREE

Homestead-Miami, FL

"How're you feeling Brie?" Daytona asked as we walked to the pre-race drivers' meeting.

"Pretty good actually," I took a deep breath. "I was worried when we took that hit in Atlanta. But with Jamie taken out in the same wreck, it didn't hurt us too much. And we managed to gain back some of those points the last two weeks with some great finishes. So I'm not too worried about today."

"Good. All you've gotta do is stay clean today and bring the car home in one piece. And as long as you're not first out, you've got the Cup," Daytona pointed out.

"Well, Drew and the team gave me an awesome car this weekend. I'm really glad he was willing to come over with Doug when we merged. And that he stepped up when Kyle left. I don't know that I want to look for a new crew chief for next year."

"You'll have to talk to him about that. But he looks happy back on the pit box. Have you gotten a lot of applications?"

"Yeah. Averaging about a half dozen every day. I seem to be a pretty popular driver to want to work for," I laughed as we walked into the meeting room.

"Wow. You're pretty happy for a woman who didn't get married yesterday," Kyle interrupted. "Guess my leaving was the right decision."

"Get lost Kyle," Jon stepped between us. "Now is not the time for it."

"Whatever," Kyle turned and stalked off, joining his driver on the other side of the room.

Drew, Ricky and Doug joined us then and we found seats in the middle of the room. Doug had started spending more time around me since our trip to Michigan, stopping by the house every couple days and hanging out in my office at the shop.

I'd gotten a couple more emails from Kathy, sending messages from Jessica and letting me know her husband had done a complete turn-around after our visit, doing more to help out.

Daytona and I had set up a fund the day after our visit to Michigan and Jessika had sent out the press release to all my sponsors. The donations had begun arriving almost right away, and I was planning to take the first check to Kathy before flying to Las Vegas for the year-end banquet.

Returning to the motorhomes after the drivers' meeting, Doug grabbed my hand, pulling me into his, closing the door behind us.

"Doug! What the hell are you doing?" I exclaimed.

"Relax. I just wanted to have a quiet minute with you before all the pre-race craziness. I know how stressful the last couple races are," Doug assured me, putting his arms around me to hold me. "And you know I'm not gonna do this out there for the whole world to see. Or for tongues to start wagging."

Relaxing, I put my arms around him and rested my head on his shoulder as he lightly rubbed my back.

"What? You don't like being part of a rumor with me?" I laughed, tilting my head to look up at him.

"Only if the rumors are true," he replied quietly, looking in my eyes. "Okay. You need to leave. Now. Or we're not gonna make the green flag." Putting his hands on my shoulders, he turned me towards the door, opened it and gave me a gentle shove.

Ten minutes later, we'd both changed into our firesuits and walked together to pit road. Most of the cars had already gone through inspection and were lined up along pit road.

I'd qualified fifth and Doug ninth. Jamie was further back and Kyle's rookie between me and Doug in seventh. As we waited for driver introductions, Doug noticed me looking at the car between our two.

"Hey! He's not gonna be stupid enough to try something today. Besides, you've got a teammate right behind him. He hits you, I hit him. No worries, right?" Doug put a hand on my shoulder.

"I hope he's not that stupid. But you know Kyle's pretty bitter today. Who knows what his mind frame is today." I crossed my arms in front of me.

"You mean more bitter than usual?" Doug laughed.

"Yesterday was the date we'd finally set for the wedding," I replied quietly.

"Oh. Yeah. I guess he has a good reason to be more bitter today," Doug agreed. "So I guess kissing you in front of him today would really make him spin?"

"Probably. But I know you won't do that," I stepped back, laughing as he reached for me.

"No. You're right. I won't do that in front of him," he assured me, looking around before he stepped closer, leaning down to whisper in my ear. "I'll wait until we're alone to kiss you."

I was saved from answering when driver introductions began. Waiting my turn, I cheered with the crowd when Doug crossed the stage and took my place in line.

As I crossed the stage, shaking hands with the various executives and special guests, I was handed a check from the race sponsor for Jessica's treatment.

"Thank you so much. I know this means a lot to a very special little girl and her family."

Leaving the stage, I handed the check to Daytona and jumped into the pick-up truck for the parade lap, waving to the fans lining the fence.

The national anthem and jet flyover passed in a blur and I slowly went through the motions of securing all the safety equipment.

Firing the engine as Drew locked the window net in place, I checked the mirrors and double-checked everything was fastened securely.

Slowly rolling off pit road, I focussed on the car, mentally preparing for the next four hundred miles.

"Okay Mom. Lights are out on the pace car. Going green next time by. Let's go racing!" Jessika radioed.

Passing under the flag stand, I steadily shifted gears and passed the car in front of me. Kyle's rookie stayed close to me and I could see Doug directly behind him.

The first twenty laps were uneventful and I slowly moved up to second. Every car I passed, Kyle's driver and Doug passed as well.

"Mom? How ya doing out there? Jamie's right up behind Doug now. Gonna be interesting," Jessika told me.

"Feels pretty good out here. There anybody in the garage yet?"

"Not yet. But the rookie looks like he's eyeing the outside line there," Jess pointed out.

"I see him," I replied, moving to block him.

"You sure it's a good idea to block him?" Drew asked.

"If he gets beside me, it'll be that much easier for him to wreck me," I explained. "Remember Atlanta?"

"Okay. I'm gonna trust you here," Drew said as the other car nudged my bumper.

"Damn," I muttered, trying to pull away. Checking my mirror, I saw Doug pull down to the inside line, looking for room to pass the car between us. I knew he had a strong car and wasn't surprised when he pulled even with the other car.

I returned my full attention to the track in front of me and focussed on chasing down the leader.

"Holy shit! Doug's into the rookie! Jamie's hit too! Got a huge mess behind you!" Jess called and I looked in my mirror full of spinning and wrecking cars.

"Whoa! What the hell happened?" I asked.

"A big mess that just clinched the championship for us," Drew shouted.

"Yeehaw!" I yelled.

As I passed the wrecked cars of Doug and Jamie, they both saluted and waved as I drove up close to them.

Once the mess was cleaned up, and green flag racing resumed, I quietly rode around following the leader, listening to Drew counting down the laps and telling me my lap times.

Pit stops were routine and I focussed on keeping the car out of trouble until the end of the race.

Finally watching the checkered flag wave over my car, I dropped the window net, happy with a tenth place finish. Laughing, I watched my crew celebrating on pit road.

As I completed my cool down lap, I spun the car around to wave to the fans lining the fence before I turned to head down pit road to the Championship Circle.

Climbing out of the car, I hugged Drew and Daytona before turning to the mandatory post-race interview.

"Congratulations Brianna on your first Championship!"

"Thanks! Wow. Talk about an awesome year. I've had a great crew and some great cars. And an amazing teammate for the last part of the year. Doug and his crew really helped out a lot for me to get here."

"Speaking of Doug Madison, what was your reaction when he wrecked and took out your nearest points rival?"

"Oh man! I can't tell you on national television," I laughed. "I didn't see what exactly happened. But I'm glad everybody was able to walk away. Looking forward to a party back at the shop and then we've got lots to do to get ready for next season."

Once the interviews were done, Daytona and I headed back to the motorhome while the crew packed up.

"So, NOW how are you feeling?" Daytona laughed, looping her arm through mine.

"Wow. Relieved. Excited. Thrilled. A little shocked too," I replied with a sigh.

Doug was sitting outside the motorhome, and stood, walking to meet us. Hugging me tightly, he lifted me off the ground.

"Congratulations! That was some race!"

"You didn't have to do that you know," I said.

"Do what?"

"Knock out Kyle's driver AND take out you and Jamie and half a dozen other cars. I woulda had the championship without you doing that," I explained.

"I didn't do it," Dug protested. "Sure. I thought about it. But HE ran into me. Just like he did to you in Atlanta. Watch the replay and you'll see. And well, Jamie was just in the wrong place at the wrong time. Again."

"Swear?"

"Yep. I knew you could win it without me messing with fate," Doug promised.

"Okay. I'm gonna go shower so we can head home," I pulled away from Doug and walked into the motorhome.

* * * * *

CHAPTER FIFTY-FOUR

I gave the crew the next week off and spent a couple days doing phone and email interviews with various media outlets around the country.

Doug, Mandy and Jonathon joined me, Jess, James and Mark for Thanksgiving on Thursday before I turned my attention to getting my speech written for the banquet.

By the time I left for Michigan to visit Jessica before flying to Las Vegas, I still didn't have anything written.

Daytona flew with me to Michigan and I was surprised she arrived at the airport with only Matthew, who dropped her off with a wave and left. She explained during the flight.

"The threat's not there that used to be. And Matt and I agreed I'll be with you the entire time until we get to New York. I feel perfectly safe with you. Plus I didn't want to drag any of the boys to the hospital. They all need some time off."

When we arrived at the hospital, we went straight to Jessica's room. Both her parents were sitting at her bedside as she slept.

"Kathy?" I said quietly as we stepped into the room. She stood to greet us and I could see she'd been crying.

"I thought you'd be busy getting ready for the banquet. Jessie was so happy when you won the championship. She's been sleeping most of the time since then," Kathy explained.

"We wanted to come back before we go to Las Vegas. I brought a check for you. Money that my fans have donated to help you out. I want you to use it to pay off whatever bills you're behind from being off work. I have another one I'm going to drop off at the office before I leave. To cover Jessie's medical bills," I handed her the check.

When she saw the dollar amount she gasped and started to cry again.

"We can't take this," she exclaimed.

"Yes. You can. I wanted to help you out and so did my fans and sponsors. Some of the drivers even. Please, take the money. I know this hasn't been an easy time for you."

"Thank you. This is an awesome gift." She hugged us both.

"I was hoping when I got here, she'd be well enough to travel. I would've loved to take her to Las Vegas with me." I looked over at the sleeping child.

"With all due respect ma'am, our daughter isn't some sort of trophy to drag around showing off," her father stood, crossing his arms over his chest, moving to stand between me and his wife.

Refusing to be intimidated, I looked him in the eye as I spoke.

"With all due respect, I'm not trying to treat your daughter like a trophy. I was hoping to fulfill her dream of attending a NASCAR banquet to sit at the Champion's table."

"Aaron. Brianna's just trying to help. Please don't start something now," Kathy begged.

"Listen. We're gonna leave. I just wanted to drop the checks off," I said quietly.

"Yeah. Maybe you should leave," Aaron sneered.

"I'm sorry," Kathy offered, walking us down the hall.

"Don't ever apologize for him. But remember, I'm here for you. And Jessie. Call me if you need anything," I reminded her as I hugged her at the elevator.

After dropping the second check at the office, Daytona and I headed to Windsor to visit with our families before we flew to Las Vegas.

* * *

Arriving in Las Vegas brought the whirlwind of Championship week activities: morning show interviews, late night interviews, and the traditional Champion parade where the top twelve drivers drove their race cars along the Las Vegas Strip.

In between interviews, Daytona and I went shopping for dresses. I finally settled on a deep green strapless, floor-length gown.

Nervous about showing my scar so prominently, I touched it lightly, checking my reflection in the mirror.

"It's part of you. Nothing you can do about it. Everybody knows it's there. Right? So no sense hiding it. Just treat it like one of your tattoos," Daytona reasoned.

"I know. It's just putting it out there on display. On national television."

"I bet nobody'll notice and if they do? Who cares?"

"You're right. And I've never hidden the fact that it's there. I'm sure everybody will be noticing I don't have a written speech more than a six year old scar," I laughed slipping the dress off and putting my jeans and sweater back on.

"The first one's always the hardest to write. Just remember to thank your sponsors, your family and your crew. As long as you do that, it doesn't really matter how short your speech is. Best thing to do is just make a list and go from that. I never wrote out my entire speech."

After picking out matching shoes and a small handbag, we paid for our purchases, arranging to have them delivered to the hotel before heading to the next appearance.

* * *

As I zipped my gown the night of the banquet, I was startled by a knock at the door. I wasn't expecting Daytona and Matt for another hour.

"Brie? It's Doug," I heard him call through the door.

Checking my appearance in the mirror, I ran my hands down the front of my dress before I opened the door.

"Hi. I wasn't expecting to see you quite yet," I said, stepping back to let Doug into the room.

"Well, I was ready early, so I thought I'd come have a drink with you. I brought champagne and wow. You look . . . Amazing. That is some dress." Doug stepped back, his gaze slowly travelling the length of the dress. I could see him checking out my shoulder before raising his eyes to mine.

"You like it?" I asked, slowly turning to show the whole dress.

"Definitely! I'm not used to seeing you all done up like this. It's nice," he paused. "But I like the natural ponytail and no make-up look."

"Well, I figured being the champion now, I'd better make an effort and glam myself up a little for the night," I explained as Doug opened the champagne, pouring two glasses.

Taking the glass he held out, I walked over to the window to look at the city below. The sun was slowly setting and I watched as the sky darkened.

When Doug stepped up behind me, slipping one arm around my waist, I leaned back against him, resting my head on his shoulder.

"Mmm, I could get used to this," Doug whispered in my ear.

"What?" I asked.

"Holding you. I'm sure you've figured out by now I like being around you. Spending time with you."

"I did notice you've been around an awful lot since Atlanta. And it's been nice having you around," I replied.

"I've been trying to work up the courage here," Doug stopped.

"Courage eh? I've never known you to be afraid of anything," I laughed.

"Well, I don't want to scare you off. But I want to be with you. I get it if you're not ready to get into a relationship, but I'm willing to wait and take it slow," Doug said quietly.

"I'm not one of your pit bunnies, Doug. It has nothing to do with not being ready. I've seen the way you go through women and then toss them aside," I protested.

"Pit bunny?" he chuckled. "I have never compared you to any of them. I know you're nothing like them. And maybe you haven't noticed, but you're the only woman I've been spending my time with for a while now."

Thinking back to the time since he'd moved his team into my shop, I realized he was telling the truth.

"Wow. You're right. I don't remember the last time I saw you with a random, nameless chick," I admitted.

"So? Do you think you could give me a chance and agree to go out with me?"

As I thought about it, we were interrupted by a knock at the door. Opening it to Daytona and Matthew, we were joined a few minutes later by Jessika and James and we headed downstairs to the banquet hall.

My team was assembled together, looking at my trophy on display. Posing for pictures, I was distracted by Doug's revelation.

When the doors were opened, Doug returned to my side, offering his arm.

"Would you allow me to escort you to your table?" he smiled.

"I'd like that very much," I smiled back, slipping my hand into his arm. Walking into the banquet hall, I took a deep breath.

"You'll be great tonight," Doug assured me, placing his hand over mine. "Just remember to breathe."

Walking me to the champions table, he pulled my chair out and leaned close as I sat, kissing me lightly on the cheek.

"Knock 'em dead champ," he whispered before straightening and walking to his table. The top twelve teams were seated together and with Doug being fifteenth, his team was at a table on the opposite side of the massive room.

My speech would be the last and I half-listened to the awards being handed out and the speeches being made leading up to mine.

As I made my way across the stage, the room erupted in cheers. Looking out over the room, my gaze stopped briefly on Kyle as he smiled. Taking a deep breath as everybody returned to their seats, I smiled.

"Wow. Thanks guys. That was an amazing introduction. And we've had an amazing year. There were a few times this year, I wasn't sure I'd make it here. But it's been quite a ride. I have a few people to thank, so I'll get right to that. A very wise friend who's been here a time or two told me this week to make sure I thank my sponsors, my family and my crew, I'm guessing in that order. So, Daytona. Thank you for everything. From believing in me enough to not only sell me your team, but to continue to sponsor me. I feel honored to know you, to be able to follow in your path and to call you my friend. I have to thank Ford and Goodyear, Sunoco and all the little sponsors who come together to keep the sport going year after year.

"Thank you to my beautiful daughter Jessika," I paused to blow her a kiss. "My biggest fan, my spotter and now, my pr rep. You were so eager to move when I bought the team and believed in me that we'd get here someday. My parents of course, for giving me the strength to be me, and the encouragement to chase my dreams, even if it meant letting me go when I moved hundreds of miles from home.

"And of course, my crew. If it wasn't for you guys, I REALLY wouldn't be here. You've gone above and beyond to give me some awesome cars week in and week out. Kyle, you helped get us to the Chase and I appreciate you for that. I hope you have an amazing career with your new team. And Drew, my crew chief that last half dozen races. You took what Kyle started and kept the momentum going. Thank you for helping bring this trophy home.

"And finally, thank you to my new teammate and business partner, Doug Madison. You've been a wealth of knowledge and I'm looking forward to seeing where the ride goes from here.

"Of course, I also have to thank the fans. Without your support, I wouldn't be here. There's one fan in particular I have to single out. Little Jessica Bonde. She's a sweet little girl I met in Michigan earlier this year and I've had her picture in my car the last few races. I think everybody pretty much knows Daytona and I have been raising funds to help out her family with their bills and the medical expenses. I had hoped to bring her with me tonight, but she's just way too sick to travel now. I think she's watching tonight from her hospital room. I'd like to thank everybody who was so willing to contribute to help out her and her family.

"Now, before I start crying, I'd better wrap this up. Thanks again and I can't wait to see what the new season holds. I'm looking forward to defending my championship."

Stepping back from the podium, I waved to the crowd before heading off the stage. I barely heard the host close the ceremony and show as I walked into Doug's waiting arms.

* * * * *

23432866R00182

Made in the USA
Charleston, SC
23 October 2013